# The Sunflower Forest

## TOREY HAYDEN

AVON
PUBLISHERS OF BARD, CAMELOT, DISCUS AND FLARE BOOKS

*While all the characters and events depicted in this novel are ficti-*
*tious creations of the author, they are based on real people and real*
*events. Documentation for the* Lebensborn *program arises from the*
*Nürnberg trials transcripts, chiefly transcript XXIII, and from dec-*
*larations made by* Lebensborn *participants.*

AVON BOOKS
A division of
The Hearst Corporation
1790 Broadway
New York, New York 10019

The G. P. Putnam's edition contains the following Library of Congress.
Cataloging in Publication Data:

Hayden, Torey L.
  The sunflower forest.

I. Title.
PS3558.A82893S8   1984   813'.54   83-27043

First Avon Printing, August 1985

# Acknowledgments

The author wishes to gratefully acknowledge all those whose patience and help were involved in creating this book. Special thanks are particularly due to those individuals who so willingly shared their *Lebensborn* and related war experiences with me. Thanks also to my long-suffering husband, Ken, my agent, Peter, and my editor, Gail, all for putting up with me. And to my good-humored friends here in North Wales, Ute, Rosemarie, Carol, Heddwyn, Maldwyn, Emyr, Dafydd and Dai-the-Hand, for answering countless questions about the war, religion, Welsh and German grammar, and the finer points of sheep farming.

This book is for ``Mara,''
with my love and respect
and with terrible compassion.

# One

IN THAT YEAR what I wanted most was a boyfriend. I was seventeen and had never had a date. I had the rest: breasts, hair under my arms, my period, the desire. I certainly had the desire.

Once, when I was little and not too informed about the mechanics, my best friend and I had pretended to make love, our legs spread apart scissor-fashion, until we were crotch to crotch, one person's sneaker under the other person's nose. My grandmother had caught us at it. She sent Cecily home and spanked me with a wooden mixing spoon and made me sit in the pantry to say Hail Marys. There was no doubt in her mind, she said; I got such interests from my mother. Perhaps I did. However, even at that tender age, I had decided that they weren't such bad interests to have.

Nonetheless, I reached seventeen with nothing more than a valentine from Wayne Carmelee and three kisses stolen by a Danish Eagle Scout under the bleachers at the county fair in Sandpoint, Idaho.

This was a source of great personal dismay to me and not helped at all by my sister Megan, who was nine that year and always willing to confirm for me that I was just as ugly as I assumed I must be. She also suggested that I probably smelled bad to boys.

My father told me that all I needed was patience. It

1

was a natural thing, and you couldn't stop nature from catching up to you. My time would come, he said. I'd replied that if we hadn't moved around as much as we had, perhaps nature would have already located me.

So, in the end, it was Mama I went to for comfort. I asked her when she first fell in love.

"Hans Klaus Fischer," she said to me. She'd been scrubbing the floor in the kitchen when I found her. Down on her hands and knees on the linoleum, her hair tied up in a red bandanna, she paused and considered the question. And grinned. Reaching up on the kitchen counter for her cigarettes, she sat down again on the floor and leaned back against the counter next to the sink. She crossed her legs and balanced the ashtray on one knee. "That was when I was living in Dresden with Tante Elfie. You see, I wasn't supposed to be seeing boys. I was just turned fifteen and Tante said I couldn't go out yet. They were very strict in those days, you understand." She lit the cigarette and over the top of it, her eyes were smiling. We both knew that what Tante Elfie said probably never had much effect on what my mother did.

"He was the baker's son. I met him because Tante Elfie made me go after the bread every day. If she'd sent Birgitta, who knows? Perhaps I would never have met him. But Birgitta was the lazy one.

"Anyhow, he was at the back of the shop each day, taking down the loaves." She paused and her eyes were still on me. "And do you think he was handsome?"

"Was he, Mama?" I asked. You always prompted Mama with her stories. That was half the fun.

"Was he handsome? Well, I will tell you. His hair was maybe the color of yours. A little darker, perhaps, and combed down like this. That's the way the boys wore their hair in those days. His eyes were blue, well, maybe more a blue-green. And light. A light, light blue-green. Like the color old glass is sometimes. And he had very fine lips. Thin. Normally, I don't like thin lips on a man, but with Hans Klaus Fischer, they gave him such a very . . . what can I say? . . . important expression. Haughty, that's the word for it. He would stand in the back room and take down the loaves, and I would think, 'Mara, you *must* have that boy for your boyfriend.' You could tell how important he was just by looking at him.''

She grinned at me. ''I was very much in love with him. I went every day for the bread, and while I waited, all I could think of was kissing those fine, important-looking lips.''

''And did you?''

''Well, in the beginning it was very hard to get him to notice me. I was just one girl, and there were many girls in love with Hans Klaus Fischer.''

''But you did get him to fall in love with you, didn't you?'' I asked.

She was still grinning. With one hand she stuck long strands of hair back up under her bandanna, and she said nothing. Mama didn't have to. She just grinned.

''What did you do? How did you get him to notice you when there were all those other girls?''

''I began to come in wearing my *Bund deutscher Mädchen* uniform. Every day. Even when there wasn't a meeting. You see, he was a group leader with the Youth Movement.'' She paused, reflecting, and studied the end of her cigarette. The smile came back to her lips. ''Sometimes I would see him in the back of the shop, and he would have his uniform on. He was very handsome in that uniform. He had a sort of strut in his walk when he wore his uniform, so I could tell he thought it made him somebody. So, I thought to myself, Mara, he's going to like you if he thinks you're a good member of the *BdM.* ''

''And did he?''

She winked at me.

''What did Tante Elfie say then? Did she mind that you were seeing a boy when you weren't supposed to?''

"Well, she did a little. At first she did. But I told her what a fine family Hans Klaus came from. I told her what a good boy he was. He was very clever at his studies, you see, and I heard his father tell Frau Schwartz once in the bakeshop that Hans Klaus might be chosen for the Adolf Hitler School. It was almost a sure thing, he said. So when Tante knew that, she said I could go dancing with him on Friday nights. If Birgitta went along. You know." She laughed. "To make sure I never really found out much about kissing those fine lips. They were very strict in those days. Not like now."

"But how did you make him love you, that's what I want to know. How did you get him to ask you out for a date in the first place?"

Holding the cigarette out, Mama gazed at it before finally snuffing it out in the ashtray. The floor all around us was still wet, and we sat together, barricaded behind scrub brushes, the pail and floor rags, our backs against the kitchen cupboard.

"I did a rather naughty thing," Mama said. Her voice was low and conspiratorial.

"What was that?"

"Well, when he came to the front of the shop once to talk to me, I told him I was really the granddaughter of the Archduke."

I laughed. "You did?"

"I told him my grandfather was the Archduke and that I had been sent to Dresden for my safety. To live with Tante Elfie, who wasn't really my auntie at all but just a nanny my family paid to take care of me."

That struck me as amusing, just the sort of thing I could picture Mama doing with such melodramatic realism that poor Hans Klaus Fischer no doubt never knew what hit him.

"Why on earth did you do that?" I asked.

Giving a shrug, she giggled. "I don't know. It was just

something I did. I wanted to make sure he liked me. I was afraid he wouldn't.''

"But it was a lie, Mama," I said, still tickled with the mental image of it.

Another shrug and she pursed her lips in a pensive expression. "No. Not really. Just a story. I didn't mean it to hurt. There just weren't enough interesting true things to tell him.''

"So, you told him the Archduke was your grandfather?"

"Well, you see, you must understand, I was quite desperate about him. I just wanted things to be nice. I thought if he believed that, then he would certainly want to go dancing with me. And once he knew me, then it wouldn't matter anymore who I was related to." She looked over at me, and the joke of it sparkled in her eyes. "You must understand, I was only fifteen. Everyone's a little mad when they're fifteen, believe me."

"Did he ever find out the truth?"

She shrugged and rose up on her knees to finish the rest of the floor. "I don't know. After I went to Jena, I never saw him again."

I was dreaming. It was about the house on Stuart Avenue where we lived before Megan was born. I was upstairs in the small attic room that my father had made into a bedroom for me. I was standing in front of the little window, looking down on the street below. But instead of the elms that had lined either side of Stuart Avenue, there were sunflowers. The avenue was empty but the sun was shining and it was very beautiful.

However, even though it seemed like the house on Stuart Avenue, I knew it actually wasn't. It was the apartment in Detroit where we had lived for a while when I was very young. While the bedroom upstairs belonged to Stuart Avenue, I knew that the stairway would lead down into the apartment in Detroit.

In the dream I could hear Mama crying. She was sitting on a cardboard box in the gloomy little storage area under the stairs. But I was still upstairs in the house on Stuart Avenue.

"Lesley, are you ever going to get up?"

I jerked awake.

Megan was standing in the doorway of my bedroom. She had nothing on but her underpants and an oversized T-shirt that said "NASA Johnson Space Center/Houston" across the front. Leaning against the door frame, she braced one foot against the shin of her other leg. "Daddy says you have to get up right now, Lesley. He has to go to work for a while this morning and he says you got to come down and stay with Mama while he's gone."

"What time is it?"

"Almost nine o'clock. Daddy says he'll be back after lunch."

She turned and left without shutting the door behind her.

I closed my eyes. I could still remember the dream. I had awakened so abruptly that it clung to me and seemed very real, even as it faded.

By the time I'd dressed and come down to the kitchen, my father had already left. Megan was there, still eating breakfast. She had her chair pushed back from the table, her legs drawn up under the generous folds of the NASA T-shirt. Mama was clearing away the breakfast dishes and putting them into the sink. The radio was playing very loudly. "Saturday Morning Swap Shop." My mother was addicted to the show, relishing all the bargains she dreamed of getting.

I reached over and took a slice of bread to put into the toaster. It was a whole-meal type, full of crunchy little wheat berries. Although it made wonderful toast, it was messy to eat because all the wheat berries tumbled everywhere. And Megan, who already had a piece, wasn't helping things. She was picking wheat berries out and carefully setting them atop her knees, which, pulled up under the T shirt, formed a knobby platform. Then she licked the wheat berries off with the tip of her tongue. Each one, one by one.

"Honestly, Megan, you eat like a pig," I said.

Megan set another wheat berry out, looked over to make certain I was watching and then languidly pulled it up with the tip of her tongue.

"Mama, look at her. Look at the disgusting mess Megan is making with her toast."

My mother turned from the sink. She regarded Megan a moment and shook her head. "You're making crumbs everywhere," she said. "Sit up and put your feet down where they belong."

I went to the cupboard for Rice Krispies.

"Megan, Mama said put your feet down," I said when I returned to the table with my bowl of cereal.

"So? You're not my mother."

"Well, she is. So, do it, Megan. Mama said to."

"So, make me."

Annoyed, I sat down.

When Megan continued to pick at her toast, I reached over and grabbed one of her legs. I yanked it down to the floor.

Mama ignored us. She kept her back to us and continued to do the dishes. She had a Brillo pad in one hand and the old cast-iron skillet in the other and was really giving it hell. Occasionally, she would pause and put to her lips the cigarette that was burning in the ashtray on the windowsill. Once she turned the radio higher. But she never turned around.

When Megan reached for another piece of toast, I clamped my hand over her wrist.

"Stop it!" Megan said, rather louder than necessary. "Stop bossing me around all the time, Lesley."

"The way you're eating that toast is nauseating and

you know it. Now, you can't have another slice. You're
making a mess on purpose."

"Leave me alone."

"Mama? Make Megan stop. She's still picking at her
bread. She didn't listen to you at all the first time."

"Lesley, let go of me. Let go of my arm! I mean it."
She leaped to her feet to yank her arm free. The motion
knocked her chair over backwards with a resounding bang.

Mama turned around.

Silence.

We both looked at her. She picked up her cigarette and
snuffed it out in the ashtray with great care. The room
went so quiet that I thought I could hear the sound of the
cigarette against the glass of the ashtray, in spite of the
clamor of "Saturday Morning Swap Shop."

Wearily, Mama raised a hand to run through the hair
alongside her face. "What is the matter with you two?
You're sisters. How can you always argue?"

We didn't answer. There was no point in answering.

"I can't understand you," Mama said. "Why aren't
you happy? You have such good lives. O'Malley and I,
we love you. We give you everything. And still you
aren't happy."

"We're happy," Megan said.

"We were just horsing around, Mama," I said. "We
didn't mean to sound like we were arguing. Did we,
Megs? We were just playing."

"I cannot understand you."

"We *are* happy, Mama," Megan said again and there
was soft desperation in her voice. "See? See? I'm
smiling. I'm happy. Me and Lesley, we're really happy.
Don't cry, okay?"

But it was too late. Mama lowered her face into her
hands. Then she ran from the kitchen. We remained, listening to the shuffling unevenness of her footsteps on the
stairs until they were drowned out by the radio.

Megan also began to cry. The tipped-over chair was still on the floor behind her. She stood, watching me, and let the tears run down over her cheeks.

"Look, Megs, you want some more breakfast? Some toaster waffles maybe? You like them, Meggie. Don't cry, all right? Shall I fix you some waffles? They're your favorites."

Wiping her eyes, she shook her head. Then she righted the chair and left the kitchen too.

My dad called them "spells." Mama's spells. When they happened, he would lift his shoulders in a bemused half-shrug and then smile, as if it were just a whimsical little quirk she had, such as the way other people might throw salt over their shoulder after spilling it. Although I'd hated the episodes, for most of my childhood I thought they were normal. I thought every child's mother acted like that. I must have been ten or eleven before I discovered other mothers didn't.

I stayed in the kitchen alone and finished up the few dishes left in the sink. Clearing off the table, I wiped away the last crumbs of Megan's toast. I dumped the soggy Rice Krispies.

Sometime later Megan came back into the kitchen. With a wide-toothed comb, she was trying to untangle the ends of her hair. "Will you help me?" she asked, holding out the comb. "I can't get all the snarls out."

My sister had beautiful hair. Like my father's, it was so dark that it was almost black, but like Mama's, it was very, very straight. You could run your fingers through it and it would fall away in a soft, undulating manner, like water. The best part about Megan's hair, however, was the length. It was nearly long enough for her to sit on. There was so much of it and it was so often left loose, since the sheer weight of it prevented her using little-girls' barrettes or headbands, that Megan always had a kind of untamed look about her. Even so, people stopped sometimes and turned around to look at her again because she was so striking. I had never been allowed to keep my hair that long when I was Megan's age, but then I had never had hair like Megan's.

"You know, Les, Daddy's going to kill you for giving Mama a spell," Megan said softly as I combed her hair.

"Me? It was your fault, you little pig. Daddy's going to kill us both."

She didn't answer. Pulling away from me, she took the comb out of my hand and went over to the table. She hoisted herself up on it and then pulled long strands of hair around to comb the tangles from the ends.

"Megan, don't do that on the table."

She didn't respond.

"Did you hear me? That's unsanitary. Go somewhere else."

Still no response. But she had stopped combing her hair. Instead, she just fingered through it, regarding the strands. "Les?" she asked without looking up. "Why do you suppose Mama does that?"

"Does what?"

"You know. *That.* I mean, we were just goofing around, that's all. How come she can never tell that?"

I shrugged.

"Why does she keep thinking we're unhappy? How come it's so important to her anyway that we be happy a hundred percent of every second?"

"It's just one of those things, Megs."

"One of what things?"

I shrugged.

At a quarter to eleven Mama came downstairs again. Megan and I were still sitting in the kitchen. She came to the table and reached for her cigarettes.

"Do you want a cup of coffee?" I asked. I was already on my feet.

She nodded. Going over to the sink, she leaned forward to look out the window above it. With fingers of one hand resting against her lips, she smoked without ever taking the cigarette from her mouth.

"There are no flowers," she said.

"No," I replied. "But there'll be plenty again when spring comes. Remember all the new ones Daddy planted?"

Megan had wrestled the teakettle away from me so that she could fix Mama's coffee herself. Carefully, she measured a spoonful of granules from the jar. "Here, Mama," she said, stirring the boiling water in. "Here's your coffee." She squeezed her body between my mother and the sink in an effort to make Mama look down at her. She held up the mug of steaming liquid. "Here, Mama. Just the way you like it." But my mother stared over her to the window.

They didn't look much alike, my sister and my mother. Megan was thin and lithe and dark, like some half-imagined thing escaped from the pages of a fairy tale. Mama was tall and pale, with broad, prominent features. Her hair was still light as sea sand. The only thing she had given Megan was her blue eyes, and they were very blue, like chambray cloth.

Mama turned entirely away from the window, and Megan had to run around to be in front of her again.

"I'm sick of this place," Mama said. "It's too cold. I hate the cold."

Mama went over to the table and sat down. With both hands she finally accepted Megan's mug of coffee.

"Does that mean we're going to move again?" Megan asked very quietly.

"I don't like it here," Mama replied.

"I do," Megan said, her voice still soft and tentative. Mama was regarding her over the top of her mug as she drank the coffee. "I think it's nice here, Mama. I got friends here. Like Katie and Tracey Pickett."

My mother lowered the cup. "There are no flowers."

"But Mama, it's January."

With a sigh my mother set the coffee mug on the table. She gazed at it. "But there are no flowers here."

"There aren't any flowers anywhere in January, Mama," Megan said.

My mother was silent for a moment. "There were in Lébény. In Popi's conservatory," she said. "There were always flowers there."

Megan's face brightened abruptly. Coming closer to Mama, she knelt down and put her arms around Mama's neck. With one hand Megan moved Mama's face away from the direction of the coffee mug so that she would have to look at her. "Tell me and Lessie about Lébény, okay, Mama? About Popi's flowers, okay? Tell us about that time you and Elek sneaked in and took Popi's camellias for your hair and then you two went to that dance. You know. That time you weren't supposed to be up late because it was a big-people's party. The time they played 'The Blue Danube' and you and Elek danced in the upstairs hallway and you could smell all the beautiful ladies' perfume. Tell us that story, okay?"

My mother's face softened. The tired, bloodless look left her and she smiled down at Megan, who was on her knees beside the chair. "You know that story, *Liebes*. I have told you that story a hundred times already."

"Oh, I know," Megan said, her expression beguiling. "But it's really my super favorite. Tell me again, okay? Please? Me and Lessie want to hear it."

Mama was still smiling when she touched Megan's face. The smile made my mother very beautiful.

# Two

My mother was born into a family of the Hungarian gentry, genteelly declining in the ruins of the old Austro-Hungarian Empire. Her father, who had fought alongside von Hindenburg in the Great War, had retired from the military a short time afterward and returned to manage his family estate in northwestern Hungary. His child bride, whom he'd met and married in 1914, was the youngest daughter of one of the old, established families in Meissen, in Saxonia.

Besides my mother, there had been three other children in her family. Her older brother, Mihály, she remembered only dimly because he had gone far away for schooling in Germany before she was two. Her beloved younger brother, Elek, however, was only thirteen months her junior, and they had been constant childhood companions. Mama's stories about Elek were so vivid he almost seemed to be *my* brother. Her younger sister, Johanna, had died of scarlet fever the year Mama was eight.

Although my mother never said as much, I suspect she had been her father's favorite among the four children. She had been a strikingly beautiful child, with that blond, clear-eyed pureness that was so prized in those days in that part of Europe. In all the photographs, she was dressed up like a little princess, in velvets and silks and

lace. Her flaxen hair was very long and carefully curled.
And even with the solemn mood of those old pictures,
she'd managed just the slightest hint of a smile on her
lips. We had only one photograph of her entire family together, and in it, my mother stood apart from the other
children and leaned against Popi's arm. If you looked
carefully, you could see his hand on her shoulder, his fingers twisted lovingly through her hair.

Popi had seen to it that she was well turned out. She
had been bilingual all her life because Mutti spoke to her
only in German while Popi spoke Hungarian. But he had
also brought a special tutor from Milan for her when she
was six so that she could learn Italian. She had had dancing lessons and voice lessons and had learned to play the
piano and the organ. When she'd wanted a pony, Popi
hired a riding instructor from Vienna and bought her a
white horse.

Like her older brother, Mihály, my mother had been a
gifted student. As always, Popi was determined to give
her the best advantages. Both he and Mutti believed in
the superiority of a German education, so when my
mother was twelve, she went to live with Mutti's sister,
Tante Elfie, in Dresden. There she attended a private
girls' school and prepared for the university.

My mother had hated leaving home. For a solid year,
she said, she was homesick, crying herself to sleep so
many nights that Tante Elfie finally moved her bed into
the hallway so that she wouldn't disturb Birgitta, Tante
Elfie's daughter, with whom Mama was sharing a room.
On this occasion Popi didn't give in to her pleas, and she
stayed in Dresden. Slowly, she grew accustomed to life
in the city, to Tante Elfie, who insisted on always setting
her table with a lace tablecloth, and to Birgitta, who
snored.

The war broke out during my mother's first year at the
university in Jena. She was sixteen and able to continue

her studies into the autumn of that year before the turmoil disrupted university life. She would have been sent back to Hungary, she told us, because Hitler was deporting everyone with foreign birth certificates, but she was recognized as an ethnic German, a *Volksdeutscherin*, and allowed to stay. Soon afterward, she went to a youth hostel in northern Germany with several other girls who had been members of the *Bund deutscher Mädchen*.

Mama didn't have a lot of stories about those years. I think she was desperately frightened for much of the time. The hostel wasn't far from Hamburg, and my mother often spoke of hiding in a cupboard to muffle the sounds of the Allied planes flying over. What we did hear about, when she told stories, was the countryside, broad, flat, humid in summer, frigid in winter. And we heard sometimes about other girls and women whom she met during the war. Part of the time she worked on a farm, and one of her best characters came from those experiences. Jadwiga was a Polish matron from Warsaw. I was never exactly clear how Jadwiga came to be on the farm, and from the way Mama told it, Jadwiga always sounded slightly surprised by the circumstances herself. What amused Mama was that it never seemed to bother Jadwiga so much that she was a city housewife out doing farmwork but rather that she was forced into intimacy with such socially inferior individuals as she thought all the other women to be. Mama, who had a wicked gift for mimicking people, would give us the whole show, imitating Jadwiga down to her walk, her buck teeth and her nasal accent. Mama would sashay around and around the room, snorting at us in mock Polish, contorting her face into a rabbity look of disdain until she would break up, laughing so hard that she was forced to stop. She'd drop into a chair then, clutching her stomach, overcome with hilarity. Inevitably, Megan and I would laugh until we had tears running down our faces.

By 1945, when the British soldiers came with chocolate and cigarettes, my mother had typhus and was so
sick she had no memory of them. She did recall the chocolate bars, however, and in her drawer in the bedroom,
she still kept the wrapper from the first one she was given
after the war.

It was then, while lying in the hospital recovering, that
my mother met my father. He was an American G.I. who
had come to visit someone else in the ward. Mama was in
bed, still weak from typhus, half bald from malnutrition,
and with her arm bandaged from wrist to elbow because
of a septic cut. As my dad was walking down the aisle between the rows of beds, Mama, who was trying to eat
soup with the wrong hand, had dropped not only her
spoon but the tray and bowl as well. Soup went everywhere. My father bent down to retrieve the rolling soup
bowl. When he stood up and gave it back to her, that was
it, he said. He loved her instantly, bandage, bald head,
soup and all. Whether that's precisely how it happened,
it's hard to say. My father always has been a romantic.

They married in Vienna on New Year's Day, 1946.
My mother's one wish as she grew stronger had been to
return to Hungary and locate her family. She'd lost contact with all of them during the course of the war.
Throughout the winter of 1945–46, she and my father
searched through the war-ravaged countryside of Germany, Austria, western Czechoslovakia and northwestern Hungary.

None of my mother's immediate family had survived
the war. Her brother Mihály, who already had a wife and
child by the time the war broke out, was conscripted into
the *Wehrmacht* in 1936. He was killed during maneuvers
in France. Mutti died of heart failure in 1940. Elek, who
had remained at home to help his father run the estate
rather than joining the military the way most boys his age
had done, was shot by German soldiers in 1942. Popi,

distraught and alone, had gone up to Tante Elfie's in Dresden to search for information about my mother. He and Tante Elfie were killed in the 1945 Allied bombings. My mother never located Birgitta.

In September of 1946 my father was again posted to his army base in southern England. After discharge the following spring, he and my mother remained in Great Britain, eventually moving to Wales. Most of the following ten years were spent living in a cottage on a Welsh mountainside. Mama told Megan and me beautifully elaborate stories about that period of their lives. The cottage where they lived had been derelict, and the farmer Dad worked for had told them they could live in it rent free, if they wanted to fix it up. He'd felt sorry for Mama, who was still in poor health, and he said the mountain air would help speed her recovery. The cottage was way up in the hills without even a road to it. They had to walk up a steep trail through a forest and over a footbridge to get there. Chiseled in slate above the door was the name of the cottage in Welsh. It meant Forest of Flowers. Mama said when they came the whole back garden of the cottage was overgrown with sunflowers. Mama took that to be a good omen, since sunflowers didn't normally do well in Wales because of the rain. But at Forest of Flowers they thrived. My parents lived there until the late fifties. Then there was a cold winter, followed by a wet summer, and the sunflowers didn't bloom. Mama and Daddy moved.

I waited until my father had finished his supper that Saturday evening and had gone up to his study. At night after a meal he liked to go there to sit among his things and listen to the radio. Occasionally he would read or write letters but usually he did nothing more than push back the lounger, put the music station on and listen.

"Dad?" I said and opened the door slightly. "May I talk to you?"

He had the lounger fully reclined and his eyes were closed. He opened them. "Yes, of course, Lessie, come in."

I shut the door carefully behind me and came over to sit on the footstool beside the chair. I touched the arm of the lounger with one finger to feel the rough, knobby threads in the upholstery.

"Are we going to move, Dad?"

He had his eyes closed again. The radio was playing quite loudly. It was classical music. In all honesty I don't believe my father knew up from down about such music. My mother did. She knew the titles, who composed what when, which type of music it was and who the performing artist was. But Dad neither knew nor particularly cared. He liked to listen because that was the only radio station with almost no commercials.

He didn't answer my question.

"I hear Mama beginning to talk," I said. "She's thinking about it."

"She hasn't said anything to me."

"No. She hasn't said anything to me either. But I can hear it nonetheless."

He didn't stir.

"So? Are we?" I asked.

"Your mama needs a warmer climate, Lessie," he said at last and opened his eyes again. "It's too cold for her here."

"We've been to warmer climates before, Dad, and she didn't like any of them either. Face it. She doesn't really like it anywhere."

I could see the pupils of his eyes dilate. They grew larger for a moment and then shrank back.

"Your mama hasn't said a thing to me," he said. "So don't go thinking up problems you haven't got."

I felt the upholstery again with my finger.

"And another thing, I don't like to hear you talk like that. The cold bothers her. You know that. It aggravates her back. So, it's through no fault of her own."

"She's got pills for her back, Dad."

He was still watching me. "Well, there's no need for her to suffer with the cold when there are plenty of warmer places."

"It's not the cold," I replied. "It's the flowers."

He pushed the lounger up into the sitting position. "What?"

"I said, it's the flowers. It's not the cold or her back or anything else. It's the stupid flowers. She wants to be somewhere with flowers. Even in January."

My father didn't say anything. It grew noticeably quiet, even with the music playing.

I studied him. My father couldn't exactly be called a handsome man. He was of Irish descent, short and wiry, with masses of curly black hair, graying by his ears. His face had a well-lived-in look, especially around the eyes, as if he'd had a lifetime of bad nights' sleep. But it was a cheerful face. He had a very ruddy complexion that gave him Santa Claus cheeks, and he was always betting Megs and me that we couldn't look at him for five minutes without smiling. Neither of us could. Yet, he was an unexpected choice to complement my mother's rather awesome appearance.

"It isn't fair, you know," I said. "As soon as we really get settled somewhere, you guys want to up and leave. And frankly, Dad, I just don't want to go anywhere right now. I'm a senior this year. I'm going to graduate and I want to do it here where I got some friends. I know kids here." I looked over. "What I really want is to go to my senior prom. I want to get asked out by some guy and go on a date and be like every other girl in the senior class. I don't want to be the only one not invited. The only one who doesn't have anywhere to go. And if we move now, that's what's going to happen.''

He smiled gently and reached a hand over to touch me. ''I know it's been hard sometimes,'' he said, and I could tell from his voice that if it came to a showdown between Mama and me over moving, I wouldn't stand a chance.

I sighed. Then once again, heavily. ''I feel like I'm going to be a million years old before I even have a date. I feel like I'm probably going to be a toothless old granny, and when I get my first kiss, he'll suck my dentures right out.''

He grinned.

''It's not funny, Dad.''

''I know it, sweetie,'' he said and chortled anyway.

''Look, if Mama decides to move—''

''Lesley, she has said absolutely nothing about it. You're creating problems that don't exist.''

''If Mama *decides* to move, I want to stay with Brianna. I've already talked to her. I told her we might be moving, and she said she'd ask her mom to see if I could stay with them until the school year ends. It'd only be until June.''

''You shouldn't be talking to people about family matters, Les. This is strictly our personal business. I don't think you ought to be sharing it with strangers.''

''Daddy, Brianna's no stranger. She's my very best friend. Besides, I wasn't specific. I was just sounding her out.''

''The cold bothers your mother,'' he replied flatly. ''If she wants to move, then I think we ought to move. We owe her that much.''

I said nothing. I put my head down and braced it between my hands. I gazed at the floor. The music coming from the radio was Rachmaninoff's. One of his concertos. I couldn't remember which one.

''Dad?''

"Hmm?"

"Do you think I'm ugly or anything? I mean, being really honest with me."

His eyes widened. "Of course you're not ugly, Lesley. What a thing to ask."

"I was just wondering." I listened to the remainder of the concerto and studied the pattern in the rug.

"Look," he said, and his voice was gentle, "you still have plenty of time. Don't put yourself in a state over it. Things'll work out just fine."

I raised my head. "How old were you when you first went out with a girl?"

"Older than you are now. I was in the army."

"Didn't you ever go out before that? When you were at home?"

"The way your grandmother felt about things like that? Are you kidding? And way out there on the farm?" He grinned. "I was lucky I even knew what girls were."

"Oh."

"So, see?" He put his hand on my head. "Nature'll take care of things. Don't worry. Your time will come."

# Three

THERE WERE no tattered remnants of European aristoc-
racy in my father's background, no private tutors, no
summer afternoons whiled away with garden parties and
violin music. The son of an Irish immigrant, my father
grew up on a pig farm on the vast plains of Illinois.

There were seven children. My dad was the fourth
child, the second son. They weren't a poor family, not
dirt poor the way a lot of farm families were in the Depression. Not the way his father had been when he'd arrived, aged four, in steerage with his parents at Ellis
Island. But my dad had recollections of just getting by.
My favorite was the one about how he got into a fight at
school because another boy had said his coat was a girl's
coat. It had been. His mother had made it over for him
from one his sister Kathleen had outgrown. When he was
recounting that episode, Dad would always end up with a
grin. Yes, he'd say, it had been a girl's coat, but he sure
wasn't going to let Jacky Barnes say so.

The mainstay of their lives had been religion. Both my
father's parents were devout Catholics. All of the children had had at least a few years at parochial school, even
with the hardship of the Depression. One of his sisters
had later joined an order of nuns devoted to helping the
poor and still lived in Colombia. His younger brother
taught theology at a university in Massachusetts.

When my father was thirteen, his father was killed in a farm accident. He had been mangled under the wreckage of an overturned tractor, and two men nearby had helped free him and bring him down to the house. My dad had been alone at the time. He was hoeing in the vegetable garden and keeping an eye on the baby, who was about two. The men had come, carrying his dying father between them. Dad wasn't one for telling stories. Unlike Mama, he couldn't spin out a small incident into a captivating drama. But when he told this, you felt it. You saw the skinny kid in worn overalls and dusty bare feet. You saw the baby with his one-eyed teddy bear. Daddy's mother had gone down to the neighbors' and so he'd been alone at the house with his small brother and his maimed father and he didn't know what to do. And every time he told about it, you felt his horror.

So I never knew my grandfather. We didn't even have a photograph of him. Once, Dad told us, a traveling photographer had stopped by the farm and offered to take a picture of all of them. His mother had made the children wash and dress in their Sunday clothes. But when the photographer returned with the developed pictures, he wanted more money than he had said initially: They hadn't said there were so many children, the photographer told them. A deal's a deal, Dad's father had replied. In the end, the photographer was sent packing, photographs and all.

Grandma O'Malley, however, I knew well. When I was very little we'd gone to Illinois every summer to visit her. She lived in a little row house in a northern sector of Chicago not far from Uncle Paddy and Aunt Gretchen's house, and I remember the cool, damp-smelling attic room where I slept. Later, when I was in grade school, I spent the month of July with her each year.

She was a tiny woman with white hair that she kept in a braided bun and skin stretched so tightly over her bones that her forearms and hands had always reminded me of the legs of a bird. Being very much my mother's daughter in respect to height and bone structure, I was bigger than Grandma O'Malley by the time I was ten.

I had always looked forward to those visits when I was in grade school. What I actually loved most, I think, were the journeys to and from Chicago with my father. They had been great adventures to me. We always went alone, just him and me, and left Mama at home to take care of Megan. All my Julys were bracketed with memories of Daddy and me sitting way in the back of the bus where my mother refused to sit because it made her carsick, of sharing Cokes and candy bars with him, of making wishes on white horses we saw in roadside pastures. We ate in steamy, dimly lit bus depot cafés and slept in motels with saggy mattresses and chenille curtains at the windows or dozed in drowsy, diesel-scented darkness.

The visits themselves I anticipated rather less. There were plenty of good aspects, particularly after Megan was born, when I was relieved to discover that I could still go alone and Megan couldn't come because she was too little for Grandma to take care of. Plus, my cousins lived just down the street from Grandma's and gave me a constant source of familiar playmates each summer, which I longed for after our frequent moves. And Grandma was usually willing to spoil me a little. She had small gifts for me when I arrived. She gave me all the pennies from her change each night. Best of all, she would make me buttermilk pancakes for breakfast any morning I asked for them, which was something my mama would never do because she'd never adjusted to the idea of making a whole meal out of something sweet.

There were, however, less enjoyable aspects about going to see Grandma. From the moment I arrived with Daddy I was always aware of a subtle uneasiness, that kind of tension you can detect so readily when you're young. And it permeated the entire stay. Regardless of the little surprises and treats Grandma had in store for me, the visits always left me anxious and on my guard.

From a very early age I knew what lay at the heart of the matter. Grandma O'Malley was devoutly Catholic and my mother was not only not Catholic, she wasn't even what could honestly be called Christian. Consequently, neither my sister nor I had been baptized, confirmed or even taken to church. This left my grandmother aghast.

Of course, Grandma O'Malley did her best to rectify what she considered an unthinkable situation. The moment after my father left, Grandma would call up the priest and have him come over to see me. She bought me Sunday dresses and patent-leather shoes and books of children's Bible stories. She marched me off to Mass and catechism classes and vacation Bible school. During mealtimes she quizzed me about the life of Jesus. While we were doing dishes, she would listen to me recite the Bible verses she'd given me to memorize. And the summer I was nine, she promised to give me five dollars if I would go home and see that Daddy had Megan baptized.

With deadly regularity, my July visits would end with a terrible argument between my father and my grandmother. Dad's first words to me as he arrived to take me home were invariably about church. Those questions doomed me. If I lied and said I'd had nothing to do with church while I was there, I got into trouble for not telling the truth. If I told the truth, he yelled at Grandma because he had expressly forbidden her to send me to Bible school or catechism classes or whatever and, of course, she always went ahead and did it anyway. Then they'd progress to his telling her that I was his child and if she didn't like his rules then I wasn't going to be allowed to come again, and to her telling him that she was not about to have any grandchild of hers burning in Hell. Within moments they'd be arguing about Mama.

Grandma knew Mama's views on religion. It was impossible not to. If you knew Mama, you knew her views. My mother was fanatically opposed to religion in any form of the word. It was because of the things she had seen in the war, she always said, and because of the way she saw religious people react. She said they knew. She said a lot of people knew—the foreign governments, the people in high places, even a lot of ordinary people. She said they knew of the various kinds of terrible suffering that was tolerated in Germany. And she said they still went home at night and had their suppers and said their prayers and went to bed. They all thought of themselves as good Christians when they were in church on Sunday. They thought they lived in Christian nations. But what kind of teaching was that? Where was the Pope when the Jews were in Auschwitz? Where were the nuns and the priests and the clergymen and all the good, righteous Christians in the Congress and the world parliaments, who could have helped, who could have passed laws to let in more refugees, who could have provided more routes of escape, or, more importantly, who could have stopped what was happening altogether? Mama always maintained it could have been stopped. If everyone had tried. Together, the Christians, the churches, the Pope, all of them, they could have formed a voice that no leader, not even Hitler, could have ignored. But they hadn't. Even if it wasn't conscious, she said, they had chosen not to help. And my mama had no use whatsoever for the doctrines that had allowed so many to turn their backs so easily on all that suffering.

Grandma, for her part, had no use for my mama. I don't think it was so much Mama's personal atheism, because I don't think it mattered a whole lot to Grandma what became of Mama's eternal soul. Even though she never said, I always suspected that Grandma felt Hell would probably suit Mama just fine. But what did matter to her was that Mama had taken my father away from the Church. And with him, Megan and me.

Despite my father's threats about keeping me home, I did go back to Grandma's every July until she died, the year I was thirteen. Almost all I knew about my father's youth came from those summers.

I think my dad, a quiet and undistinctive boy from the sounds of things, might have escaped notice in the rough-and-tumble anonymity of such a large family, if it hadn't been for his poor health. He had suffered a mild case of polio as an infant and later, scarlet fever, and these left him with what Grandma called ''a weakness of the chest.'' Consequently, he had been sick a lot, often seriously, and much of his childhood was marked by long periods of isolation and convalescence. Because of it, he'd grown into a shy, introverted boy, not bookish, the way his brother Colin was, but just self-absorbed. Grandma said she'd never been much worried by that. With the casual certainty about destiny that is so common in devoutly religious families, it was assumed my father would become a priest, because he was the second son and that's what second sons did. So Grandma was comforted by the knowledge that he was not inclined toward fast cars, parties and the high life, the way Paddy, Kip and Mick were.

Of course, my father didn't become a priest. Nor did he achieve Grandma's other aspiration for all her sons: a college education. When my dad was finished with high school, the Second World War had started and like so many other young men of his day, he'd ended up in that. What always went unsaid in these conversations with Grandma but was implied was that Dad had met my mother while he was in Europe. Grandma was capable of attributing virtually anything my father didn't accomplish to the fact that he had married my mother.

So, my father had joined the army and was posted to England. He was only twenty-one when he married my mother, who was almost two years his senior. After that, he never found the time nor the money nor the energy to pursue a higher education. And frankly, I don't think my father ever particularly minded.

What did bother him were the kinds of jobs he ended up with because of his lack of skills. Between moving so often and no real training, my father had always done whatever he could find, taking dead-end jobs that were easy to get and easy to leave. They never paid enough money, and they usually required physical effort, which made him less employable as he grew older. When we'd moved to Kansas from our previous home in Nebraska, my father had been unemployed for over two months before he found work at Hughson's Garage. No one was looking for a fifty-year-old unskilled laborer.

I knew he hated his jobs. He never said so but it was one of those things you could feel. He would linger a moment too long over his morning coffee. He would come home with his hands black and his clothes dirty and apologize to Mama even before he kissed her, although Mama had never complained. But mainly it was the study. In every house we'd ever lived in my father had always insisted on having an extra room for his study. Even if it meant Megan and I had to share a bedroom. Someday, he told me once, he'd have a job where he'd have to bring home work from the office to do at his desk and he'd need a study—somewhere quiet to get away from the noise of the TV and Megs and me and Mama's records, so he could do his paperwork. So far he had never found such a job but every night after supper he went upstairs and sat for a while behind the desk and waited.

While my father dreamed, my mother acted. We lived like Gypsies because of Mama. She pursued happiness down a real road. Wherever we were, my mother assumed peace of mind must be waiting over the next hill. Nowhere suited her for long. She wanted it cooler; she wanted it warmer. She wanted to be in the country; she wanted to be in town. Always searching, never finding.

There was a regular routine to our moves. First Mama would grow restless. Pacing around the house, uprooting things and transplanting them in the garden, paging through Megs' or my schoolbooks and constructing fabulous tales about what she imagined the places in the pictures must be like, while my sister and I would sit captivated, eating our afternoon snacks at the kitchen table. Then would come the depression. Any little thing my sister or I'd do would upset her, and she'd start having more and more spells. Her anxieties would increase, in particular, her fear of leaving the immediate environs of the house and yard, because she'd begin thinking the people in the community didn't like her anymore. Then Dad and I would get stuck with all the grocery shopping and the errands. When those things started happening, I knew it was only a matter of time before we would head off for some new horizon.

I hated the moves. I hated the awful weariness right afterward when I would wake up in the morning and realize that all the people out there were strangers except for Mama, Daddy and Megan. I hated the discouraging task of starting over, of trying to make new friends, of even wanting to try.

My feelings, however, never appeared to make much difference. When my mother was in that state, she had no energy left over for other people's feelings. As far as my father was concerned, relieving her discomfort was all that seemed to matter. He never questioned the process. If Mama wanted to move, we moved. If Mama thought we'd be happier in Yakima or North Platte or Timbuktu, then that was all it took for my father. He would drop everything, give notice at his job, sell whatever was necessary to raise the money, then pick up and go to wherever it was Mama believed she'd be at peace this time. And he expected the same devotion from Megs and me. We were not allowed even to question the move in front of Mama: This was just something you did when you were part of a family.

The guidance counselor was waiting for me again when I came out of my calculus class on Wednesday of that week. She was leaning against the lockers on the other side of the corridor, and when I came out of the door of the classroom, all she did was nod and I knew it was meant for me. Without exchanging any words, we went back to her office together.

The counselors, six men and Miss Harrich, were together in the new part of the school building. Each one had a little cubicle just large enough to accommodate a desk, a desk chair and a second chair and still have space to close the door. In Miss Harrich's cubicle there was a large framed print hanging over her desk that said, in letters that were nearly impossible to read, "A wrongdoer is often a man who has left something undone." It took me the better part of three visits to puzzle it out.

Sitting down at her desk, Miss Harrich lifted a file with my name on it from the stack by the dictionary. For several moments she riffled through the contents, stopping to read occasionally with such absorption that it was hard to believe she had read it all so many times before.

"So, how's it going?" she asked me.

I shrugged. "All right."

"Are you thinking, as I asked you to? About where you want to go to college?"

"Yes," I said.

"Have you decided?"

I shrugged.

"Lesley, I hate to have to keep reminding you about this, but the time is coming. You'll have to get an application in. You can't procrastinate forever."

I nodded.

There was a pause and she looked back down at the file. I was sitting across from her and could see what she was reading. I already knew what was in the file: my IQ score, my achievement-test results, a long note from my old chemistry teacher that said he thought I was an underachiever. I could read upside down easily.

"You're exceptionally good at languages, Lesley. German, French, two years of Spanish. Do you still speak Hungarian at home?"

"Sometimes," I said.

"There are some promising career opportunities for linguists. Have you thought about doing something like that? You're very good. And it's an open field, job-wise."

I nodded.

Miss Harrich sighed. I wasn't trying to be difficult, although I could tell she thought I was. Or at least that I wasn't being very cooperative.

"You know," she said, "I am trying to help you, Lesley. I know you think I'm just hassling you, but I'm not. I'm worried that you're going to just keep putting this off and putting it off until it's too late. And you're such a bright girl. You have so much potential. I just don't want to see you waste it."

I stared at my hands. My stomach hurt and I wanted to leave.

There was a long, uncomfortable silence. She watched me, and because I couldn't bring myself to look at her face, I studied her clothes. She was an older woman, perhaps near sixty, but she dressed very fashionably. Soft wool skirts and silk-look blouses, in muted, earthy colors. If she'd been someone else, I would have liked to ask her where she bought them. They didn't look like what you found in our town.

I shrugged wearily as the silence grew too heavy for me. I didn't know what to say to her. I didn't even know what was wrong, why it was so hard to look at the applications and do something about them, why I hated coming in here so much that it made me feel sick to my stomach.

"Is anything wrong?" she asked. "I mean, how's it going for you? Generally speaking. Classes all right? Are you having any trouble?"

I shook my head.

"Are things okay at home?"

I nodded.

She regarded me for a long moment before finally opening her desk drawer to take out the pad of hall passes. "If you ever need anyone to talk to," she said, "you know I'm here."

"I have history now," I said when I saw her hesitate over that blank on the form. "Room 204. Mr. Peterson."

"You heard me, didn't you? That's why I'm here, Lesley. To help out when things get rough. I do care. You know that, don't you?"

I stood and held out my hand for the pass. When she laid her pen down, I snatched the form from the pad and left.

Claire, one of my group of friends from school, was having a party the next Friday night. Her mother was helping her clear the furniture from the family room, and there was going to be a live band. It was a local band, made up of three boys from our high school and someone named Frog Newton from Goodland, who played the drums. Frog was a friend of Brianna's cousin, and Brianna said she thought he was one of the weirder monkeys not in the zoo. She always referred to him as Fig Newton, which in my mind was an improvement over Frog.

Claire's party was the big social event of the term among my crowd, which by and large didn't seem to generate many big social events. None of us girls who were friends that year was exactly femme fatale material. Claire still had a generous amount of what her mother affectionately called "puppy fat." Brianna wore glasses and braces and had hair like Little Orphan Annie's. And of course there was me. Naturally, Claire intended that we all bring dates. But she did tell us that her brother and a bunch of his friends were coming, which was a diplomatic way of saying that there would be at least some boys on the premises.

After lunch on Wednesday I went down to my locker to change books for my next class. I stood alone, sifting through the debris in the bottom of the locker, searching for my German vocabulary notebook.

"Where were you in history class today?"

I looked up.

His name was Paul Krueger. I didn't know him well because the only class I had with him was history and he sat clear across the room. All I knew for sure about him was that he was reckoned to be a whiz kid in physics. Otherwise, he was an ordinary sort of boy with brown, wavy hair and a lumpish build, like a wrestler's.

"I was down at the counselor's office. Miss Harrich is always hassling me about college applications."

Shifting his books from one arm to the other, he leaned back against the locker next to mine. "Too bad you got her. I got Mr. Perryman. He's not so bad."

"Yeah. It's because my last name begins with *O*."

"Yeah. Mine begins with *K*."

"Yeah," I said.

Silence. We both looked away.

"Luckiest kids are those with last names starting with
*S,* because they get Mr. Kent. He's really nice. I know.
My friend Bob's got him."

"Yeah, they're lucky."

"Yeah," he agreed.

"Yeah."

Silence.

"So. Where are you going to college?" he asked me.
"Have you been accepted anyplace yet?"

I shrugged.

"I'm going to Ohio State. They've got a good statistics department there. That's what I'm going to major in.
Statistics." He shifted his books again. "My old man
says there's lots of jobs available in statistics. And you
know how it is. You pretty much do what the old man
says."

With a smile, I nodded. I had located my vocabulary
notebook, so I shut the locker door. By the hall clock I
could see I had only two minutes left to get to German
and I didn't want to be late because Mr. Tennant gave us
marks when we were tardy.

Paul was studying the fingernails on his left hand. "I
wanted to ask you something—in history class," he said,
still regarding his hand. "But you weren't there."

"No, I wasn't."

"No."

Still the intense interest in his fingernails.

"See, I'm a friend of Kurt's—you know, Claire's
brother. And about this thing on Friday night." He
looked over. "You going to it?"

"You mean Claire's party?" I asked.

He nodded.

I shrugged. "I guess so."

"You want to go with me?"

My jaw went slack.

"I mean, assuming you're not going with anyone else or anything. Are you?"

"Yes. I mean, no, I'm not. I mean, yes, I'll go with you. If you want." I grinned. "Yeah. Okay. I will."

"Great, then." He hoisted up his books. "I gotta go to English. Listen, I'll talk to you more after school, okay?"

I nodded.

With a smile he turned and took off down the hallway.

I stood next to my locker, a stupid grin plastered all over my face, and watched him disappear. Astonishment had me spellbound.

So this was it.

Still grinning like a Cheshire cat, I tossed my pencil way up into the air and tried to catch it. The teacher monitoring the hall gave me an odd look. I hooted at her, then grabbed my books and ran for German.

# Four

WHEN I ARRIVED home from school, I went into the kitchen to fix myself a snack. Megan was sitting at the table and spreading butter on soda crackers. I took down the bread and then went to the cupboard to get the peanut butter.

"There isn't any peanut butter," Megan said.

"There was this morning."

"Yes, but I ate it already."

Frowning, I turned. "You know I always have a peanut-butter-and-honey sandwich when I get home from school. Always. Since before you were born, you little brat. That was my peanut butter."

"Not anymore!" She giggled. "Here. You want some crackers?"

"Aren't there any apples left either? Did you pig them all up too?"

"No. But all that's left are the old wormy ones that fell off Mrs. Reilly's tree."

I sat down at the table and took the crackers away from Megan. Intently, I worked on extracting one from the wrapper without breaking it. "Where's Mama?"

"In her bedroom." Megan was concentrating on spreading butter to the exact edges of her cracker.

"Is she okay?"

Megan shrugged. "I guess so. She's still got her bath-

36

robe on. And she doesn't look like she combed her hair yet today. But when she was out a little while ago, she said 'hi' to me, so I guess she's all right.'' Megan paused to look up. ''But you know what she's doing?''

''What?''

Megan wrinkled her nose. ''She got all those photographs out. You know. The ones of Popi and Mutti and Elek.''

I sighed.

''You know something, Les,'' Megan said, ''what I really feel like doing someday when she isn't looking is taking all those old pictures and burning them in the fire.''

''What an awful thing to say, Megan. All Mama's family got killed in the war. And she misses them. If something happened to all of us, would you want some kid of yours to burn up our pictures?''

She took out another cracker. ''Well, I dunno. If it kept me from remembering I had real live kids here in front of me, then I might.''

''She remembers us, Megs. Don't be so selfish.''

Megan didn't reply.

''Hey, you want to hear some super news,'' I said, hoping to distract her. ''You know Claire's party on Friday?''

''Yes?''

''Well, guess what? I got a date for it.''

Her eyes widened. ''Really. Who with?''

''This guy at school. You don't know him. His name's Paul Krueger and he's in my history class.''

''Can I meet him? When he comes to get you, will you introduce me?''

I rolled up the wrapper on the crackers and rose to put them away. ''Well, he isn't exactly coming over.''

Megan's brow wrinkled.

''I told him to pick me up at the nursing home.''

"The nursing home? But you finish there at 5:30. Claire's party doesn't start at 5:30, does it?"

"No," I replied. "But I thought I could study until it was time. Mrs. Morton lets me use the staff room to study when I want to."

Bafflement still clouded Megan's features.

"Besides, it's a lot closer for him. He lives on Cedar Street. That way he doesn't have to come clear over here to pick me up."

Megan had the knife in one hand, and with a finger she scraped off bits of butter from it and put them into her mouth. "Cedar Street isn't really that far, Les. How come you don't have him come over here and pick you up? Then we could meet him." But before I had to explain, I saw a look of understanding cross her face. She gazed at the knife and finally put it into her mouth to suck the last of the butter off. "Yes," she said softly, "I guess it probably is a better idea to meet him somewhere else."

That was the good thing about Megan. She was young but she wasn't stupid.

When my father came home and saw that Mama was still wearing her bathrobe, he went up into the bedroom and stayed there quite a while with her. Later, when Mama came out, she was dressed and had her hair pulled back in a rubber band, the way it always was when Dad brushed it for her. She made us pork chops and French fries and green beans for supper, and while we were eating, she started joking with Dad about Mrs. Beckerman, who lived across the street. Mrs. Beckerman's main activity seemed to be standing behind the net curtains in her living room and watching what everyone else on the block was doing. Mid-meal, Mama, carried away with the pleasure of her story, was on her feet, waddling across the floor precisely the way Mrs. Beckerman waddled, imitating that suspicious, beady-eyed expression Mrs. Beckerman had so exactly that we all were in hysterics. Megan laughed so much she choked over her milk.

While we sat around the table after the meal and ate ice cream, I told my family about Paul. Or rather Megan did. But once the beans were spilled I elaborated willingly.

Mama was pensive. "This boy, you know him from school?"

"He's in my history class."

"Is he a good student?" she asked. She was stirring her ice cream around in the bowl. The coldness bothered her teeth, so she always stirred ice cream into milk-shake thickness before eating it.

"Yes, he's a good student. He's practically a genius in physics. He takes honors physics, would you believe. And he won this prize at the science fair last fall. It was for this contraption that even Mr. Wallace, our physics teacher, didn't understand."

"So, will he go to university?"

"Yes, Mama. He's going to Ohio State. To study statistics. His dad says that's a really good field for jobs now."

Mama lifted her spoon and sucked the ice cream off. "What is his other name, this Paul?"

"Krueger."

A frown. "Is he German?"

"No, Mama, he's American."

She nodded. Briefly glancing in my father's direction, she turned back to me. "Very well. You may go out with him."

"Thank you, Mama," I said and looked down at my bowl. I hadn't realized I was asking.

Thursday, my mother was not home when I returned from school. This came as a surprise because during the previous weeks Mama had become increasingly anxious about leaving the house. When Dad came home from

work at 5:30, he was just as surprised as I was. Did I
know where she'd gone? he asked, and I could tell he was
concerned. No, I said. No, said Megan. So we waited.

Mama returned just as I was beginning to worry that
she'd forgotten about supper. I was standing on a chair
and rummaging around in the top cupboard for one of
those macaroni and cheese dinners in a box, when the
back door burst open and there was Mama.

"Ho!" she said cheerfully to me. The winter air had
reddened her cheeks and nose. Snowflakes fell out of her
hair as she shook it. Setting down a bag of groceries, she
came over to me. "Here, come down from your chair.
I've bought you something." Excitement edged her
voice. Her lips pulled back into a grin that showed all her
teeth. "Come on. Come with me upstairs, I'll show it to
you."

Still wearing her jacket, she went on through the
kitchen and into the hallway. Jumping off the chair, I galloped after her.

"What is it?" I asked. She climbed the stairs ahead of
me and would not say.

I sat down on my bed, and Mama, brown paper
wrapped parcel in her hands, sat down beside me. She
put the package in my lap, but before I could undo it, she
reached over and broke the tape and pulled back the paper. Inside was a shawl. It was a deep, rich turquoise.

"Oh Mama, it's gorgeous!"

Gently, she lifted it up and laid it on my shoulders.
"It's for your date. When you go out with this boy,
Peter."

"Paul, Mama."

"Well, Paul then." She smiled. "See how soft it is?
One hundred percent wool. It's made in Guatemala. Feel
it. Isn't it soft?"

I touched the shawl. Rising, I wrapped it around myself and stood in front of the mirror. It was magnificent.

Not exactly the thing to wear with jeans to a party, but still, it was beautiful.

"Remember, I told you about Hans Klaus Fischer, the baker's son?" Mama asked.

I nodded.

"The night I went to my first dance with him, I was wearing a white dress. It was cut like so in front. Like this." She gestured. "It was very much a little girl's dress, and I hated it. I was so embarrassed to have to wear it. But there were shortages because of the war." She smiled. "So you know what Tante Elfie did?"

"What?"

"She saw me standing in the hallway at the mirror and she brought me her shawl. Her white one. Made of crocheted cotton. I've told you about it, *ja?* Anyhow, she gave it to me to wear that night. I was very touched. You see, I thought she was still *böse*—angry—with me for wanting so badly to go out with Hans Klaus. But she said, 'This is to make you feel beautiful, Mara, because now you are a woman.' "

Mama rose from the bed and came to stand behind me. She touched the soft material of the shawl on both my shoulders. "That meant very much to me, that she understood. I thought I would want it that way for you."

I was watching her reflection in the mirror. She was smiling. Her hands remained on my shoulders. "This is a very good color for you. When I saw it, I was thinking, this color will make my Lesley very beautiful. This will make this boy know how lucky he is to take her dancing."

"Thank you, Mama. It's really super. Thanks for thinking of me."

For several moments she continued to stand there. The smile played itself out on her lips to be replaced with a more thoughtful expression. Still she studied my face in the mirror. Her head tipped to one side. "This boy, this Paul," she asked, "is he a virgin?"

*"Mama!"* In astonishment I whirled around to look her directly in the eye. She could do that to you, Mama could, just ask you those kinds of questions. "Mama, how on earth should I know that? I just met him. I hardly even know him. Cripes, Mama, what a thing to ask."

She smiled pleasantly. Turning away from me, she went over and gently closed the door of my room. She leaned back against it. "I will tell you something about men," she said. "I want you to know how important it is to be very gentle with men who are virgins. You must be good to this boy."

"Mama, for Pete's sake. I'm just going on a date with him. I'm not planning anything else."

"Men are very different from women." She tapped her chest. "In here, they are. You see, in here they're different. Not as strong. Men hurt more when they love. They give themselves more. Women don't. Women always keep a little piece of themselves back just for themselves. Women are more complicated in that way. But men, they aren't. They just love. And you see, they get hurt."

The shawl still around my shoulders, I walked back to the bed and sat down. Mama continued to lean against the door, hands in her pockets. She was still smiling slightly, her eyes going dreamy.

"O'Malley, he was a virgin," she said. She called my father O'Malley. His first name was Cowan but I never knew my mother to ever call him that. When I was young, I thought my father had only one name, rather like Ann-Margret. "He was a boy still. You know. With a baby face." She grinned. "And me, I was no winner either. I was just over typhus, you see. I was skinny as a toothpick. My hair stuck out. It was only this long." She measured with her fingers. "But O'Malley, he thinks I'm beautiful. He was so afraid. Of me. Men, they have many fears. You must be very gentle with a man, because if you let him love you too much and then hurt him, he'll never get over it. A woman will. But not a man. He'll be afraid. He will never be able to love as well again, if you hurt him. It gives you power over him. You must remember that.''

"Mama," I said, "I'm just going on a date with this guy."

She nodded and pushed herself off the door. *"Ja, ja,* I know. But I am telling you this so you remember it. You must be aware of what you do. You bind a man to you in the way you love him. And if he's a virgin, then he will always love you just a little bit, even after you are gone. So you must be good to this boy.''

"Mama, it's not just him. What about me?"

She chuckled and reached out to touch me. "I just want you to find a good boy to make you happy. I want you to have a boy to make you as happy as O'Malley's made me.''

# Five

ON FRIDAY NIGHT Paul picked me up at the nursing home about 8:30. He had his mom's car, a little red Ford that smelled of wet dogs. Paul knew it smelled. Even as I was first putting my foot into the car, he apologized and explained that they had two Labradors that rode around in the backseat when his mom was driving. Their names were Fortnum and Mason, which referred to a high-class store in London that I'd never heard of. I made a joke out of it, saying what a good thing it was that she didn't name them after Barnum Hooker's Drugs downtown, because I didn't want Paul to feel too self-conscious about the stink. He thought my comment was hilarious and laughed. I was surprised how easy it was to talk to him. Normally, when I became uncomfortable around people, I tended to go dead silent, and that had been one of my major worries about the evening.

We were among the last couples to arrive at Claire's party. The band was already playing, and most of the others were dancing. The small room was oppressive with the heat of moving bodies.

Throughout most of the evening Paul and I sat on folding chairs and drank Cokes. He said that he didn't really like dancing particularly, and I told him that was okay because I didn't either—which wasn't precisely true, but I said it anyway. The music was so loud that it was im-

44

possible to carry on a conversation. So we just sat and drank. I watched Frog Newton playing his drums. He wasn't as grotesque as Brianna had made him out to be. His hairstyle was rather unique, but aside from that, I thought he was good to look at. He had a nice body.

A little after eleven Paul suggested we go. The volume of the music was making my insides vibrate, and I was hoarse from shouting over it, so I agreed.

Coming outside was a shock. After all the noise and humid, sweaty heat, the January cold ripped my breath away. Shivering violently, I tried to zip my jacket.

"You want to go for a drive or something?" Paul asked, as he unlocked the car door for me.

I glanced at my watch. I was supposed to be home by midnight, which Paul knew, and it was already 11:15. I showed him the time. "A short one, maybe."

We drove down the street that led to the highway. Paul turned west and we sped out beyond the reaches of the town lights. It's very flat in that part of Kansas. All of Kansas is more or less flat, but out there in the western reaches, I reckon you could see the headlights of a car in Colorado, if you tried.

"That's not really my scene," Paul said as he drove. "That back there. Claire's brother told me I had to go. It was all right, I guess, but it's not for me. I hardly ever go to parties."

I didn't answer. I was wondering if Claire's brother had also told him to invite me.

Leaning back on the headrest, I closed my eyes. Paul had turned the heater to its highest setting, and the car grew very warm. It also smelled incredibly of dog.

It was a nice feeling, speeding silently along the highway in the darkness. For a split second I let myself slip into dreams, imagining that this warm, shadowy quiet was my life to come, that Paul was my husband and we were off across the country, speeding to some secret destination in the west. It wasn't that I wanted to be married to Paul or even that I wanted to be married at all. It wasn't that specific. Just the sudden feeling of well-being I had at that moment made me wish I could keep it. I wanted to prolong that instant of dark, drifting laxity forever.

"You don't talk much," Paul said, shattering the silence.

"I don't have much to say," I replied.

He smiled over at me. "You want to stop? I know this place. On Ladder Creek. My brothers and I used to go there to hunt rats."

*"Yuck."*

He laughed. "It's not as bad as it sounds. It's pretty there. The water bends around and there're these little willow trees. I saw a deer there once."

This is it, I thought. *It.* He was taking me to make out. With sudden sharpness I became alert to the fact that we were a mighty long way from anywhere, and I wasn't very sure precisely where we were. He had taken off on a series of tiny county roads until we were far out on the plains without a light to be seen anywhere.

Paul pulled the car off the road as we neared the creek. Turning off the motor, he sat a moment, and I waited for him to make a pass. I ran my tongue around my teeth to dislodge any bits of potato chips and wondered if my breath smelled of Cokes. Cautiously, I glanced sideways to see what was going to happen next.

Nothing.

Pulling the keys from the ignition, Paul opened the door on his side. "Come on. I'll take you down and show you where Gary and Aaron and I used to get the rats."

Great.

It couldn't have been more than fifteen degrees outside. I had my jacket zipped up to my nose as I followed him down along the creek bed. It was dry then, in January, without even a glassy trickle in the bottom.

"I used to pretend I was Luke Skywalker," he was saying as he forged ahead of me. "You know, from *Star Wars*. See, here was the Death Star, and Aaron and I would pretend we were flying our fighter planes and trying to hit the place that'd blow the Death Star up. That's what we pretended the rat holes were."

This is a date? I was thinking.

In the east the moon was rising. It hung on the horizon, not quite full, but big as a house. Overhead were scattered a billion stars honed to brilliance in the cold night air. Prairie grass crackled with frost as we walked through it.

Near a clump of leafless willows, Paul paused. He put his arm around my shoulder with clumsy affection. It tightened my muffler. He paused from his story about rats and *Star Wars*.

"Isn't it beautiful?" he asked. "I think this is the most beautiful place in the whole world. You can have your mountains and oceans and cities. Give me this any time."

I stared out from the creek bed. It was so flat. In every direction, as far as you could see, the horizon came right down even with our feet. There were no lights to be seen, no trees except for the four or five willows beside us. Nothing but sky and stars and darkness. It struck me as novel to think of somebody actually loving Kansas.

I shivered. "It's cold though."

His face brightened. "Yup. But I've thought of that. See here?" He held out matches. "I thought we could gather up sticks. I'll make us a fire. And see, I brought apples. You put them on sticks and roast them over the fire." He had a peculiar expression that reminded me of Megan when she desperately wanted to do something but was afraid of being laughed at for it.

"I'm supposed to be back by midnight," I said. It was already ten to twelve. We looked at one another and both knew I wouldn't be.

Paul built a small fire on the dry stones of the creek bed. Clearly, he had done this sort of thing often. Hands in my jacket, chin buried in my muffler, I watched him as he cut willow sticks, peeled them back, stuck them through the apples and put them over the fire. I had never heard of doing that to apples but I didn't say anything. They gave off a wonderful smell, like autumn and old barns. When they were done, they were charred and crackly on the outside but the inside was steamy, smooth and slurpy. We ate in silence, hunkered down beside the small fire. Paul was gazing at me across the flames, and it struck me then how differently the night was turning out from what I had expected. I had expected a date. One of those pick-you-up, go-to-the-party, make-a-pass, take-you-home sort of evenings. The kind of thing I could tell Brianna about on Monday. And I would have liked that. What I was getting was more of a communion.

"I haven't ever brought anyone out here before," Paul said as he banked the fire. "But you know, I've been sitting in history class watching you. All term. You seem different from other girls."

"Oh?" I said, flattered. "How's that?"

He shrugged and reached an arm out around my shoulder. We went walking a ways down the empty waterway. We didn't speak again. We walked about a quarter of a mile in the moonlight until we came across a trickle of water under thick panes of ice. Paul crunched the ice with his shoe and we followed the water until it disappeared into a culvert running under a farm road. He stopped a moment to bend down and watch the water. Then we turned and walked back.

Paul stabbed the fire to life again. He threw small, dry

branches on it. Sparks rose up into the air, and he stood back, watching them.

I thought how I wouldn't mind at all if he did make a pass. A kiss from him would be nice. He had a sensual mouth, full lips. I wondered if I dared to start something.

Paul tipped his head back and stared up to the sky. The fire cast grotesque shadows on his throat. "You know," he said, "whenever I'm out here at night and looking up at the stars, I always wonder. I mean, I feel like such a small thing compared to all that up there. I think that I'm just one little person and there're billions of people and this is just one little planet and there're billions of planets." He looked over. "Do you ever think about stuff like that?"

"Sometimes."

There was silence. The fire crackled.

"And yet," he said, his eyes on the stars again, "every one of us still has dreams."

We stayed out very late. Paul and I talked for so long that the fire fell into embers and the cold held us rigid in its grasp. I had never come across anyone like Paul before, who found places like these bare plains beautiful and who thought about things like the stars. When we finally gave in and drove home, heater and dog stench going full blast, it was after three in the morning.

"What are you carrying in there?" he asked as we neared my block. "I saw you get in with it." He indicated a brown grocery sack.

"It's a gift I got," I said and opened the bag to show him.

He touched it. "It's soft, isn't it?"

I nodded and took the turquoise shawl out, laying it across my jeans.

I had become frightened on the way home, thinking that my father might be waiting up for me. I dreaded to think of the state he would be in because I had stayed out so late. And I was so tired that I didn't feel able to cope with anyone's anger just then. So, when we reached my house, it was with great relief that I saw all the lights were out except the porch lamp.

As noiselessly as possible, I let myself into the house and tiptoed up the stairs. My eyes had long since grown accustomed to darkness. I undressed and prepared for bed without bothering to turn on any lights. The room seemed unnaturally warm to me after being out so long in the winter night.

Carefully, I took the turquoise shawl out and draped it across my chair so that if Mama came in early in the morning, she would think I'd worn it. Then I went to the window and pulled back the curtain. The moon was high. It had lost its hugeness and now threw out a cold, lifeless light. The wind had picked up and drew debris from the street into noisy eddies below the window. I watched intently, still half lost in the dreamy strangeness of the evening. I was tired, but for some curious reason, I was not sleepy.

Then the door opened. I started violently. It was just a whisper of a sound but my heart popped into my mouth, and I jumped enough to hit my head on the upper edge of the window sash.

It was Megan.

She closed the door quietly but deliberately behind her, so that the latch sounded in the silence. Then she turned and looked at me but came no closer.

"What are you doing up?" I whispered.

"I heard you come in."

We stared at one another across the expanse of the room. It was almost too dark to distinguish her when I let the curtain drop back down.

"Why aren't you in bed?" she asked.

"Why aren't *you?*"

Again, no words. Megan reached up and pushed back her hair.

"Is something the matter?" I asked. "Why are you awake?"

She continued to try and keep her hair back from her face.

"Come over here," I said.

She came, hesitantly, stopping just before she was within my reach.

"Did you have a bad dream or something?"

She shook her head. "No. I wet the bed."

"Oh. Oh well, Meggie, don't worry about it. Do you want some help getting it changed?"

"No. I did it already." She scratched her nose. Her long hair was wild about her, like a secondary garment. She looked up again. "No, I was just sitting there and I heard you come in."

"Well, you better get back to bed then. It's really late."

A pause. "Can I sleep with you?"

"Are you having bad dreams or something?"

She shrugged. "No, I'm just sort of lonely."

"It's like the old days," Megan whispered after we had gotten into bed. She had the quilt right up to her nose and it muffled her words.

I had my eyes closed.

"Remember how I used to come in and sleep with you when I was little? When we lived in Yakima. Remember that, Lessie? I came in all the time."

"No lie."

"It was because of those dreams. Those nightmares I got. Remember them? And I'd wake everybody up? Remember?"

"Yes, I certainly do."

Megan shifted. We didn't fit together in my single bed

like we used to. I had almost outgrown it myself. And Megan was no longer tiny. I lay with my cheek resting against the top of her head.

"Did I ever tell you what I believed then?" she asked.

"I don't think so."

"Well, you know how Mama was in the war? And she couldn't go home to her family?"

"Yes," I said.

"Well, when I was little and in the school in Yakima, I thought maybe they were going to do that to me. That teacher, remember, she used to always keep me after school. Mrs. Hoolihan. Because I kept doing those worksheets wrong. And I thought it was going to be like it was with Mama. That pretty soon she wasn't going to let me go home at all."

"That would never have happened, you know," I said. "You should have told somebody you felt like that, because we could have told you. It wouldn't really happen."

"But it happened to Mama, Lessie. And it was when she was at school. She told us that. She was there and she couldn't go home."

"Yes, but that was different. There was a war on. And she was at the university, not in grade school. Besides, that was in Germany a long time ago. Not America. It wouldn't happen here."

"Well, yes, I know that. I'm telling you what I believed *then*. Remember, I was just little."

"Yes."

"And I mean, you can understand it. They *did* keep Mama there and not let her go home. So I thought they might do that to me too. Especially when Mrs. Hoolihan made me stay after school and wouldn't let me leave until I did those papers right. It really wasn't such a stupid notion."

I put my arms around Megan.

"It was you guys I was scared about most," she said.
"That they'd keep me there and I'd never see you or
Mama or Daddy again. That's what happened to Mama,
and I think I'd just die if the same thing happened to me. I
would. Even now. So, I kept dreaming about it. Over and
over and over."

"Was that tonight too?" I asked.

"No. I just wet the bed, that's all. Then I got up and
changed the sheets and I was just sitting around. It made
me feel lonesome."

Silence settled over us. It was horribly late.

"Did you have a nice time?" Megan asked.

"You mean tonight? Yeah, I did."

"Is he okay?"

"Yes, he's okay."

"Did he kiss you?"

"Yes."

"Did you like it?"

"You know, Megs, it kind of wrecks a thing like this
when you have to come home and discuss it with your
little sister."

Megan shifted. "I don't see why."

The darkness closed in around us, and Megan grew so
quiet that I assumed she had fallen asleep finally. I was
very sleepy myself. Closing my eyes, I dozed.

"Les?"

"Hmm?"

"Can I ask you something?"

"I'm getting awfully tired, Meggie. I want to go to
sleep."

"But can I ask you something first? Before you go to
sleep?"

"You will anyway."

"Well, you know about the war?"

"Mmm-hmm."

"Well, we're studying about it at school. And you

know, my teacher was telling us about some of the things
the Nazis did to people. To the Jews, you know? She had
some pictures. They were in a book.''

"Mmm.''

"Have you ever seen those pictures, Lessie?''

"What book is it?''

"Well, I can't remember its name. But have you ever
seen pictures like that? Of what they did to the Jews?''

"Yes,'' I said. "I have.''

Megan was silent. I was wide awake again.

"Is it true? Did they really, really do things like that to
people?''

"I guess they did.''

"Mama never makes the war sound very bad. She
makes it sound like, well . . . I don't know. You hear
her stories. Like about Jadwiga. About how silly she was
and stuff.''

Again silence.

"Well . . .'' and then she stopped. I could feel her
breath against my arm as she exhaled. "Well, Les, do
you think they ever did things like that to Mama, things
like in those pictures?''

"Is that what's bothering you? Are you worried about
that?''

"But did they, Lesley?''

"Megs, Mama wasn't a Jew, was she? Those were
Jews in those pictures.''

"But how come she never went home when the war
started?''

"I don't know. She was working or something. I don't
know. But it was different than with the Jews, Meggie. I
know that for certain. They liked Mama. See, they
thought Mama was really beautiful. Because she was so
blond and stuff. You know. She's told us about that.
About how the Nazis liked people to have blond hair and

blue eyes. Aryan. That was their name for it. They liked people to be Aryans. And Mama was.''

"But Mama had a hard time in the war. You know it. Like she's got all those little scars and stuff. You know that's from the war. Daddy said.''

"Well, who knows. It was a difficult time there then. People got in trouble pretty easy. And you know Mama and her opinions. She'd get in trouble anywhere.''

No response from Megan.

"But it wasn't anything like what happened to the Jews. The Nazis hated the Jews. They planned to kill them all.''

"But what was it like where Mama was?''

"I don't know.''

"Then how can you say it was different from the places the Jews were? For all you know, maybe it wasn't.''

I sighed. "I'm too tired for this, Megan. It's the middle of the night. Cripes, it's practically morning. I want to sleep.''

Megan squirmed around. She was well past the cuddly stage. Instead, she was mostly knees and elbows. She had her shoulder jammed against my breasts.

"But what was it like for Mama, Lesley? I got to know. I keep thinking about those pictures and I got to know.''

"But *I* don't know. Listen, just forget about it. It happened a long, long time ago before you were born or I was born, before a whole lot of people were born. A *long* time ago.''

"If it was so long ago, how come it still bothers Mama?''

"Megan, go to sleep.''

"But I need to know. I just keep seeing those pictures in that book. I shut my eyes and that's what I see. In this one picture there was this little boy with his hands above his head. And they shot him. I keep seeing him in my mind. I keep seeing the way he was looking out of the picture. He was littler than me.''

"Well, stop seeing him. Don't think about it, because it's over and done with. And Mama's circumstances were not like the Jews'. I do know that much. Mama would have told us if it had been like what happened to the Jews. But she hasn't, has she? So stop worrying and don't think about it.''

Megan sighed. "You sound like Daddy."

Again, another long silence. But this time I didn't grow sleepy. I lay staring at the wall.

"Les?"

"What is it now?"

"You know Mama?"

"Of course I know Mama, Megan."

"No. Stoppit. Be serious. You know *about* Mama. The way she is. That's because of the war, isn't it?"

"Megan, I mean it. Stop worrying about it. If you don't shut up right now, I'm going to make you go back to your own bed.''

"I'm not worrying. I'm just wondering."

"Well, then stop wondering."

She sighed again. Then she wiggled to make herself more comfortable against me. She sighed one more time, heavily.

"Your teacher shouldn't be talking to you kids about stuff like that. You're too little. She's just scaring you. And I think that's wrong. I think in the morning we ought to tell Daddy what she's doing.''

Megan didn't answer.

"So just forget about it and we'll take care of it in the morning, okay?"

Megan squirmed and then relaxed. She expelled a long breath of air and then closed her eyes. "Doesn't matter really," she said quietly. "I already knew about it anyway.''

# Six

BOTH MEGAN AND I slept late. It was after ten o'clock
when I woke up. Megan was still in bed with me, still
asleep. I had a painful crick in my neck from not having
been able to move easily during the night, and it hurt like
heck to turn my head. So I sat up cautiously and then
tried to climb over my sister without waking her.
Quietly, I dressed and brushed my hair. Megan remained
dead to the world.

Downstairs in the kitchen, my mother and father were
still sitting at the table and drinking coffee. On days
when my father didn't have to work, my parents enjoyed
long, leisurely breakfasts. Often they spent as much as
three hours at the table, talking, eating, reading the newspaper, discussing world events, listening to the radio and
drinking the strong, dark coffee my mother made in a
special pot. When I came down I could tell they had eaten
their main breakfast quite a while earlier, but by the way
things were spread out, it was apparent they were still a
long way from finishing.

Warily, I glanced at my father to see if he was angry
about my late return. But after greeting me, he returned
to his coffee and newspaper. Mama was browsing
through the want ads. She looked up.

"Did you have a nice time?"

"Yes, Mama, I did."

She lit a cigarette and leaned back in her chair. "This boy, did you like him?"

"Yes, Mama." I smiled at her as I went to the refrigerator to take out the eggs. "I like him a lot. He's different."

Lifting down a bowl, I broke a couple of eggs into it and scrambled them. Mama had turned in her chair to watch me. Her hair was loose. Apparently she had washed it earlier and had not gone to tie it back yet. Like Megan, she had extraordinarily straight hair, and it lay across her shoulders, reflecting the glow of the kitchen light. Putting her cigarette into the ashtray, she pulled out one strand of hair and twisted it around her finger.

"Guess what, Mama. Paul liked the turquoise shawl. He said how soft it was. He thought it was beautiful."

Pleased, she smiled.

"And guess what else? They have dogs. Two of them. Labradors. Named Fortnum and Mason. His mama lets them ride around in the backseat of her car when she goes to do the shopping."

My mother laughed. She adored dogs. We'd had one once, a great hulking brute of a dog, a cross between a dalmatian and a Newfoundland retriever. Mama had named him Piffi, which was a very unlikely name for that dog. He should have been called Brutus or Killer, or at the very least, Rover. But in spite of his appearance, he had been gentle and good tempered. Megs used to ride on him, and I dressed him up in doll bonnets or tied yarn to his tail to make him look more like the pony I was longing for then. However, Piffi's real allegiance had always been to Mama.

All the while I talked, I kept an eye on my father. I was concerned that if I let the conversation between Mama and me flag, he would pounce on me for having stayed out too late. I stalled as best I could, talking faster and faster, elaborating way beyond what I actually knew about Fortnum and Mason. But Dad said nothing. He sat with his newspaper and his coffee and a piece of toast Mama had gotten up and made for him while I was talking. When I couldn't detect a flicker of life from behind the newspaper, I gave up and ate my breakfast.

I knew he knew I had come in late. Because it was my first date alone with a boy, Dad had sat me down for a thorough talk the night before. Unlike Mama, my father wasn't the least concerned about Paul's virginity. He made me Scotch tape a dime inside my shoe so if I needed to call him to come get me, I'd be prepared. I knew it mattered to him and my lateness wouldn't have gone unnoticed. Besides, he seldom went to bed before midnight anyway.

But my father said nothing. I could tell he was listening to my conversation with Mama, but he never came out from behind the sports section. My mother saved me. Delighted with all this talk of dogs, she began reminiscing about Piffi. We exchanged little memories about him, and Mama was laughing and illustrating her stories with animated gestures. Dad, I suspect, was reluctant to spoil her happy mood by getting mad at me.

The weather that Saturday was wretched. It rained in the morning, the drops half-frozen before they hit the ground. Around noon the sleet stopped and the sky hung low and swollen. When we had lived in Washington state, the snowdrops and crocuses would begin to show in late January, and I had always shared Mama's deep relief at seeing them, even though the weather often persisted in being miserable. But here there was nothing to indicate that winter wouldn't go on forever. All I could see out the window was dead grass, bare trees and lead-gray sky.

After breakfast, Dad rummaged around the house in an attempt to assemble all the bits and pieces he needed to do the income taxes. It put him in a foul mood. He yanked out the junk drawer in the kitchen while I was doing the dishes and he rooted sullenly through the mess. Unable to locate all of the prescription receipts, he hollered for my mother, and she came running. For some reason my father always assumed that Mama had done something with whatever he could not find in the house. Still unable to unearth what he wanted even with Mama's help, he left the junk drawer sitting up on the counter, its contents strewn everywhere. Wiping the counters down with a dishrag, I paused, unsure if I should put the stuff away or leave it alone.

Mama seemed nearly as moody as my father. Wearing a pair of faded jeans and one of my old sweat shirts, she drifted around the house restlessly, hands in her back pockets. She was trying to help Dad find everything but she wasn't much help, chiefly because doing the taxes put my father in such rotten humor that no one could have pleased him. So she shadowed him at a distance, hands still in her pockets, until he would growl impatiently at her for always sticking things in strange places. Then I would hear her mutter softly that she *didn't* stick things in strange places, that if he would only file them away in his desk like she asked him to . . . But by that point Dad would have disappeared somewhere else. So she would wander over and sit on the edge of the kitchen table and watch me struggling through college applications. Until my father hollered for her again.

Boredom, I think, had always been my mother's principal foe. She needed more to keep her occupied than she could ever find around our house, especially now that neither Megan nor I were babies any longer. If she could have had a job of some kind or something similar, I think it might have helped. I had said this to my father on numerous occasions because, since he was working, I didn't think he was as acutely aware as I was of how empty Mama's days were. But he didn't agree. In fact, he

was flatly against her working. Mama was too unpredictable, he would always reply. What with her moods and
her strong opinions and her idiosyncrasies, you couldn't
expect people to be very tolerant.

My mama had a lot of what Dad labeled "idiosyncrasies." Many of them were rather endearing behaviors, if
no one you particularly wanted to impress was watching.

For instance, my mama talked to radiators. And to
most other inanimate objects, if the occasion arose. In
her mind everything had the possibility of being alive.
"Well, you don't really know, do you?" she'd say to us
when we laughed at her. "Would a stone know you're
alive? Well, then how can you know for sure that the
stone's not alive too and *you* just don't perceive it? How
do you know? It could be." And in her mind, it could. So
it only stood to reason that you treated everything courte-
ously, just in case. Our radiators, which were forever
banging and clanging, were the recipients of three-
quarters of Mama's conversations on cold winter mornings, when Dad, Megs and I were still stumbling around
bleary eyed. "You got air in your belly?" she'd inquire
politely of the one in the kitchen as we sat, eating jam and
toast.

Some of her idiosyncrasies, however, were less
charming. She had, for instance, a morbid fascination
with food. Starchy things, like potatoes or pasta or rice,
were her favorites, and many were the occasions that we
would chance across her in the kitchen, eating a bowl of
plain, cooked macaroni or a dish of cold, leftover potatoes. And my mother ate *everything,* including the fat off
the meat, the skins off the potatoes, the liquid left in the
vegetable bowl. Her idea of scraping dishes before washing was to eat whatever the rest of us had left and then
wipe the plate clean with a piece of bread to get the last
bit. The most distressing aspect of this inability to ignore
food concerned things that fell on the floor. My mother

would eat dropped food. She didn't confine herself to retrieving those things that could be washed off, but also went after and ate such things as Jell-O or mashed potatoes or butter. Both Megan and I had always found this horribly embarrassing behavior, and we were often reduced to bouts of berserk screaming when we demanded that she leave it alone and she in turn called us wasteful little louts. But we never broke her of the habit. She still did it every time something dropped. So we were forced to keep the kitchen floor literally clean enough to eat from and we prayed like zealots when we went to a restaurant that God might intervene before anything hit the ground.

And others of Mama's idiosyncrasies were downright intolerable. Perhaps her most incorrigible habit had to do with her speech. My mother still spoke four languages and used three of them in daily conversation, yet out of all those words, she had never acquired a euphemistic vocabulary. Consequently, tact and diplomacy certainly were not Mama's strong suit. She had a colorful, multilingual way of offending everyone by always saying precisely what she thought. This habit, more than any other, drove my father wild. "Why can't you think sometimes before you speak?" he would yell at her. "How can you say things like that?" Yet Mama made no serious attempt to curb her tongue. "I am just being honest," Mama would say. "It's *you* who are wrong, always saying what isn't true. I'm just saying what I think. I'm just being sincere." Or on other occasions, particularly when her language had gotten a little salty as well, she would just give him a completely blank look. "What does it matter?" she'd ask. "They are only words. Shit is shit. Fuck is fuck, no matter what you call them." And Dad would explain that you *didn't* call them that, period, at least not in polite company. Mama would nod wearily and shrug, and I knew she didn't care one way or the other. Then, the next time, there they'd be, together in the checkout line at the supermarket, Mama sliding cans of pork and beans or whatever down the conveyor belt for Dad to pack, and she'd casually remark what a bastard she thought the man who cut the meat was. My father would go white with horror, and once they were in the car, the argument would start all over again.

So these were the reasons, my father explained, that he did not want Mama out working. She'd end up being humiliated or treated shabbily or made fun of, he said. Or she'd get herself into trouble.

I still didn't agree. Some of the things Mama was capable of doing were excruciatingly embarrassing, and I was as bad as anyone about trying to keep her separate from people I hoped to impress, but nonetheless, I couldn't help thinking that if she had something more to occupy her mind, perhaps she wouldn't have so much time left over to think up good reasons for engaging in eccentric behavior.

I am not sure how much Mama felt her confinement. Everything always had intensity for her, wherever she was, and she could go about the most mundane tasks with almost electric vigor. She liked listening to her various phonograph records and often jotted down notes to help her remember to show Megs or me some small nuance she had discovered in comparing one piece with another. She pored over the newspaper for so long each morning that she was far better informed on the state of the world than either my father or I. Then she'd reread the editorials, clip out articles, write short, sharp, to-the-point letters to people like our congressmen or the President. She always made me proofread the letters to make sure she'd made no grammatical errors. They were good letters, well thought out. She read voraciously. She would read anything we brought home from the library for her, from murder mysteries to books on family finance. She browsed through Megan's and my schoolbooks, and sometimes I would find penciled-in answers to the questions at the ends of the chapters. She exchanged magazines with Mrs. Reilly next door. And every payday she made Dad buy her a paperback at the supermarket.

Mama's contacts with people outside the family were limited, partly because of our frequent moves and the difficulties in meeting people that engendered, partly because of her fluctuating agoraphobia, and no doubt partly because of my father's inclination to keep her home. She did have coffee with Mrs. Reilly quite often, and when she was active, she went downtown, and I knew she had some acquaintances in the stores because she always came back with local news. Otherwise, her only long-standing contact was with a German Jew from Berlin, who now lived in New York. She had never met him. She'd simply struck up a correspondence with him after reading an article he'd written in a magazine. Over the years their friendship had flourished. My mother had developed very strong Jewish sympathies arising from what she termed her "enlightenment" during the war; yet I knew she was still wracked with guilt about having been born Aryan in a time and place when that had mattered and about never having questioned the Hitler regime until she was forced to. She spent hours composing the letters she sent Herr Willi. Writing them out in longhand, revising them, writing them again, typing them, she struggled to untangle turgid emotions and troubled philosophies. Occasionally she would let me read the letters, to see if I thought what she was trying to say was clear. But she wrote to him in German, her sentences far more complex than anything she ever produced in English, and often I could not fully understand them. One thing, however, was always plain to me then: we underestimated Mama.

So I felt sorry for her. It seemed wrong to me that she should spend so much time sitting around the house all day, reading novels and watching soap operas. That would depress anyone. But one time Mama overheard me when I was talking to my father about it and telling him I didn't think he was right to keep her home. She took me aside afterward and told me to leave the matter alone. She was okay, she said, she didn't mind. What she meant, I think, was that she didn't want me to hurt my father.

Mama seemed at loose ends that Saturday, trying to help Dad assemble what he needed for the income taxes. Finally, she wandered into the living room and turned on the phonograph. She had a collection of old 78s she'd bought while they were living in Wales. The music on them was a type unique to the Welsh, and Mama was fascinated by the complex harmonies.

"Do you want to hear *The Lark Ascending?*" Mama called to me after a short while. I was still in the kitchen.

"All right, Mama," I called back.

That had been Elek's favorite piece. Mama had told me so often about Elek's sitting in the gazebo, playing his violin, that I could see the house near Lébény myself, and the gardens with their broad expanse of lawn curving around the linden trees. The white gazebo I pictured was one of those with all the ornate Victorian fretwork. Behind it was the mill pond, glassy in the midafternoon sun. The ducks quacked sleepily as they drifted in the shallows. And soaring over it all was the eerie, grave beauty of *The Lark Ascending*.

She played the record twice, turning it up louder to make certain I could hear it. I was trying to fill out college application forms at the kitchen table, so I ended up putting my hands over my ears in order to concentrate enough to understand what I was reading.

My father came down the stairs from the study. Mama lifted the needle off the record. He came into the kitchen to sharpen a pencil. She followed him to the doorway.

"O'Malley, dance with me," she said to him as he

stood over the pencil sharpener. She came and put her arms around his waist.

"Not now, Mara. Let me get this done first."

She had her cheek pressed against his back. Her hair, still loose, flowed over her shoulders. She was watching me, smiling at me, because my mama knew she could get pretty much anything she wanted out of Daddy. He stood in front of the sharpener and felt the point of the pencil.

"Dance with me now, O'Malley," she said. "I'm in the mood."

Grinning, he unhooked her arms. My dad was a sucker for dancing. On Friday and Saturday nights he would put on records and push back the couch and the coffee table in the living room and whisk Mama off, as if it were the Stardust Ballroom. Both Megan and I had learned to dance before we were in school. Perhaps my favorite memory of my father came from when we lived on Stuart Avenue. Mama was very pregnant with Megan at the time and she could hardly get close enough to my father to put her arms around him. Plus, she tired easily and her back hurt. So my dad played waltzes all night because they were slow. When they were taking a break, my father lifted me up on his lap and showed me the cover of one album with a picture of the Vienna Woods on it. He and Mama had been there in the woods of Vienna, he told me. Right there by that tree. They had eaten bread and cheese on a picnic, but no sausages because meat was still too hard to get in those days. They had gotten married not very far from that spot in the Vienna woods. Then when he started the music again, he bowed deeply to me and asked if I wanted to be his partner. I was eight and couldn't waltz very well. So he told me to stand on his feet and he whirled me around and around the living room.

I remember that evening with timeless clarity. I remember the color and plaid of his shirt. I remember the way he looked down at me, his smile, his eyes. I remember his warm man's smell as he hugged me to his stomach. I felt like a princess, dancing magically around the room on my father's feet.

"Dad?" I said, standing in the doorway of the study. I was trying to discern if he was still working on the taxes, because if he was, I didn't want to interrupt. The papers were strewn all over the top of his desk: tax forms, receipts, slips for this and for that. But Dad had a magazine open on top of the lot.

He raised his eyes as I came into the room. It was almost evening. On such a gloomy day, the passage of day into night was not noticeable until it had happened. He had the desk lamp on, and it bathed his hands and the litter of paper on the desk in a yellowish glow. The rest of the room was a deep, grainy blue.

"I need to talk to you," I said. "It's about going to college next year. I have to get these applications in."

He rocked back in his chair and put his hands behind his head.

"They got deadlines. My counselor at school keeps hassling me about it because I've put it off so long."

"Put what off?" Dad asked.

"Put off deciding where to go."

"Where do you want to go?" he asked.

I set the applications down on the edge of the desk. Stuffing my hands into my pockets, I gazed at him over the top of the lamp. Silence.

"It's something I thought you might kind of like to help me decide," I said. "Like Paul's dad. His dad decided that he ought to go to Ohio State. See, they have a good statistics department there. His dad thought that the job opportunities would be good in statistics."

My father reached over and took the applications. "Have you figured out how much these places cost?"

"Yes, Daddy. It's at the end. I was doing that earlier. That's why it took me so long. See. I calculated the tuition and my room and board. If I used that savings bond Grandma gave me, plus my money from work . . . Well, just look at it. I got it all figured up."

He studied my calculations.

"I could go to Fort Hayes. Or KU. If I get a really good scholarship, I thought I might try for Columbia. It costs a lot, I know, but if I got a big enough scholarship . . . It's a very good school. That's what Miss Harrich says." I paused. "What do you think, Daddy?"

He said nothing. He just read. Standing in front of his desk, hands still in my pockets, I rocked back and forth on my heels and watched him. I felt nervous without really knowing why. It caused a crawlly feeling, primarily in my hands and feet and in the pit of my stomach. Desperately, I wanted my father to help me, to tell me where he wanted me to go and what he thought I should do, the way Paul's father had done. That was the chief reason I had procrastinated with the applications for so long. I kept waiting for Dad to say something when I told him about the places I was interested in. I knew he cared about what I did, so I could never figure out why he left me to decide so much on my own.

"It'd be nice," he said, "if you could go somewhere close to home. In case we needed you or you needed us or something."

"Fort Hays? That's nearest. If we don't move. Are we going to, Daddy?"

"I don't know. No one's mentioned it to me."

"Should I apply there?"

Again he paged through the various applications, checked my figures at the end. Then looking up, he handed them back to me across the lamp. "I trust you to do a good job, Lessie. You know better than anybody what you'd like to do."

"But Paul's dad pretty much decided for him."

"How can that be right?" my father asked. "You're the one who's going to end up living at the college and doing whatever it is you get trained for. Not me. You've got a level head, Lesley. You know best the things you're interested in. You just go ahead and decide."

"Even Columbia?"

He grimaced. "That is a long ways away." Then he smiled. "You're a lucky girl. You got all your mama's brains. And your daddy's going to be proud of you, wherever you choose to go."

I stared at the papers. "May I have money for the application fees?"

He nodded. "You let me know what you come up with and I'll write you a check."

# Seven

I APPLIED to the University of Kansas in Kansas City. I told them I wanted to study languages. Who knew? Maybe I would. It ended the visits to Miss Harrich's office anyway. On the 27th of February they sent me a letter of acceptance. I showed it to my father, and after work the next evening he came home with a box of chocolate éclairs from the bakery at the supermarket and we had a family party.

No one ever did speak of moving, so eventually I concluded we weren't going to. Mama continued to cast around the house restlessly during the month of February. Her agoraphobia worsened abruptly, and she refused even to go next door to see Mrs. Reilly for a while. But she never said anything about moving. On my way home from school one afternoon, I stopped by the florist's and bought her a bowl of forced hyacinths. It was only a tiny point of brightness in the winter-ridden days but it was the best I could do. The ground outside remained brown and unbroken.

Megan took up crocheting. She wasn't very coordinated at doing things with her hands, so it took my mother almost three weeks of undiluted patience to teach her. Once Megan caught on, she crocheted and crocheted, turning out a thing that was five inches wide and about three feet long, because she didn't understand how to cast off. It looked like a woolly blanket for a snake. I thought my mother was going to break a blood vessel trying not to laugh when Megan showed it to her. But she didn't laugh. Instead, she said how nicely all the stitches were made and how she'd always wanted a crocheted belt. I don't believe that's what Megan had thought she was making, but she was so tickled by Mama's comments that she immediately set about making another one.

I spent as much time as I could get away with at Paul's house. All on his own he had converted the attic into a room for himself, so that he would have space for all his projects. Paul lived for the quiet, free moments he could spend up there and I lived for the moments I could spend with Paul. Sometimes I would sit on his bed and watch while he tinkered with one project or another. Other times we would lie, arms around one another, stretched out across the bed, and talk. We talked about ourselves, about school and our classes, about the future, about life, about dreams.

Our relationship moved with languid gentleness. Indeed, I suspect that if Paul's family had realized how very little went on behind Paul's closed door when I was with him, they would have laughed at us. As it was, I always had the distinct feeling from his mother that she was distinctly relieved to have me around. I think she'd begun to despair that Paul, happily shut up in his attic with his gerbils and his telescope and his dozens of notebooks full of observed astronomical minutiae, would ever get around to taking girls out. So sometimes I said things to Paul in their presence that intimated we were doing more than we were. I didn't want them to know that we had such an innocent relationship because I think Paul would have gotten a real razzing. His mother kidded him a lot anyway in a cheerful, good-natured fashion, because he blushed really easily and it made everybody

laugh. Paul hated her to do it, but I must admit, she was
funny, and her teasing was a whole lot less caustic than
my mother's was, when she got on to someone.

I did, however, find myself anxious for the relationship to move more quickly, but intimacy was difficult
around Paul's house because, even up in the attic with the
door closed, there wasn't an abundance of privacy. His
brother Aaron was worse than Megan had ever dreamed
of being. If we were in the attic, Aaron would continually
go back and forth outside the door, making smoochy
noises, even when Paul and I were doing nothing more
than homework and kissing was distant from our minds.
Once Aaron changed thermoses on Paul when we were
going skating, and when Paul opened it to pour hot chocolate, out dropped a pile of condoms instead.

The only place we could go for peace was to the spot
on the creek where Paul had taken me on our first date.
Aaron didn't have his driver's license, so we were safe
there. And God knows, no one else was dumb enough to
be out picnicking in a spot like that in February. We went
out often, perhaps once or twice a week, but still we did
nothing serious. We just petted and necked. I was a little
worried. I enjoyed the slow, easy-going friendship we
had and was fearful of losing that, if I pressed him. But at
the same time, I was ready for more. I didn't know what
to do. I talked about it with Brianna, to see if she thought
I should say something or do something. I asked her if
she thought anything might be the matter with Paul, because Brianna had four brothers and I reckoned she'd understand how boys worked better than I did. I even toyed
with the idea of talking to Mama. But I didn't. Not because Mama wouldn't understand. To the contrary. A lot
of things Mama seemed to understand completely and, in
an obscure way, I resented that. Paul was *my* boyfriend
and these were *my* feelings. So, in the end, I just kept
quiet. Most of the time Paul and I did no more than lie in

the brown prairie grass, arms around each other, and watch birds wheel over the enormous expanse of sky above us.

I had rapidly grown to adore Paul's family. They were noisy, energetic and extroverted—the antithesis of mine. One of Paul's two brothers was already married and living in Garden City. The other, Aaron, was fifteen. With a face full of acne and peach fuzz, Aaron knew he was God's gift to girls. Every time I saw him, he was either washing his hair or blowing it dry. He deafened the household with his stereo. To me, Aaron was a kid right out of a television comedy: bold, brash and full of one-liners.

My favorite member of the family, aside from Paul, of course, was his mother. The very first time I came to the house at the end of January, she'd put her arm around me and told me to call her Bo. None of this Mrs. Krueger stuff. After all, if I was a friend of Paul's, I was a friend of hers.

She was a tall woman. Her features were rather plain; she didn't have the classic bone structure that made my mother's face so dramatic, but nonetheless, Bo was an attractive woman. Even in February she had a tan. Her body was long and lean from diets and dance classes and daily swims at the Y. Twice a month she had her hair highlighted and trimmed to keep the short, stylish cut. Bo dressed in jeans with designer names and turtlenecks under oxford-cloth shirts, not like my mama in her old cords and Daddy's shirts and sweaters.

Sometimes when I was over on Saturdays and Bo wasn't busy, she would take me into the bathroom off the master bedroom and show me how to put on makeup. She'd pull my hair into a ponytail and draw with soap on the mirror to show me the shape of my face. Look at those cheekbones. Why couldn't I have cheekbones like that? she'd always say. Or else she'd take out balls of cot-

ton and orange sticks and little jars of cuticle remover and
help me do my nails before putting on pale, dreamy colored polish. On other occasions she would let me come
into her bedroom and she'd show me her clothes. This
blouse is a Bill Blass. Ralph Lauren designed this
pullover. See what good use of colors he makes? Feel
this. It's genuine silk. Bo knew all the really exotic
places to shop. She had been to New York City and
shopped in Saks Fifth Avenue. She'd been on Rodeo
Drive in Beverly Hills. Once she had even been in the
same shop as Shirley MacLaine. I would stand in the
bedroom beside her and listen and feel drab and colorless, my bones, like Mama's, peasant huge, my hair,
like Daddy's, uncontrollable. The eye makeup would
smudge when I put it on. The blusher made me look like I
had a fever. And once when I came home after Bo had
made me up, Mama just stood there, arms folded over
her breasts, and shook her head. When I asked what was
wrong, she burst out laughing. But with every passing
visit to the Kruegers, I grew to love Bo more. She never
seemed to doubt that I could enter her world, if I tried.
She never seemed to lose faith that I was really a peacock
in sparrow's clothing.

Paul's father I really never came to know. He was
gone much of the time. He was a lawyer and was thinking of running for the legislature, so he spent a good
share of his time in Goodland or Topeka or clear over in
Kansas City. The few times he was home when I was
over, he was usually in his study. Unlike my daddy, Mr.
Krueger really did have paperwork to do.

The majority of the time I spent at the Kruegers' was, of
course, spent with Paul. Usually we shut ourselves upstairs in his room and worked on his projects. He would
explain them to me in patient, loving detail. Some of the
things I did eventually understand. Most of them I didn't,
but it mattered little. I found it fun to be with him, to

work on them, to see how they would come out. He could so easily conceptualize what he wanted to do and then create it, that I was excited just to be a spectator to the process. Through January and most of February we worked on a contraption to photograph Kirlian auras and then hunted for various items to try in it, including money and gloves and once, the seat off the upstairs toilet. But Paul's real passion was for astronomy and his dream was to build a telescope larger than his current one. So we spent hours and hours together, paging through catalogues that sold ground lenses and mirrors and numerous bits and pieces that I had no understanding of, in preparation for creating what I came to think of as "our telescope." Actually, I was impressed with the telescope he already had. I'd never seen one that powerful in someone's home before and I knew it must have cost a great deal of money. We spent a lot of our evenings looking through it. I learned how to locate Procyon and Andromeda and Mira, "the Wonderful," and helped Paul keep his observation notebooks. Sometimes we attached his father's camera to the telescope, and once I got to take photographs of the moon. Later, we made plans to get them blown up into posters, some for his room, some for mine.

At my house, life remained very much the same.

"Daddy," said Megan one evening as we were sitting at the dinner table, "can I have a slumber party?"

Dad looked up. "You can. The question remains whether or not you *may.*"

Megan groaned. *"May* I have a slumber party? I got to thinking about it today and I thought, well, maybe when my birthday comes around, we might've moved and I won't know any kids to ask. So can I have a slumber party now while I still got friends?"

"We're not moving to my knowledge," my father replied.

"Well, we might. You never can tell. Besides, my birthday's right in the middle of summer vacation, and there's never any kids around then anyway. So can I have one now? And we can count it for my birthday, like an advance against it or something. I won't ask for anything then."

"What's a slumber party?" Mama asked.

"Oh Mama, it's where kids bring over their sleeping bags and sleep on your floor. And you eat food and stuff. It's real fun." Megan obviously had it plotted out already in her head.

"Well, Meggie," my father said, "I can see why you'd like to do it, but I don't think it's a very good idea right now."

"Why not?"

"Well, for one thing, it'd be a lot of trouble for your mama."

"No, it wouldn't. Just a little party. Just a little, little, little one. Just maybe me and Katie and Tracey Pickett and Suzanne Warner. And maybe Jessica. And, oh yeah, Melissa. I can't forget Melissa because I went to her birthday party in November. Remember? But that's all. Just them. And I already got it thought out. They could bring their sleeping bags and we could do it in the living room. And we could have dinner, you know, like hot dogs or something. Nothing big. I could make hot dogs myself. Then we'd just watch TV and go to sleep. We wouldn't be any bother at all, Daddy."

By the set of his jaw, I could tell my father had already decided against it.

Megan studied his face.

"No, Meggie," he said, "I'm afraid not. Maybe some other time. Maybe when we get a bigger house."

"But we'll *never* get a bigger house."

"Sure we will. Maybe we'll get a house with a rec room in it. Then you can play games and everything."

"By then I might be old and not want a slumber party."

"Sure you will."

Megan fell silent a moment, her lower lip jutting over her upper. "I want a party now, not some far-off time, Daddy. Not someday."

"I know you do, kitten."

Putting her elbows on the table, Megan braced her face on her two fists. She rolled her eyes in my father's direction. "It's not fair. I never get to do anything. Katie had a slumber party just last week. Katie's had *three* of them."

"Yes, and you got to go to every one of them, didn't you, Megs?" Dad said.

"That's not the *same.*" Megan's voice had grown whiny. My father's brows began to knit together when she spoke like that. "Well, it's not, Daddy. Sometimes *I* want to do these things too. Sometimes I just want to be like everybody else."

"But you're not everybody else, are you?"

"No," Megan said in a low voice. I could see she was about to cry. Mama, next to her, was busying herself with the mashed potatoes.

"Well then," said Dad, "that's that. Just as soon as we're in our new house, Megan has a party. I'll mark that down in my diary so I remember. Just as soon as we're settled." He looked over at her. "But in the meantime, young lady, take your elbows off the table and start on all that food."

Megan was still teetering dangerously on the edge of tears. With one foot she kicked against the leg of the table. Milk danced in our glasses. Mama turned around and lifted the coffeepot from the stove. She asked Dad if he wanted more.

"You know something," Megan said, her voice low and hoarse, "I don't really like being in this family very much. In fact, I hate it."

Without even looking up from his food, my father said, "You're excused. You may go to your room, Megan."

Megan just sat, kicking the table leg.

Lifting one eyebrow, he looked over at her. Megan threw down her napkin, rose and left.

I felt sorry for Megs. I knew exactly how she felt. Besides, it was easy to hear from her voice that she'd had the slumber party all planned out. You could tell that she'd most likely sat through all of Katie's party the previous week, saying to herself, at *my* party we'll have hot dogs, at *my* party we'll watch *Happy Days,* at *my* party there'll be even more girls than here. Megan always did have more dreams in her head than sense.

After the dishes were done, I stopped by her room. She was lying on her back on the bed, doing nothing but staring at the ceiling.

"Look, I'm sorry about your not getting to have a slumber party, Megs."

"Go away," she said.

"I know how you feel. I remember wanting stuff like that too."

"It's not fair," she said. "He's just mean."

"He's not trying to be, Megs. He thinks he's doing the right thing."

She looked over. "It's because of Mama, isn't it? He just doesn't want to bother Mama. Well, I didn't hear Mama say anything against it. I didn't hear her complain."

"Megs, it's not his fault. It's just one of those things."

"Well, whose fault is it, then?" she asked and rolled over onto her stomach. The instant she said that, she knew the answer. Gently, she kicked at the bed with her foot. Silence followed. I picked at the wallpaper by the light switch. "You know what, Lesley?" she said at last.

"What's that?"

"I hate Mama."

"No, you don't."

"Yes, I do. Sometimes I do. And you know what else? I meant what I said. I don't really like being in this family very much."

Then at last it was March.

"Lesley? Lessie? Wake up."

"What do you want?" Sleepily I rolled over to see Megan leaning over my bed. It was not even 6:30.

"Are you awake? Get up. Come on. I want to show you something."

"Go play in traffic, Megan."

"Get up. Come here. Come in my room." She gave me a mighty shove.

Without any show of good humor, I got out of bed and followed her back to her own room. She ran across and bounced up on the bed.

"Lookie here, Les."

"This better be good. Or I mean it, Megan, I'm going to murder you."

*"Look."* She had the curtain held back.

It was not quite dawn. Early March and the world for the main part was still winter gray. From Megan's window I could see the big, leafless sycamore in the Reillys' backyard, the street, the roofs of other houses, and out beyond them the dull, yellowish stretch of plains. The day was dawning clear and cloudless, but at that hour the sky was mostly without color.

"I don't see anything, you little pig. What did you drag me in here for anyway?"

"Down there. Look in the grass under the window."

On the small stretch of lawn between our house and the Reillys', I could make out crocuses growing in the grass. White and yellow ones, forming letters. M-E-G-A-N.

"Look at it. See? Someone's made my name in flow-

ers down there on the lawn. See them? I never noticed
them until just this minute when I woke up and looked
out. And there they were.''

I pressed my nose against the glass to see them better.
The letters were surprisingly clear in the grass. Then the
windowpane fogged over with my breath.

"It's like magic, isn't it?'' Megan said. Megan was
the kind of child to believe in magic. Although she didn't
admit it, I knew she still hoped for the possibility of fairies and elves and a real Santa Claus.

I tried to see down the strip of lawn to tell if there were
flowers under my window too. When I saw crocuses
there, I pointed them out to Megan and she bolted off her
bed and down the hallway to my room.

The letters making my name were not nearly so well
formed as Megan's. They looked like L-E-S-L-F. There
was no *Y* at all, just random flowers. But still, I could see
it was my name.

"Who did it, do you think?'' Megan asked, as she
tried to wrench open my window to stick her head out.

"I don't know.''

"Mama. I bet it was Mama. I bet Mama did it.'' The
window wouldn't come open after the long winter of
being shut. Megan pressed her face and both her palms
flat against the glass. "Or maybe it's really magic. It's
like magic, isn't it? I never seen it before now and there it
was, like it came up overnight. There was my name in
the grass.''

"I don't think it did,'' I said. "We never go over on
that side of the house. It could have been up for ages.''

"But I *look*. I'm always looking out my window, Lesley, just like now. And there it was. Just this morning.''

The discovery excited Megan all out of proportion to
what it was. I couldn't restrain her from galloping in and
bounding into bed with Mama and Daddy. They were
both asleep when she crawled in between them. My fa-

ther woke, yawning. Mama turned over sleepily and kissed Megan on top of her head. Megs was squirming down between them and chattering like a chipmunk. When Mama saw me standing in the doorway, she beckoned. I got into the bed with everyone else.

Mama put her arms around us. Megan was between her and Daddy and I was on Mama's other side. She pressed us against her with strong arms, and my nose was filled with her warm, familiar smell. It was a broody scent, of baby powder, stale cigarette smoke and sleep.

"Did you plant the flowers, Mama?" I asked.

She nodded. She was smiling drowsily.

"It's like real magic," I heard Megan say. Her voice was growing soft and sleepy sounding. I lay with my head pressed against Mama's breast. She had her left hand on my face. Her skin was almost hot, and I could feel the faintly different temperature of her wedding ring against my cheek.

"It was magic, *Liebes,*" Mama said to Megs.

There were a few moments of sleepy silence.

"I love you, Mama," Megan whispered.

Then my father rolled over with a motion that rocked the whole bed. He settled deeper into his pillow. "There're an awful lot of female voices nattering on in this bed," he said without opening an eye. "And this being Sunday and the day of rest . . ."

With a finger to her lips, Mama winked at me. No one spoke again. I lay for a while, quite wide awake. I could hear Mama's heart beating. I lay listening to it. Then eventually, I closed my eyes and went back to sleep too.

# Eight

WHEN I WAS very young, we lived in West Texas for a while. I don't remember much about it. I was only about three at the time. I don't recall anything about the house at all. I do, however, remember that there was no yard in back of the house. The ground just stretched away from the back porch down a hill and out onto alkali flats before dissolving into the interminable plains. Sitting on the porch, I used to look out over the landscape and think to myself that if I could only see far enough, the plains would stretch all the way to the ocean and on the other side was Madrid, Spain. Why Madrid, Spain, I don't know. How I even knew there was such a place, when I was that age, I don't know either. But that was one of only two clear memories of the house in West Texas. My other memory was of the sunflowers.

Down on the alkali flats below the hill grew sunflowers. They may have been wild ones, springing up after the summer downpours had flooded the flats. Or maybe they were cultivated. My memory doesn't serve me there. What I do remember is sitting on the porch and looking down on all those sunflowers.

They were beautiful from the hill. The big golden heads would track the sun through the day, and that made them seem as if they were looking at me part of the time and looking away the other. Sometimes children would come and play there. From where I was sitting on the hill, I could see them, small as insects, disappear amid the flowers, and the huge heads would nod and sway as the children ran among them. Laughter would ride up the hill on the wind.

I longed to go down there myself. The sunflowers beckoned to me welcomingly. Certainly I didn't have permission the day I did go. I remember slipping down the rough prairie grass of the hillside, keeping low to the ground to stay out of Mama's sight, in case she glanced out the window. Then I ran across the flats and into the shadows of the flowers. My biggest concern was not getting caught.

When I ran among the sunflowers, I discovered they were gigantic, a veritable forest, not small, the way they appeared from the hilltop. The flowers were high above my head, and before I realized what was happening, I was deep among the tall stalks. With each step I took, the green-and-gold wilderness closed silently behind me. In no time at all, I was lost, trapped.

I screamed.

I flailed about amid the sunflowers, hysterical, crying in terror to get out. The flowers went on and on in all directions, and I could not escape. Panic-stricken, I thrashed and screamed and was swallowed up.

Mama found me. From the house on the hilltop she could hear my terrified crying. She'd come crashing in among the sunflowers, bending them aside, pushing them down. They were even taller than she was.

In her hurried slide down the hillside to reach me, she had slipped and scraped her knee. I remember clutching frantically at her and tasting blood mixed with my tears. She pulled my fingers apart and lifted me up on her shoulders so that my head was above the flowers and she carried me out.

What I remember with brittle sharpness is that final

moment, being on my mama's shoulders. I remember
turning and looking back at the forest closing behind us,
the flowers bright in the Texas sun, and innocent and
heartless.

For my mother, however, sunflowers had an entirely
different connotation. They were of almost mystical sig-
nificance for her. Sunflowers had grown wild in the back
garden of their cottage in Wales after the war. The way
Mama told about it, it was easy to tell that she perceived
the appearance of those unexpected sunflowers as practically a religious experience. They were the sign of her
resurrection, and she knew she had managed to pass
through her season in Hell.

My mother loved to tell us about those years in Wales.
They were among her very best stories, spun out in epic,
almost mythlike proportions, laced with lyrical descrip-
tions of an aged land. I loved them above all the others,
not only because she made them so beautiful to listen to,
but also because they were the only stories about her life
after the war that had the same magnificence as her tales
of Lébény and her girlhood. They reassured me that she
still had the capacity to be happy and that all her joy had
not been dragged from her by the horrors of the war.

The translated name of the cottage was Forest of Flowers. It was high up a mountainside in North Wales.
Mama always told us how she and Daddy had had to
climb the last half mile to the cottage on a small, steep
path. I had a very romantic image of Forest of Flowers in
my mind. I could see the narrow, meandering trail passing through sun-dappled woods, the forest floor a carpet
of snowdrops and bluebells and populated with little
Thumpers and Bambis. And there in the clearing, like
Snow White's cottage, was Mama's holly hedge and the
winter jasmine and the quaint wooden arch, all leading
up to the whitewashed Forest of Flowers.

Those were her sunflower years.

In Kansas, sunflowers are grown commercially. If you go out in the late summer along the small county roads in western Kansas, you'll come upon field after field of flowers, a sea of golden, nodding heads. In the time since we'd moved to Kansas, it had become a family ritual to drive out every few weeks to watch the progress of the sunflower fields from planting in March to harvesting in mid-autumn. In spite of that childhood experience, which still came back to me in nightmares, I enjoyed these journeys, although I never could bring myself to walk down the narrow rows between the stalks, planted in military straightness, the way Mama and Megan did. For my mother especially this observation of the sunflower crop was a most pleasurable way of marking the year. The sunflowers were the single redeeming feature of Kansas for my mother.

By mid-March the ground underfoot was spongy and smelled of newness. The sun had grown surprisingly hot in the space of a few weeks. It was a Saturday afternoon, but despite the weather, I was in my room studying. On the next Monday we were having an exam in calculus, and I'd be the first to admit that calculus was not my best subject. It wasn't going to be an easy test either. Mrs. Browder told us on the previous Friday that she was intending to give us a set of ten problems and we had to solve eight of them. So I was frantically going back over old assignments to make sure I knew how to do them.

Mama came to the open door of my room. "I feel like a walk," she announced.

This caught me completely unawares because my mother had not been out of the yard since the end of January. I turned from my desk to see her standing in the doorway. She was dressed in old tan corduroys and a plaid shirt. She had one of Dad's pullovers on, and her hair tied back with a yarn ribbon. She smiled at me, knowing, I think, that she'd surprised me.

"They'll be starting to put the sunflowers in," she said. "And I want to walk out and see."

"Mama, it's quite a walk. Most of those fields are at least a couple of miles away or more. If you wait until Daddy comes home, I'm sure he'll take you out in the car."

She remained in the doorway. She had a small smile that gave her a look of amusement. "Come on with me, baby. We can walk that far. It's such a beautiful day, and I'm longing to move my legs."

"We don't even know for sure if they're putting them in the same fields as last year. I think we ought to wait for Dad."

"I have cobwebs in my legs. Come along with me. I want to walk."

I turned back to my books for a moment. "I can't, really, Mama. I have a calculus test on Monday morning. And I honestly think I might not pass it. Not if I don't study; because I don't understand how to do all these problems. In half of them I can't even tell what they're looking for."

She continued to stand there, silent but insistent. It was difficult ever to deny my mother things.

"Maybe Daddy can take us all out in the car tomorrow," I said. "We could have a picnic. Why don't we do that?"

Mama still had the small smile on her face. She looked young to me then, standing there in those old clothes. She had an ageless quality to her facial expressions that made it very difficult for people to guess her age.

"What about Megs?" I suggested when it was apparent Mama wasn't going to give up the idea. Megan was downstairs doing something in the kitchen. I knew because I'd been hearing her throughout my studying. Megan never had been what you could call a quiet child.

"I bet Meggie would love to go with you. Why don't you ask her?"

Mama considered that. She waited a moment longer in case I was going to change my mind. Finally, satisfied that I wasn't, she turned and left.

I could hear them preparing downstairs, fixing a picnic of fruit and soft drinks. Mama was talking in Hungarian, her voice full and undulant. Megan was beside herself with excitement, and her glee floated up the stairs in squeally, high-pitched syllables.

From my window I watched them leave together. They had the little knapsack with them. Bulky in Dad's brown sweater, Mama strode off down the street, moving purposefully, like one of Odin's Valkyries. Megan flitted around her like a small, dark wraith.

"Where's your mama at?" my father asked when he returned from work midafternoon.

"She and Megs went to see the farmers putting in the sunflowers," I replied. He had come upstairs, still carrying a bag of groceries in one arm. He was in his blue work coveralls and had his cap on. He set the bag down on my bed. Taking off his cap, he ran his fingers through his hair. It stood straight up.

"Mama asked me to go," I said, "but I have this test on Monday to study for."

"That's an awful long way," he said.

"That's what I told her. I said you'd probably take her out in the car, if she'd only wait till you got back. But you know how Mama is. She wanted it right then."

He wandered over to the window and pulled back the curtain. "It's been such a long time since she's been out," he said, more to himself than to me. Then he turned in my direction. "Did she say where she was going?"

"No."

I knew what he was thinking, even though he didn't say it. He was thinking I should have asked her specifically, that I was being irresponsible to let my mother wander off with Megan without finding out at least which way they planned to go. It had not occurred to me until just that moment that Mama might have had no idea of where she was going. That was the problem with Mama. Like the time she had dismantled the refrigerator because it wasn't working, Mama would set her mind to do something and she'd do it, not caring whatsoever that she had no clue about how to go about it. The sheer pleasure of action was enough for her, even when her willingness to tackle something far outweighed her actual knowledge of what was involved. Suddenly the simple Saturday afternoon walk seem fraught with every kind of possible disaster.

"Maybe I should take the car and go look for them," Dad said thoughtfully.

"I don't think you need to do that," I said. "If they get lost, they can call. Megan'd know to do that."

"Do they have any money with them?"

Again, I realized I hadn't checked. "Well, they could go to a farmhouse and use the phone there."

"How long have they been gone?"

"Since about one."

My father sighed. "She's been inside all winter. She should have waited." Letting the curtain fall back into place, he went over and picked up the bag of groceries from the bed. "Well, I'll give them until five. If they're not back by then, I'll take the car out and look for them."

There was no need to worry. By 4:30 the storm door slammed, and I heard the sound of Mama's voice calling for my father. When I came downstairs, I found them embracing, involved in one of those chaste but terribly long, complete-with-droning-bees-sound-effects kisses that they got into. Dad never said anything to her about being gone without telling him. Instead, he told her that Mr. Hughson from the garage had paid him double over-time for working Saturday afternoon and that he'd bought us steaks for supper.

When it became obvious that I'd get stuck helping with the meal if I stayed downstairs, I returned to my room to study. Megan had gone thundering up the stairs past me when I'd first come down, so on my way back to my room, I stopped at her door. It was shut.

"Can I come in, Megs?" I asked and opened the door without waiting for an answer. "How was it? Did you and Mama find any sunflowers being planted?"

Megan was crying. She was sitting on the edge of her bed and had her stuffed tiger cat shoved against her mouth to block the noise.

"Whatever's wrong with you?" I asked in surprise.

"Nothing," she said and furiously mopped at her face. I came over and sat down on the bed beside her. That immediately caused her to throw the stuffed animal down and get up. She crossed to the window. Reaching for a rubber band on the window ledge, she lifted her hair up and put the band around it. I remained on the bed.

"Megs?"

Another prolonged effort to stop the tears. I waited.

"Lesley, who's Klaus?" She turned to look at me.

"Klaus who?"

Tears flooded her eyes again. "That's what I'm asking *you*, dummy."

We stared at one another in silence. She had snot running over her upper lip.

"What are you talking about, Megan?"

"Well, you know we went out? We were walking on this road by the creek. By those fields where you and me got the fireflies last summer, remember? Anyway, there was this little boy there. He was playing in the underbrush."

Megan paused. She came over to the bed and picked

up the tiger cat again. Taking its two forelegs, one in each of her hands, she held it out in front of her and gazed at it. "All of a sudden," she said pensively to the cat, "Mama looks at this kid and she says to me in this really excited voice, 'There's Klaus!' You could just tell from the way she said it, she was *super* excited." Megan looked above the stuffed animal's head to me. "I mean, really, really super excited, Les. She shouted, 'Klaus, Klaus, come here!' And this little kid looks up and he sees her and of course, 'cause he hears this lady yelling at him, he gets this scared look and he takes off down into the underbrush. And Mama's hollering 'Klaus! Klaus!' after him."

"What did he look like? Did you know him?"

The tears reappeared and Megan paused a moment to quell them. Pressing the tiger cat to her chest, she sat down on the bed beside me. "He was just some little kid. I don't know who. He was just little. Maybe five or something. He was wearing overalls and one of those brown jackets that's got the flannel lining inside. And he had this really white hair."

"What did Mama do then?" I asked. "After he ran away?"

"We were on the road. So she ran down the road a little ways, and I was running after her. Then she turned to me and said, 'Maybe he doesn't understand German.' See, she had shouted at him in German. So then she shouts at this kid in English. Same thing. 'Klaus, come back here.' But the little boy was on the other side of the fence by then and he was still running. She stopped when she got to the fence. But she kept yelling for him to come back."

I shrugged. "I wouldn't worry about it, Megs. Really, I wouldn't. It's not worth getting so upset about. It's probably just one of Mama's funny things."

"But she kept saying to me, 'He must not speak German. They must have raised him here.' "

"Look, don't worry about it. You know how Mama is sometimes."

"But who *is* Klaus?"

"I don't know, kiddo."

"Where would Mama know him from?"

"Like I said, it's probably nothing at all. Just a funny idea of hers. Maybe somebody she remembers from before. You know. From Germany or somewhere. I wouldn't get all upset about it."

"You weren't there. You don't know what it was like."

"Just the same, I wouldn't worry about it."

"But who is he?"

"Megan, I said I don't know. I don't. I've never even heard of anyone around here named Klaus. So don't cry about it anymore, okay? It's probably nothing."

"You know what she said, though? She said to him, 'Klaus, come back here. It's Mama. Come back, it's me, Mama.' "

Megan remained upset. I was unable to talk her out of it, and she was unable to forget it. She stayed up in her room and told my father that she was sick to her stomach when he came up to see why she hadn't come to supper. She put on her pajamas and crawled under the covers and stayed there. I didn't bother her. Nor did I tell Dad what had happened. If it was one of Mama's imaginings, there was not much to be done about it, and I saw no point in upsetting him too. And I couldn't fathom what else it could be.

All through supper and into the evening, I watched Mama closely and wondered. That was a strange thing for her to do. Even by Mama's standards, it was weird. I wondered what she could have been thinking of.

If anything, my mother was more buoyant that evening than she had been in months. The wind had burned the skin along her cheekbones, giving her a ruddy, healthy look. She had removed the yarn tie, and her hair lay thick and pale over her shoulders, catching the glow of the kitchen light as she moved. She and my father joked around. While he was drying the dishes, he flicked her playfully with the dish towel, and she squealed like a schoolgirl. Later, they went upstairs, hand in hand, and left me to watch television by myself.

Mama was pacing. I woke slowly to the sound, not quite realizing it wasn't part of my dream until I was fully awake. I turned to look at the alarm clock. Four-fourteen. Putting the pillow over my head, I tried to shut out the sound.

Mama had always had trouble sleeping. Her insomnia was periodic. Sometimes she'd go seven or eight months without difficulties, then she'd start waking up in the night and be unable to go back to sleep. She said it was her back. Her back would ache, and she couldn't sleep because of the pain. Then she'd go to the doctor for a prescription, sometimes for her back, sometimes for the insomnia. Nothing worked for long. If she was in the midst of one of her wakeful periods, she woke up, pills or no pills.

"Mama, what's the matter?" I stood at the bottom of the stairs. She was by the living-room window. In her long cotton nightgown, she looked like a ghost in the darkness. The only light came from the glowing end of her cigarette.

When I spoke, she started and turned. I came farther into the room and bent down to switch on one of the table lamps. She squinted in the sudden brightness.

"Can't you sleep?" I asked.

She shook her head.

"What's wrong?"

At first she did not respond. Then slowly she dragged a hand up and touched the small of her back. "It's just the old hurt, *Liebes.* I shouldn't have been walking so far today. I overdid it. That's all."

"Do you want me to rub it for you? You want to go up

to my room and lie down on the bed? I think we've got some rubbing alcohol."

She shook her head.

Shivering in the predawn chill, I watched her. Her hair, mussed from sleep, splayed over her gown. She had broad shoulders, which the gown emphasized. I noticed she was losing weight again. Long-term dysentery during the war had played havoc with her system, and she still suffered frequent, severe bouts of diarrhea; consequently, she never could keep weight on, even with her prodigious appetite. And when she did gain and was well within the norms for someone her height, she still looked underweight. Her skin fit loosely, making her always appear too thin.

"Shall I make you a cup of hot milk, Mama?"

No answer.

"A cup of tea? Would you like a cup of tea? India tea, maybe? I wouldn't mind a cup myself. How 'bout if I fix you one too?"

"No thanks," she said. She kept her back to me and watched out the window. I doubted that she could see much, because the lamplight obscured any view into the darkness beyond the glass. But she watched anyway, absorbed.

I noticed her feet were bare. "Mama, come sit down. It's too cold for you over there. Cripes, I'm freezing."

Her eyes remained focused on some point in the darkness.

"Mama, *was ist los?*" I asked. She was always most comfortable in German. Even more so than Hungarian, I believe. German had been her language with Mutti, the one of nursery rhymes and children's songs and a mother's secret words for her small daughter. We never could settle on a language in our family. Mama slid back and forth at will between German, Hungarian and English, often in the same conversation. But it was German she took her comfort from.

Still she gazed at the glass. Bringing a hand up, she scratched along the side of her face in a slow, pensive motion and then dropped her hand and locked it behind her back. In the reflection of the glass, I saw her eyes narrow, as if she were seeing something out there, and her forehead wrinkled into a frown of concentration.

"I saw him," she said very, very softly.

"*Wer*, Mama?" I asked.

She said nothing.

"*Wer*, Mama? Klaus?"

Sharply, she turned and looked at me.

"I know about him. Megan told me about this afternoon."

She sighed and once again turned away from me. I saw she was shivering too.

"Mama, come away from the window. It's too cold there for you. Here, take the afghan."

She didn't move.

I had had the afghan around my shoulders. Bringing it over, I tried to hand it to her but she didn't take it. So I wrapped it back around myself. My stomach felt sick, and I thought perhaps Megan really did have something and I had caught it. I almost hoped so. Then my mother would have to take care of me.

"I saw him," she whispered, her breath clouding the glass. "I've found him. The *Scheisskerle*, they could not keep him hidden from me."

"What, Mama?"

"Him," she said, nodding her head slightly at the window. "The bastards, they thought I'd never find him. The stupid swine. They thought they'd had the better of me. But they never did. I've found him now."

"Who, Mama?"

"*Mein Sohn.*"

# Nine

"DAD," I SAID, "I need to talk to you."

He had a shovel in one hand and a cardboard box in the other. Sunday, like Saturday, had come up warm and bright and smelling of spring. Mama was still asleep on the couch in the living room when my father had gotten up, so he had made himself breakfast and put on his gardening clothes and went out into the backyard. Mama was still sleeping when I rose too. I didn't eat. My stomach felt all right, but I wasn't hungry. Instead, I pursued my father into the garden.

"What about?" he asked and put a shovel into the damp earth. He turned a spadeful over.

"Well, I got to thinking," I said. I watched him. With slow, almost rhythmic movements, he spaded up the length of the flower bed. When he came to the end, he paused and leaned on the shovel handle.

"About what?" he asked.

"Well, you know how back in January Mama was acting like she might like to move?"

"Yes?"

"I got to thinking. And I think maybe we should. Maybe right away."

"I thought you had your heart so set on graduating with your friends, Lesley."

"Well, not really, I guess. I mean, it doesn't matter

that much to me. Graduating's graduating, isn't it? It can happen anywhere. There's nothing so special about it.''

My father rocked thoughtfully forward on the shovel. A worm squirmed in the upturned soil. He reached down and pushed a bit of dirt over it.

"I think I'd like to be in a different place," I said. "And I think it would be good for Mama too."

"Your mother is doing just fine where she is," he said, still watching where the worm was buried. He rocked again against the shovel. "We don't need to disrupt things on her account. She's quite happy here."

"Really, I don't mind going, Dad. Somewhere warm. Mama's back's bothering her again. She was up last night with it. And I was thinking that if we were somewhere warmer, maybe she wouldn't have so many problems with it."

"It's March, Les. It'll be plenty warm enough for anyone right here in no time at all."

"Well, I was just thinking maybe it'd be better."

"I thought you liked it here," he replied, looking over. He was wearing a red-plaid flannel shirt. I noticed two buttons were missing, replaced by a safety pin. "You've got all your friends here. And Paul. I thought you and Paul were . . ." He didn't finish the sentence.

"Yes, well, I just thought I'd tell you that it doesn't matter at all to me. That you don't have to stay here for my sake. I'd rather move, I think."

He was searching my face. "Did something happen to cause this sudden change of heart? Did you and Paul have a falling out?" There was a tenderness in his voice that I hadn't anticipated.

"No. No, no, nothing like that. I just thought there was no point hanging around here just because of me."

"I don't think we are. I don't think I ever heard anyone around here mentioning moving except you. Your mama never has."

"Well, I was just thinking it might not be such a bad idea."

I could tell that Dad thought it was me. He thought I'd had some kind of disagreement with someone and was trying to get away. That hadn't been what I'd intended but at least he didn't think it was Mama.

Megan, however, was nobody's fool. She was sitting out on the front sidewalk with her roller skates when I found her.

"How're you this morning?" I asked.

She shrugged and continued to adjust her skates. They were an ancient pair that had belonged originally to one of Auntie Caroline's children back in the fifties. Mastering the art of putting them on and making them work should have qualified Megan for an engineering diploma.

"Do you feel okay? Is your stomach all right?"

She tightened the skate further. They pinched into the sides of her running shoes. "Nothing was wrong with my stomach," she said acidly. "You know that."

I hitched my thumbs into the waistband of my jeans.

"We got to ask her, Les."

"No, we don't."

"Yes, we do. I heard you two up last night. I know she wasn't asleep. And I can bet you a million dollars I know why. So don't bother to lie to me." Carefully, she rose and put the skate key into her pocket. Taking a step backwards, she let herself roll down the sidewalk away from me. I followed her.

"No, we don't have to ask her, Megan. What Mama is thinking about is her own business."

"Lesley, are you deaf or something? Did you hear what I told you last night? Mama thought that little kid was one of us."

"No," I replied. "She didn't. She thought he was her son."

Megan's eyes widened. "Well, that's *worse*. She hasn't got a son."

Neither of us spoke after that. Megan was skating along very slowly and with deep absorption. In the same way, I focused all my attention on simply keeping up. To the rhythm of the skates against the cement, I counted out my steps.

We went down around the corner and up Bailey Street and over to Third without saying anything to one another. When we reached the park on Third and Elm, Megan stopped. She ran her skates off into the grass and paused, balancing on the toes. Taking the skate key from her pocket, she sat down on the grass.

"What exactly happened to Mama?" Megan asked. Her voice was very calm. She was adjusting the skates again and did not look up. "I mean, during the war. Just what really did happen then?"

"I don't know."

"Have you ever asked?"

I shrugged. "She's told us plenty of stuff, Megs."

Megan rested her cheek against her knees. I sat down on the grass beside her. "I want to know what happened," she said. "Not just the funny stuff. Not just about old Jadwiga. I don't want Mama to stick out her teeth and do old Jadwiga's funny voice and make me laugh. I want to know the rest of it. I want to know how come Mama's got scars on her butt and her legs. I want to know how come she was so sick in the war, how come she got starved. I'm not so stupid as you think, Lesley. I see all that stuff. And I need Mama to tell me what really happened. It matters to me, because I never can really forget about it. And I don't think she does either. So I need her to tell me. It's better than guessing all the time."

"Megan, don't you dare ask her stuff like that."

"Why not?"

"Just don't. I mean it."

Megan eyed me with annoyance. "I will, if I want to."

"You do and I'll make you sorry."

Silence between us. From her expression, I could see she wasn't backing down.

"You're not old enough," I said. "That's what they'll say to you. I asked Dad once and that's what he said to me. That I was too young to understand."

"When was that?" Megan asked.

"When I was about your age."

"So what about now. Are you old enough to find out now?"

I shrugged. "I'm not so sure I want to know now. I can see what it does to Mama. Besides, it's old stuff, Megan. It's over and done with. The war got finished in 1945 and that's years and years and years ago. There's no point in knowing, really."

Megan sighed and reached down to pull tight her shoe-laces. Then wearily she rose and skated off.

# Ten

MEGAN WAS SITTING in the kitchen when I arrived home from school on Monday afternoon. She had her school-books stacked on the corner of the table and her stock-inged feet up on the chair across from her. One apple core lay beside her already. She was crunching her way nois-ily through a second apple while deeply absorbed in a book that lay open in her lap.

"Hey Lessie, come here and look at this," she said when I appeared. I crossed over to the table.

It was a book on the Third Reich, an adult book, some-thing for readers far older than Megan.

"Where did you get that?" I asked.

"The library. I went in after school and asked the lady there where they had books about the Second World War. She gave me these. See?" She indicated a couple of other books on the table too. "I'm going to read about it. I'm going to learn all there is to know."

"Those books are too old for you. You won't even un-derstand them."

"No, they're not. I can read them. The lady at the li-brary gave them to me."

"What did you do? Tell her you were a kid genius? Megan, those books are for adults."

"Not necessarily. Lookie. This one's about kids. See?" She pulled a thin paperback from the stack.

"There are poems and stuff that these kids wrote while they were in a concentration camp for children. See what it says here in the back? The library lady showed it to me. Fifteen thousand children went into this camp. And only a hundred ever came back."

There was a sudden, potent silence. Megan remained intent a moment longer over the book. "This could have been us," she said quietly without raising her eyes.

"Megan, you shouldn't be reading stuff like that. It's macabre."

"It's the truth though," she said. She looked up. "It happened, for real. And it could have happened to us. This here, in this book. If we'd been born, they could have tooken us away just like these kids and put us in a camp."

"They couldn't either. Those were Jewish children. They took them away because they were Jews."

"But we still could have been one of these children. If we'd been born then. They were kids just like us. See, look at the way this one kid writes. He makes his *G*'s just like I do."

"Megan, listen to me. It wouldn't have ever happened to us. Those were Jewish children. We aren't Jews. We never were and we never will be. So it could never have happened to us."

"It could have."

"Megan, it could *not* have. Wash your dirty ears out. I said, we're not Jews. It could *not* have happened to us. So don't be stupid and keep insisting. You're as bad as Mama with your ridiculous opinions."

A frown formed across her features. "How come you keep on saying that? 'It couldn't happen to us; we're not Jews.' Why do you say that all the time? It happened to people, Lesley. Real people. And because we're people too, it could have happened to us. You're the one who's stupid."

"You shouldn't be looking at stuff like that. It makes

you crabby," I replied. "Besides, what do you know about anything? You're too little to understand what's really behind it anyhow. You don't know anything; you're just a baby."

Megan's scowl deepened.

I set my books down and went to the cupboard to get down the peanut butter and honey for my sandwich. "All I'm saying, Megs, is that we're in no position to be even discussing it. We don't know what happened. That's my point. We just don't know. So it's stupid to go reading about what happened to the Jews and generalizing it to everyone else who was in the war." I turned around and looked at her. "And if you ask me, you just shouldn't be reading that kind of junk."

"No one's asking you."

"For one thing, Megan, all you're going to do is end up hurting Mama. She'll come in and see those books and it'll make her remember all the bad stuff that did happen to her and then she'll be unhappy."

"She's remembering already, Les."

"And for another thing, I mean it when I said you're too little. That's *horrid* stuff in those books. You won't be able to forget it, once you've read about it. They were wicked, really evil things that happened and it's so terrible that I wish people didn't even have to think about it."

Megan was still glowering.

"Anyway, you want to know what you're going to end up with out of this?"

She didn't reply.

"Nightmares, that's what. I know you, smarty-pants."

"I will not."

"And you'll wet the bed."

There, that shut her up. I shouldn't have said it. Even as I did, I regretted it a bit. It was spiteful and nothing more. But she could go on so, and I was sick of her incessant questions. Why couldn't she tell when things ought to be left alone? That was the problem with Megan. One of the many problems with Megan.

I didn't feel much like a sandwich anymore. I had the bread out and the peanut butter and the honey, and when I looked at it all, I knew I wasn't hungry. In the end I left everything sitting on the counter and went out of the room.

Upstairs, all was silent. I put my books in my room and changed clothes.

"Mama?" I said softly. Thinking she was lying down for a nap, as she often did in the late afternoon, I eased open the door to their bedroom. No one was there.

Returning to the kitchen, I stopped in the doorway. Megan was still engrossed in her book. "Megs, where's Mama?"

She shrugged. "I don't know."

"Isn't she home?"

Megan looked up. "I thought she was taking a nap."

"Did you look? Have you seen her since you've been home?"

"No. I just thought she was sleeping and I didn't want to disturb her."

Cripes. I looked around the kitchen, despairing for an idea of what to do next.

"Listen, Megs, if I go get the car from Daddy, do you think you can show me where you and Mama were walking on Saturday afternoon?"

"I think so."

All the way to the garage Megan did not talk. She was still angry with me for the earlier conversation, and I don't think she wanted to come. Still dressed in her school clothes, still munching apples, she trailed along behind; but she did not talk.

When we arrived, Dad wanted to know why I wanted the car. He was lying on his back under Mr. Toppano's old Dodge pickup and couldn't hear me well.

"I said, we're going shopping," I shouted, getting down on my hands and knees.

"What for?"

"Groceries," I said, thinking fast. That would require a car.

"Do you have any money?" he asked.

I had $1.27. Hardly enough for a car full of groceries. My father slid out from under the truck and sat up. He fished the keys from his coverall pocket. Then he went and got his wallet and gave me five dollars.

Unlike the weekend, Monday was overcast. It was mild but blowy, and the plains stretched so far out they finally disappeared into the grayness of the sky. Together Megan and I went along country roads by the creek. Megs didn't remember things as clearly as she could have. It was different riding in a car, she claimed, and I had to return to town three times and start over before we found the road they had taken.

Again we did not talk. It was a silent chore, searching up and down the roads for Mama. I wasn't sure what I would do if we found her, but as time wore on, I grew increasingly desperate because I hadn't. Megan sat, stone silent, her face pressed against the glass of the passenger window.

There were no signs of anyone on the long, straight dirt roads. You could have seen a person walking from a great distance away because the land was so flat. Even around the stream there was little undergrowth. The only way someone could keep from being seen was to go right down and walk in the creek bed. But I didn't believe Mama was trying to stay out of sight. She just wasn't there.

I looked over the fields. There were no sunflowers being planted. Most of the fields in this area were already cropped in winter wheat. The rest stood idle.

"There's where that boy was," Megan said, pointing. "Over there. See where the underbrush is?"

"Where did he run to?"

"There. Down by the creek."

I stretched my neck to see down an intersecting road. Nothing. No one. I turned the car around and drove by a farm. Waterman, it said on the mailbox. There were no other houses to be seen.

Finally, we had to give up. It was nearly six o'clock. The daylight was giving out. Besides, I knew my father would be arriving home. Even if he walked instead of hitching a ride with someone, he'd be home by six. Despondent, I headed back.

"Do you think we would have made it?" Megan asked me. It was the first thing out of her mouth in perhaps twenty minutes.

"What are you talking about?"

"If they'd put us into one of those camps like they did those children in that book. Do you think we would have survived?"

"Oh, Megan, please, do stop going on about that kind of stuff, would you? Please?"

"I can't help it," she replied, her voice faint against the window on her side. "I think about it. They were just little kids. Littler than me in lots of cases. It'd be hard to survive. A lot of people didn't. So I just keep wondering, what if it was me? Would I make it out okay?"

I didn't reply.

"Living with Mama, it's pretty hard not to wonder about those things."

I still did not say anything. I wasn't even thinking. Just driving.

"Well, don't you?" she asked.

"Don't I what?"

"Don't you ever wonder if you could have survived?"

I chewed my lip. The town ahead, I noticed, was like a little sore on the great expanse of plains.

"Yeah, Megs," I said. "I guess I do wonder about it sometimes."

* * *

Mama was not home when we arrived. Dad was. He was standing in the unlit gloom of the front hallway as we entered. There was a long moment's assessment of Megan and me as we came through the door when he saw that Mama was not with us and that we had no groceries.

"May I ask precisely what is going on in this house?" Neither one of us answered.

"Just what the hell is happening, girls?" The hall was remarkably dark. His figure was gray and grainy and indistinct, like an overenlarged photograph.

"Mama's gone," Megan said softly.

"I can see that for myself. What I want to know is where."

"I don't know," I said. "Neither of us does."

Abruptly turning, my father went down the hallway to the kitchen. He flipped on the lights.

"We tried to find her," Megan said. Her voice was rising with the threat of tears. I wasn't feeling too jolly myself. Dad was clearly angry with us. Perhaps it was because we hadn't told him something was going on with Mama. Perhaps it was only because he was worried. I couldn't tell. But it was not an emotion either Megan or I needed.

"So where is she? What's been going on around here?"

Megan told him about Saturday afternoon, about the walk and the little boy whom Mama called Klaus. My father covered his mouth with the ends of his fingers as Megan spoke. There was an odd, paralyzed expression in his eyes as he watched Megan. Then slowly he turned and walked over to the table and sat down. He put his head between his hands in a disheartened gesture. For an instant, I thought he might cry himself. Megan kept talking, faster and faster. She filled in all the little details of where they had walked and where we had searched this afternoon. Her voice remained high pitched and fragile. She clenched and unclenched her hands as she spoke.

Then nothing. My father sat at the table. Both my sister and I stood, rooted in the doorway of the kitchen. Beyond the window I could hear the wind pick up. The clock over the refrigerator ticked.

"Daddy?" Megan ventured very tentatively. "Who is Klaus?"

He did not answer immediately, and I began to believe he wouldn't. His head was still between his hands. Then he moved slowly, rubbing his fingers across his eyes. He turned. "A long time ago, a very, very long time ago your mother had other children. She had two little boys."

"I didn't know Mama had any kids but us," Megan said in disbelief.

"Once. Long ago. Long before you were born."

I was as incredulous as Megan.

"Then is that little boy one of them?" Megan asked, her voice hushed with awe. "That little boy we saw on Saturday?"

"No. He was someone else," my father replied.

The front door opened and we, standing in the kitchen, felt the gust of wind and saw Megan's schoolwork, pinned to the bulletin board, flutter. Mama came striding into the kitchen.

"Hello, everyone," she said cheerfully. Her hair was tousled wildly, her cheeks were red. She could have been a girl then, with her pale loose hair and casual clothes and hearty, bright-eyed expression. The three of us were standing there, feeling like death, and my mother never looked better.

"Where have you been, Mara?" my father said. It wasn't as much a question as a demand. But my mother, whose radar normally was so acute, seemed oblivious. With one hand she unwound her muffler while she walked past us to the cupboard. Bending down, she took out a pan from under the stove.

"Macaroni and cheese tonight? With tomatoes in it?"

She turned to Megan. That was one of Megan's favorite meals.

"Mara, where have you been?" There was definitely no mistaking my father's feelings that time. "Mara?"

Mama looked over at him. For the first time there was alarm in her eyes.

He jerked his head. "May I see you in the study?"

Mutely, my mother regarded him. The color drained away from her face and with it went the look of youth she had had coming through the door. She grew old before our eyes.

"Mara, come in the study with me. I need to talk to you." The emotion faded from my father's voice. He too must have seen the way the gaiety ran out of her so quickly. His voice softened, and he extended a hand to her.

Mama was still holding the pan in her hand. She looked down at it, as if it were a foreign object. A troubled expression wrinkled her brow as she regarded it. She set it on the stove, turned and went with him. She didn't accept his hand, so he laid it gently on her shoulder. Megan and I remained in the kitchen. My parents' footsteps sounded on the stairway, but the study was too far away for me to be able to hear the soft click of the catch as Dad shut the door behind them.

Wearily Megan collapsed into a chair at the table. Her books from the library were still stacked on the other end. Bracing her cheek with one fist, she stared at them. "I'm really wishing right now that I was someplace else," she said.

I too sat down.

She looked over. "I wish he hadn't found out. Or at least I wish he could have left it alone. Too bad we couldn't have just sort of gone on like it hadn't happened."

I nodded.

My parents seldom had serious arguments. They disagreed with one another as often, I suppose, as people generally do when they live together. Usually, however, the arguments were one sided. My mother would want to do something and my father wouldn't. Or he would be after her for one of her more provocative idiosyncrasies. Just small things. Then one of them would become annoyed, and they'd seesaw back and forth over the issue for a while before one of them would grow sick of it and go off. Or they would end up laughing. Mama could make you laugh at the damnedest times, and she knew it. But it made for few serious fights.

When they first went upstairs, we could hear nothing. As disconcerting as this whole incident was, in the beginning I could not force myself to become too worried. It was just one of Mama's little things. Dad would set her right. He'd tell her not to go running off without letting someone know. He'd explain that she was mistaken about that boy, that he was just some farmer's child. Mama would sulk and most likely have a spell, but then we'd be over it. We could have supper and go on with things as usual.

The difficulty with sitting at the table, waiting for them to come out was that it gave me ample time to contemplate what my father had said to us beforehand. Those few simple sentences of his were so incredible to me as to border on the irrational. Other children? Had Mama really had other babies besides us? Why had we never known about them? Who were they? *Where* were they? The issue and its implications began to mushroom into such gargantuan proportions that I was unable to grasp even the possibility of it.

Then above the silence of the kitchen came my father's voice. He was shouting at my mother. As far as my sister and I were from the study, we could still hear him. What he was saying was not distinct, but the emotion certainly carried. My mother must have been holding up her end of it, because although her voice was inaudible, my father kept on and on for so long that it was obvious she had to be responding.

Megan and I sat like zombies. We didn't even dare look at one another. I was trying to think of what to do. I wasn't hungry. I was afraid to go upstairs to my room. I could hardly just go in the living room and turn on the television as if nothing unusual were happening. Beside me, Megan was motionless. She gave no indication of life at all, except for the fact that she was running her finger up and down the length of her bare forearm. Up and down, up and down, with hypnotic slowness.

Then the door to the study opened, and I could hear them in the hallway. My mother was sobbing.

"He's *my* baby! They took my baby *away* from me, O'Malley!"

Then my father's voice, restrained. "Mara, come in here. For God's sake, don't stand in the hallway."

"I want him *back!* You must help me, O'Malley. You promised you'd help me. You promised me. He belongs with me."

"Mara, get out of that hall this minute. Get back in here."

Muffled sobs, and my mother said something I couldn't hear.

"Mara, I mean it. Get out of that hallway. The girls are going to hear you."

I felt like shouting up at him that the girls had already heard plenty.

Then he must have come out into the hall to get her because there were several muffled, angry sounds, and Mama muttered something about his leaving her alone, that she needed a glass of water because she couldn't breathe. More noises. The bathroom door. The study door. The bathroom door again. Then they were fighting in the bathroom right above us.

Megan was inching her chair around the table. Her

head was on her folded arm on the tabletop, but very slightly, inch by inch, she was moving in my direction. Tears had filled her eyes but they didn't fall. She said nothing; she did not even look at me. And I was too paralyzed to be any comfort.

Suddenly I could plainly hear what Dad was saying. He was still in the bathroom, and his voice rose in volume. It was about Klaus. About Klaus being dead and gone. About Mama living in a dreamworld and how if she couldn't help herself, no one else could.

There was a small, strangled shriek of rage from my mother. Then she roared at him, first in a mixture of English and Hungarian, before sliding into pure German. My mother could give a wrath to the German language as she could to no other. She knew all the most vulgar and hateful phrases in that language. And she was furious with my father. Klaus is not dead! she shouted. He had no reason to say Klaus was. Do you, O'Malley, she screamed. Do you? Look me in the face and say that. Say you know he's dead. Look me in the face.

I couldn't hear my father's answer.

Then the subject was Megan and me. I heard my father tell my mother that she didn't pay enough attention to Megan. Why had they bothered to have another child when she never paid enough attention to her? What did they have Megan for anyway, if all Mama did was dream about Klaus? I glanced over to see if my sister was listening. It was difficult to tell. She remained immobile, her head still resting on her arm. I was embarrassed for her. Although hoping desperately that she hadn't heard, I realized that if I'd heard, no doubt she had too.

Then the bathroom door opened and they were back in the study. They argued for what seemed to me a small eternity. It went on and on and on. All the peaceful years vomited up their small bitter moments.

Finally, the study door opened and shut noisily. Dad's footsteps were on the stairs. He thundered into the kitchen.

"Lesley, do you know the name of those people whose little boy your mother saw?"

I shook my head.

He sighed, cast around the room for a moment, as if lost for what to do next. Then grabbing up his jacket, he headed for the door.

"Where are you going?" Megan cried, leaping up.

He paused, stock-still, like someone caught in a frame of film. Still wearing his work coveralls, he hadn't even gotten around to washing the garage grease from his hands. Then abruptly he came back to life.

"I'm going out to get us something to eat," he replied. "Fried chicken or something. Look at the time," he said and sounded as if it were somehow our fault that it had grown so late. "And no one's had any supper."

"I'm not really very hungry, Daddy," Megan said.

"No, neither am I," I said.

He stared at us, flustered, as if we were speaking foreign tongues. Then he yanked on his jacket. "Well, I am. I'm starved. So I'm going to get myself something to eat." He looked over Megan's head to me. "And for Christ's sake, get your sister to bed. It's way past her bedtime." Then he left.

Megan started to bawl. After the agony of enduring their argument, the sudden silence overwhelmed her and she broke into loud, inelegant sobs. There was no point in trying to talk her out of it. She was beyond caring.

It took a long time to muster the courage to go upstairs. I put it off as long as possible. I comforted Megan and got her to sit down in front of the TV. I made us both mugs of hot chocolate with more marshmallows than milk. But I realized that before Megan would be willing to go up to bed, I was going to have to go upstairs first myself.

Mama was still crying. Huddled in my father's lounger

in the study, knees drawn up, head down, she sobbed wearily. It was a heavy, hopeless sound that carried all the way to me on the staircase.

"Mama?" I said softly. "It's just me, Mama." I walked into the room. She didn't acknowledge my presence.

"Mama?" I knelt down beside the chair and touched her shoulder. "I've made me and Meggie some hot chocolate. Do you want some? Do you want to come down and sit with us?"

My mother always had about her a truly heart-breaking kind of vulnerability. Even in the good times, even when she was being wickedly funny and full of laughter, there seemed to be some tender part of her exposed. That fragility had always terrified me. From the time I had been very, very young I'd felt it, and it made me reluctant to ever take my eyes off her. You just didn't, not if you loved her. You had to be there right on top of her to protect her, because it never seemed that she could ever be fully trusted to protect herself.

From the bathroom I brought a damp washcloth and again knelt down beside the lounger. I pressed the cloth to her face and could feel the heat come through to my fingers. Her cheeks were swollen and red, but in contrast, her eyes were almost an electric blue. While kneeling there, my emotions rocketed through extremes, varying from fury at my father's willingness to leave her like this to a frenetic desperation about my own ability to cope. I was nearly in tears myself before I was finished.

When I went back downstairs, Megan was still in the living room watching television. It was after eleven o'clock, and she had switched to a raucous cop show where they were killing everyone in sight.

"Get up those stairs, Megan. Honestly, didn't you hear Daddy? Do you know what time it is?"

She ignored me. Still wearing her school clothes, she was draped over the chair, feet up on the arm.

"Does somebody always have to tell you everything? Now I just don't have patience for this. It's ten after eleven and you're supposed to be in bed. You're going to be like murder in school tomorrow."

"Get lost, Lesley. I'm watching this."

I walked over to the set and turned it off. Megan shot up angrily. "Who gave you the right to do that? You're not the boss in this house. I was watching that show."

My back against the television set, I glared at her. "I'm the boss now, Megan. You heard Dad. He told me to put you to bed. Ages ago. So get up those stairs or believe me, I'll damned well make you, the way I'm feeling right now."

Tears were in her eyes.

"Look, the last thing I want to do is fight with you."

"I hate you," she muttered and stomped out of the room. I reckoned that at that particular moment everyone was hating everyone else just a little.

Mama had fallen asleep. Still in the lounger, she slept in a tight, cramped position, her head resting heavily against the side of the chair. Her breathing was deep and still faintly congested.

Wandering idly around upstairs, I picked up my schoolbooks with an intention to study but did not sit down. Instead, I went into my parents' bedroom and parted the curtains to see out to the front of the house. The car was still in the driveway. My father was still in it. I had never heard it leave.

Megan had changed her clothes but then gone to sleep before she'd gotten under the blankets. She lay in the midst of the clutter of things on top of her bed, the tiger cat stuffed against her face. The light was still on.

Seeing her, I was unexpectedly awash with regret for having been so snappish with her. The emotion came as sodden remorse, oversized for the crime, and made me want to wake her up to get forgiveness. Going into the room, I tried to move her sufficiently to get her under the blankets, but she was too deeply asleep to cooperate. All I could do was double back the spread over her. I gazed at her. On impulse I kissed her before I turned off the bedside lamp and left the room.

I wanted to wait until my father came in, so I took my schoolwork down to the kitchen table. By midnight Dad was still out there, and I knew I was going to have to go to bed myself. I had gone past the point of being tired and into a sort of taut, desperate exhaustion. I looked out the window and wondered if he was intending to sleep in the car. I wondered if I should take him a blanket. But I decided against disturbing him in case he was still angry. So, leaving the back door unlocked, I turned out the kitchen light and went upstairs. Hesitating in the hallway, I considered whether or not to wake Mama and get her into bed. She wasn't going to be able to move at all in the morning if she slept in a position like that. But the thought of having to cope with Mama awake at that point seemed unbearable. So I left her alone.

Tired as I was, once in bed, I couldn't sleep. I heard my father come in eventually. Then the house returned to silence. After another hour or so of trying to sleep, I rose, took a blanket and my pillow and went downstairs. Turning the radio on and tuning it to the all-night station, I curled up under my woolly blanket on the couch.

I fell asleep dreaming that Aaron was actually Klaus and that Paul and I couldn't see each other anymore because that made us brother and sister. The funny thing about the dream was that Mama was not in it. It was Bo. She was my mother.

# Eleven

IN THE MORNING I woke stiff and sore from sleeping on the couch and uncomfortably tired. Dad came into the kitchen while I was making a pot of tea. Rumpled and weary looking, he rummaged out the instant coffee and a mug, poured hot water from the teakettle into it, stirred it with the handle of a fork lying on the counter and walked out of the kitchen with it. He was already in the hallway before he paused, turned around and looked back at me. Then without saying anything, he came back and embraced me. It began as a one-armed hug because he was still holding the coffee. But then he set the mug down on the table and hugged me with both arms. Holding me painfully close for just a moment, he then let go and left with his drink. He said absolutely nothing.

The shower went on upstairs. Within half an hour my father was back, his hair wet and slicked down. He drank a second cup of coffee while standing beside the counter, watching me pack his lunch. He asked if I would mind staying home with Mama. I said, sure, I'd do it, without even stopping to think whether I minded or not. He nodded, smiled and rumpled my hair in an agitated caress.

My sister, who did not have a particularly thick veneer of civility in the best of times, was hopeless that morning. She was too tired to want to get up. The blouse she planned to wear was in the dirty clothes. I refused to make her a boiled egg, and by the time she finished complaining about it, there wasn't time for her to do it herself. Then she couldn't find her gym shoes or her social-studies book. There was no change in the house for lunch money, and I wasn't about to let her take the five dollars I found where my mother kept the grocery money. In the end, Megan left for school crying because I made her peanut-butter sandwiches and Mama always made her tuna.

Mama was still asleep. Sometime in the night she apparently had awakened and gone in to the bedroom, because when I looked in, she was stretched out on her stomach across their big bed. It must have been very close to morning when she did, because she had not bothered to get under the covers but had Dad's bathrobe over her instead. The remainder of the bed was in jumbled confusion from my father's getting up.

She still wore her clothes from the day before. Only her shoes were off, and they lay, one on top of the other, at the foot of the bed. Some of the tension had gone from her face. Her jaw was relaxed. Her forehead was smooth. But even asleep her expression remained troubled.

She slept a long time. On the occasions when she could do so, my mother had a tremendous capacity to sleep. She slept like one dead, and next to nothing woke her. I sat downstairs, bored and unsettled. Clearing away the dishes, I washed them, dried them and put them away. I scrubbed out the sink. I sorted the laundry and started a load. I vacuumed, picked up the debris of newspapers and magazines and other paper that seemed to collect in the living room. Even doing the ironing did not fill up enough time.

At one point I came across Megan's books about the war. Aimlessly, I paged through them. The worst aspect of the war to me was that it happened so much before I was born. I hated thinking about it because of that. Where *had* all the good people gone? Why had no one stopped all the atrocities? I would have. If I had been born in time, I would have done something. But I didn't even stand a chance. It seemed brutally unfair to me that I should have to live with the consequences of something I had never been given the opportunity to prevent.

Shortly after noon, Mama woke up. She came stumbling drunkenly into the kitchen, her hair disheveled, her face swollen from so much sleep. Dropping into a chair at the table, she struggled with her package of cigarettes. I made a cup of coffee for her.

"Oh *Scheisse*," she muttered under her breath, and with eyes still half-closed, she braced her head with one hand and smoked the cigarette. She wasn't beautiful then. My father was forever saying how much he thought Mama looked like Princess Grace. Sort of a Germanic Grace Kelly. From over by the sink I stood watching her. My mama was nobody's princess.

She looked up. "When did O'Malley come back?"

"He never really left, Mama. He was just sitting out in front in the car."

She lit a second cigarette from the end of the first. Thoughtfully, she rubbed along the skin of her left temple and stared off into space. I turned and took a can of tomato soup from the cupboard to make lunch for us.

She was still sitting, still staring when I came to the table with crackers and the soup in enamel mugs. With the fingers of one hand, she'd begun working the tangles from her hair, but it was a casual, undeliberate motion.

"He's a good man, O'Malley," she said, "but he has no dreams."

"He's got dreams, Mama," I said, wondering how she could say that when my father's dreams seemed so plaintively obvious to me.

She shook her head. "No. He has no dreams. He has

fantasies. But no dreams. Nothing to pursue." She looked over, focusing her eyes on me for the first time. "When you marry, don't make that mistake. Marry a man with dreams."

I said nothing.

Silence. She lifted the mug and sipped the soup. She was staring off again.

"I had dreams," she said. "Once." Then she looked at me again. "How old are you now?"

"Seventeen. I'll be eighteen next month."

She nodded. Looking into the mug of soup, she nodded a second time. I could hear birds singing somewhere. Not terribly melodically. Sparrows, most likely.

"I was seventeen," she said. "Then. When he was born."

A pause. Elbows on the table, she clasped her hands together and put the tips of her thumbs between her teeth. "Did I ever tell you what they were doing there? At that hostel? Where they took me from Jena."

I shook my head.

"It was a *Lebensborn* hostel." She glanced over at me. "Do you know about that?"

Again, I shook my head.

"Fountain of Life. That's what it means. They were breeding us. We were selected for our Aryan qualities. We were the source of their fountain."

There was a slight lisp to her words because she still had the ends of her thumbs against her teeth. She gazed at the tabletop. "Some of the girls knew. Some of them volunteered, I think. I don't know for sure. I wasn't allowed to talk to them very often."

She paused for breath and then fell into pensive silence.

"I was sixteen when I first arrived. Sixteen and four months old. It was November 15th. And there were trees outside my window. Lime trees. And I thought, Mara, you are such a silly goose to be so scared." She looked at me and smiled slightly. "You see, I *was* scared. I was terrified. I didn't know what they wanted, why they'd sent me there. All the other students with foreign birth certificates they deported from Jena. But me . . ." She looked away again. "But when I looked out the window, I thought, this can't be such a bad place. There are lime trees here, like at home."

Her voice grew very soft, hardly above a whisper, and I had to lean forward to hear her clearly.

"I was very innocent then. A child really. I'd only had my periods for two years and I did not think of myself as a woman. I was very much a virgin, even in my mind. I didn't know things." She shook her head. "I just did not know."

She paused, searching the grain in the tabletop for something I could not see. "He was born there. On a bed with no sheets. I said to them, 'Please give me a sheet.' I was lying on a rubber mat and I was cold. I was freezing. And it hurt so much. I hadn't thought it would hurt like that. 'Please,' I said to them, 'let me lie on a sheet.' And when he was born, I wept."

She unclasped her hands and took up the mug of soup. She stared into it. "I was so full of milk for him. It came in fast, and I couldn't stop it from leaking. They would hold him up in front of me and he would cry and the milk would just run. It ruined all my blouses. My breasts, oh God, my breasts hurt me. And I was so ashamed. I felt like a little child who cannot get to the toilet in time. They'd hold him and watch to see my blouse get wet. But if I cried, they laughed." One hand in a gentle, unconscious movement came up to cup a breast.

She glanced briefly in my direction. "You see, I was just a child myself. Hardly turned seventeen. And I will tell you, I did not know much. I decided to put toilet paper in my bra. Wads of it. To keep the milk from showing. It seemed so indecent to stain my blouses like that. And I was humiliated when they made me cry. So I put all these wads of toilet paper against my breasts. And put on my blouse. It was the one Mutti gave me, the white one with lace at the collar that Oma had tatted. It was my only good one. The only one left without stains.''

Her voice grew faint. ''They came with him. It was just before lunchtime. Eleven-thirty, I think. And he was crying so hard. My breasts were full. They ached, and I felt them leaking. But it didn't show.''

She reached for another cigarette. ''When it didn't come through onto my blouse, the woman holding him said, 'She has no more milk.' So, you see, they took him away. I was of no more use to them then.'' Her voice went flat. ''And I never saw him again.''

Mama went upstairs and took a long shower. She must have been in the bathroom the better part of an hour and a half. I did the dishes and put them away. When my mother returned to the kitchen, she had changed into clean clothes. Her hair was wet, the comb marks still showing. The earlier mood was dispelled. She was brisk and full of purpose again.

''Will you come with me?'' she asked. I didn't need to ask where.

''Mama, Daddy's not going to like this. He doesn't want you to go out there, I think.''

She shrugged. ''He doesn't understand.''

''Mama . . .'' It was a plea.

She glanced over at Megan's books, now sitting on the counter. Going over to them, she picked up one and opened it. ''Whose are these?'' she asked. ''Yours?''

I shook my head. ''Megan's. She got them at the library.'' I watched fearfully as she paged through it.

''Megan's, hmm?'' she said.

122     *Torey L. Hayden*

"I told her not to. She didn't have anyone's permission. She just did it. You know Megan."

Mama stopped to study one of the photographs. "Is Ravensbrück in here?" she asked.

"I don't know."

She lifted her head and regarded me across the book. "You know what Ravensbrück was, don't you?"

Slowly, I nodded.

Her expression grew into a taut, sardonic sort of smile, and she flipped through the rest of the pages. "Someday, Les, I'll tell you about that. When you want to know, you don't have to get books. I'll tell you."

"They aren't my books, Mama."

She nodded. "I didn't think they were."

I went with her. There was no point in not going. She would have gone without me, if I hadn't.

Mama knew where she was headed. We walked silently through town and then out along the most southerly county road. She never talked to me. She never said a word. Hands in the pockets of her jacket, she just walked.

We came to the spot Megan had shown me the day earlier. Mama squeezed between the strands of barbed wire and went down a gully toward the creek. We walked there for a few hundred yards until we came to a decaying cottonwood trunk, fallen across the creek bed. Mama sat down on the lee side, her back against the brown, rotting trunk.

The day was cold. It remained overcast, and although it did not rain, you could feel the damp chill. The gully afforded very little protection from the wind. Mama took out her cigarettes and matches. Cupping her hand, she lit one, then leaned back and waited.

About half past three we saw him. He was a small boy. I doubt that he could have been six. He wore patched overalls over a T-shirt and an old denim jacket a size or two too large.

"Hello," Mama said to him.

He whooped with delight. Hopping down over the rocks deftly, he settled into the lee of the fallen cottonwood beside Mama. He cast a brief, wary glance in my direction but that was all.

He was an odd-looking boy. His hair was lank and fair, that ashen tone of blond that is more gray than yellow, and it was cut in a curiously old-fashioned style, as if someone had put a mixing bowl upside down on his head and trimmed around it with dull scissors. But what was more striking were his eyes. They were very, very pale, like the eyes of a blind dog. Whether they were blue or green I never did decide because there was literally almost no color in the irises at all, just the black of the pupils and a faint rim separating the irises from the white.

"Here," Mama said, "I've brought you something." She took a Hershey bar from the pocket of her jacket.

"For me?" the boy asked and bounced up onto his knees with excitement. He grinned. I noticed he still had all his baby teeth. In one of the top front ones there was a conspicuous silver filling. It gave him an unexpectedly run-down appearance, the kind of sullied imperfectness you don't associate with young children.

"I'm going to call you Mrs. Nice," he said to Mama and patted her cheek. "You know what? That's what I told Teddy. He's my brother. He's eight. I said, I met Mrs. Nice down at the creek. He don't believe me. He thinks I made you up." He unwrapped the Hershey bar and shoved a full half of it into his mouth at once. "I don't care. You're *my* Mrs. Nice, ain't you? Don't got to share nothing with Teddy!"

Mama smiled.

"Who's she?" the little boy asked, looking across Mama to me.

"My daughter."

"Oh," he replied without much interest. He broke the rest of the candy bar into squares and ate them quickly, one by one. I could smell the chocolate on his breath.

They talked, my mama and this little boy. He was full of a sort of heartless innocence, chatting with immodest directness, passing judgments, caring mostly for the candy. He laughed at Mama's accent. He said she was a very old woman. She laughed back at him and told him he was a very little boy. Then he was up on his knees beside her, talking animatedly, bouncing up and down, stretching his hands out in wide gestures as he spoke. Then he climbed on top of her, straddling her legs, patting her on the head. Mama seemed not to mind his audacity nor the fact that he was a dirty little thing. His clothes were old and poorly cared for. His hair needed washing. He smelled of stale urine.

I grew cold, sitting in silence while they laughed and competed with one another to be heard. My toes were numb. Mama was lounging back against the tree trunk, oblivious to both the temperature and my discomfort. Finally, the little boy rose to his feet to go. He bounded up onto the cottonwood trunk with the agility of Peter Pan.

I sat up. "Hey you," I said as he was about to bolt off. He paused, teetering back and forth on the trunk above me. "What's your name?"

"Toby."

"Toby what?"

"Toby Simon Waterman." Then he jerked his head in the direction of my mother. " 'Cept her there, she calls me Klaus. I call her Mrs. Nice and she calls me Klaus." He smiled. "That's our deal, ain't it?" He grinned at Mama. Then he turned, scrambled up the bank and disappeared over the edge of the gully.

Mama remained leaning back against the tree and smiling.

"That isn't him," I said to her as we walked back home. The wind was to our backs and it blew my hair around my face. I kept my shoulders up and my head tucked down.

Mama didn't reply.

I looked over. "You realize that, don't you, Mama? You're not really thinking he is, are you? You aren't. He's just some little boy." I walked on. "In fact, a rather awful little boy. Did you see how filthy he is?"

Still no reply from my mother. She was braced against the wind also, hands in her jacket pockets. Her blowing hair completely obscured her face from me.

"I mean, if he reminds you of Klaus, that's probably okay. I guess it is. And maybe it doesn't hurt to visit him. But you're not imagining he really is Klaus, are you?"

"The motherfuckers," she said softly. "I told them they'd never manage to keep him from me." Her words were almost borne away on the wind before I caught them.

"*Mama.* Mama, you listen to me. That isn't Klaus. You know that, don't you? Of course you do. Klaus would be a man by now. If you were only seventeen, he'd be nearly forty. You do realize that, don't you?"

"I told them I'd find him. They said I wouldn't. But I swore I would. I knew I would. I always kept looking. Kept on going and looking."

"*Mama!*"

She looked over at me. She had to hold the blowing hair out of her face to see me. There was a peculiar expression on her face, reminiscent of the look she had when she'd pulled a really good joke and my dad fell for it. The kind of expression she had when she was very pleased with her cleverness. I felt relief to see her smiling like that.

"Good joke, Mama," I said. "You caught me."

She kept grinning. "I never forget."

# Twelve

As ABRUPTLY as it had surfaced, the furor over Klaus died down. Both Megan and I remained intensely curious about this extraordinary revelation, but the matter rapidly receded into silence. The subject was closed. There were no more discussions between Mama and Daddy, no more arguments, not even allusions. It was as if the entire thing had not occurred.

Mama was in high spirits. As the weeks passed and the flowers began coming up, she busied herself around the garden. The weather turned pleasant and seasonable and filled her with noisy exuberance. When Megs and I came home from school, she was always eager to show us what she'd been up to during the day, whether puttering around the house making elaborate desserts for supper or ironing the dish towels. Constantly, she was singing under her breath to herself in her not particularly marvelous voice. She wanted to know everything that was happening to us at school, about how I was getting on with Paul, about graduation coming up in June. She and Mrs. Reilly started going to garage sales, and she came home with some remarkable items, including a gigantic tarnished brass fork that she made Dad hang in the hallway outside the kitchen.

Of course, I assumed Mama was still making daily pilgrimages to the tree trunk by the creek. She was discreet about it. It was never mentioned; she was always back before Megan or I returned from school. But I was almost positive she was doing it. What I was not certain of was whether or not my father knew she was going to see Toby Waterman. It was hard for me to guess what kinds of discussions my parents had with each other in private. I knew they talked a lot because I could usually hear the buzz of their voices long after they'd gotten into bed at night. But I don't think Toby was ever one of their topics. If my father had known, the whole issue would not have been relegated to silence the way it was, and Megan and I, I believe, would have felt freer to ask about Klaus.

However, if Dad didn't know, he should have been able to guess. Not only was Mama in a vastly improved mood, which always meant that she had found something interesting to occupy herself with, but she was focusing her attention in different directions. For instance, she became quite keen to know what kind of treatment poor people got. She'd always been the more politically aware of my parents, and her views had always been considerably to the left of my father's, but suddenly she wanted to discuss them. What's going to happen to the poor people? she would ask him at the dinner table. What do we do when people can't take care of themselves? When their children are hungry? When they don't have proper clothes? We need to help out. We need to do something. It's wrong to have things when other people don't. My father would point out to her that we weren't exactly rich ourselves. But we're not poor, Mama would reply. There are some people right here in town who are a lot poorer than we are.

Over those weeks I spent a lot of time thinking about Mama and Toby Waterman. Once I recovered from the initial shock of discovering I had a brother I'd never known existed, I realized that the shock came from Klaus's existence, not Toby Waterman's. My mother's

spending time with Toby seemed harmless enough to me.
He liked her. He obviously enjoyed her company as
much as she did his. As long as his teeth didn't rot out
from all the chocolate bars, I didn't think there was anything seriously wrong with the relationship. Just two
lonely people finding pleasure in each other's company.
But at the same time I felt guilty for knowing she was
doing something like that and not telling my father. I was
a little annoyed with Dad too because it seemed to me
that he should have been able to see it, but I was almost
positive he didn't. And I didn't tell him. It wasn't really
my business, I reckoned, as long as it didn't impinge on
our lives. So I went on as if it weren't happening.

For me the month of March was fairly peaceful. With
graduation nearing, most of my teachers seemed to realize that no one felt like working hard. My only difficult
subject continued to be calculus, but even Mrs. Browder
was easing up.

I spent most of my free time in the language lab, listening to tapes or talking with my French teacher, Miss
Conway. She was young, and I thought she was very
pretty. She knew I was going to study languages at the
university, so she gave me extra things to read and let me
listen to the records she'd bought in Paris when she had
been there in her junior year abroad in college. And she
told me that someday she would have me over to her
apartment and show me her slides.

Each week I spent three or four hours extra in the language lab, usually alone after school, working with the
cassettes. I liked French best, due mostly to Miss Conway, who was my favorite teacher, but also due to the
fact that French was not a language my mother spoke, so
I felt I deserved some credit for doing well in it. Miss
Conway did not know that the reason I was such a star
pupil in German was because when I went home at night I
had to speak it to get the butter passed to me at the dinner

table. That makes you quite outstanding in a second-year German class. But French I had to do all on my own. I had a surprisingly difficult time because when I was at a loss for a word, English, German, and even Hungarian would come to my mind first. Miss Conway would stay after school with me sometimes and sit at the console to correct my pronunciation. *"Accent allemand!"* she would always shout through my earphones. Later, she'd tease me about it, saying I was just paying too much attention to old Mr. Tennant, the German teacher, and why wasn't I that awake in French? She could never understand how I had developed such a harsh-sounding accent. And I never told her.

The rest of the time I spent with Paul. We were starting to build his new telescope. Or at least he was. I'd lie on his bed and browse through Edmund's Scientific Catalogue while he tinkered with mirrors and lenses. I told him I wished he was in my calculus class so he could help me, and he said physics and calculus were quite separate disciplines and he wasn't any better than anyone else in calculus. I asked him how come he was going into statistics then? Why wasn't he going to study astronomy or something like that? No jobs, he said. His father said that he had to learn something that would make him employable.

One weekend afternoon when the sun had become hot, I took off my shirt while Paul and I were lying together in the grass out on Ladder Creek. Then he unhooked my bra. We had no blanket to lie on, so all along my back I could feel the damp, scratchy prairie grass. Paul, beside me, touched my breasts, moving his fingers around the nipples. It made me shiver with an electric sensation that I found too intense to be pleasurable, and spasmodically, I would jerk away from him when I couldn't tolerate it any longer. Paul unbuttoned his pants. Closing his eyes, he clutched me tight against him and rubbed his body against mine. I could smell his sweat. It was a pleasingly sexy odor that belonged with the smell of prairie grass and with the warmth of late March sun. Then suddenly I felt a spurt of wetness over my belly and I sat up abruptly. Paul laughed. Didn't I know that was going to happen? he asked and dropped back onto the grass. Hadn't I realized he was going to come? Raised up on one elbow, I looked at the semen, creamy and white like liquid soap from the dispenser on the kitchen window ledge. I had never seen semen before and I *hadn't* known it was going to happen and for a moment I was tempted to deny my ignorance, feeling stupid for having been so surprised. But instead, I just giggled and fell back on the grass beside Paul and we laughed about it together.

When it was time to go, I wiped the semen off my stomach with my shirt. At home that night I examined the shirt, smelled the faintly musky odor. I meant to pitch it into the laundry afterward, but I didn't. I kept the shirt out and put it under my pillow for that night, if not to smell Paul's closeness, then to dream of it.

During those days of late March and early April the only person in the family to have any problems was Megan. She went through a peculiar stage. She grew obsessed with reading about Jews and concentration camps. The rest of us basked in untroubled happiness, while Megan went from day to day, distracted by thoughts of tortured Jews. Although she never came right out and asked my mother, I knew she wanted Mama's version of the war. Whenever I thought she might ask, I threatened her with whatever dire consequence I had available to me at that moment. It unsettled my own peace slightly because I never entirely trusted Megan and now, more than ever, I didn't want her to jar Mama's good mood.

I couldn't understand what Megan was getting out of it. I had never gone through such a bizarre stage when I was her age, and I couldn't fathom why she should. All the books on the subject were far too advanced for her. She wasn't what could be called a spectacular reader, even by third-grade standards, so I didn't believe she could actually be distilling much from the material. But that didn't seem to deter her. She kept at it, cloistering herself in her room for hours at a time. In a perverse way it was almost laughable. I reckoned Megan to be the only person in the world reading *The Rise and Fall of the Third Reich* who still believed in fairies.

But the fact was, it wasn't laughable at all. Megan was miserable and she was making us miserable. The two of us argued constantly and over everything. But it wasn't just me. She argued with Dad. She argued with her friends. She'd had a big blowup with her best friend, Katie, and came fuming into the house one afternoon, saying she was never going to see Katie again as long as she lived. To my knowledge, she was keeping that threat. And she even argued with Mama, which was strange because she'd developed a fixation about being with Mama all the time. My mother couldn't even go into the bathroom without being bothered. But still Megan argued with her. Perhaps she argued with Mama most of all.

It was then too, during that early part of April, that I learned about Paul's parents. We were, of all places, in the playground of the park on Third and Elm when he told me. I'd been working at the nursing home that afternoon and Paul had come to pick me up afterward. He hadn't been able to get the car from his mom, so he'd walked. We were cutting through the park when he sat down on one of the swings.

"They're going to get divorced," he said. He twisted the swing around. Leaning back, he stared up at the chains, wound around one another. "I heard them talking the other night. They haven't said anything to me or Aaron yet. I just overheard them in the kitchen."

"I'm sorry," I said.

He lifted his feet from the ground and the swing spun around. "Nothing to be sorry about really, I guess."

Regarding the other swing, I debated about whether or not to sit down. I was still wearing my white nurse's aide uniform, and Mama was always complaining about how dirty I got it.

"I think I knew it was coming," Paul said. "It's been coming a long, long time. They don't love each other. Maybe they never did."

I tried to imagine what it must feel like to know your parents didn't love each other. It was an entirely foreign concept to me. I couldn't fathom what my mother or father, either one, would do without the other. They fit together like one person. Apart, they would be incomplete.

"What are you going to do?" I asked. I sat on the swing, realizing that compared to Paul's problems, Mama's yelling at me about my uniform wasn't much.

"Dunno."

Silence. He had begun to push himself back and forth on the swing. I lifted my head and looked up at the sky.

"I'm just thankful I'm going away to school," he said. "I wouldn't want to have to live with either one of them, quite frankly. My dad, he wouldn't want me anyway. I think maybe he's said six whole things to me this year. 'Hey boy,' " Paul said in a sneering mockery of his father's voice. " 'Hey boy, what you doing there, boy? How come you aren't on the football team like Aaron? How come you hang around with all those fairy queers in the physics club?' 'Hey boy, don't look at me like that. You earn the money, then you call the shots.' That's all he ever said to me."

I pushed my swing and let it come forward. "I'd live with your mom."

Paul snorted. "Maybe you would. I wouldn't." He made a second futile-sounding little noise. "I embarrass the shit out of my mom. You've seen her. With all her fancy, phony crap.''

"You shouldn't talk like that, Paul. It isn't true."

"A lot you know about it."

There was a long silence. It was growing late. The sun was down on the horizon, and I was finding it not a particularly warm evening.

"I embarrass the shit out of you too, don't I?" he said. "You want to be just like her, don't you? And you're embarrassed by me.''

Slamming my feet down to stop my swing, I stared at him. "What do you mean? Why do you say something like that?''

"Because."

"Because why, Paul. You don't embarrass me. Why would you say that to me?''

"Think, Lesley. It shouldn't be too hard."

Disgruntled, I turned my head away. "Cripes, Paul, don't make it a stupid guessing game." I looked back. "If something's wrong, just say so. Don't be so coy.''

"Well, if you think I'm so godawful wonderful, how come you've never once invited me over to your house? Jesus, you practically live over at our zoo. And I've never even met your folks.''

I was shocked. I couldn't believe that was how it seemed to him. "Oh cripes. Oh God. God almighty, Paul, you think it's *you?*''

Shrugging, he launched the swing backwards with a push.

Now what? I looked down at my fingernails.

He was seething. I watched him pump the swing higher and higher and I could tell he was easily as mad at me as he was at his folks for their divorce. In a way perhaps he was madder.

"Listen, stop the swing, would you?" I asked.

He kept going.

"I can't talk to you when you're flying through the air like some stupid trapeze artist. Stop it, all right?"

Without aiding it any, he let the swing slow down. But he still did not stop it.

"You're dead wrong, Paul. It doesn't have anything to do with you. If that's what you think, then it's just your swelled head. It has nothing to do with you."

He gave the swing another push. "So, what is the reason then?"

Silence.

I looked over. "Nothing special. I don't know."

Silence.

I sighed. "It's just that my family's different, that's all. Not like yours."

"That can't be all bad."

"No, I really mean it. Like, we're poor compared with you guys, Paul. My dad's a mechanic down at Hughson's Garage. My sister and me, we got nothing like you and Aaron have. We don't have our own stereos or TV's or phones or stuff. There's nothing to do but sit around. It's boring."

"Well, I wasn't asking for an amusement arcade, Lesley. I don't care about that," he said.

"Yeah, but it's still different. My parents are nothing special. My dad's never gone to college. And my mom's from Hungary. She's been in this country since 1957 and she still speaks German and Hungarian better than she does English. And she doesn't wear nice clothes. She doesn't even wear her own clothes half the time. She wears my dad's. Or mine. She wouldn't know Bill Blass if he kicked her in the teeth."

"Oh," said Paul acidly. "I get it. You're not embarrassed about me. You're embarrassed about them. God, that shows a deep personality. Nice move, Lesley. That makes me real reassured."

"That's *not* what I meant. I'm not *either* embarrassed

by them. You're twisting my words. I was just saying there's no point to going over there. You're not missing anything.''

"Nice move, Lesley."

I looked out across the park. Twilight was settling into the shadows. I was frozen half to death, sitting there. Paul in his shirt sleeves seemed unfazed.

He was watching me. He had stopped his swing entirely and was even with me. "You don't have to cry about it," he said and there was no sympathy in his voice.

"I'm *not* crying."

"Oh Jesus," he said in disgust and launched the swing again.

"Stop it!" I said and grabbed the chain on the swing. "Stop that goddamned swing." We glared at one another. "You want to know? Mr. Know-it-all with your stupid brains. You want to know what the truth is? My mother has mental problems. I don't bring people home because I don't want them to laugh at her for some of the things she does. And I don't want them to talk about her behind my back. And I don't want them to make fun of me because she's my mother and I love her."

"Oh," said Paul. There was a moment's sharp silence, piercing as a dart, and he turned away.

"So there. Are you satisfied now?" I wiped the tears back with the heel of my hand. "Are you happy?"

"Nice move, Paul," he said softly under his breath. He turned back. "Look, Les, I'm sorry."

Snuffling, I grimaced. "Don't be sorry. It's not your fault she's got problems."

He shrugged. "But I'm sorry for talking like that. I didn't realize."

"Look, just forget it."

# Thirteen

I BROUGHT PAUL OVER. He came on a Wednesday evening to study, and except for Megan, who was pretending to be Supergirl and was leaping off tables and wearing her swimsuit with a towel stuck down her back for a cape, my family acted quite normal. So I chanced inviting him for supper on Friday evening.

I woke up Friday morning with an upset stomach from nerves. While sitting in bed waiting for it to go away before I got up for school, I drew up a little list of things I didn't want my mother to do while Paul was eating with us. Later, I carried it down and showed it to Mama. I'd waited until after Dad had left for work because I knew he'd be horrified if he found out. Mama, who was sitting in the kitchen reading the newspaper and having another piece of toast with her coffee, studied the list thoughtfully as she sipped from her mug. I had tried to be as tactful as I could. Mama appeared to take it seriously. She nodded and said she understood.

And she didn't do any of the things on my list. Instead, she caused Paul to howl at the dinner table by mimicking me from the morning when I had presented her with it. She had every little detail, from the way I'd smoothed out the paper on the tablecloth to the way I'd tried to explain why some of the things on the list were embarrassing to me. I was absolutely mortified and thought I was going to murder her before she was done. But Paul loved it. And he loved my mama. Far more than I did that particular evening.

As the days passed I relaxed more and more. I even thought about asking if I could have a party for my birthday in the middle of the month. The closest thing I had ever had to a party was the year I was twelve and my father took two of my friends and me to a movie on my birthday. I didn't ask my parents immediately, however, but I sat in school for days, doodling up invitations and thinking about things like refreshments and dancing and lots of boys rather than Newton's laws or irregular French verbs.

I had a dentist's appointment. Although I intended to go back to school afterward, I went home instead. I had had three fillings, and my mouth was swollen and sore. Since the only classes I had in the afternoon were German and physical education, I decided it wasn't worth the agony of returning.

When I arrived home, my mother was out. I knew where she was. It was payday for Dad, and he had dropped her off downtown on his way back to work from lunch so she could put the check in the bank and go pay the bills. My mouth felt very uncomfortable, so I went into the living room, turned on the television and lay down on the couch with the afghan over me.

There was a loud rap at the back door.

I ignored it.

Another series of taps, louder, more insistent. Then again. Dragging myself off the couch, I went into the kitchen to see who it was.

Toby Waterman stood with his face pressed up against the screen in the back door. With his odd, colorless eyes he studied me. "Where's Mama at?" he asked through the screen door; it was less a question than a demand.

"Your mother isn't here, Toby," I replied. I didn't let him in.

"Where's she at?" His face was pushed flat against the mesh of the screen, giving him a piggy look.

"You're an awfully long ways from home. You know that, don't you? Do you know how to get back without getting lost?"

He reached up to let himself in but I put my foot against the bottom of the door to prevent his opening it. When he couldn't exert enough pressure to move the door, he gave up and dropped his arm back down to his side. He gazed through the screen at me.

"Does your mom even know you're here?" I asked.

"Not her. *My* mama. This mama in this house."

"*My* mama? Whose mother are you looking for anyway?"

"*Her!*" he said with impatience. "Her that lives in this house. My mama here. Let me in."

Startled, I did.

He had a grungy little bouquet of dandelions in one hand. He lifted them up toward me as he walked in. "I'm her little boy," he said. "To this mama here. I was just staying with that other family till she founded me. They was just taking care of me for her."

"Listen Toby, I think you've got something awfully mixed up."

"And for another thing," he said and smiled disarmingly. "I ain't Toby no more. Not really. My name is Klaus. They just called me Toby at my other family, but that ain't really my name. I'm her little lost boy. When I was a baby, see, the bad people, they takeded me away from her. And they gave me to my other folks. But real honest truly, my name is Klaus."

He was so unclean. His hair stood out in all directions like the hair on a too-often-played-with doll. His face was smudgy with food stains. The windbreaker he wore was far too large, and underneath was a ratty-looking T-shirt. He smelled like he wet his bed and the sheets weren't changed afterward. Of all the kids my mother could have chosen, why had she picked one like this?

"Look, Toby—"

"It's *Klaus!* How many times I got to keep telling you?"

"Whoever you are, look, you're going to have to leave now. You understand? No one's here but me, and I want you to go."

His brow furrowed, but he didn't speak. Instead, he regarded the dandelions. Lifting them up, he inspected each flower carefully and then held them higher. "You want to see if you like butter?" he asked engagingly.

"No!" I replied. "I just want you to go. Mama isn't here now."

"I want to wait for her."

*"No!* You have to go. You can't stay here."

"Why not?"

*"Because."*

"Because ain't no reason."

I glared at him.

"But when's she going to come get me, huh? I been waiting. I been waiting all day for her."

"Toby, you have to go. Right now. This minute."

"I told you. My name is Klaus. How come you can't remember that?"

"Just *leave!"* I cried. Putting my hand against his back, I shoved him physically toward the door.

"But when's she gonna come for me?" he asked, his voice trailing off into a whine of protest.

One hand still on his back, with the other I opened the screen door. "I don't know. It won't be today. You hear me? So just go home. Right this minute." And I pushed him outside, closed the door sharply and locked it. He stood a moment in the sunshine.

"Tell her I comed to see her," he said, his eyes narrowing in the brightness. "You tell her her little lost boy was here." It sounded like a threat.

I was shaking. I went around the house and locked all the doors and windows and pulled the curtains. Not daring to look out for fear he might still be there, I sat down on the couch and wrapped the afghan around me. Still unnerved, I shook so badly that my hands could hardly grip it.

Shortly, my mother returned. She came up to the front door, tried it, expecting it to be unlocked. When it did not open, she tried it a second time, harder. I heard her mutter something under her breath in German. Then keys jingled and the door opened. Smiling at me, she breezed past with an armload of groceries.

I stayed in the darkened living room a moment longer. My mouth still hurt. The novocaine was half in and half out, making my jaw feel unpleasantly peculiar.

Mama buzzed by to get a second bag of groceries off the front doorstep. "You're home early," she said to me as she headed back for the kitchen.

"I had a dentist's appointment, remember? I decided not to go back to school afterward." She had already disappeared around the corner.

Forlornly, I rose and followed her. "Mama, that little kid was here."

She was putting groceries away, and whether she did not hear me or whether she was simply ignoring me, I couldn't tell.

"Mama, please stop what you're doing a moment, would you?" I took hold of her arm. "Listen. That little boy was here. That little Toby Waterman."

She looked at me.

"What have you been telling him, Mama? He came here all full of tales about being Klaus."

Mama moved away from me, went over to the table and took more groceries from the sack.

"Mama, you can't be telling him stuff like that. It isn't right."

She emptied a plastic bag full of apples into the colander, put it in the sink and turned on the water. Turned the water off and shook the colander. Dumped the apples into the fruit bowl.

"Mama, do you hear me?"

My mother took a thick paperback book from one of the sacks. She paused a moment to page through it. Then she held it up. "I've been wanting to read this," she said. "It's supposed to be very good. Mrs. Reilly, you see, she read part of it in *Family Circle* and she told me about it."

"Mama, we're not talking about books."

My mother remained absorbed in the pages of the paperback.

"Please, Mama, put that down. Please? Now listen to me. You can't go around telling Toby Waterman things like you've been doing. He's just a little kid. How old is he? Six, maybe? Not even that, I bet."

Mama set the book down and turned away toward the table.

"I know you've been going out there, Mama. I know you and he have been having a lot of fun together lately. And I know it's making you happy. I'm glad about that. But you can't go telling him things that aren't true. He's too little. He doesn't know not to believe them."

"But they are true," she said softly, not looking at me. She pulled a chair over and climbed up to put away a package of spaghetti in the top cupboard.

"*Mama.* Don't say that. They *aren't* true. You know as well as I do. Don't go trying to convince yourself they are."

She didn't answer.

"I know you wish they were true. I can understand that. But it doesn't make them true."

She got down from the chair and returned it to the table.

"Fun's fun, Mama, but this is going past it. This isn't fun anymore. To be honest, I'm getting sort of scared by it."

No response.

"Are you listening to me?"

A can of pork and beans in each hand, she stopped stock-still in the middle of the floor and looked at me. "Can't you see that's him?" she asked me. Her voice was faint. "Can't you see that's Klaus? He's my son. I'm going to recognize my own son. He's my own flesh and blood."

"*Mama,*" I wailed. "Oh cripes, Mama. Oh God. You don't think that, do you? Not for real? Mama, that was forty years ago. That was in Germany in the war. This little boy couldn't be Klaus."

"That's what they want you to believe," she said. "You see, they didn't think I'd find him here. But I'm going to know my own son."

"Mama. Oh Mama. *God,* Mama. Please don't talk like this. It scares me."

She looked down at the cans, still in her hands.

"Toby Waterman is not your Klaus. He's just some Kansas farm boy."

"That's what they *want* you to believe," she said, exasperated.

"Because it's *true,* Mama. Your Klaus would be a man now, not a little boy. Toby's only a child, maybe five or six years old. Klaus would be all grown up. Time's gone by, Mama. Klaus wouldn't be a child anymore. This kid isn't him. Oh God, Mama, say you don't really believe he is."

She turned away from me and back to the groceries.

An air of desperation strained around us. We had both grown upset. I grabbed hold of her arm to make her stop moving around. *"Listen.* You have got to stop this. Right now. You've made a horrible mistake. Toby is not Klaus. You cannot keep thinking he is. And you can't keep telling him he is. He's not. Do you understand me? Do you understand what I'm saying?"

She inhaled sharply and jerked her arm, but I continued to hold on to it.

"Say it to me, Mama. I want to hear you say it. Say that he is not Klaus."

"He's not Klaus," she said and broke my grasp.

Frustrated and upset, I went back into the living room and sat down while my mother finished what she was doing in the kitchen. This was madness, I thought, and was then overwhelmed by the sickening realization that indeed, it was.

A short time later I heard Mama coming down from upstairs. When I turned, I saw she had her sweater on. She was wearing walking shoes.

"Where are you going?" I asked.

"Out in the garden."

I leaped to my feet and bolted after her. In my haste I nearly knocked her over. "Mama, stop. You're not going anywhere."

In her hand was a Hershey's chocolate bar.

"I'm going to tell Daddy. I'm going to tell him that you've been going out there every single day, and he'll make you stop."

She gazed at me, her eyes steady and unafraid.

"Look, I'll make a deal with you. You don't go out there anymore and I promise not to tell Daddy that you've been going out. Okay? Just take off your shoes and stay right here, agreed?"

No response.

"Mama, come on. Please?"

We stared at one another. It was a showdown, eyeball to eyeball. I didn't know what to do. Glancing down, I saw her turning the Hershey bar over and over in her hand.

It was a chocolate bar with almonds.

The fight just went out of me. I found myself suddenly awash with a very hopeless kind of sadness. The emotion was made even more powerful by its unexpectedness. One moment I was furious and full of exasperation. The next was all pain and sadness.

"Mama, what are you doing to us?" My voice quavered. "That's Meggie's favorite kind of candy bar, didn't you know that? Why are you giving candy to some strange child when you've got your very own children right here? What's wrong with us?"

She raised her hand and looked at the candy.

"Chocolate with almonds. That's Meggie's very favorite. Yet you never buy candy bars for Meggie."

She studied the chocolate bar.

"Mama, *we* love you. Not that little boy. He's just some kid who likes you because you give him candy. He's just greedy and if you stopped . . . Meggie and me, we're your children. I don't know where your other children are or who they are or what's happened to them, but, Mama, you ended up with Meggie and me."

There was a small, sharp silence.

"Please, Mama, give the candy bar to one of us. Give it to Megan. It'd make her so happy if she thought you'd gone and specially bought her a chocolate bar with almonds because you wanted to. Because you knew she liked them. Please give it to Megs."

With the fingers of one hand, Mama was twisting her lower lip. She was still contemplating the candy in her other palm.

"But I said I was going to find him," she said in a near

whisper. "I swore to God I'd get him back. I swore it on my life."

"Mama."

When she looked up, there were tears in her eyes. Reaching out, she took my hand and placed the candy bar in it. Then she turned and ran up the stairs. I heard the door to my parents' room open and slam shut. She was gone.

My father sat at the table, hands braced on either side of his head, fingers twisted through his hair. He studied the tablecloth. I had told him about what had happened when he came in from work. From his expression then, I had been unable to discern whether or not he'd suspected that Mama was continuing to see little Toby Waterman. He had sighed and put a hand over his eyes. He had whacked the banister with his cap all the way up the stairs.

There was no argument, as I had feared there would be. No yelling. No nothing. He went into the bedroom and spent a long time talking to Mama. Later he came out. She never did that night.

I made supper for us. Soup and sandwiches, because no one was especially hungry. Megan took her sandwich apart and ate the middle out of it, and my father threatened to send her to her room for making such a mess. I didn't tell him that she'd eaten a whole Hershey bar while he was up with Mama.

Afterward, we stayed amid the clutter of dirty dishes at the table.

"Oh golly," he said wearily. "What do we do now?" He brought a hand down and traced along one of the flowers in the material of the tablecloth. Megan was sitting on the far side of the table. Slouched down in her chair, head resting against one arm, she shoved crumbs around with her finger.

"Maybe I ought to go over there and see those people and talk to them," my father said.

"What good would that do?" I asked.

"Let them know that we know. Honestly, they must wonder. Honest to Pete. If someone were doing that to Megan, I would have been ready to shoot them by now." He shook his head. "I don't know. I just don't know what gets into her sometimes."

Silence. I was wishing Megan would leave. It was difficult to discuss anything delicate. But apparently she wasn't going to.

"Does Mama really believe that boy is Klaus?" I asked.

"I don't know."

More silence.

I glanced around the kitchen, at the dirty pots and pans, at the stove and refrigerator and the spice racks on the wall. It was a very ordinary kitchen.

"I don't see how she can," I said. This was crazy thinking. Before—the other things Mama had done— were just eccentric. Annoying, yes, but just eccentric. They made Mama different from most people but then Mama was. This, however, was crazy, plain and simple.

"I don't know," my father said again.

"Dad?"

He looked over.

"Do you think Mama ought to go see a psychiatrist or something?"

For several moments he was pensive. Then he shook his head.

"It might help."

"It isn't that big a deal, Les," he said. "We can handle it ourselves."

"But it might help."

Silence again. Dad scraped a bit of food off the tablecloth. It was dirty. It needed to be changed.

"No," he said softly.

"Why not?"

He lifted his head, looked out around the room, ran a hand through his hair. Then his attention returned to the tablecloth. He searched for another dirty spot and scraped at it with his fingernail. "She wouldn't understand, Les."

I watched him.

"There were psychiatrists there," he said. "In Ravensbrück. Where she was during the war. They were, well . . ." He shrugged. "Well, they did things. You know what I mean." He rubbed his hand through his hair again.

"But that was then," I said.

"She wouldn't understand. You know how she gets her opinions of things. She wouldn't be able to see that they wouldn't hurt her. You know your mama when she believes something."

I sighed. "But couldn't you make her understand?"

"I wouldn't try. I took her away from those things, Les."

I sighed again.

"I know it's hard, sweetheart," he said and reached his hand over to touch my shoulder. "But this just isn't that big a deal. Just a little thing. Just another one of your mama's little things. She'll get over it in time. I know it's annoying, but it'll pass just like everything she does." He looked at me. "You do understand."

I did, I guess.

Megan shifted in her chair. "Daddy?"

"Yes, love?"

"Daddy, I know about those things. I've been reading. I understand too."

He reached across the table to caress her cheek. Megan smiled.

Then she looked down at her fingernails. She gazed at

them thoughtfully before looking back. "That was a camp, wasn't it, that place? It was like where the Jews were, huh?"

My father nodded.

Lifting her chin, Megan gave me an I-told-you-so glance. I said nothing.

"So you see what a brave woman your mama is, Meggie?" my father said to her. "See what good strong blood you have running in your veins?"

Megan nodded.

"That's why we help Mama a little bit when she slips and isn't as strong now. That's what families are for."

I drifted into thought, sitting there in the bright kitchen light. My sister and my father continued to talk, but I ceased listening to them. What came to me was a vision of a girl. A young girl, not even my age. With pale hair and pale eyes, with strong, broad features, perhaps not quite beautiful yet, but rather ungainly, the way tall girls are at that age. A good girl, who ate her peas, kept her fingernails clean and tried hard not to fight with her brother. Wearing the blouse with lace around the collar that her mother had given her. I could see her quite clearly then. Not my mother but a stranger.

I looked over at my father. "I want to know one thing," I said.

His eyes met mine.

"Did they rape her?"

He nodded. "Yes, they did."

# Fourteen

THE NEXT DAY I stayed home from school. It was my father's decision, intended to buy him more time to figure out what to do to keep Mama from seeing Toby Waterman. My mother was not pleased about this. The night before, she never had come downstairs after her spell. When my father finally went to bed, I could hear them talking. I heard her voice rise in protest to something that he said. My dad didn't argue with her; his voice was barely audible. She went on for quite a while and then left the room, slamming the door behind her. She went into the bathroom. The faucet in the bath came on, and then my father was out in the hallway saying, Mara, open the door. Let me in there. She did. The door to the bathroom shut again, and the sound of the water drowned out their voices. I fell asleep before either of them came out.

During the night Megan was up. She had gone out to the linen closet in the hall to get clean sheets and had pulled half the contents of the closet down on top of herself. I climbed out of bed and went and helped her change her sheets. When I was back in my own room, I lay in the dark and hoped that Mama would sleep late in the morning. I felt exhausted.

Of course, Mama didn't. She was up with Dad at seven.

The morning that followed was miserable. Angry with

me for being there, for having told my father, for having interfered, my mother said virtually nothing to me all morning. Bored and restless, she paced through the house, leaving clouds of cigarette smoke in her wake. I sat in the living room and watched game shows on television.

The afternoon, I feared, would be worse. That was normally the time she saw Toby, and I was frightened she would go to him regardless of me, in which case I couldn't realistically do much to stop her. Or worse, Toby would come over to our house as he had the day before.

The whole experience was intensely uncomfortable for me. I felt like a jailer.

Mama made lunch for the two of us. Afterward, she returned to the kitchen with a box of photographs. Making herself another cup of coffee, she sat down at the kitchen table and began to sort through them. Relieved to see she had found something to occupy herself, I returned to the living room and watched soap operas.

When I rose some time later and went into the kitchen to see what Mama was doing then, I found her still sitting at the table with the pictures. She was drinking Kool-Aid and eating potato chips and had her feet up on the chair across the table from her. Although I noticed she was wearing her walking shoes, I said nothing. Instead, hoisting myself up on the counter in back of her, I reached down and took a handful of snapshots.

Most of them I had seen. They were ones of my sister and me when we were younger.

"Look at this one, Mama," I said and handed her one of Megan. It was taken when we lived in Yakima, in the backyard of our house there. Megan was standing stark naked in her little plastic wading pool.

I looked through the others. "Where's this?" I asked.

"Wales," Mama replied.

"I didn't know you had a camera then."

"We didn't." She reached a hand up for the snapshot. I gave it to her. "Jones the Farmer took this. He owned Forest of Flowers. It's by the cottage. The cottage would be over there, beyond the right side of the picture. See? You can see a bit of the holly hedge."

I leaned down from where I was sitting on the counter and put a hand on her shoulder to steady myself. The photo was of my father and a black-and-white dog. The hedge in the background was no more than a vague blur because the entire photograph was slightly out of focus.

"When we stood there," Mama said, "in the place where O'Malley is standing, we could see all the way down to the valley."

I studied the young man in the picture. He didn't look much like my father. He was thin and reedy like a boy who didn't eat well. But it was obvious what a good time he was having with the dog. Even through the blurriness, his casual joy was apparent. I wondered whose dog it was.

Mama remained silent. With one finger she touched the figures of the man and the animal, probing them gently, as if she expected to feel the texture of them. "It's a strange place there," she said quietly. "I don't know what it was. You felt it. But I never knew what it was." Her voice was soft and distant. "The light, perhaps. I would sit at the window and wait for O'Malley to come home and I would look down into the valley. The light was different there, a different color." She smiled faintly at the figures in the picture. She touched the dog. "I loved it there. The land was so old. So gray and green and sad. It broke my heart. You know the way some things do. When you are sad with joy."

"Would you like to go back, Mama?"

Her features softened with a smile. "Oh baby, *ja. Ja,*

*ja*. Oh, it is the one place I wish we hadn't left. I would go back there in a minute, if I could.''

She held up the photograph and gazed at it. "I don't have an American heart. I belong in an old country. You must be brave and new to live in this place. I have too much sadness. I belong in an old country."

A thousand ideas loosed themselves in my mind and went scattering in all directions. "Mama, why don't we go back?"

Turning away and reaching for her glass of Kool-Aid, she shook her head. "It takes money. We have no money for things like that." But I could see by the expression on her face that I had made her dream.

I jumped down from the counter and came around to sit in one of the chairs. Frantically I was thinking. There had to be a way. If we could get Mama away from here, out of Kansas, away from Toby Waterman . . .

She sat, glass between her hands, and did not speak. Deep in distant memories, her features relaxed. She smiled inwardly, and the smile never fully left her lips.

"It was the flowers," she said softly. "There were more flowers there than I had ever seen. Even in Popi's conservatory. Forest of Flowers. Up on the hillside. The valley was gray and green. It was always in the mist. But we were on the hillside and had the sun."

After school Paul stopped by. He was in a sour mood. The whole day had gone wrong for him. He was disappointed to find I was not in class. Aaron had gotten to take the car for driver's ed. There had been a pop quiz in English over a book he hadn't read.

Mama had gone upstairs at last to take a nap, and Megan was in the kitchen, so Paul and I went out to sit on the front lawn.

"Were you sick or something?" he asked.

"No," I replied. The sun was very warm. After being

in the house all day, the heat on my back felt good. "Mama's having a little trouble so I stayed home with her."

He looked at me. I think Paul believed everything about Mama had been made up. "What's the matter with her?"

I shrugged. I didn't want to tell him about Klaus because there was too much about Klaus I didn't know myself. I certainly didn't want to tell him about the crazy business with Toby Waterman. "She's just had a couple bad days, that's all."

"What do you mean? Is she depressed?" he asked. Clearly, he wanted to know exactly.

"Yes," I said because that sounded better than the truth did.

Concern wrinkled his forehead. "Is she . . . I mean, she isn't suicidal or anything, is she?"

"Oh no," I said and laughed, which I abruptly realized wasn't an ideal reaction to a question about suicides and depression. So I clamped a hand over my mouth. I was a rotten liar.

I was wishing I hadn't told Paul about Mama's having problems. It was almost worse than not having him know at all. Wistfully, I thought about the fact that the lies never stopped in something like this. Now that I didn't need to hide the fact that Mama was different, I was having to disguise less acceptable differences under more acceptable ones.

"Your dad let you?" Paul asked. "Just skip school, I mean."

A bug was crawling along through the grass beside my leg, so I put a finger down to let it crawl up. "I wasn't skipping. I stayed at home with my mother. My dad told me to. I do it all the time. I always have."

He watched me.

"So?" I asked. "Who else is going to? Megan can't.

She's too young. And too irresponsible. I used to do it when I was her age but you could never trust Megan like that.''

Paul picked a clover blossom from the lawn. He had collected half a dozen or so in his lap. With his fingernail he split the stems and tried to chain them together. They fell apart. ''I'd go stark raving mad if I had to stay home with my mother,'' he said. ''You couldn't pay me.''

''I've never thought too much about it,'' I replied. ''It's just something I've always done.''

''Do you resent it?'' he asked, looking over. ''I would. Even if my mom was tolerable, which she isn't. I'd still resent my old man telling me what to do. Boy, if he told me I had no choice but to stay home with my mom, I'd sure say a thing or two.''

''No, you wouldn't,'' I said.

''You want to bet? I would. I mean, you got your own life to lead, don't you?''

I paused. ''I don't see where it's very different from having your father tell you what school to go to and what subject to major in.''

An angry glare. ''What's that got to do with it?''

''Seems the same thing to me. Seems worse. You don't want to go into statistics. You know very well you don't. You're not even especially good at it. It's just him telling you to do it.''

Leaning over, I searched through the grass for a four-leaf clover. Neither one of us said a word. Paul still struggled to make his clover chain; it still fell apart. I found what I thought to be a four-leaf clover and pulled it out. It wasn't. I balled the leaves up between my fingers, and the juice ran out to stain my skin.

''It's a lot different,'' he said, resentment still echoing in his voice. ''I have to go where my dad says because he's paying for it. If it's his money, I'm pretty much trapped, aren't I? But how much are you getting for this?

You're not being paid to stay home. There's no money involved. You don't have to do it."

The small wad of green pulp was still between my fingers. I lifted it up and smelled it. I liked the smell of grass. Letting out a long breath, I shrugged. "You do have to, Paul," I said. "Know what I mean? They're your family. You just do it. I don't know why. You just do."

My father didn't return until almost seven that evening. I knew where he had been. Over at the Watermans, telling them about my mother and their boy. Of course, I didn't want to say that to Mama. When she'd come downstairs from her nap about 5:30, she'd wondered aloud why my father was late. To keep her from worrying, I said the first thing that popped into my head. I told her he'd phoned from the garage while she was asleep and had said he had to stay late to service the mayor's car because the mayor had some big function first thing in the morning and his car didn't run. I had no idea whatsoever if the mayor even patronized Mr. Hughson's garage but then I assumed Mama didn't know either.

When six o'clock came and went and my father still was not back, Mama made us a cold supper with a salad so that we could eat and yet Dad wouldn't have to eat warmed-over food when he came in. Megan had hauled out her Barbie-doll camper and about two hundred miscellaneous Barbie-doll accessories and had strewn them all over the kitchen floor while Mama was preparing the meal. After having dodged Megan and her toys for long enough, my mother finally told her to get out of the way with her things. "See, you can't do that anymore," Megan said to the Barbie doll, jamming it into the camper. She whizzed it off across the floor. "Barbie's going to concentration camp now," she said to herself as she crawled along the floor and propelled the plastic camper out into the hallway. My mother went white. I told her that we had to do something about Megan's reading those awful books.

When my father returned, he appeared exhausted. He'd apparently cleaned up at the garage before going over to the Watermans, because he returned home wearing a shirt and tie. While he was up in the bathroom washing for supper, Mama said in a scandalized whisper to me that the mayor was expecting a bit too much to have the men who serviced his car work in white shirts. I said no doubt it had been a nerve-wracking experience for Daddy, so it was probably best not to mention the mayor to him at all.

Mama sat with my father at the kitchen table while he ate. As she talked to him, she leaned way across the table toward him. She told how we spent the day, about the pictures and our lunch and seeing that the lilacs by the garbage cans were starting to bud. She told him that she had read in a women's magazine that you had to watch out for too much lead in the water in old houses because of lead pipes and did he know if our house had lead pipes, since it was, after all, a rather old house. All the time she spoke, she kept her fingers moving toward him, fiddling with the placemat and the coffee cup and the cuff of his shirt. She spoke in Hungarian, and it occurred to me, as I stood with my back to them, listening while I did the dishes, that Mama wasn't speaking English very much at all lately, even when she wasn't tired.

After supper I gave my father a while to unwind before I went up to the study. As always, he was stretched out in the lounger. He had it pushed all the way back into a horizontal position. The radio was blaring out marching music, which I would not have found particularly relaxing. But Dad had his eyes closed and his arms hanging loosely over the sides of the chair.

I did not say anything. I simply let myself in and sat

down on the footstool next to the chair. Listening to the music, I decided that I didn't care greatly for marches.

My father opened his eyes slightly and looked at me.

"How did it go?" I asked.

He groaned and let his head loll back.

"What did they say?"

"She's been making a damned nuisance of herself out there. They didn't know who she was but they were getting ready to call the police."

"Oh great."

He nodded wearily.

"Were they at all understanding? I mean, you know . . ."

"Not especially. But then you can hardly expect them to be, can you? By now, I would have drawn and quartered anyone I'd caught hanging around one of you girls like that. I wouldn't be very understanding either."

It had been humiliating for him. He didn't say it but he didn't need to. It was evident from the way he related the event. People never were very tolerant about putting up with other people's crazy relations. They always thought they were. Very liberal and very understanding. But when push came to shove, I had never witnessed it to be true.

"Dad, I have an idea," I said. "Mama and I were talking this afternoon, and something occurred to me."

He glanced over.

"Could we go to Wales?"

His eyes popped open. "Wales?"

"Yes. Mama and I were looking through some old pictures and she was telling me how much she regretted leaving there. So I was thinking . . ." I let the words trail off, hoping he would pick them up. Hearing my thoughts said aloud made them sound much less plausible.

My father said nothing at all.

"Well, I was thinking that if maybe we could go somewhere, it'd take Mama's mind off Toby Waterman."

"Oh Lessie," he said, smiling. Gently, he reached out and touched my face just the way he did with Megan when she was being endearingly stupid.

"But it would get her away. It'd solve things."

"Lesley, it's a nice idea but there's no way we could do it. Wales is another country. You can't just pick up your bags and go there. It takes job permits and visas and lots of money. And I'm afraid no one would want to give a permit to an old man like me."

"You're not old."

He smiled.

"Well, anyhow, I wasn't thinking necessarily of moving. How about just a vacation? Back to somewhere Mama really wants to be. Until she gets this idiotic notion about Toby out of her head."

"No money, sweetheart," my father said. Putting his head back, he stared at the ceiling in silence for a moment. "That's what it all boils down to in the end: money. What I would do, if I were rich. I'd take her anywhere her heart desired. I'd go to Lébény or Wales or Vienna. Anywhere." Then he looked over. "The problem is, I'm not rich."

Crestfallen, I looked down at my hands. He caressed my cheek.

"Don't feel bad," he said. "It was a sweet idea."

"Would it really cost that much? Just to have a vacation? Even a little one?"

"I have no money, Lesley. Not even for a little vacation."

I sat, thinking. The music on the radio had changed. I didn't recognize it. It was a slow melody played on panpipes, wistfully sad.

"I've got almost $250 in my savings account from

working at the nursing home," I said. "I was meaning to save it for college but I wouldn't care if you took it now. I can earn more in the summer when I can work full time. We could use that. Would that be enough?"

"No, darling," he said. "I'm afraid it wouldn't."

Again, I lowered my head. I studied the strands of fiber in the rug and thought. "Remember my bond?" I asked. "That one Grandma got me when I was little. For me to go to college. Could we use that?"

He shook his head.

"That's a thousand dollars, Daddy. I can cash it when I turn eighteen. Surely that would be enough. Wouldn't it? That's a lot of money."

"That's college money, Lesley. That's for you to take and go get a good education like your grandmother intended. Colleges don't come cheap either."

"But it would be enough, wouldn't it? To go to Wales, I mean. We could take Mama to Wales on the thousand dollars, and then I could just work or something when I get to college. I've always found jobs. I'll manage."

"No, I want that money for your education. That's what it was meant for. That's why your grandmother gave it to you, Lesley. Not for anything else."

I didn't reply. My mind was running elsewhere, producing rapid visions of Wales. We could do it with a thousand dollars. We could take Mama to Wales, and she'd forget about Toby Waterman and about Klaus and everything would go back to the way it was before. I smiled. We'd all go home to Forest of Flowers.

# *Fifteen*

BEFORE SCHOOL the next morning I went into the study after my father had left for work, and I rifled through the files for Grandma's bond. When I located it, I took it out and put it in the underwear drawer of my dresser in my room. My eighteenth birthday was eight days off. After that the money was mine. Grandma had said so.

School was becoming more difficult to stomach. It was one of those places I always wanted to be when I wasn't there but never enjoyed as much as I'd anticipated when I was. Even in the best of times I never quite fit in. I would try. I would wear the same makeup, put on the same clothes, attempt the same expressions as the others, but I knew I came out looking stupid, like a little girl in dress-up clothes. And no one was fooled. In the more difficult times, like when we were moving or when Mama was being awkward, I didn't even bother to try to fit in. I knew I didn't. I knew the other kids didn't go home to what I went to. I knew they didn't care that I went home to it. During those times school was a love-hate relationship for me. I loved it for its freedom, for its dreamworld, for all its passionate, meaningless conformities. But when I was there, in my classes, in the cafeteria, I hated it.

In calculus Danielle, the girl who sat in front of me, was always talking to the girl who sat in back. They were very much part of the school elite, both on the cheerleading squad, with boyfriends in school athletics. Danielle never spoke to me. For Danielle I did not exist except as an object she had to curve her head around to see Chris, who sat behind me, or occasionally as someone to borrow answers to homework from when she hadn't had time to get them done herself. But I wasn't a good enough student to merit an actual relationship based on that.

They were talking about boys. Dudes, they called them. Foxy dudes. And about Missy who was having to go out the next Friday with Timothy Gold. Timothy? Gawd, Chris said. Gawd, she must be desperate. Gawd, if I had to go out with him, I'd *die*.

I was thinking about how little Chris probably knew about dying. I wished passionately that Mrs. Browder would turn around and make them shut up. She was drawing hyperbolic curves on the blackboard, and with ESP I tried to will her to turn around. When she finally did turn, she looked directly at me and said, Lesley, would you please be quiet. Chris sniggered.

At lunch when I was down in the cafeteria with Brianna and Claire, the lunch aide came to me with a slip of paper that summoned me to the office. My father had phoned and I was supposed to call him back.

"Your mother is out at the Watermans'," he said when I did. "Would you come down and get the car and go take her home?"

"Oh Dad, do I have to? Can't you?" I felt certain everyone in the office was listening. My cheeks burned.

"Lessie, somebody is going to have to stay with her or she'll go right back out. You know your mama. And I just can't leave the garage right now. Mr. Hughson's at lunch. I'm the only one here . . ."

Mr. Waterman was sitting in a straight-backed chair on the front porch. My mother was in a wicker rocker beside him. She had a grim, displeased expression on her face, but it was nothing compared to Mr. Waterman's.

"You keep her away from here, you understand?" He was a bigger version of Toby, but fat, his stomach hanging out over his belt like overrisen bread dough. He wore a string vest and stained gray flannel trousers. "Now I told Mr. O'Malley that I don't want her coming around here no more, bothering my boy. You hear? You keep her away from here or I'll have the law out. I will. The next time I see her. You understand, girl?"

I nodded.

Mama rose.

"You tell your father that. You tell him the next time I catch her out here, he'll be fetching her from the police station. I ain't having no more of it. I mean it. I ain't having no crazy woman hanging around here. You make that good and plain to her."

"Yes, sir," I said. Then I turned and went back to the car with Mama.

Once seated, I slammed the car door and turned the key in the ignition. Mama sat on her side, arms folded across her breasts, mouth set in a tight, annoyed expression. I could see that she was just as angry with me as she was with Mr. Waterman. I was supposed to be on her side. She was thinking that, and I could tell it. And she was immensely irritated by my disloyalty.

"You just can't keep going out there, Mama," I said. "Daddy told you not to. You're supposed to stay at home."

"I'm going to get him back," she said resolutely.

"Oh, for pity's sake, Mama. This has gone far enough. It's got to stop."

No reply. She sat in silence, looking like one of those warrior women in the old German operas, expression fierce, arms folded firmly. Resentment emanated from her.

"Do you realize how humiliating that was for me?" I asked. "Do you have any idea how embarrassed I feel? Geez, I wanted to fall into a hole." I glanced over. "I'm getting sick of this. I was in school and I had to leave to come get you. Paul and I were going to go to Torres Café after school. And now Dad's called me up and made me come out here and get you. I'm sorry you're mad at me. I'm sorry you don't see things the way the rest of us do. But honest to God, Mama, I'm getting to the end of my rope with you too."

A heavy release of breath.

"Now, you're just going to have to stop all this non- sense. You got to accept the fact that that little kid is not Klaus. What would you want that little kid for anyway? He's dirty. And he's that nasty man's son. Not yours. That's all there is to it."

"You should help me," she said accusingly.

"I'm hardly going to do that."

"They're clever. You're not old enough to know. You don't understand them, how they can make you believe things. But I'm not fooled. They fooled me once, but not again. No one's taking him away from me this time."

"Mama! Honestly, Mama, no one is trying to take him away from you. He isn't *yours.*"

"You're just too young to realize."

I sucked in a long breath between my teeth to quell the frustration. We'd reached the house. Pulling the car over to the curb, I parked it. "Now, listen, Mama. I'm going to tell you one more time and I want you to listen good. You've made a mistake. You're remembering things and they've gotten mixed up in your mind. That boy is *not* your Klaus. Maybe he looks like him. Maybe he seems like him. But it isn't him. I'm right, Mama. Nobody's tricked me. No one's fooled me. I'm right and I'm telling you the whole truth. I don't know where your Klaus is, but that boy isn't him."

My mother simply unlatched the door on her side of the car and got out.

Furious and frustrated, I followed her up the walk. The humiliation of having had to face Mr. Waterman and bring Mama home like a wandering pet intensified my exasperation.

Coming behind her through the back door and into the kitchen, I said, "Why can't you understand, Mama? Why do you always have to be so stubborn about things?"

She turned. Her expression blackened but she said nothing. Instead, she went to the refrigerator and took out the milk. She began opening the top and I could tell she was going to drink the damned milk right out of the carton. I leaped over the kitchen stool, grabbed a glass out of the dish drainer and slammed it down on the counter in front of her.

"I'm getting tired of this," I said. "I'm getting sick of you wrecking my days with all the stupid things you think up."

She took the glass, poured the milk, drank it and poured herself a second glass. She behaved as if I weren't in the room, when I was standing so close to her that she couldn't shut the door of the refrigerator without difficulty. Frustration was making me wild. I didn't know what to do to get through to her. She could simply close her mind off to all reason. She could act like a perfectly normal human being on one hand and on the other be dense as a rock.

"You're imagining this, Mama," I said, bringing my voice down to normal volume. "It's only in your mind. Just the way that whole deal about Uncle Paddy cheating Dad out of that money was. Just the way it was on Stuart Avenue. Remember that? Remember when you kept thinking you heard rats in my closet when we lived on Stuart Avenue? Remember how Daddy kept taking you up there and setting all those traps that never caught anything? But oh no, you wouldn't believe him. Oh no. No matter what he did, no matter how much I loved it there, we had to move. Rats would get into Megan's bassinet, you said. What a stupid idea, Mama. How would they get into a bassinet? What would rats want with Megan anyhow? But would you believe that?''

Ignoring me, she squeezed past and went to the far counter to pick up her cigarettes.

"I don't want to talk to you like this, Mama, but somebody's got to sooner or later.''

She pulled the wrapper off the package of cigarettes and knocked one across her fingers. She searched around for the matches.

"You know what's going to happen, if you keep making a nuisance of yourself with your stupid notions? They're going to cause trouble, those Watermans. They're not like Daddy and me. They're not going to just put up with you. And they'll have a right, if you keep bothering them.''

Still no response.

"You heard what he said. They're going to call the police next time.''

She paused, cigarette in hand, unlit match in the other.

"They'll call the police, and who will go out and get you then? It sure won't be Daddy or me. It'll be some policeman.''

"The police can't arrest you in America,'' she said firmly.

"Mama, the police in America sure can arrest you, if you go around trying to make other people's children believe they belong to you. That's wrong. Just think how you'd feel if someone were doing that to Meggie. What you're doing to that little boy—that's against the law in anybody's country.''

She set the match down a moment and ran her fingers

through the hair near her left temple. Her lips pursed into a thoughtful expression. She then picked up the match again and lit it.

"I hate to be the one to talk to you like this, Mama, but if Daddy won't, then I will. If you keep this up, the police'll come and arrest you. And if you don't stop altogether, they're going to put you in jail or something. Or in the state hospital. They'll say Daddy and I can't control you and they'll put you in Larned and there won't be a single thing we can do about it. Those are the consequences for doing stupid things like this."

Her eyes dilated. The pupils expanded nearly to the edges of her irises, eclipsing the blue. Thank God, something's finally gotten through to her, I was thinking, and I relaxed back against the counter. She was standing stockstill. She'd lit the match but had frozen somewhere midmove. The match burned down, and she dropped it onto the Formica counter top. We both watched it burn out.

"So, you got to promise me, Mama, that this is the end of this nonsense and you won't go out there again."

She had begun to shake. The cigarette, still between her fingers, twiddled.

"I'm not trying to scare you, Mama. I just want you to understand how things really are. Try to think of it as being Megan. Imagine how awful we'd feel if someone kept coming around, talking to her. Don't you understand how the Watermans must be feeling? Try to put yourself in their shoes. That's all I'm trying to point out."

The shaking continued.

"So, look, just promise me, okay? I got to know you mean it. Promise me. Say, 'Lesley, I promise I'm not going to go out there to the Watermans again. I'm not going to bug Toby Waterman anymore.' Tell me that. Promise me."

The unlit cigarette tumbled from her grasp and rolled

across the counter. Hands clasped together, she brought them up over her mouth.

"Okay, look, I'm sorry. Don't get upset about it. I just wanted you to understand the consequences, that's all. But don't worry about them. Just promise me that you won't bother the Watermans anymore and then nothing will happen."

No response. I reached my arm around her shoulder and gave her a little hug to reassure her. I wanted her to realize that I wasn't angry with her anymore, that the things I had said had been simply for her own good, because I loved her and didn't want her to get into trouble. People have to be honest sometimes.

But she could not stop shaking. Within moments she was shaking so hard that she shook me too.

"Look, Mama, I said I'm sorry. I am. Don't get all upset about it. Don't worry."

"He said I was safe here," she said in a hoarse voice. Lowering her head, she clasped her hands on either side of her face.

"Mama, listen to me, all right? Don't shake. Come on now, quit shaking. Nothing's the matter. Nothing's happened yet, has it? I was only telling you. I know it's hard for you, Mama. I know you wish the little boy was yours. I can understand that. But get hold of yourself a little bit, can you? Don't shake."

The tears were there then, over her cheeks.

"Mama." It was more of a moan than a word. "Oh, Mama, for Pete's sake, listen to me, would you? I'm sorry. Let's just forget what I said, okay? Here, sit down. Let me help you. Do you want a cup of coffee? Shall I fix you some coffee?" I almost had to push her down into the chair. Her muscles were iron hard beneath my fingers. "Mama," I said, coming down on my knees beside the chair. "Look at me. I love you. We all love you, Mama. And we won't let anything happen to you. You know that. I was just talking. Trying to make you understand.''

"This is America," she whispered. "O'Malley, he said I was safe here."

"Oh, Mama, you *are* safe. Oh cripes, Mama, don't cry like that. Don't.''

"I thought I was safe."

"Oh Jesus. Oh God. Mama, stop it. Mama, don't. You're making me upset. See me? Look what you're doing. Do you want me to cry too? Mama, don't. I love you. Don't. Please stop.''

"They cannot take you away in America. O'Malley, he tells me this. He says I'm safe. I believed him.''

"Oh, do believe him. He's right. I'm sorry. Honest, I am. I was just running off at the mouth. I was upset and I just said what came into my head. Forgive me, Mama. I'm sorry.''

Tearfully, she looked over at me. "You won't let them rape me again, will you?" Her voice had grown very small. "Oh please, they won't rape me again, will they?"

"Oh Mama, *no!* " I reached to hug her, to cling to her. She was sobbing.

"He said I was safe. I believed him. Oh please, please, don't let them come again. Please. Please don't let them come. I thought I was safe.''

I felt like hell. Like shit. Why had I done that? Of all the stupid, half-assed things I could have said, why had I chosen to say what I did?

I pleaded with her to calm down, but she grew more and more agitated. She went on and on and on about being safe in America where the police could not come into your home and get you, where the doctors could not lock you up without your permission. Clutching the material in my blouse, her fingers going white with the strength of her grasp, she begged me to protect her. And

I, hideously frightened myself, still kneeling on the floor beside her, began to cry too, too panicked to pull myself together. Like Pandora, I had no idea how to get the lid back on what I'd opened.

I couldn't calm her down on my own. Even after I had managed to get her out of the kitchen and upstairs to the safety of her own bed, she couldn't stop crying. She sobbed hysterically, and I heard myself screaming at her to stop. Finally, I went into the bathroom and sorted through the bottles in the medicine chest. Some of the prescriptions were ancient. I uncapped them, smelled them, rolled a few tablets out into my palm before throwing the majority of them into the toilet. At last I came across a name I recognized. It was a tranquilizer prescribed by our old doctor in Nebraska. The label said take two, so I took out four pills. I went downstairs with them, mashed them up, dissolved them in milk. I added a little chocolate syrup and took the glass back upstairs. She had a hard time drinking it, and I worried that it might taste too awful. But in the end she got it down. Then I stayed with her on the bed and rubbed her shoulders, hoping she wasn't so tense that she'd throw the medication up.

When the pills began to take effect, I went downstairs again. I located *The Lark Ascending,* took it from the record cabinet and put it on the phonograph. I turned the volume up so loudly that the high, melancholy wail of the violin pierced every small corner of the house and the floor vibrated with the deeper sounds of the other instruments.

"Listen, Mama. It's Elek's violin. Do you hear it?" I sat on the bed beside her and ran my fingers through her hair, working the long strands out across the leg of my jeans. "Everything's going to be okay, isn't it, Mama? I won't let anything happen to you. You don't have to worry about anything. You can just relax. Me and Daddy and Megan, we love you. We'll always take care of you. No matter what. So you never have to worry. Just listen. Listen to Elek's violin.''

She closed her eyes. I lay down not so much beside her as on top of her. She was on her left side, and I lay with my two hands locked over her right shoulder, my face pressed tightly against her arm. The music swelled around us. Exhausted, we both fell asleep.

The phone was ringing.

I sat up groggily. What time was it? It could have been any hour of the day or night as far as I was concerned. Dazed with the unexpected deepness of my sleep, I felt completely disoriented.

The phone persisted. I leaned across Mama to turn the clock on the bedside table toward me. It was just after four in the afternoon. With slow, heavy movements I got out of bed.

"Mrs. O'Malley?" the voice said a little impatiently when I finally picked up the receiver.

"No, I'm sorry. This is Lesley. My mother isn't available right now. Who's this?"

It was the secretary from Megan's school. She wanted my mother, and when I explained that Mama wasn't there to be talked to, she wanted to know when Mama would be home. I explained that my mother was ill and not able to come to the phone. In that case she wanted my father. I said he was at work. She asked for his telephone number there.

Within minutes my father rang. What was Mama doing? he asked. Sleeping, I replied and didn't go into details. Would I please come get him in the car? he asked. He had to go over to Megan's school immediately. I asked what was wrong. It seemed a day for wrong things. My father replied that he didn't know for sure.

When we arrived at the school, the principal shook hands with my father. Megan was sitting in the front of-

fice. Scrunched down in a plastic chair, she did not ac
knowledge our arrival. Instead, she picked at a scab on
her arm.

The principal invited my father into his little office and
for the first time seemed aware of my presence. Would I
mind waiting outside, please? He motioned to Megan.
She could go with me.

Shoulders up, head down, long dark hair lying over
her like a cloak, Megan looked a trapped elf, miserably
ensnared in this room of plastic chairs and fluorescent
lights. Full of unexpected sympathy for her, I went over
and put my arm around her shoulder. She pulled away.
Sliding off the chair, she left ahead of me and went into
the corridor.

The school was old, built sometime around the turn of
the century when the town was thriving. On the inside
over the vast entrance was a huge carved wooden panel
inscribed PROGRESS and depicting the pioneers on their
way west. I studied it for a few minutes before sitting
down on the bench beside the door. Megan made a point
of sitting on the other bench instead of beside me.

"What did you do?" I asked.

"Nothing."

"How come they called Daddy out of work then?"

"How come you don't stick your head in a hole, Lesley?"

"You might as well tell me. Dad will anyway."

She raised her head slightly to glare at me before turning her attention back to the sore on her arm.

"So?" I asked.

"I got a swat."

"You did? Cripes, Megs. What for?"

"Nothing," she said and pulled up the scab. She
studied it.

"I hate to inform you of this, Megs, but they don't
generally give swats for nothing."

"Buzz off, Lesley."

"So what did you do?"

"Nothing, I said." And that was the end of the conversation.

Dad came out about twenty minutes later. The principal put his hand under Megan's chin and lifted her face. She wouldn't be doing something like that again, would she? No, Megan muttered in an almost inaudible voice. Was she sorry? Yes, she said in the same tone.

My father got into the car in silence. About halfway home he looked over at Megan in the front seat beside him. "Whatever made you do that?" he asked. I still didn't know what she had done.

Megan shrugged.

"Listen, don't shrug at me when I ask you a civil question, young lady. I'm not at all happy with you. You're in enough trouble as it is."

"Well, they said it wasn't true," she replied in a defensive tone. "They were teasing me. I didn't mean to hit him that hard. That was an accident. I just meant to hit him a little. Just to sort of knock him down. To make him stop."

My father sighed.

"Him getting hurt like that, that was an accident, Daddy. I tried to explain to Mr. Gaines. I didn't mean for him to hit his head. It was *his* stupid fault for doing that. I just wanted him to shut up. He kept saying it wasn't true."

"But Meggie," Dad said, "it *wasn't* true."

Megan did not answer.

My father pulled into the driveway and stopped the car but he didn't get out. Instead, he removed the keys from the ignition and laid them on the dashboard. He turned in his seat, leaning back against the car door. Megan remained pinioned by her seat belt.

"It wasn't true, was it, Megs?"

"I didn't mean for the kid to be hurt. I said I didn't. Why doesn't anyone believe me?"

"I believe you. But that's not what I'm asking. Frankly, Megan, I don't care anything about that child. That's a whole other matter. And I'll take your word it was an accident. You shouldn't have been fighting in the first place, because you know better. But, like I said, that's another matter. What I care about is this other thing. About what got you into this mess to begin with. That's what I want answers for."

Megan unbuckled her seat belt.

"No. You stay right here. We're not going into the house and upset your mother with this kind of talk."

Megan sank deeper into her seat.

"So?"

"It was true," she said in a tiny but defiant voice.

"Megan."

"It *is* true. You said so yourself."

"I said nothing of the kind."

"You did too," she said, tears beginning. "You said Mama was strong and brave. You said so yourself. It *could* have been true. You weren't there either, so you don't know."

The story she had been spreading around school about my mother was dramatic and wildly heroic, about how Mama had been imprisoned during the war, how she had single-handedly fought off the worst advances of the SS, how she had saved so many Jews' lives that the prime minister of Israel wanted to give her a medal for it. Mama became Wonder Woman, Golda Meir and Sheena, Queen of the Jungle, all rolled into one.

My father was tender with Megan. He reached over and pulled her onto his lap, even though at nine and a half she wasn't such a little girl anymore. My sister wept, still protesting bitterly that her stories *might* have been true, that he didn't really know for sure because he hadn't been there either. He kept her head tucked under his chin, his hand pressing against the side of her face, obscuring most of it from my view.

"It was a nice story," he said to her gently, "but it's just for us. Not for the children at school."

"It's true," she sobbed. "I just wanted it to be true."

# Sixteen

THE SEVENTEENTH OF APRIL was my birthday. By then I had been home with Mama for seven school days. No one said anything about it anymore. Each morning my father seemed to take it for granted that I'd stay.

The night before my birthday had been a bad one. My mother had been awake through most of it, pacing in the silent house. She refused to talk to us about Toby but she'd not given him up. My father had heard her in the night and had come downstairs to discover her dressed and putting on her shoes. So he had stayed awake. Somewhere in the wee hours Mama had finally fallen asleep on the couch in the living room. She was still sleeping there when I came down for breakfast about seven. Dad, his eyes red rimmed with weariness, was sitting in the kitchen with the newspaper and a cup of coffee.

Megan was there too. She had her feet twined around the rungs of her chair and was rocking herself back and forth on the chair's back legs. "Happy Birthday!" she shouted jubilantly. "Happy Birthday to you!" She proceeded to sing with all the tunefulness of an intoxicated sparrow until my father told her to be careful not to wake Mama.

At my place at the table there was a package wrapped in wrinkled white tissue paper. I sat down and began undoing the tape.

"That's from Daddy and me both. And Mama too," Megan said. "I got to choose it. I went downtown all by myself on Monday afternoon and bought it. Did you notice I was gone then? That's what I was doing."

It was a book, an extremely thick novel by someone I had never heard of. From the bright orange sticker, not quite fully removed, I could tell Megan had found it on the bargain table at the book shop.

"See?" she said enthusiastically. "It's a book. It's the biggest book I could find there, except, of course, for the dictionaries."

"That's nice," I said, trying not to sound disappointed. I hadn't had anything special in mind for my birthday. Nonetheless, I had had rather higher hopes than this.

"I got it for you to read," she said. "So you'll have something to do when you're here all day with Mama. I looked for the thickest book I could find so that it'd last a long time for you."

I smiled at her. "Thank you, Meggie. That really was thoughtful of you."

Once my father and sister were gone, I cast around the house morosely. I washed up the dishes from breakfast, swept the floor in the kitchen, went upstairs and made all the beds. Housework had developed a magnetic attraction for me since I'd been staying home. It was the only available activity that sufficiently absorbed the long hours.

By ten I had everything done, including having ripped Megan's bed entirely apart and remade it from scratch because she could never do it right. I'd even dusted over the tops of the curtains.

Mama remained asleep on the couch. Quietly, I walked in to check on her. On her side, one arm extended over the edge of the couch, she slept deeply, the sound of her breathing filling the room.

I watched her.

"Mama?"

She slept on.

"It's my birthday, Mama."

She wouldn't remember. She never remembered how old I was. There were more important things on her mind. There always had been. But I had it better than Megan. At least she remembered I was around. Half the time she acted like she was genuinely surprised to find Megan there, as if she were some little stranger whom we'd accidentally picked up somewhere.

"Mama, why don't you wake up?"

She slept in her clothes, her long hair partly hiding her face. She could have been one of those sleeping princesses from fairy tales, her sleep was so deep, her face so ageless and still. There might as well have been a wall of thorns protecting her.

"I'm eighteen. I'm an adult today, Mama. You hear that? I'm grown up now."

She never stirred. I did not even ripple the surface. She caused us all that trouble and then could sleep like a baby.

Despondent, I turned and went upstairs. Alone in my room I picked up the book Megan had bought me. Sitting down on the bed, I paged through it. The loneliness would not go away.

A short time later the doorbell rang. I went downstairs with a certain amount of hesitation, still afraid I would find Toby Waterman there.

Miss Harrich stood on the front porch.

"Hello, Lesley."

I smiled and nodded.

She had a yellow legal pad and some files in her arms. "I was out and I thought I would stop by to see how you are. You've been absent quite a while now."

"I know," I said. "But my dad's been calling the attendance office every day."

"I just thought I'd—"

"I'm not skipping, Miss Harrich. My father's called and told them each morning. See, my mother's ill. I have to stay home with her."

"How is your mother?"

I shrugged. "All right."

"Is she improving?"

"Yeah. Sort of."

Then there was a pause. I didn't know what she wanted or what she thought might be wrong with Mama. I prayed she wouldn't ask any specific questions that would force me to lie.

"I do hope she's feeling better," Miss Harrich said.

What occurred to me as we stood in the doorway talking was that Miss Harrich was probably about the same age as my mother. It was a bizarre thought. I could never imagine my mama dressed in a tweed suit, standing on someone's doorstep, passing the time of day. By the same token I couldn't picture Miss Harrich in the war, although I realized that she must have in some way experienced the war too.

"Well," said Miss Harrich after a while, "I just wanted to stop by and see how you were doing."

"I'm fine."

"I don't want you to miss too much school, not with graduation and everything."

"I won't."

"All right then. Good-bye, Lesley," she said and turned. She started down the sidewalk.

"Miss Harrich?"

She paused and looked back.

I regarded her, my tongue tied.

"Have a nice day, Lesley." She began to turn away again.

"Miss Harrich, it's my birthday today. I'm eighteen."

She smiled. "Happy birthday, Lesley."

Afterward I sat on my bed in my room and read Megan's novel. It wasn't such a horrible book. It had a fantastic amount of passionate sex and really dirty talk in it, so if you were sufficiently bored, it was almost interesting. At least the sexy parts were. About 12:30 I heard the shower running. I stuck a pencil in the book to mark the place and went downstairs to make something to eat.

"Mama, did you know it's my birthday today?" I asked at lunch.

She smiled. "Happy birthday, baby."

"Well, what I was thinking was that since it's my birthday and I'm eighteen, you know that bond? That money Grandma O'Malley put in the bank for me? That bond matures today. I can cash it now. And I was thinking that what I might do is take the money out and use it to take us to Wales."

Mama looked up sharply from her tuna fish.

"You know. To Forest of Flowers. It'd only be for a vacation. There's no way for us to live there or anything. But we could go visit. Would you like that?"

"Your grandmother's bond?" Mama asked.

"Yes, you remember? The one that she gave me when I was little."

Mama guffawed into her sandwich. "She'd turn over in her grave if you spent that money on me. She'd turn right over."

I ignored that comment, true as it probably was. "It's a thousand dollars. That's a lot of money, isn't it? And we could have a nice long vacation. Just us. Just you and Daddy and me and Megs. Over at Forest of Flowers. Does that sound good? Would you like to do it, Mama?"

She turned her head and looked toward the kitchen window. She smiled. "There'd be rhododendrons in May," she said, her voice dreamy. "Did I ever tell you about the rhododendrons? They grow wild. All up the sides of the mountains. Everywhere, rhododendrons.''

"We could go see them."

"I miss so much from there." She sighed. "This is a good country but it isn't the same. I miss so much."

I leaned forward to touch her hand. "I don't really care what Grandma would think. It's my money now and I can do as I want with it. And I want to take you to Wales."

Paul phoned late in the afternoon. His brother Gary had come up unexpectedly from Garden City and they were going rat shooting together at the dump. So, he said apologetically, he wasn't going to be over. It's my birthday, I pointed out. Oh come on, he said, he didn't get to see Gary very often. I didn't really mind, did I? I did mind. Bored and restless anyway, the thought of being jilted for rats did not please me much. We had a few words, and I hung up angry.

By supper time I was in a miserable mood. I had pinned my last hope for the day on Dad's bringing home a birthday cake. It was a stupid thing to want. I didn't even particularly like the cakes from the supermarket. But I got the desire for one into my head and couldn't shake it.

Naturally, he came home without one. He hadn't even bothered to stop and get something special for the meal. Instead we had some truly horrible stuff that comes out of a box and you mix hamburger with it. I helped Mama prepare supper, and all the while I kept hoping someone was going to mention going to get me a birthday cake. I hinted broadly that I wouldn't mind one, that we didn't have a thing in the house for dessert. At one point I thought perhaps my father actually had bought a cake and was planning to surprise me with it after we'd eaten. But there was no logical place to hide a cake that I hadn't looked. I even took the keys to the car and checked the trunk. Nothing.

During the meal Megan occupied herself by making mountains and valleys out of her mashed potatoes and by kicking me under the table.

"Megan, stop it," I said.

"I'm not doing anything."

"You're kicking me. Now stop it."

"I am not."

"You are too. Now cut it out."

"I'm not."

"Megan, you are kicking me in the legs. Now I know if you are or not and you are. So don't deny it."

"Well then, move your dumb legs, Lesley. I got mine right here under my chair and yours are clear over where they don't belong."

"Girls," Dad said, "be quiet and eat, please."

Megan kicked my legs again. As she did it, her mouth widened into a smart-alecky little grin.

"Cut it out, Megan."

"I'm not doing anything."

"You little snot, you are too. Now stop it. I mean it."

"Did you hear that, Mama? Lesley's calling me names."

Mama looked over.

"Girls, mind your own business and eat," my father said without even bothering to look up from his plate. The garage had been overbooked, and he'd worked through his lunch hour. So he had come home very hungry. The tone of his voice warned that he was not up to any nonsense from us.

After a few moments Megan picked up a little itty-bitty wad of potatoes on her knife. She held it up so that I could tell what she was going to do with it. Quickly, she glanced to see if either Mama or Daddy was watching.

Assured they weren't, she flicked the knife at me. The potatoes hit my shirt.

"Daddy!" I cried. "Megan's throwing food!"

"Megan Mary," my father said and leveled a reptilian glare in her direction.

Wide-eyed innocence was all over Megan's face.

"Look, she hit me right on the front of my shirt. And I put this on special today because it's my birthday. Now Megan's wrecked it."

Dad turned from Megan to me. My mother looked over too. Dad said, "Lesley, what is the matter with you tonight? All I've heard out of you since I've walked through the door is bellyaching." He looked back at Megan. "And you, young lady, don't you dare let me catch you throwing food. Sit up straight and eat."

Megan made a face. "I don't like this very well."

"Just eat it." He reached past her for another slice of bread.

I seethed. It was unfair. It was *my* birthday, and no one seemed to care. No one did anything special. There should have been a good meal. Something I liked and not some ratty thing out of a box. There should have been *something* special about this day.

Megan stuck out her tongue at me.

"Megan, just stop it, would you?"

Mama was watching us. I could tell we were right on the verge of giving her a spell. She had that sort of expression on her face. But honestly, at that point I couldn't have cared less.

When Mama looked away, Megs picked up another little wad of potatoes. She checked to make sure the coast was clear and everyone's attention was diverted except mine. She waved it on the end of her knife. I gave her my meanest look, meant to scare the hell out of her. She grinned.

Mama looked over. Megan lowered her knife quickly

and pretended to eat. I think Mama knew something was going on. She watched Megan carefully for several seconds before turning around to get the coffeepot off the stove.

*Whap!* The wad of potatoes sailed across the table and hit me on the neck.

"You little asshole!" I shouted.

"Lesley's swearing!" Megan sang out in delight.

That did it. I had had it with the entire rotten day. Reaching my foot out, I curled it around the rung of her chair and yanked. Hard. The chair toppled and Megan with it. She came crashing down, her chin hitting against the edge of the table. She screamed.

Confusion erupted, and both my parents were on their feet.

"Well, it's not my fault! The little snot's there bugging me the whole lousy meal. Why don't you ever make her mind! She's throwing the goddamned potatoes, and you and Mama sit there like a couple of lumps on a log."

"You are excused to your room," my father said.

Mama was on the other side of the table, cuddling Megan against her breast. Megan's lip was cut, and Mama knelt, cupping her hand to catch the blood. Resentful, I glared at her. I would have preferred to see her have a spell than hold Megan.

"I said, you are excused." My father was standing beside me. We were very nearly the same height. If anything, I was slightly taller. But I could see I was better off obeying him.

I stomped up to my room. Once there I slammed the door shut. No one downstairs responded to the noise, so I opened it and slammed it again. As hard as I could. Still no response. So I stormed over to the bed and flopped down. Why did he get so mad at me? Megan was the one throwing the stupid potatoes. I examined the spot on my shirt where the first wad of potatoes had hit. The area was dry and crusty. If I scraped it off, it wasn't going to show. That made me even angrier.

I thought I was going to explode. It was an actual physical sensation, pushing upward and outward through my torso. I looked around the room. Spying the novel lying open on the bedside table, I lunged at it and flung it across the room. There. See how I like your dim-witted gift? I raced after it, picked it up and threw it again. I kicked it. Then I kicked the wall. Hard. And again. Paint chipped off the woodwork.

I paused a moment, regarding the mopboard and feeling the heady rush of loosened anger. What I really wanted to do was destroy something of Megan's. Roaring out of my room and into hers, I was confronted with her usual clutter of toys and clothes. Groping in the half-light, I found her tiger cat. Midst the rest of the mess, it had been carefully tucked into her doll's bed. I snatched it up. Stupid Megan, nearly ten years old and still sleeping with a stuffed animal.

Where would my parents have been, I thought, if Megan had been born first and not me? What would Dad do with no one to take care of Mama for him all the time? No slave labor around the house?

Fiercely, I stalked out of the room, taking the tiger cat with me. I was going to hide it from her. I would hide it and never give it back. She could cry and cry and I wouldn't tell her where I'd put it. Dropping the stuffed animal, I kicked it like a football. It hit the far wall and fell with a muffled thunk onto my dresser. I would flush it in the toilet. Ruin it forever. I grabbed one stuffed leg and flung the animal against the door. I stepped on it, right in the belly. I would toss it on the roof. Then nobody could get it down because we didn't have a long enough ladder. Then it'd be gone for good.

Bending down, I picked it up. Megan called it Big

Cattie. Trust Megan to think up an original name like that. Big Cattie. I touched the fur. It was soft. Mama had bought it for Megan. It was made by Steiff and it'd cost a lot of money. Far more money than we could afford to spend on toys. But Mama bought it anyway, making us all eat hamburger for God knows how long. She'd had a Steiff rabbit in the same shape when she was a little girl, she explained. Mutti's mother had sent it from Meissen one year for her birthday. Mama had named it Hansi. She didn't know what had happened to it. Although she'd searched through the house when she and Daddy went back after the war, she'd never found it.

I stroked the fur. It was so soft. I hugged it. Smoothing back the big round ears, I examined it carefully. Its face was remarkably realistic. All of Megan's loving attention hadn't harmed it yet.

Mama had bought it for her the year Megs was held back in school. I wasn't allowed to say she flunked. Mama became furious with me when I said Megan had flunked. She hadn't. Mama was adamant about that. Megan was just littler than most of the kids, Mama said, because her birthday was in August and that made her the baby in the class and didn't give her a fair chance. Besides, we had just moved during that summer, and the school Megan had gone to in Washington wasn't very good, Mama told me. So that was the reason the school people in North Platte thought Megan ought to go into first grade again instead of second. And Mama bought Megan Big Cattie because Megan was still crying about it in the night.

Gently, I held the animal against me, rocking it a little, like Mama was doing downstairs with Megan, cradling her and wiping her bleeding lip.

Then my father walked in. He had not knocked.

I was feeling considerably less angry. My rage had fizzled like a small camp fire after a drenching. In its place was sheer, undiluted misery.

"Just what is the matter with you, Lesley?" my father asked. He shut the door firmly behind him.

I had sat down on the bed. I didn't answer him.

"What do you have to say for yourself?"

"Didn't you see Megan? She was throwing food at me."

One eyebrow raised. "And so you think that gives you the right to half kill her? Honestly, Les, I don't expect that kind of behavior from you."

I pressed the tiger against me, feeling its solid but inanimate weight.

"Look at me when I'm talking to you."

I lifted my head.

"You're a big girl, Lesley. I don't expect you to act like a child. Megan's half your age. But you, you're growing up. You're no child."

I began to cry.

He sputtered. He was angry with me, and I think he had assumed I'd still be angry too. In a gesture of frustration he flapped his hands. Another baffled sputter followed.

"What *is* the matter with you?" he asked.

I couldn't answer.

My father continued to stand over me. Folding his arms, he shook his head. I couldn't stop crying, so he unfolded them again. There was another disgruntled flap of his hands, and then he sat down on the bed beside me.

"It's not all that bad, is it?" he asked, his voice a little more gentle.

"I wanted a birthday cake."

"A birthday cake? A *birthday* cake? All this is over a birthday cake, Lesley?"

"Daddy, it is my birthday."

"Well, yes, of course it is, but—"

"Daddy, I just wanted something special. I just wanted someone to do something special for *me.*"

"Oh honey," he said and reached an arm around my shoulder. His sudden tenderness I found harder to bear than his anger. The tears intensified, and I kept the stuffed animal pressed against me like a nursing child.

"We did get you a present, remember," he said, his voice buoyant with mock lightheartedness. "You ought to have seen Meggie going down to get that for you. She had it all planned out. Because she knew how long the days have been for you. It was her very own idea."

I felt like telling him that it was not too difficult to discern that the book had been a nine-year-old's idea of a present.

I caressed the tiger, pushing its soft ears back. The tears remained, blurring my vision, clogging my throat, running down along my cheeks and dripping into the orange plush fur of the stuffed animal.

"Dad," I said, "you have to do something."

"About Megan?"

I shook my head. "No. About Mama. About this. I can't keep going on like this. I want to go back to school. I want to be with my friends again and be like other kids."

"Oh sweetheart, I know it's hard on you." He pulled me over against him with one arm and brought the other up to encircle me. "I know you've had a lot of responsibility."

"But what are we going to do about it? I just can't stand to go on like this forever, baby-sitting Mama."

"Yes, yes, I know," he said and hugged me. He had me almost sitting in his lap, and the tiger cat was squashed in the embrace between us.

"But what are we going to *do?*"

"Shhh. Shh. Don't cry." His arms were strong and solid and warm around me. Against his flannel shirt, I was enveloped in his man's fragrance, deep and faintly musky with sweat. It was such an evocative scent, bringing with it memories of thousands of childhood hugs. I stirred to speak but he pressed my face down against him. "Shhhh. Shh. Shh. You're just tired, love. It's been hard and you're just tired, that's all."

"It isn't, Daddy."

"Hush, lovey. Just relax. I know. I know how you feel. But everything's okay. Just relax."

I did relax, and the tears got worse instead of better. I let him hold me. He had a powerful embrace for such a small man. It was easy to listen to him and his tender words, especially then when I was feeling so frail and unprotected. I relaxed into the safe warm strength of his arms much the way I suspect my mother must have done so often when he comforted her.

"We're so lucky," he whispered into my hair. "I love you so much. We all love each other. Each one of us. We're such a lucky family, to have so much love."

I struggled for a deep breath and kept my eyes closed. I could hear the staticky sound of hairs crinkling as I was pressed tighter against his chest.

"We're so lucky," he whispered.

What a wizard my father was. Because luckless as I felt, he still made me believe he was right.

# Seventeen

THE NEXT MORNING while Mama was still asleep, I went down to the bank to cash the bond. For a moment I feared that the man behind the counter was not going to do it. Even worse, I thought he was going to call my father. It's mine, I told him. My grandma gave it to me. For going to college. It's in my name and it matures on my eighteenth birthday. Yesterday. I pulled out my driver's license and looked him right in the eye as I spoke. Everything I said was the truth anyway.

After several minutes of dithering over it, he went into a back room. When he came out, he asked how I wanted it paid. Did I have an account? No, I replied. I wanted cash. That made him halt again, and once more he disappeared into the back room. Then a second man came out. He asked for identification, where I lived, what kinds of banking my parents did. I showed my driver's license again and my student I.D. card. I said my father banked with them but that the money wasn't supposed to go into his account. It was my money. For college. And I needed it immediately. What about a cashier's check, the first man asked. No, I said. I wanted cash. After more twittering between them and a third disappearance into the back room, they cashed it. I left with ten hundred-dollar bills.

Once outside the bank I fell back against the stone wall

and gasped with relief. My hands were shaking. My
heart thudded in my throat.

"Do you sell tickets to Wales?" I asked. It was the
only travel agency in town. The girl behind the counter
didn't look much older than me. Sitting at a typewriter,
she was doing her nails. There was no one else in the
cramped, cluttered office.

"Whales? You mean like at Marineland in California?"

"Wales, not whales. Like in Great Britain. You know.
Can I buy a ticket here to go there?"

Confusion still touched her features as she rose from
the desk. She fished out a thick book resembling a telephone directory and came over to the high counter where
I was standing.

"When do you want to go? A regularly scheduled
flight? Charter? This is the shoulder season. You want it
for now or in the high? You want to connect internally?"
she asked, leaning over the book. She was chewing gum
with the elegance of a camel.

Staring blankly, I shook my head. I had no clue as to
what she was talking about. Carefully, I tried to explain
what I wanted, that I needed to get from here to Wales. I
tried to tell her the name of the village near Forest of
Flowers, but I had no notion of how to spell its lyrical,
foreign-sounding name. Which did not matter much
since Wales was not listed in her book anyway.

"You'll have to go through London," she said and
popped the gum. Fingers on a pocket calculator, she
added sums. "$834.97." She held up the calculator for
me to see.

"For four?" I asked.

She laughed. It was a loud, snorty guffaw. "Nah. For
one." When she saw my face, her expression softened.
"It is terrible, isn't it?"

"Can you do it cheaper than that? I have to get there.

See, I'm taking my mother . . ." I watched her eyes. "But I only have a thousand dollars. Isn't there a cheaper way?"

"Well," she replied, opening the thick directory again. "Let me have a look. Can you stop back later? Give me some time to try and figure something out."

When I returned home, Mama was up. She had washed her hair and was sitting in the sunshine on the back step, toweling it dry. My mother had a fixation about clean hair. Every single day she had to wash it. Sometimes, if she'd been out walking or working in the garden, she washed it twice.

"Look here, Mama," I said and sat down on the step beside her. "I have money. For us to go to Wales."

Her brow furrowed with suspicion when she saw the money.

I laughed. "I didn't rob a bank, if that's what you're thinking. It's from my bond. The one Grandma gave me. Remember? It's a thousand dollars. Look at it. A whole thousand dollars."

Her forehead was still wrinkled with concern as she reached over and touched the money. I don't think she'd ever seen that much either. "Your grandmother wouldn't want you spending it this way," she said, her voice cautious.

"Grandma's not here to mind, is she? Besides, you know Grandma. If it'd make me happy, it'd make her happy."

"Not this." Mama was still touching the money, her fingers gingerly running over the edges of the bills in my hand. "What about university? Don't you want to go to university and study languages?"

"Don't worry. I'll still go. I'll just have to work, that's all. But in the meantime, we'll go to Wales."

"But will you still go to university?" Her eyes were full of concern. "It's very important that you do, you know. I want you to. I went. Popi always said how you should never waste a gift you've been given. And he was right. You see, you're very bright. You'll go and you'll finish, *ja?* I didn't finish. But I want you to."

"Yes, Mama, I will. Don't worry about it, okay?" I smiled and bumped against her shoulder affectionately. "But this money is for us. For you and me and Daddy and Meggie to take a vacation to Forest of Flowers."

That night Paul came over. He and Gary and Aaron had been out rat shooting earlier in the evening. They would go down to the dump after dark and shine the headlights of the car toward the piles of garbage. Then they'd sit on the hood of the car and pick off rats with their .22s. Paul and Aaron went out two or three times a week in warm weather. Sometimes Aaron's latest girl friend, Marie, went along with them. But I couldn't bear even to think about it, much less go. I always felt sorry for the rats.

Paul had let off Aaron and Gary before coming over. But he was still wearing his denim overalls, rat-shooting clothes, he called them, when he arrived.

Mama and Daddy were in the living room playing a game of cards with Megan. I had been upstairs in my room waiting for him. Coming in, Paul sat down on the arm of the couch and watched the game over Megan's shoulder until she told him to buzz off. He laughed, thumped her playfully on the side of the head and moved over to sit next to Mama.

Paul and my mother got on terrifically well despite my misgivings about her scaring him off with her nutty behavior. In truth, he seemed to get on better with her than I did. He teased Mama constantly, telling her things like he was going to run away with her to Mexico and leave me behind. Mama would laugh and tell him he was too old for her. Other occasions she could mimic his voice exactly and put him into fits of hysterics. And once when

Paul was visiting, she rolled up the legs of her pants and danced in her socks for him. I was embarrassed beyond being able to stay in the room with them, but Paul was laughing and dancing with her.

"Can I go out?" I asked my parents. "We won't be long." Paul was picking out cards from Mama's hand and putting them down on the table.

Dad nodded, not paying much attention. Gleefully, he laid down his cards. "I'm out. I win."

Before we left, I made Paul bring the guns in and lean them against the wall by the hall closet. It made me nervous to have them and all the ammunition around me. I told him I certainly was not about to ride all over creation with that stuff in the car. Paul rolled his eyes about it, but he acquiesced.

As soon as we were in the car, we kissed. Paul put his arms around me and pulled me against him. "Jesus, it seems like forever," he whispered. We clung to one another in the light-and-shadows darkness created by the streetlight. "When are you ever going to come back to school? It seems like you've been gone for months."

"It feels like months, believe me."

Another kiss, long and slow and greedy. Then Paul straightened up and put the keys into the ignition. He started the car.

I turned my head to watch our house disappear as the car rounded the corner. "This seems like another life."

"Where do you want to go?" Paul asked.

"This is just like I walk out of one life and into another. And then out of this one and back into that one. You can't imagine it. It's like being two people sometimes."

"Do you want to go riding? Or shall we do something in particular? Want to go to the Astra? That Burt Reynolds movie's still on. Aaron's seen it twice."

Silence. I hadn't meant to pay no attention to what he

was saying. I turned away from the window and looked at him. The silence suddenly filled with things not being said.

"So," Paul said slowly, "how is your mom?"

I shrugged.

"She isn't really depressed, is she?"

"Depression's tricky, Paul. You can't always tell when someone's suffering from it. Believe me. I'm getting to know a lot about these things."

"Yeah, but come off it, Les. You're not fooling me. She's not depressed. Not your mom. Not the way she acts. If she's depressed, then the rest of us got to be dead by comparison. I know about these things too."

"Let's not spend the whole night discussing my mother, okay? The object of this is for me to get away from Mama for once, not take her with me."

Paul nodded.

Coming to the end of Third Street, he turned the car out onto the highway. In no time at all we'd left the lights of town behind and were swallowed up in darkness.

"Let's not go to Ladder Creek," I said.

"Where do you want to go then?"

I shrugged. "Don't you know anyplace different for a change? I'm tired of going to Ladder Creek all the time."

"It probably wouldn't be much good our going over to my house. Aaron's got Maria over. And Gary's there. He's helping Mom sort her junk out from Dad's."

"I don't particularly want to go there either. I just want to get away to someplace entirely different. Go somewhere I've never been. I'm feeling really bored tonight. I want to get away from all the old stuff."

The car picked up speed. We were heading westward and there was no one else on the highway for as far as we could see.

"Aaron's going to live with my mom after the divorce," Paul said.

"Where are you going to live?"

"With neither one, thank God. I'm going away to school, remember?"

"But I mean on vacations and stuff. Where will you go then?"

Paul shrugged. "My mom says if I don't take my telescope with me, then I'm going to have to sell it. She says there won't be any room for that kind of stuff in her new apartment. I can go back there on vacations. That's what she said. But I'm not going to have a room of my own. She says there's no point when I'm gone nine-tenths of the time anyway. So she said the telescope would have to go."

"Couldn't you just dismantle it?" I asked. "We could use the parts on that other telescope. The one you and I are going to build. You know, the big one that we got the lenses for."

Lifting one hand off the steering wheel, he chewed a hangnail on his little finger. His eyes remained on the road. "I don't know if we're ever going to get it built."

"Sure we will," I said.

Neither of us spoke for quite a while. My thoughts were pulled back to the night of Claire's party and the first time we had gone out. I remembered how riding through the darkness had made me feel so good that night. Ages seemed to have passed since then.

"We could go to New Mexico," I said.

"Huh?" He glanced over, perplexed.

"If we stay on this road. We could go to New Mexico."

"We'd go to Colorado first. Actually, if we stayed on this road, we'd end up in California."

"Well, we'd go somewhere. Somewhere else besides here. We could go on and on and on and just not turn back."

Paul looked over. "You want to?" I couldn't tell if he was serious.

I smiled and lifted my shoulders. "I wouldn't mind."

A brief pause followed and I looked out the side window.

"We could run away," I said and my breath fogged the glass in the window. "We could go to California and live on the beach. And you could bring your telescope and study the stars and I'd support us by being a beachcomber. And we could forget about everybody except ourselves."

Paul reached his hand over and took mine. Squeezing it, he smiled at me.

I leaned back against the seat. "I got to admit, it's Mama I want to run away from," I said. I stared at the shadowy pattern of dots in the vinyl on the ceiling. "I'm so sick to death of my mama and her weird ways."

Silence.

Around us the plains stretched forever in all directions. It was a clear night and only the stars differentiated the sky from the earth. Occasionally there would be a light near a farmhouse but otherwise, there was nothing but blackness and stars and the small path forged by the headlights.

"You mind if I say something a little personal, Les?" Paul asked. His voice was quiet, almost disembodied in the darkness.

"What's that?"

"I think maybe you're a little too sensitive about your mother."

"Let's not talk about it. I don't even want to think about Mama tonight."

"Yeah, but you are anyway, aren't you?" he said. His voice was still very soft. "I mean it, Les. I think maybe you've gotten too focused in the fact that your mom is different. She is. But I don't think there's anything wrong with that. I mean, geez, I think it's fantastic. She's got all this energy, you know, she's really alive. A hundred percent alive. Not like most adults. Sure not like my folks."

"There's more to it than that, Paul."

"I think you're lucky. Your mother has such a joy about life. And she's got her own thoughts. She doesn't wait around for television or something to cram what she's supposed to be thinking into her head. She's got originality."

"She's got that, all right."

"Yeah, but what I'm saying is that that's *super*. You're too close to the trees to see the forest, Les. Not to put you down or anything. But I think she's just this really creative, alive person. A genuine nonconformist. So maybe she is different, but there's nothing wrong with that. It doesn't mean she has problems. I think you ought to appreciate your mother more. She's not so bad. And I just don't think she's really got such problems."

I looked over at him in astonishment. "What a lot of gall you have, Paul. Christ. Where do you come off saying something like that to me? What do you know about it? She's *my* mother. What do you think having problems means? Hanging from the curtain rods by your toenails? Running naked through the streets? This isn't a subject you know one thing about, Paul, so don't go setting yourself up as an expert."

"I'm not setting myself up as an expert. I just said I thought you were too sensitive and I still do. I mean, I can understand where you got trouble. You live with her and stuff and I know what that's like. I probably don't see my family very clearly either. You just don't when you live with people. Which is why I'm telling you this. I understand."

"I don't particularly want your understanding, because you don't understand a thing. My little sister knows more about it than you do. Maybe you got brains galore on everything else, but on this subject, you're a zero. So, I don't think you're in any position to judge."

Silence.

"Besides," I said, "if I'm just being hypersensitive, what am I staying home for all the time? Am I making that up too? Does that mean my dad's as blind about my mother as I am, Professor?"

"I don't know," Paul said. "Why *are* you staying home?"

I didn't reply. Weariness overtook my irritation and pushed me to the verge of tears. Desperate not to have another evening end with my crying, I said nothing more.

Paul, alert to my discomfort, reached a hand out and touched my leg. "Well, let's not get into an argument. It's not that important."

"It seems to me like we're already arguing."

"Okay, listen, Les, I'm sorry. I started it. I apologize. Let's just forget it."

Rubbing my hands over my face, I let out a long, slow breath. "It's just that I want to get through one evening without Mama dogging every moment of freedom I have."

"Okay. I understand."

Paul pushed a tape into the car tapedeck. *Star Wars*. It was the only music expansive enough to fill the darkness. He grinned at me, his features made ghostly by the green dimness of the dashboard lights. He pressed his foot down on the accelerator, and we tore off into hyperspace.

We drove all the way to Eads, Colorado, almost a hundred miles across the dark plains. It made no difference. It was as flat there as anywhere and looked very much like where we had been. I was disappointed. Whenever I thought about Colorado, I pictured lakes and forests and towering mountains. But Eads was surrounded by the same open loneliness as all of western Kansas.

We were still talking space talk, still being Luke

Skywalker and Princess Leia when Paul pulled into a drive-in and ordered us hot-fudge sundaes. We couldn't remember any *Star Wars* names for food, so we made up our own. Paul kept his arm around me, pressing me close against his side as we waited for the carhop to bring out the order. The drive-in, empty of other cars, was a little island of orangish fluorescent brightness against the darkness. We had a deep discussion about whether the carhop, when she finally appeared, was an alien foe in disguise at our spaceport. Perhaps we should zap her. By the time she arrived at the car, we were dissolved in fits of laughter.

Instead of eating the sundaes at the drive-in, we drove to a nearby roadside park and got out of the car. Paul left the tape playing and the window down so we could hear it. We sat shivering at the picnic table, and devoured ice cream in the chilly April darkness.

After he finished his sundae, Paul folded his hands over the empty plastic dish and watched me.

He smiled.

I smiled back. Savoring the flavors and the almost painfully pleasant contrast of the hot fudge against the cold ice cream, I was still eating. I leaned across the table to give him a kiss tasting of ice cream.

He returned the kiss. Rising up and clasping my face in both his hands, he pressed his lips heavily against mine. His kisses grew wet and urgent and within moments, Paul was on the table between us. Hands now tangled through my hair, he kissed my lips, my jawline, my neck. Keen to avoid his collision with my ice-cream dish, I whisked it aside.

"I got Aaron's thermos along," he whispered. I didn't understand immediately. But when he reached into his pocket, I knew what he meant. The thermos filled with condoms. "Your birthday present," he said.

We moved down onto the grass in an almost fluid way,

arms still around one another. Or perhaps because I was not concerned about it, even an obstacle as clumsy as a picnic table was not noticeable.

The tape came to its end and stopped. Paul turned his head and I felt his muscles tense in readiness to get up and change it over to the other side. Touching his face, I said leave it. I didn't want more *Star Wars*. This wasn't a children's game. I wasn't pretending anymore.

We cuddled in the long grass, still untrimmed since winter. Paul's hands moved with confident tenderness over familiar territory. He undid each button of my blouse, then slipped it from my shoulders. The night air was too cold to be comfortable and I pressed against him. His kisses were everywhere. Pleasantly aroused, I found my way beneath his loose-fitting overalls.

It wasn't until Paul paused to put on the condom that it really occurred to me what was happening. *This is it*, I thought, lying in the grass beside him. The thought came to me in a startlingly cold-blooded way. Whatever arousal I had felt before he took out the condom quickly faded. His penis looked huge. Although I had seen it before, this time I couldn't help but stare. What was it going to be like? Was it going to hurt? What if I did it wrong? Was I going to make stupid noises? Was someone going to hear us? I had read about that in books, about how women, in particular, would lose control and abandon themselves to writhing and screaming ecstasy. At least that's what they were forever doing in Megan's novel. I began thinking that maybe we ought to put the *Star Wars* tape back on because I was just a little concerned about having quite so much ecstasy within yards of a public highway.

Paul lay down beside me again and took me in his arms.

"You do want to do it, don't you?" he asked and I knew he had sensed my tension.

"Yeah."

"You're sure?"

I nodded. I did. But I was a lot more scared than I had anticipated.

We returned to gentle petting, and I hoped I'd recapture the relaxed pleasure I usually felt with Paul. But the disconcertingly detached feeling remained. My body responded but my mind drew back, tense, alert, aware, like an unrelated observer.

With meditative slowness Paul touched me. I wondered if it was his first time too. I'd never asked, mostly because I had assumed I was his first serious girl friend and if I wasn't, I didn't want to know. But now I wondered, because although his movements were slow and studied, he seemed a lot more sure of himself than I felt just then.

My body began responding with an unnerving urgency of its own. Paul's fingers became electric and sent out tickling currents every time he touched me. The sensation would have been pleasurable, I think, if I could have relaxed more but as it was, it was too intense. Without meaning to, I jumped when he touched the small of my back. It startled him, and he pulled himself up to look at me. I grinned and shook my head and kissed his hand.

Then I felt him enter. It hurt. Not badly but more than I had expected. Again I jerked under him and he had to try a second time. He lay atop me and his weight helped calm the sensitivity in my skin. Knowing what to expect, I could relax a little more, and it didn't hurt so much when he tried again. It still didn't feel particularly wonderful but it grew better.

Paul came very quickly. Almost before he was all the way in, I could feel the warmth swell inside the condom. It was a luxurious sensation, subtle and deep and by far the pleasantest I had experienced since we'd begun. Moaning, Paul clasped me to him tightly. The tension in my body drained away, and I felt very much in love with him.

We returned to necking for a while before relaxing into the damp grass, grown warm with the heat of our bodies. The air around us was full of a deep, ripe odor like the smell of apples, only heavier, and with a faint saline scent underlying it. It was a good odor and I inhaled it repeatedly, trying to decode it. The sharp, electric sensitivity had faded entirely, and I felt warm and happy. Paul kept his arms wrapped around me, but his eyes were closed. He was smiling faintly. I lay, watching him. He wasn't asleep but he was very, very still. His penis had retracted up close to his body, and the condom hung loose and full. I touched it gently with my fingertip, and he smiled again but still did not open his eyes.

Paul didn't seem to want to rouse himself very quickly, so with his arms still around me to ward off the night chill, I lay quietly and thought about the experience. Did it take practice? I had thought I was going to enjoy it more than I had. Had I done something wrong? Or did it just take a while to get it right? I wondered why my skin had grown so hypersensitive. I wondered why instead of sinking into the usual relaxed and sensual pleasure I got from petting, my mind had leaped to such absurd alertness. Turning on my back, I peered up through the branches of the trees to see the stars.

I was no stranger to sex. I could hear my parents making love quite often. The house was just too small not to. They weren't noisy about it, but if you were in the study at the wrong moment, you could overhear them very plainly. They would laugh together intimately and giggle. It made Mama incredibly talkative. She would say very silly things to my father, not at all the kind of things I was used to hearing out of her. She talked a kind of baby talk to him, as if she were a little girl. I never really heard my father's responses because his voice was too deep to carry when he spoke softly. But it embarrassed me to hear my mother talk like that, more than overhearing the actual sex act did.

Anyway, I was thinking, I had never heard Mama screaming and writhing in ecstasy either. Probably no one did except in books.

Then with painful suddenness the thoughts all melted together. Making love, screaming, my mother. They had raped her, and she had been a virgin. Like I had been tonight. Only not in the arms of an innocent lover. I sat up sharply.

Paul opened his eyes. "What's wrong?"

I tried to clear the images from my mind.

"What's wrong, Lesley?" he asked again and there was concern in his eyes. He thought he had done something. He thought he had hurt me, that he'd done it wrong, that I hadn't wanted to.

I shook my head. "It's nothing," I said. But the mood was ruined. The warmth dissipated into chilly spring dampness. Paul remained troubled.

"Are you sure?" He picked up his overalls and put them on.

I nodded.

"Was it okay for you? Did you like it?" he asked.

Again, I nodded.

He bent and kissed the top of my head. "I love you."

Still cold and exposed without my clothes, still on the grass, I nodded a third time. I meant to say it back to him. I meant to tell him I loved him too. But I could only manage to nod.

# Eighteen

On Saturday afternoon I went down to Torres Café with Brianna. Dad was out in the backyard mowing the lawn, so I told Mama, who was in the kitchen making a rhubarb pie, that I would be home around supper time.

I hadn't been seeing much of Brianna or Claire or my other girl friends, mostly because of having to stay home from school with Mama, but also because I was usually spending what free time I had with Paul. So Brianna and I met at Torres Café, where we could sit for hours over just a Coke and an order of French fries and not be hassled to buy more, and caught up on all the news. I told her all about my night in Eads with Paul, about the interminable boredom of being home from school every day, about trying to keep up with my homework, about having to give up my two nights' work at the nursing home each week because it was impossible to coordinate with everything else going on, and how Mrs. Morton, the nursing-home director, had said she wasn't sure that she could promise me a full-time position in the summer if I quit for the rest of the spring. Brianna, in turn, caught me up on the gossip from school. Mainly, Brianna told about Jenny Soames and the fact that her parents were sending her off east somewhere instead of to the university like she'd planned. Brianna thought Jenny was pregnant.

"You want to go over to my place?" I asked. It was

about 4:30, and Brianna was counting out change to see if she had enough to buy us more Cokes. "I think we got some Coke in the refrigerator. I know we got Mountain Dew. That's what my stupid sister drinks."

Brianna wrinkled her nose.

"Maybe I can get us some corn chips. I think I saw Mama get corn chips last time at the supermarket. You want to come over? We can sit outside on the steps and you can tell me about Danny. You think he's going to maybe ask you out?"

As we turned the corner onto my street, Brianna nudged me. "Look, Les," she said. "There's a police car in front of your house."

I froze.

Brianna also stopped.

"Listen, Bri," I said as calmly as I was able, "do you think you'd mind, if—well—if you didn't come over right now?"

"What's happening?" Her voice was hushed.

"I don't know."

We were standing at the corner. I gazed at the police car. It was definitely at my house. I could see one of the officers in the doorway.

"Don't say anything about this, okay?" I asked. "Don't tell anybody."

"I understand," she said, and I knew she did. Her dad tippled a bit after paydays, and he was always getting brought home by the police.

"Promise me, Bri. Promise not to tell, okay?"

She nodded. "Okay. I promise." Then with one more look at the police car, she turned and went back down Bailey Street.

Megan was sitting on the back steps, crying. I'd gone around to the back door to go in and found her there, all hunched up. "They've arrested Mama," she said.

"How? What happened?"

"She got out. When Daddy was trimming the grass over by the lilacs. She went over to the Watermans and then she tried to make Toby go with her. They called the police."

"Oh geez." I sat down beside her. I could hear heated voices coming from the living room. "Who all's in there?"

"The policemen. And Daddy. And Mr. Waterman's there and it's awful."

"Is Mama there too?"

"No," Megan wailed. "They got her in jail."

"Now look, Megs, don't cry. That's not going to do any good, is it?" I said, although I didn't sound very convincing.

Car doors slammed out front and an engine started. A short time later my father appeared at the back door. We moved over on the step so that he could get the door open, and he stepped out between us.

"We have to go down to the police station and get your mother."

"Megan said they arrested her and put her in jail."

He shook his head. "No. They just took her down there. But I'll have to pay a fine for harassment the next time it happens." He frowned and looked off across the lawn at all his mowing and trimming tools, lying in disarray. "I had to agree to have her see a psychiatrist. Mr. Waterman was going to press charges. The only way I could get him to drop them was to promise him I'd make her see a psychiatrist. The police are going to set up an appointment at the mental health clinic in Garden City."

When we arrived at the police station, we found Mama sitting on a long wooden bench in front of the sergeant's desk. Someone had given her a cup of coffee in a white Styrofoam cup. She sat, holding it, staring into the liquid. My father leaned over the desk and talked with the policeman behind it. They had a handful of papers for him to look at. Someone was phoning the mental health clinic. Good; there's a Monday cancellation, he said to my father. Dr. Carrera. Monday morning at ten. Yes, all right, my father was saying, his voice soft and deferential, he'd see she got there.

Apparently, it had taken all the effort my mother could muster to stay composed in the police station. The moment she got the door to the car shut, she burst into tears. My father leaned over and wrapped his arms around her, pushing her face into his shirt. We sat for several minutes in the police parking lot while he comforted her. Mama was trying to say something through her sobbing, but from the backseat I couldn't understand. No, Dad was saying to her in a gentle voice, the police aren't like that here. This is America, Mara. There's no one who wants to hurt you.

How my mother had managed to hold herself together in the police station, I couldn't imagine, because she had obviously been terrified. Once able to release the tension, she sobbed against my father's side all the way back to the house. At home in our kitchen with Daddy's arm around her, she still could not stop. Shaking and crying, she threw up the coffee she'd drunk into the kitchen sink.

Megan and I watched, terror stricken ourselves. To see my mama retch into the sink from the sheer fear of being inside our little two-room police station left me in awe of the inescapability of her past.

My father tried to calm her. Sitting her down in a kitchen chair, he wiped her face with the dishcloth from the sink. He was down on one knee, his hands pushing back her hair. But nothing did any good.

Rising finally, he put a hand under Mama's elbow and brought her to her feet, and they went upstairs to their bedroom. For once I was grateful for the sound of their door closing. Mama's sobbing became only a distant murmur, like the running of a washing machine.

Megan and I went out in the backyard. I brought out the things I'd intended to get for Brianna and me—the corn chips, dip, pretzels, Megan's Mountain Dew.

Megan lay back on the freshly mown grass. Her arms were behind her head, and she gazed up into the leaves of the elm tree. "What's going to happen to us now?" she asked and looked over. "Is Mama always going to be like this from now on? Is she going to keep thinking that little boy is her son forever?"

"No," I said. "I don't think so. If we can figure out something to do, she'll forget it. I think she just doesn't have enough other things to think about."

"But *why* does she do it? Why can't she understand he isn't Klaus?"

I shrugged. "I don't know. She misses Klaus, I guess. She misses him so much that she can't get him out of her mind."

Megan fell silent. She reached across to get a pretzel out of the box, and when she had it, broke it up into dozens of small pieces. One at a time she threw them to a robin hopping on the grass nearby. "What do you think has happened to the real Klaus?"

"No idea."

"Do you think he's still alive?" she asked.

"Probably. He wouldn't be really old yet. In his thirties or so. But not Toby's age, that's for sure. Not needing a mama."

Megan took another pretzel. "Les, is he really our brother, this Klaus? Really, truly?"

"Our half brother."

"It's weird to think about, isn't it? That there's somebody else walking around who's part of our family. Who's related to us." She paused. "What about the other baby? Didn't Daddy say there were two?"

"Yes, but I don't know anything about him. I don't even know his name."

"It's weird to think about. Really super weird."

We lay in the grass without speaking. I munched my way through half a package of corn chips and most of the can of bean dip. When I had emptied the package, I scooped out the remaining dip with my finger. I was surprisingly hungry.

"Les?" said Megan, rolling over on her stomach.

"Hmm?"

"I want to ask you something."

"So, ask."

"Well," she said, "if that was us, do you think Mama would have tried this hard to find us?"

"You mean if it had been us the Nazis had taken away instead of Klaus?"

"Yeah."

I reached for my can of pop. "Probably. I don't think she'd ever want to lose us either. I think all Mama really wants is to have all her family together in one place, like they should be."

"I wonder sometimes," Megan said, "I wonder if because she's *got* us, she cares as much about you and me as she does about all the things she's lost."

"Well, she lost a lot, Megs. You have to be understanding."

"I do understand. I'm just saying that, well . . ." She paused over another pretzel. "Well . . . that sometimes inside me, I don't."

We stayed in the yard for the better part of two hours, until dusk came. Then we went inside. Megan settled in front of the TV to watch the Muppets. I stood in the front doorway and stared out into the street. Feeling heavy with the need to get away from the house, I decided to go over and see Paul.

Upstairs, I knocked gently on my parents' door. There had ceased to be any noise from their room quite a long time before, so I was very quiet in case they were both asleep.

"Come in," my father said, his voice barely above a whisper.

Carefully, I eased the door open. They were on the bed. The bedclothes were rumpled, and my parents lay on just the sheet. My father wore only his T-shirt. Mama had nothing on at all. His one arm stretched out across the sheet, my father lay on his right side with my mama curled up, lying very close to him, her head tucked down against his chest. Her hair was loose and hid her face, but I could tell she was asleep. Dad had his left hand over her, his arm on her arm and shoulder, his fingers twined through her hair. The room was very warm and humid, and he asked me to crack the window open for him. I did.

The sun had set, and the room was murky with April twilight.

"I was wondering if it would be all right for me to go over to Paul's," I asked, still standing by the window. A rush of cool air pushed into the room. "I called, and his mom said it's okay."

"What's Megan doing?" my father asked.

"Watching television."

"Have you two eaten?"

I nodded.

He gestured for me to hand him the top sheet, from the foot of the bed. I came and drew it up over them. "All right," he said. "But don't be too late, will you? And take your keys."

I nodded. "I will."

What I thought about as I walked to Paul's house was sex. Seeing my mother and father like that, I wondered how Mama could do it. How had my dad made sex good for her again? How was it that she could come home from the police station, hysterical with fear about their raping her, and a few hours later be in bed like that with my fa-

THE SUNFLOWER FOREST            211

ther? I couldn't fathom what kind of communication they had together. How had he managed to comfort her and breathe life back into her right in the center of the vortex? I wished I understood. I wished I could ask one of them, although I knew I never would.

Paul and I sat together on the curb in front of his house. A neighbor had been watering, and the gutter flowed with runoff. Paul made up little boats from leaves and twigs and set them sailing under our legs. Then he rested his face on his knees to watch them.

Behind us, Aaron's stereo blared. As always, it was so loud you could feel it if you were in the house. But outside where we were, it was tolerable. I found it a comfortingly normal sound.

"My family's driving me insane," I said, leaning down to trail my fingers in the water running alongside the curb.

"*Yours* is?" said Paul. "You ought to see what's going on around here. You know what my half-assed brother did today? You know Marianne MacAlister?"

"No, Paul," I interrupted. "I don't mean things like Aaron does. I mean insane. The real thing. The thing you get locked up in Larned for."

I told him. I told him precisely why I wasn't going to school. About Klaus and Toby Waterman. About my mama and the war. I think in a way he knew. Not the details. But he'd gotten the substance by osmosis.

He sat on the curb, feigning an interest in his leaf boats I knew he didn't have. I was unable to tell how shocked he was by what I was saying. At that point I didn't care. The need to share was so pressing to me that I had no room left to worry about anyone else.

"What I wish," I said, "is that my father would do something. I keep telling him that—that we ought to be doing something to change things. That we ought to have been doing something all along. But my father ignores me. He never does anything but hedge."

"But he's doing something now, isn't he?" Paul asked. "If your mother's going to see a psychiatrist."

"That's only because Mr. Waterman threatened to press charges if he didn't. He wouldn't have otherwise."

"But what more can he do than that?"

"I don't know. There's got to be something. Why do I have to think of it? He's the adult. He ought to know more about these things than I do."

I rested my cheek against my knee. The night was warm, and it being Saturday, the area was alive with activity. You could hear the cars zooming up and down Main Street a couple of blocks over.

Paul leaned forward and studied something on the street's surface. "You're lucky, though," he said. "You know what I think's so super about your family?"

"What?"

"That you all love each other. I mean, God, I've never seen two people who love each other like your mom and dad. You all do. You all love each other like mad, Lesley. You stay home with your mother, and your little sister is always trying to do things to help and everything. Believe me, you don't know how lucky that makes you. A million kids in this country would probably be more than happy to trade places with you, to have to put up with the problems your mother has, just to be in a family like yours."

"Are you *kidding?* Criminetly, Paul, is that what you seriously believe?"

"Yes," he said without looking up. "Most people would give anything to live in a family where everybody loves everybody else and they all know it. I sure would."

I sloshed my fingers through the water and said nothing.

"It isn't enough," I finally replied. "Love helps, but

it isn't enough. You've got to change things. You got to get out and find why things are wrong and make them better. That's where my dad and I are different. That's where he's wrong. If you're going to make the world better, you've got to change things. Daddy comes along and puts his arms around you and you *feel* better, but things aren't better. That's what he does with Mama. He hugs her and he kisses her and he makes her think she's wonderful. But she's still got all her problems. Nothing's changed."

"But how do you change that kind of stuff?"

I sighed. Watching the launching of another leaf boat, I sighed again. "I don't know. But there's got to be something."

# Nineteen

THE POLICE HAD PHONED down to the regional mental health center in Garden City on Saturday afternoon and made a Monday appointment for my mother to see one of the psychiatrists there. We all realized that Mama was going to be decidedly underwhelmed by this information. When my father and I met early Sunday morning outside the bathroom door, he said to me that he thought breakfast would be the best time to broach the subject with her. He reckoned the sooner she was told, the better, and Sunday morning breakfasts were always very relaxed. He said that if Mama got upset, he didn't want Megs or me to aggravate things by taking sides. Then he went down the hallway, back to their bedroom. Left standing outside the door, gripping my blow dryer, waiting for Megan to get out of the bathroom, I was filled with dread, convinced that the morning was doomed to deteriorate into a repeat of the horrific earlier scenes of hysteria. I wondered if I could get away with skipping breakfast altogether.

My father was capable of great gentleness. He had an innate sense, in particular, of how to touch you to convey a caring so deep it was almost raw. Hands on Mama's shoulders, he stood behind her as she sat at the kitchen table and he explained carefully how the police had released her on the condition that she go to this appointment, how Dr. Carrera was there to help her work out some of the things troubling her about Klaus and how she would eventually feel so much better for it. My mother sat with her elbows on the Sunday paper, her hands clasped together in front of her mouth. Her expression blackened. Even though he could not see her face from where he was, my father began to massage her shoulders. In a tender voice he said he had supported the decision to get some help for her.

Mama, as characteristically unpredictable as ever, showed no fright whatsoever. Instead, she exploded. Like a kitchen-sized atom bomb she went off, right then and there, without excusing herself and my father to another room, without telling Megs and me to leave them alone. There we all were together, having finished Sunday breakfast, all still absorbed in the leisurely business of having a second or third piece of toast and browsing through the newspaper, when my mother let go of a wrath that would have done justice to a betrayed warlord.

"Those bleeding motherfuckers! Are you on their side? They steal my son and you are standing there. *Agreeing* with them! Why the hell don't you help *me*, O'Malley? You big fucking bastard, whose side are you on?"

She roared up from the table, knocking my father's arms back. He moved away from her. First to one side of the kitchen, then around to the far side of the table. She pursued him, screaming furiously at him. She didn't need anybody's help working out what was troubling her about Klaus, she yelled. Nobody's help but my father's was needed. Because he was her husband and he was supposed to help her. So why was he just standing there? Why was he telling the policemen she would go to a psychiatrist? *He* was the one who needed a psychiatrist. To have his head examined. To see who had bewitched him.

To find out what kind of man he was, who wouldn't even stand by his wife.

I was afraid she was going to hit him. All the hitting I'd ever seen Mama do was confined to occasional smacks on the bottom when Megan and I were little, but just then, I thought she was going to hit my father. She grabbed hold of a chair by its back, and I closed my eyes. But when I opened them, she was still in the same spot, still holding on to the back of the chair. My father kept the table between them.

Embittered by our refusal to support her, by our recent treatment of her, as if she were an untrustworthy child, she raged at us, saying vicious, tortured things. All these weeks she had borne what was to her our humiliating, degrading treatment, all these weeks she had suffered our betrayal and had said nothing. Now the hurt and rage came spilling out of her like vomit.

Our unwillingness to help her reclaim Klaus had clearly caused her deepest wound. Time and again she came back to that point. Why had we abandoned her? She was right. She knew about these things. She understood these kinds of experiences better than any of us. Why wouldn't we trust her? How did we let ourselves be fooled by their dirty tricks? How had they convinced us to believe them and not her? She knew she was right, and she was horrified that they had the power to make the people she trusted most, suddenly desert her. Or was it just that we were weak people?

"I can't understand this! Why are you just standing there, O'Malley? You said you would help me get Klaus back. You promised me. You did, O'Malley. You swore you would. And now you betray me!"

Then abruptly she turned on me. "And what about you, you big lout? Why do you always sit there like shit in a bucket? Why don't you listen to what your mother tells you to do? You are soft. You are spoiled by this good life. You don't know what it's like to have people beat you every day, to have no food to eat except what you wouldn't give a dog here. You don't think it can happen to you. You're spoiled. You're nothing but a lazy lout."

I ducked my head and stared at the newspaper.

"Well, what do you say for yourself? You just sit there. Did I come out of Ravensbrück just to have a child like you? I might as well have died there. It would have been better. I can't understand you. I tried to make you a good person. Why won't you help me?"

"Because you aren't right about this, Mama," I said.

My father frowned and put a finger to his lips for me to keep quiet. Frustrated and upset, I lowered my head again.

Mama began at last to cry. They were hardly tears of defeat, however. She was still furious, but finally all three languages had failed her. Standing in the middle of the kitchen floor, she wept for several minutes, shoving the tears back roughly with her forearms, her fists clenched.

"You treat me like a child," she sobbed. "You all do. Even her, even the baby does," she said, gesturing toward Megan. "Don't you think I know how you treat me? Do you think I want this? Do you think I'm happy?"

I felt wretched. Mama had a good deal more insight into this dreadful situation than I had realized, and obviously we must have been crucifying her over these past weeks. There was no way to listen to her without being heartbroken. And there was no way not to listen to her.

"Why in God's name are you doing this to me? Why do you treat me like this? Like I'm defective. Like I'm stupid. *Ein Dummkopf. Bin ich ja kreuzdumm?* Eh, O'Malley? *Bin ich?*"

My father remained stoic. He was leaning back against the counter to the right of the stove. He stood, hands on his thighs, and studied the linoleum. He did not look at her. He did not refute anything she said. He did not answer her questions. He just stood. I felt sorry for him. He was the recipient of almost all my mother's anger, and she grew so provocative that I found it difficult not to come to his defense. But I didn't. I knew only his exterior was calm, and that if I said anything, it would be me he'd get angry with.

The whole of that Sunday morning was excruciating. Mama went on and on and on without pause from breakfast time until nearly half past eleven. Still choked with tears, she raged and cursed and cried. It was like having a septic sore burst, pus running everywhere, only to discover that the pain that followed was worse than the pain before. Megan sat petrified over the comics section of the newspaper. Her knuckles had gone white where she gripped the edge; her eyes went back and forth over the panels of Charlie Brown and Snoopy and Lucy. Back and forth, back and forth, back and forth. Otherwise, she was entirely motionless. I couldn't keep myself that still. Muscles twitched. I became acutely aware of needing to use the toilet as the morning wore on. My feet were cold. But like Megan, I didn't dare move. And eventually, I went numb, body, soul and spirit.

In the end Mama broke down into sobs, heavy with weariness. She sagged into a chair across the table from me, covered her face with her hands and wept. The three of us all remained frozen, watching. No one dared touch her. She sat only a few moments, then rose and left the room. We heard her go upstairs, come down again, rattle around in the back cupboard and finally go outside. And still we remained silent and immobile.

My mother spent the rest of the morning and the early afternoon in the garden. On her knees, she fiercely ripped weeds from the flower beds. Her face was smudged from where she had wiped back tears with dirty hands.

Then in the late afternoon I again heard my parents, Dad once more explaining things to Mama. This time her voice was only plaintive. She was exhausted and unhappy and all she wanted from him was sympathy. Again she was in tears. My father continued on calmly, patiently, relentlessly, to explain how Mr. Waterman was going to get his lawyer, if she didn't go see Dr. Carrera. They were upstairs in their bedroom, and I could hear them through the open window as I sat on the lawn. I felt like screaming at them to shut up. But of course, I didn't.

Monday morning, I expected Mama to be, if not resigned, at least too worn out from all the hysteria on Sunday to be troublesome. She wasn't. The appointment was for ten in the morning, and when I came upstairs to tell her it was time, I found her sitting on the bed, absorbed in a book.

"Are you ready, Mama?" She wasn't. She was wearing a pair of old blue jeans and one of Dad's shirts with the sleeves rolled up.

"Mama, it's time to change. Come on now. Put the book down." I went over to the closet and sorted through her clothes. She didn't have a large assortment, mostly because her communal spirit kept her rifling through Dad's and my wardrobes. But there were a few nicer things, and Mama could look really beautiful when she tried.

"What about this?" I asked, taking out a pink wool dress. I turned around.

"No," she said, not lifting her head.

I put it back in the closet. "What about this brown skirt? Yes, this looks nice." I pulled it out. "You like this, Mama?"

"I don't want to wear that."

"You could have my white blouse to go with it. You

know. The one with the pointy collar. That would look nice with it.''

''No,'' she said, and I was not convinced that she'd even bothered to look up.

Piece by piece, I took out each garment. Piece by piece, she vetoed them.

''Look, Mama, you got to change your clothes. That's all there is to it. You can't go wearing stuff like that.''

''This is clean, what I've got on,'' she replied. ''If it's good enough for O'Malley to see me in, then it's good enough for that doctor.''

''Mama, this is different. You have to put nice clothes on. Clean clothes aren't enough. You try to look nice when you go to see a doctor like this.''

''These look nice.''

''They don't, Mama.''

''They're good enough.''

''Mama, they're *not*. Those jeans are all baggy and out of shape. Besides, you just don't go wearing jeans to something like this anyway. And you don't go wearing one of Daddy's shirts. It looks awful.''

She paid no attention to me.

''*Mama*. Please change your clothes. Do it for me, okay? For once I just want you to go out looking like everyone else's mother does.''

Nose in the book, she ignored me. I snatched the paperback up out of her hands. Erica Jong's *How to Save Your Own Life*.

''What are you reading a book like this for?'' I asked.

She shrugged and gave me a good-natured smile. ''Research?'' she offered and chortled.

I didn't think she was being particularly funny.

She stalled for so long that finally I had to physically boost her to her feet to get her moving. ''At least tuck the stupid shirt in,'' I said, grabbing the waistband of the jeans and stuffing the shirttail into the back. "Honest to Pete, you're worse than Megan sometimes."

The entire way to Garden City she sat silently, arms folded across her breasts in her warrior-goddess pose. I grew increasingly angry, not only about her continued resistance but also at my father for not doing this nasty chore himself. Anger, it seemed, was becoming our household emotion.

The mental health center was a new building, reaching out in two long arms around a graveled entrance drive. The reception area inside was brightly painted in primary colors. The woman behind the desk greeted us with more cheer than a Monday morning warranted. How had the journey been? Was the wind bad? Did it look like thunderstorms for the afternoon? Mama, in a sudden burst of friendliness, chatted enthusiastically with the receptionist. It occurred to me then what was happening. She was going to go in there, bright as a penny, and charm the damned socks off everyone. As I sat glumly in one of the waiting-room chairs and watched her operate, what came to my mind was the war. No wonder she had survived. She could roll with the punches. And this was just one punch more.

I sat and read out-of-date magazines while my mother spent an hour with Dr. Carrera and another hour with their psychometrist, taking various tests. Then Dr. Carrera and my mother came out into the waiting room. The doctor was a very tall man, older than Mama, and built like a football player, with powerful shoulders and a broad chest. He was handsome in a distinguished, Latin way, and dressed nicely in a well-tailored gray suit and crisp-looking white shirt. Only his tie seemed out of place. It was wide and bizarrely colored, which made me think he must have a good sense of humor or horrible taste in ties, or a kid like Megan at home, to buy him presents.

He shook my hand. "Your mother will be coming back to see me next week," he said and handed me a folded slip of paper. "In the meantime, here's a prescription for her."

"Will she be coming in the morning, like this?" I asked. "Or do you think we could have a different time? See, I'm having to take off from school to bring her down . . ."

"There's a late clinic on Wednesday nights. Until nine. Would that be better?" he asked.

"Yes," I said and smiled. Great. Then Dad would get stuck with bringing her.

The doctor walked all the way out to the car with us. For the first time my mood lifted. Perhaps we were finally accomplishing something. Dr. Carrera seemed pleasant and competent. Mama appeared to have gotten along well with him. They chatted genially together in the parking lot as I unlocked the car. They were discussing London. Mama was telling him about the roses in Regent's Park. He was saying his oldest son was living near there and studying drama.

We stopped at a drive-in for lunch. Mama, in exuberant spirits, suggested that we really treat ourselves. So we ordered the biggest hamburgers on the menu, as well as French fries and onion rings and some deep-fried mushrooms, an item I'd never seen offered on a drive-in menu before. They looked dreadful to me and tasted the way Megan's socks smelled, so Mama ended up eating them all.

We had a riotous time together in the car over lunch. Mama was telling me about the tests she had taken at the clinic, about the psychometrist, whose job it was to administer them. I had nearly forgotten what great fun my mother could be when she was in a good mood. That, in turn, made me realize how depressed her behavior, as well as mine, had been during the events of the last few weeks. But in a torrent of laughter, her stories and jokes came back.

I asked afterward if she wanted to go someplace. The day was gorgeous, and I was sick to death of being cooped up at home. With the car at our disposal, it seemed a pity to waste such a beautiful afternoon. Yes, she agreed, why not have a good time.

"Where do you want to go?" I asked.

She was pulling up the last of her milkshake through the straw. It made a raucous noise.

"The museum?"

She shook her head. "We can be indoors in our own house."

"Where then?" I asked. "You want to go shopping?"

"No," she said, as I had assumed she would. She never had been one to enjoy shopping.

"We could go to the zoo, I guess."

Mama laughed. "Go see Twinkle the Elephant," she said, mimicking an official-sounding voice. There had been numerous billboards on the highway coming into Garden City that commanded "Go see Twinkle the Elephant" at the local zoo. It surprised me that in spite of her aroused state on the trip down, she'd been reading billboards about elephants. I certainly hadn't.

In the end we decided to go to the reservoir. Neither of us was a devotee of elephants, and we couldn't think of any other interesting-sounding alternatives. So the reservoir it was.

"This is a very pretty place," Mama said to me. Picking up a stone, she lofted it into the water. The surface, already riffled by the wind, spread out in choppy rings. "When Klaus is back with us, we'll bring him out here. He'll love to play here."

"Mama," I said, "just for this once, let's halt the conversations about Klaus. Let's talk about other things instead."

She nodded.

The sun was brilliant. It was the type of day to spawn thunderstorms: clear, slightly humid and rather too warm for the end of April. There was just enough wind to keep it from being hot. We sat on a sloping bank above the wide stretch of water.

"Did you tell Dr. Carrera about Klaus?" I asked.

"I thought you didn't want to talk about him."

"Well, I was just wondering. Did you?"

"I told him that they took my baby away from me during the war."

"Yes, but did you tell him specifically about Klaus now? About Toby Waterman?"

She picked up another stone. With her fingers she rubbed dirt from it. The stone was round and smooth, gray and ordinary. Carefully, she lifted it up, sighted and threw it out into the water. There was nothing to sight on from what I could see, except small waves. She watched the arc of the rock intently before it splashed into the depths. She didn't answer my question, and I could tell from her studied inattention that she wasn't going to. I also reckoned that she hadn't told the doctor about Toby.

We sat together in untroubled silence. Absorbed in hitting her target in the water, Mama repeatedly picked up stones and lofted them, each time studying the way they fell. I watched off across the reservoir toward the other side. It was early enough in spring for there still to be a slight greenish tinge to the normally yellow prairie grass. Above, the sky stretched endlessly away, endlessly blue.

My mind wandered. I thought about Klaus, the real Klaus, wherever he was. And about the war with its influential, unyielding grasp on my life.

"Mama?" I asked, turning my head to see her. She had her chin resting in her folded arms, atop her knees.

She too was watching the far horizon. "Who was Klaus's father?"

At first she said nothing, and I became self-conscious. It occurred to me then how private that question was and how perhaps I shouldn't have asked it.

She shook her head. "I don't know. I never really knew any of them. They just came. I never knew their names."

"What about my other brother? What was his name?"

"József."

"Where's he at now? Do you know? Was it like it was with Klaus?"

She shifted her weight and sighed. Lower lip over upper, she let out a long breath that made the hair around her face flutter.

"I'm sorry," I said, "I shouldn't ask you stuff like this, should I? I'm sorry. I know it's really personal. I can understand that you mind telling me."

"No, I don't mind telling you," she replied. She smiled, not at me but at the horizon, before looking over. "But the question is, do you mind knowing?"

Chastened, I turned away.

There was silence.

"It was a terrible time," she said. "That's what's hard to tell. Ordinary life just disappeared. *Poof,* like smoke. And you were left with no rules to go by anymore. You had to make up your own. And if you haven't lived like that, it's hard to make it sound real."

She reached out for another rock, dusted it, sighted it against the invisible target and lofted it. Silence followed the splash.

"You see," she said, "some of the things you do in times like that, they're dreadful things. But you do them anyway. You do them because they're better than the alternatives."

She ran her fingers through the dirt on the ground beside her, searching for another stone.

"Do you understand what I mean?" she asked and looked over.

"I think I do," I said.

"Here, in this country," she said, "things are easy. No one is forced into evil decisions. Here, choices are just choices. Good is good. Bad is bad. There are no gray shadows around everything you do." Lifting up a hand, she regarded the nail of her little finger. "That is the hard part to tell. Because I can't explain it well enough."

"You're doing okay, Mama," I said. "I think I know what you mean."

Silence. Only the sound of the crows in the pine trees behind us. Mama turned her head to look at them. Then she leaned over to locate another stone. Picking it up, she rubbed it against her shirt, examined it, rejected it, letting it fall back to earth. She searched the surroundings for a second stone.

"I was very young," she said. "I was only seventeen when Klaus was born. Seventeen and two months old. And I was a very stupid girl for seventeen. You're smarter than I was. Much. I was too protected. It was all pretty clothes and dancing and good marks at school for me. Popi wanted a lady of the manor. He should have been raising a soldier."

She paused.

"I went with no knowledge, no understanding," she said softly. "I'd been at university studying, but I knew nothing about the world. Nothing at all. I still thought you got babies from kissing with your tongue.

"When I first arrived at the hostel, they put me in a room and made me undress. I was ashamed, so ashamed to have to do that. Popi was very harsh about that at home, about showing our bodies. He was so strict with me when I wasn't modest. And here I was, naked, in front of strange men. Even I didn't really believe they were all doctors. Some of them had uniforms of the SS.

"This one, he measured me. *Everywhere.* He put these things, what do you call them?—*Greifzirkel*—around my head to see how much room there was for my brains."

She leaned over and ran her fingers through the grass. Finding a pill bug, she tapped its shell with her fingernail.

"Then afterward they put me in a little room with a wardrobe and a bed and that was all. No chair. No table. If I put my arms out, I could touch opposite walls. Most of the girls were in pairs at the hostel. They shared their rooms. Some of them had curtains and colored bedspreads. You see, I think some of them were volunteers. They knew why they were there. And they got the nice rooms. And the pretty things. But I didn't, and because I was a foreigner, they kept me separate."

She stopped.

The pill bug was still trapped beneath her fingers, and she sat, her gaze fixed on it.

"When he came to my room that first night, I didn't know what he wanted. I didn't even know who he was. I'd never seen him before. He was older, perhaps twenty-five or so, and he told me to lie down on the bed. I did. I don't remember now why I did it so willingly. I suppose I just didn't really have any idea of what he was going to do. But he said, 'Lie down.' And so I did. But I wouldn't take my nightdress off. He said, 'What is the matter with you?' He thought I was teasing him, that I was pretending to be shy. *'Warum tust du so spröde?'* That is exactly what he said to me. *So spröde.* What is the word for that? Coy? He thought I was teasing. 'But I'm not,' I said. 'Then take off your gown,' he replied. But I wasn't going to. What would Popi think of me then, if I went around taking my clothes off every time a strange man told me to? I wouldn't do it. I told him so. So he grabbed my nightdress at the shoulder and pulled at it. I was angry with him then because he'd pulled so hard it ripped. Right at the top of the sleeve. I remember shouting at him. It was the only nightdress I had, and I remember saying, 'You think these grow on trees, these gowns?' But he grabbed hold of me and pushed me back onto the bed and got on top of me. And then I was too scared to think of the nightdress anymore. He still had his uniform on. He just lay on top of me and he was very heavy.''

She lifted her head and looked out over the reservoir. ''He said, 'What's your name?' And I said, 'Mara.' And he said, 'You're the Slav, aren't you?' And I said I was a *Volksdeutscherin* from Hungary. I could feel his breath on my face. He had been drinking schnapps, and I could smell it. And he was so heavy I could barely breathe out. Then he kissed me on the lips. Like no one had ever kissed me before. When he tried to do it again, I bit him. 'No one does that to me,' I said to him. And he laughed. 'You're full of fire, my little Hungarian whore.' I told him I was no whore. He said, 'You're a whore, Mara, or you wouldn't be here. You're nothing more than a little Hungarian cocksucker.' Well, I tell you, I started to cry then. I was so full of shame and humiliation. And fear. I just broke into tears.

''I began to tell him everything. I told him about my home in Lébény and how I hadn't seen my mama and papa for so long and I was worried about them with the war beginning. I told him how I'd been sent away to school in Dresden. And about Tante Elfie and having to sleep in the hallway because I bothered Birgitta with my homesickness. I said I'd just started university in October and I was only sixteen. I said I hadn't had any choice about coming, that they had made me come and all I wanted to do was go home to Mutti. But he laughed at me. He said I was no more than a filthy little cunt.''

She licked her lips and wiped them against her left wrist. The crows rose up and went wheeling over the water to the far side.

"One time I ran away from there. It wasn't very long after I'd arrived. I managed to make it to the train station, but of course, I had no money to buy a ticket. So I was going to try to get on the train to Vienna unnoticed. But there wasn't one going south. So I thought, I'll get on any train. But they found me before I could. And they took me back. The man with the big boots, the one who had been in the room when I'd had to undress in front of all of them, he said to me, there were camps. Did I know about the camps? he asked. If I didn't like life here, I could choose to be in a camp.

"After that time they locked my door. During the day I didn't mind much. They brought me newspapers and books and I had my meals in there, in my little room. But at night . . ."

She shook her head. "I could hear them coming. I would lie in bed and listen to the sounds of them walking in the halls. And I could tell. Always I could tell if they were just walking or if they were coming to my room. I grew to know them by the sounds of their boots. I never knew their real names, but I gave them names. Big Boots. Sure Step. Clodhopper. But that was in the day-time. At night, I'd just lie in bed and hear their boots on the wooden floor and always I'd know when they were coming for me."

She paused.

I wanted to tell her to stop altogether. I did not want to hear more of this. Unlike her usual stories, there was an aching simplicity to this account. No dramatics, no pregnant pauses for me to guess what happened next. She just talked, quietly, without embellishment. The contrast to her normal style made it even more difficult to listen to because suddenly it all seemed terribly private to me, as if I were eavesdropping or reading a personal diary.

The wind ceased, and the afternoon grew very warm around us. In the heat the prairie went absolutely soundless. You could have touched the silence.

"I became pregnant," she said when she finally spoke again. "It was much better then. Big Boots still came sometimes. He was the one who stopped the other men from coming because I was already pregnant. But he still came.

"Just the same, it was better. There weren't all of them. It was easier. And I thought I would be going home. Some of the girls, you see, were allowed home as soon as they were pregnant; they just came back for the delivery. Some of them, I think, might even have been married to SS officers. But I'm not sure. No one talked there. Anyway, I asked Big Boots and he said, *ja, ja,* I could go home when the baby had come."

She looked over at me, and there was a small smile on her lips. "I could feel the baby," she said, bringing a hand gently up to her stomach. "It was a wonderful feeling, him in there moving. I would lie on the bed and dream of him. I'd think, 'Mara, you'll be free. This time next year, you'll be home and helping Popi plant the flowers. This baby, he's going to be your savior.'" Then unexpectedly, Mama laughed. She looked at me and giggled again. "I must admit, I was a little afraid of going home. Can you imagine me explaining to Mutti and Popi how I got a baby? I thought about that the whole time. I invented such fantastic stories to explain. For nine whole months I was thinking, 'Mara, how *will* you tell Popi this?'

"Then he was born. I told you about that. I told you already how he was born. In the delivery room at the hostel. On the rubber mat." One corner of her mouth pulled back. "Anyway, I named him Klaus. For Hans Klaus

Fischer, the baker's son. Because I'd loved him. When I was fifteen, I'd thought I would marry him. I was *so* certain of that. I had my whole life mapped out, when I was fifteen.'' Then she shook her head. ''But no. No, I didn't, did I? But I named the baby after him anyhow. Because I wished so much the baby was his.''

A slight, inward smile. ''He was such a good baby. Calmer than either you or Megan. You were both such squirmy babies, so anxious to be about your business. But he loved to be cuddled. He was very . . . what should I say? . . . peaceful. Like the sea when it's quiet. He would just lie in my arms and look at me and was so at peace with himself.'' She glanced over. ''And he was tiny. Just tiny. Just so.'' She measured with her hands. ''You were bigger. You were a big galoot,'' she said, grinning.

There was silence then, that grew long and brittle. She looked away from me, raising her head and gazing off into the distance. Her eyes narrowed, and she sat back. Still she said nothing. I studied the ripples on the water.

''I was so stupid. *Die grosse Idiotin,*'' she said at last. ''It hurts to remember that kind of stupidity. You see, I believed them. Even after the baby was born and they thought he was so beautiful. He was not black haired like some of the babies. He was blond from the beginning, and the nurses would come to me with him. All of them were in love with him. Even Big Boots came once and gave me squares of chocolate and told me what a good son I had borne. *Grosse Idiotin.* I kept thinking, 'Mara, you're such a clever girl. You've not made a very big fuss about being here and so now everyone is happy with you and you're almost free. And you have this wonderful little baby besides.' You see, I still believed them. I thought I was very crafty to get through all that. I thought I was a fox.''

She let out a deep breath. ''I thought the baby and I—I

thought—'' Words failed her. She lowered her head and rested it on her arms, momentarily obscuring her face from my view. I found myself suddenly alarmed that she would cry. Not now, I was praying, because I didn't know if I could bear the tears that would come from this. Then she lifted her head, and to my relief, was dry eyed. She looked upward at the sky.

Then nothing. We sat together in total silence. Time passed, seconds, minutes, maybe years.

"They just took him. He was twenty days old, and they thought I had no more milk for him." An abrupt pause. "No. No, I'm wrong. It wasn't the milk. They'd always meant to take him. It was the *Idiotin* here," she said, touching her chest. "She was the one who needed reasons. They never did.

"I swore I'd get him back. I cut my arm. Here, see. This is the scar. I cut it and I marked my blood on the door and said they'd never keep him from me. He was my flesh. I'd find him. They laughed at me. 'Mara, our little Hungarian cunt,' they said, 'she makes such a fuss.'

"Then it started all over again. I said I wasn't going to let the men come in. I pushed the wardrobe in front of the door. 'You can't do this to me,' I said, 'I'm human.' I just wasn't going to stand for it, now that I understood: I wasn't going to let them treat me like that. But him, with the big boots, he came with the dog whip. He said, 'You are nothing but a bitch to us, and this will show you that I'm right,' Every night he came with the dog whip. Every night until my periods came back. From then on he sent the men."

She shrugged. "What else is there to say? It was the same. Except that I no longer got privileges. No more books. Never out of my room.

"I got desperate to hear what was happening outside the hostel. It was 1941 then, and I could hear the Allied planes. I hid in the wardrobe at night. The planes would go over and I'd hear the bombs hitting. I was scared to death. I never knew who was the enemy and who wasn't. Not that it made much difference. At that time they were all enemies.

"When the men came, I asked them what was happening. Each one of them. Each night. I would give them a better time, if they told me a lot. Who was winning? I would ask. What is going on out there? What are the Allies doing to us? One man told me that soon Hitler would smash the British and be in London. Any day now, another officer said, we will prove the strength of the Thousand-Year Reich. They all said, and I think they all believed, that we were winning the war.

"Well," she said with a shake of her head, "I will tell you, I thought I was going to be locked in that room forever. If they could keep making me give them babies, there was no reason to think it would end with the war. And of course, I was terrified of the Allies. I believed they would kill me outright, if they won. So it got bad for me. I thought then, no matter what happened, no matter who won, I would never be free again."

Hands on either side of her head, elbows on her knees, she stared across the reservoir. There was an animal there, a cow most likely, making its way down a small rise. It walked slowly and without apparent aim.

"By December I was pregnant again. That was all they wanted out of me. So once that happened, they were better to me. I got books again. And sometimes, when the nurse was with me, I could come out of my room for meals. But I was terribly sick with that child. I hadn't been with Klaus. Or you. Or Megan. But I was with him. I'd vomit from the moment I awoke in the morning until I fell asleep at night. I thought for sure I'd vomit that child right out.

"But they took good care of me. They sent a special nurse. And she said, 'Don't worry. You'll keep this child; you won't miscarry. Because sickness always means a child's well planted.' And she stayed with me all the time, even in the nights.''

The wind blew again faintly, and her hair was lifted from her shoulders. She gazed away, lost in thought. I sat, paralyzed, beside her.

''Yes,'' she said resolutely, ''there are decisions one must make. When all the choices are evil ones but one must still decide. I had to make one then. I was only eighteen. Just a girl. Not such a stupid girl anymore, but still just a girl. And that was a real decision. All the other decisions I've ever made have been nothing in comparison to that one.''

She stopped speaking for a moment.

''The baby came early. He was due in August but he came in July, only three days after my birthday,'' she said. Her voice was flat and detached. ''I asked them to name him Josef, after my father. But I made them spell it József. That's the Hungarian. I wasn't going to let him be a German. I told them to christen him and to bring me the certificate so that I could see that he'd been christened József.

''They did,'' she said and then stopped. Hands clasped together, resting against her lips, she said nothing more. Minutes built up. She stared at the grass.

''My breasts would get very full. You see, when you haven't had the baby to nurse for a while, your breasts become very round and hard. Especially in the beginning when you are just getting in your milk.'' Her voice was soft and fragile but without discernible emotion.

''So when they brought him to me in the afternoon . . . that afternoon . . . they gave him to me and . . . I held him. He turned so hungrily for the milk. He hadn't been fed since the morning and he rooted against me. Like babies do. So, very, very gently, I just pressed his head against my breast and smothered him.''

She shrugged her shoulders. "I was sent to Ravensbrück, Big Boots, he said he had no other choice." Her expression was almost a smile, mirthless and sardonic. "The choice, you see, had been all mine."

# Twenty

"HE ENJOYED SEEING HER," my father said to me in the study that night.

I leaned back against the lounger. "But what does he think is wrong with her? Why does he think she's doing that?"

"He said he found her delightful. Very articulate."

"Daddy, she was purposely trying to be delightful. You know Mama."

"Well, then," he said with a smile, "things can't be too bad, can they? Not if she can do that."

*"Daddy.* What did the doctor *say?* What's the matter with her? What are we going to do about it?"

"He said he didn't think it was too serious. Something about a personality disorder, about her being obsessed at the moment with this thing about Klaus."

"We didn't need a psychiatrist to tell us that. We *know* she's obsessed. Even Megs can tell that. But what are we going to do about it? About the Watermans? What about my ever getting to go back to school again?"

My father reached down and picked up one of the framed photos of Mama he kept on his desk. "He wants to keep seeing her. Every Wednesday. To try and sort it out for her. And he gave her some pills. He said those should help."

"And what if they don't?"

236

"They should. He said so." Dad turned away. He still held the picture in his hands. He studied it. "You know what the doctor told me? They gave her tests. You know. To measure how alert she was. An IQ test. And you know what?" He turned back to me. "Dr. Carrera said she got every single question right. He said she was a very, very brilliant woman."

"Daddy, she's not applying for college."

"She's beautiful," he said softly to the photograph.

*"Dad!"* I cried in exasperation. "Stop it, okay? It's Mama we're talking about. Her, downstairs, who keeps going out to the Watermans. And what's going to happen to her if those pills don't work? That's all I want to know. Nothing else. What if they don't work?"

"They should. He said so. He's a psychiatrist, Lesley. He's used to these kinds of problems. He knows what he's talking about. He said they're special pills, tranquilizers, and they're very strong. They're what's given to schizophrenics to make them stop hallucinating."

"But Mama's not hallucinating. And she's had billions of tranquilizers before. What if these don't work on her? I want to know. I'm sick to death of waiting. I want to know right now what we're going to do next, if this doesn't work."

"You have to have patience, Les."

"You weren't the one sitting there today, Dad. You didn't see her conning all of them. You don't have to spend every day with her, day in, day out, trying constantly to stay one step ahead of her. You haven't had to give up your school time and your job and your friends because of her."

"Your mother didn't 'con' anyone, Lesley. That man is a psychiatrist. A very highly trained specialist. He knows about things like that."

"She didn't tell him about Toby."

"He already knew about Toby." Dad was a little angry with me, and it echoed in his voice.

Nettled, I turned and went over to the bookshelf. I browsed among the titles. "I just don't have that kind of faith in anything anymore, Dad. I need to know where we go from here when this fails."

He lifted one shoulder in a weary, defensive gesture. "We just cross that bridge when we come to it, kiddo."

I returned to stand in front of the desk.

He looked over, and when he saw my face, he looked away and shook his head. "Don't be so difficult, Lesley. It's hard. I know it's hard, believe me. But other families go through this too. And a lot worse than we've got it. Families with retarded children. Or senile parents. Having to change diapers on someone twelve years old, like the Martins do with Kenny. Or Perry Edelmann with his autistic son. It's not easy. But you do what you can do. If you don't want them in institutions, Les, you do what you can. It's hell sometimes. I know that awfully well. But it's part and parcel of loving someone."

I said nothing.

"And the thing is, Lesley, I do love your mother. She doesn't belong in a hospital or an institution. That'd kill her. And if it takes my last breath, I'll make sure she never goes in one."

"Dad, I'm not asking that."

"You are. Because if you and I and Meggie can't cope with her, then that's what's left."

I lowered my head.

"But I won't have it happen. I don't care what kind of sacrifices that means for us. I won't let anything happen to your mama. She's where she's at through no fault of her own."

Swiftly, without any prior warning, tears rose to my eyes. They did not simply blur my vision but rather swelled up and came down my cheeks before I even anticipated them.

Concerned, my father came around the desk to me. I shook my head, unable to speak.

"I'm sorry it's so hard on you, sweetheart. I'm sorry you're having to take the brunt of it. I do understand."

"It's not that," I said, strangling.

His brow puckered.

"She told me," I said. "This afternoon when we were out. She told me about the hostel and József and how she got to Ravensbrück. I was trying not to think about it but I can't. It's the only thing on my mind."

The pills made my mother listless and drowsy. The doctor prescribed two a day, and they took effect immediately, making her unable to keep her eyes open. She would sit on the couch in the living room, hands on either side of her head, trying to stay awake. Eventually, she gave up and lay down, dozing fitfully. My father rang Dr. Carrera to tell him that he thought the pills were too strong, but the psychiatrist said she would adjust to them.

I returned to school that Tuesday afternoon after two weeks' absence. It felt odd to be back. I think I'd thought I was missing it more than I apparently was, because when I arrived back, it did not turn out to be nearly the high I had anticipated. Old Mr. Tennant in German called on me, as if I'd been there all along. No one asked me where I'd been or how it felt to be back. The day left me lonely and depressed. I felt adrift between two worlds.

The tranquilizers literally immobilized Mama. There was little worry about leaving her alone. When they didn't put her right to sleep, they left her too sluggish to accomplish much. When I left for school in the morning, she would be lying on the couch, watching TV. When I returned in the afternoon, she was still there. She didn't even bother to make herself lunch.

Megan found Mama's torpid behavior under the tranquilizers very unnerving. She worried constantly that
Mama needed someone to take care of her in such a stu-
porous state. She fretted when she noticed Mama had not
been making herself coffee during the day, because
Megan knew how much Mama loved her dark, aromatic
coffee. If we'd just not give Mama the pills, Megan
begged, she'd be willing to stay home and take care of
her. She didn't mind missing school. Which was probably true, given the state of Megan's previous report card.

On Thursday Mama finally appeared to be adjusting to
the tranquilizers. At breakfast she was more alert, and by
the time I came back from school in the afternoon, she
was practically her old self, puttering around the kitchen,
humming under her breath. I watched her carefully as I
was having my after-school sandwich to see if I could detect any renewed interest in Toby Waterman, but there
was none. She wore a pair of old, holey tennis shoes, not
her walking shoes. Most of her conversation was about
mundane things, cheerfully put and in English.

Later when I was in the living room, I noticed dust col-
lecting along the mopboards. Housework really had become a fetish with me, and realizing that Mama hadn't
been up to doing any during the week, I went to get the
vacuum from the back cupboard.

Down on my hands and knees behind the couch, I
came across a slip of paper. It had fallen down from a
stack of magazines and papers under the end table.

I picked it up, turned it over. What'd caught my eye
was that it bore my mother's handwriting. She had written on the back of one of Megan's school papers. Megan's work was dated the previous Monday, so I knew
Mama had written this recently. I inspected it. It was
written in German, in my mother's flaired, foreign-
looking script. She had a bold, distinctive hand, the letters large and easy to read in spite of their European

appearance. Apparently, it was some kind of list. Brown shoes, it said. Three shirts. Bread.

"Mama?" I asked, coming into the kitchen. "What's this?" I held the paper out.

She looked at it but did not take it from my hand. She shook her head.

"You wrote it, Mama. What is it?"

"I don't know," she said. "This medicine, it makes my head funny. I do things I don't remember."

"It looks like some kind of shopping list or something."

"I do these things," she said, her expression guileless. "It isn't good, this medicine. It makes me do things and I don't know I do them."

I raised an eyebrow but she gazed steadily back at me. She was sly as a fox, my mama, pills or no pills.

I went into the study to join my father about half-past eight. He was sitting at the desk reading a magazine.

"Dad," I said, "I've done something. I don't think you're going to be too happy when you hear about it. But I think it had to be done."

He looked up. He'd washed his hair in the shower when he'd returned from work, and it had dried without much combing. Wild, black and curly, it gave him the look of an Irish Albert Einstein.

"I took Grandma's bond and cashed it. I've bought tickets to Wales." I threw the travel agent's folder onto the desk. "There's only two there. I wanted us all to go, but it costs too much money. The girl at the agency, she did these pretty cheap. So there's three hundred dollars left over. That and my savings from work. See? Here." I put the money on the desk too. "I want you and Mama to go to Wales. I'll take care of Megan. But I want you to take her back."

My dad said absolutely nothing. He stared at the ticket folder and the money.

"I know you're going to be mad at me. I know you didn't want me to do it. But I had to. I had to do something. I just couldn't stand around and watch Mama go through this. It's my money, after all. And this is how I decided to spend it."

He shook his head slightly. Color had risen into his cheeks. "Oh, Lessie, sweetheart, you shouldn't have." His voice was barely above a whisper.

"I know you're going to be mad. But you're always talking to me about love. You're always saying that this thing or that thing we do is just because it's something you do when you love someone. Well, so is this. I love you and Mama. And this is just something I had to do."

He put his palm against his mouth and slowly let out a long breath of air. He wouldn't raise his head to look at me.

"It's for June. I had to get it at least twenty-one days ahead of time to get the discount. Is that all right? Can you get off at the garage?"

"Oh Lessie, you shouldn't have done this," he said again. "How are we going to pay for college now? What will we do?"

"Well, like you're always saying, we'll just have to cross that bridge when we come to it. I'll get by. I'll work. I'll go and I'll manage. But for now I just want you and Mama to go back to Forest of Flowers."

I wished he would speak more. I'd been prepared for him to go into a tirade. I had not been prepared for him to sit, speechless.

"Dad, I had to do something."

"I just wish you had told me about it first."

"I couldn't," I replied. "You wouldn't have let me do it."

* * *

It was purely by accident that I went back up to my room the next morning. I should have already left for school, but a few steps up the sidewalk, I recalled that I'd left my French essay on my desk. I went running back.

My bedroom was right next to the bathroom, a facet of the room I hated because I could hear everything that went on in there. So, when I came back to get my assignment that morning, I paused. I could hear someone in the bathroom vomiting.

Going to the bedroom door, I looked out. Megan had been downstairs at the kitchen table when I came through. However, for some reason I assumed it was she. "Megs?" I said at the bathroom door. "Are you sick? Let me in."

No answer. I tried the door. It was locked.

Running back to my room, I got a coat hanger. Our bathroom locked only with a hook and eye because Dad worried about what a dangerous room it was. Someone could slip in the bathtub or have some other accident, he was always warning, so he made certain that you could push the door ajar and easily unlatch it in an emergency. I knew the system worked because Megan was always breaking in on me.

Mama was in there, sitting on the edge of the bathtub beside the toilet. Her expression was wary. The toilet had been flushed.

"What are you doing?" Sudden realization dawned on me. "You threw up the goddamned pills, didn't you?" Anger roared into full flame.

Her cheeks were flushed. She was running her tongue around the inside of her mouth.

"Oh, honestly, Mama," I said and flapped my hands in frustration. "What are we going to do with you?"

"They make me too sleepy. I can't think."

"You're not *supposed* to think, goddamnit. We don't *want* you to think. That's what's causing us all this trouble, your thinking. Damn it, Mama, those pills were for your own good.''

She was incredible. Always one step ahead of us. Unlike my father had said, there was a vital difference between caring for Mama and putting diapers on Kenny or Perry Edelmann's autistic son. With Mama it wasn't custodial. She was all too willing to take care of herself. So looking after her degenerated into one long, futile battle of wits.

I blew out a heavy breath. "Just wait until Daddy hears. Wait till I tell him about this." I looked at her. "I'll have to, you know. I'm not going to school either. If you think you can do things like this, that you can deceive us and get away with it, then you got another think coming.

"Just what did you have in mind to happen next? A trip out to the Watermans, I bet. Were you planning to see Toby?" I folded my arms over my chest. "Well, you can just unplan it, Mama, because you aren't going to get away with it. I'm not going to let you.''

Still furious, I stormed out of the bathroom and back into my bedroom. Yanking off my school clothes, I threw them onto the bed and pulled on a T-shirt and a dirty pair of jeans. When I came downstairs, Megan, who was still at the table with the morning paper, looked up in surprise.

"Aren't you going to school?" she asked.

"No," I said and I couldn't keep the unspent anger from echoing in my voice. "But you better. Right this instant, if you know what's good for you.''

She gave it a moment's consideration and then rose. "Yes, I think I will.''

While I was standing in the kitchen doorway, I chanced to notice the slip of paper I had discovered while cleaning the living room the previous day. Going over to pick it up from the far counter, I puzzled over it. What had Mama had in mind when she wrote this? It was just a list, written in blue felt-tipped pen, but it grew sinister as I regarded it. Was she planning to run away? Abduct Toby and go somewhere?

What intruded into my thoughts as I held the paper was the realization that even now, even here in Kansas with her own family, everything was in a state of war for her. She had survived the experiences in the hostel; she had survived the camp; she had survived the SS; and she was damned well going to survive us. It was a courageous trait, that kind of perseverance, but a ruthless one, wholly without mercy. She was killing us. Yet, this wasn't Germany. The war wasn't on. We weren't the enemy. Taking the list with me, I went over to the table and slumped into a chair.

A short time later, my mother came into the kitchen. Apparently, her stomach was still upset, because she kept a hand tenderly over it. Taking down a glass from the cupboard, she went to the refrigerator and poured herself some milk. She said nothing to me, did not even look in my direction. Her feelings were hurt. There was that kind of injured rawness to the silence between us, so evident it was palpable.

Still slouched in my chair, I watched her. What did she have to feel hurt about? I was the one whose day had just been ruined. I wasn't feeling at all charitable toward her; in fact, I wanted to keep afire the devouring fury I'd felt coming into the kitchen so I could confront her again about the stupid list, about how she was mucking up my whole damned life with her ridiculous ideas. But within seconds of her arrival in the room, my anger slipped away, dissipating like smoke into darkness.

"What are we going to do with you, Mama?" I asked, chin braced in my hand as I watched her.

She turned and we regarded one another across the infinity of a table, two chairs and maybe four feet of floor space. The anguished, unhappy silence persisted. She turned back, took up the milk carton and poured herself a second glass of milk.

"I'm not a child," she said, looking not at me but at the glass. Her voice was heavy with feeling.

Suddenly and with a startling lack of warning, I was overpowered by a truly daunting sense of hopelessness. The magnitude of the feeling was incredible; it might as well have been a physical blow. My mother still stood beyond the table, the extent of her own misery showing plainly in her expression, and in that split second the amount of damage that these events had wreaked on our family was profoundly evident to me. My world had gone upside down, completely topsy-turvy. We were being destroyed.

For what seemed like the hundredth time in recent days, I realized I was going to cry. There wasn't much I could do about it, other than let the tears come. This sudden, desolate moment of insight had overwhelmed me to the point that all my energy was used up just staying upright on the chair.

My mother raised her eyes to me. She continued to hold the glass of milk in one hand. Lifting it to her lips, she drank slowly, watching me over the rim of the glass. It left her momentarily with a milk mustache before she wiped it off. But her expression was wary, as if she distrusted my abrupt loss of composure. I think I had caught us both unawares by bursting into tears.

"How did we ever come to be like this?" I asked. My voice cracked. I brought a hand up to wipe away the tears. "Mama, what is happening to us?"

Guarded concern remained in her eyes.

"This is too much for me. I hate it like this. All I want is for us to be a normal family again. I don't want to keep hurting you. I don't want you to hurt me. I just want things normal. Like they used to be. But I don't know what to do anymore. I'm scared to death by all this, Mama. I don't understand what's happening, and I don't want it like this, but I just don't know what to do.''

Compassion suffused her features, the way water does dry soil. The cautious hesitance that had governed her earlier movements melted away. Pushing aside the chairs between us, she came to me, and with both her hands she clasped my face for just a moment before opening her arms and enveloping me. She pressed me deep into her breasts in an embrace that was strong and reassuring and solidly maternal.

*"O mein liebes, liebes Kind,"* she whispered as I clung to her. *"Liebes, liebes Kind."* She kept me tight against her, her fingers entangled in my hair, her lips against my head so that I could feel the hotness of her breath.

Then very gently she pulled back and with both her hands she lifted up my face. "I do love you," she said and smiled. She kissed my lips.

I could see the tears in her eyes too.

# Twenty-One

I TOLD MY FATHER. I said I had discovered Mama vomiting the tranquilizers. I told him about the list and said Mama would not say what it was for. I said I bet she was planning to snatch Toby Waterman. Mara, he called when I was finished. Mama's head appeared around the door. Come in here, he said, I want to talk to you.

For the umpteenth time my parents argued over Mama's behavior. Only this time it was my father's voice that rose and my mother did not reply. When they came out of the study later, Mama was not crying. Her face was flushed with emotion but instead of running off in a spell, she came into the kitchen and made herself a cup of coffee. Then she sat down at the table alone and drank it, while tracing invisible designs on the tabletop with one finger.

I stayed clear of both of them. Megan wanted me to French braid her hair, so I went up to her room with her and we both remained in there until bedtime.

I was in a deep, dreamless sleep when my mother woke me. She lay a hand on my shoulder and, startled, I jerked up. She was leaning close to me, her hair loose and trailing against my cheek.

"What is it? What do you want, Mama?" The bedside clock said 3:47.

"Come down and be with me," she said. She had a deep voice, husky from all the smoking, and when she spoke very softly, all you could hear were the explosive letters in the words. She said her *r*'s and *t*'s strangely anyhow.

Sleepily, I sat up and rubbed my eyes.

When I came into the kitchen, there was a cigarette still burning in the ashtray on the table, so I realized her decision to wake me must have been impulsive. The teapot was out. She had brewed a pot of the black India tea that she drank with milk. Without asking me, she brought another mug to the table and poured me a cup too.

"Can't you sleep?" I asked as I sat down.

"I don't know what it is," she said, still softly, although there was no need to be quiet down here. I could detect the tightness of unshed tears behind her voice.

She puffed thoughtfully on the cigarette and stared off across the kitchen. I wondered what had prompted her to get me up. That was unusual. Generally, one of us would hear her and get up, but if we didn't, she very seldom woke us. Particularly lately. And particularly me. If she felt she needed company, it was normally my father's. So I wondered. Perhaps it was because of the argument. Perhaps it had hurt her more than was apparent, and she couldn't sleep but was afraid to wake my dad. I didn't know and I couldn't tell. She sat silently smoking. Dressed in a worn, well-washed print nightgown, she had pulled a cardigan over it for warmth. The front of the gown was untied, and I could see the outline of her breasts.

"What am I doing?" she asked softly, speaking to the cigarette. "I ask myself that. I say, 'Mara, what are you doing to them?' O'Malley, he's so mad at me. Furious. I'm afraid he's starting to hate me. I'm afraid everyone is. I ask myself, 'Are you wrong?' "

She looked over at me. "Am I wrong?"

She was beginning, at long last, to lose heart. She said that in quiet, hard German syllables, struggling to hold back the emotions behind them. She continued to speak mainly to the cigarette. We still had not convinced her that Toby Waterman was not her son; but, for the first time in all these weeks, her courage was beginning to fail her. The cost of getting Klaus back was becoming apparent to her. She could see what was happening to all of us because of it and she was losing heart.

Relief washed over me like cold, fresh water. These were the words I had been waiting to hear from her. I had dreamed of hearing her say them. My muscles sagged with sudden relaxation, as tension began to give way.

She pulled out one of the long ties on her nightgown and wound it around her finger. "I don't know what to do now," she said.

"It's time to just forget it, Mama. To go back to the way we were."

She looked over, took a deep breath, reached for another cigarette. "I wish it were that simple, baby. God in Heaven, I do." Again, there was the heavy weight of unsaid things behind her words. She shoved a hand into her hair.

I rose to make another pot of tea.

"It's the guilt really," she said.

I turned from the stove.

"It's living with the guilt."

"What guilt's that, Mama?" I asked. I assumed she meant what had happened to József. Or maybe just the destruction she had wrought in the last few weeks.

"I don't know," she said. "Of just being."

Bringing back the fresh pot of tea, I sat down again.

"When I was at Ravensbrück, I was so angry with Elek," she said. "Because I was there and he wasn't.

This is the way it's been my whole life, I thought. He
was such a rascal. Always thinking up these terrible
things, always setting me up to get the blame. We'd do
something and, every time, I'd get punished for it. Popi's
strap was for me. 'Elek doesn't know any better,' Popi
would always say. 'But you, Mara, you're older.' For
God's sake, I was only thirteen months older! And I
hadn't even thought the things up. Elek had.'' She
paused and touched the rim of her tea mug with one finger. ''But they were little things, weren't they? Children's things. Nothing important. I didn't think so then.
When I was in Ravensbrück, I was furious with him.
This is just like always, I thought. I am here and he is
safe at home.

''Then,'' she said, ''I learned they simply shot him. I
survived, and they simply came and shoved him against
the wall in the mill house and shot him. The blood stains
were still there, still on the stones when O'Malley and I
went back. I can never forgive myself for being so
petty.''

I watched her. She sat, studying the tabletop.

''You can't imagine what it is like to wish people dead
for silly little things and then learn they have died. Especially when you have done so many more evil things
yourself.

''I wanted to live so badly. You don't understand that.
You must be there in that terrible time to know how precious the ordinary world is. How much you want to live
in it again and do ordinary things once more. I betrayed
them because of it. All of them. Elek. Popi. Mutti. I have
betrayed Hungary. I wanted to make myself German just
so I could survive.''

I leaned forward across the table and reached my hand
out. ''Oh Mama, I don't think you betrayed anyone.''

''I did. To stay alive I betrayed everyone.'' She looked

at me. "I must have, mustn't I? Because I survived and
no one else did." Then a pause. "Why didn't I see it
coming? I ask myself that question a hundred times a
day. I was there. Why didn't I see what they were doing?
Why did I let them take me away from Jena? I just got on
the bus when they told me to. I never questioned it. Why
didn't I realize what was happening?"

"Mama, you were sixteen. People a lot older than you
never saw it coming."

"But why was I so stupid?"

"Mama . . ."

Pressing her fingers against the bridge of her nose, she
expelled a long breath. "And then there I was. It was
worse there at the hostel than in Ravensbrück. My soul
was gone before I ever got to Ravensbrück. I had betrayed everyone I loved by then. Just to survive. I should
have done more than I did. I am always thinking that.
When the men came, I should have tried to kill them.
They were all officers in the SS. I am always thinking,
how many Jews might I have saved, if I had killed one of
them while he was with me? But I never even tried. And
they were important men, those officers that were in
*Lebensborn*. And they had much blood on their hands. If
I had killed them, I might have saved the lives of many
people. Somehow, I should have killed them. Or killed
myself. Or something. But I was so scared. I only wanted
to get out of there alive."

"Mama, that's very understandable."

"I would sit in my little room before the night came. I
would sit and think, only I am real. Only my body, only
my thoughts, only my feelings. Nothing else is real. The
men would come and I would see them and know in my
mind—*mein Verstand*—that they were there. But to *me*
they became very unreal. I could make them have no importance. And it worked, you see, because it made me

have no feelings about what they did to me." She shook her head. "But it was wrong. I see that now. I should have tried to kill them."

"Mama, you were only a young girl. What you did, most people would have done. I don't think you meant to betray anyone."

"They tied me. They took off my clothes and they tied me, like an animal. I let them. I let them piss on me. I crawled on my knees in front of them and kissed their boots. I was just too scared of them."

"Oh Mama, don't. Please, let's don't talk about it anymore, okay? Please? It's over. It happened but it's over, so let's try to forget it. Please, for my sake?"

"Popi would have been so ashamed of me." There was a pause. It grew long and heavy and she sat with her head braced in one hand. She looked over at me. "Do you know what? Shall I tell you a very terrible thing?"

I did not move.

"I did a very, very terrible thing," she said softly. "Such an evil thing. After the war when O'Malley and I were searching, I prayed." She glanced at me again. "You know what I prayed? I prayed we would not find Popi. It is the very worst thing I have ever done. I am still so ashamed, when I think of it. I prayed we would not find him. And he was my own father. He loved me." She touched the tabletop with one finger. Pensively, she regarded it. "I was afraid of him."

Silence.

It grew.

Still, she sat, feeling the Formica with her fingertip.

Motionless, I watched her.

"I could never be what he wanted," she said very quietly. "He wanted so much. When I was little, he would take me from the nursery and walk with me down to the drawing room and let me sit in the leather chair beside his desk. Then he would take out his pipe and sit down and smoke it. And he would look at me. 'Of all of them, you are the best,' he would say. 'You are best. Many people in the village say to me how beautiful my daughter is. Such a little lady. People think, what a fortunate man I am.' He said that to me. I don't know how many times. And I would sit in the leather chair and my feet didn't touch the floor.''

She paused. Tears puddled in the corners of her eyes but she ignored them. She continued gazing at the tabletop.

''Why me?'' she asked, her voice plaintively questioning. ''Why was he always so ambitious for me? I was not good. Why did he keep telling me those things? Why not Elck? Or Mihály? They were his sons. I never understood. Why was it me?''

Again she paused. She did not look up.

''I was so afraid we would find him. He would have known. He would have looked at me and been able to tell what I had done in the war.''

''Mama, let's not talk about it.''

''Why did I survive? I should have died. It would have been better to die than to have let them do those things to me.''

''Please, Mama . . .''

Then silence. She became briefly absorbed in her tea mug, tipping it and staring into it.

She looked over. ''Did you understand about József? About what I was saying about decisions?''

''Yes,'' I said. ''I did, I think.''

Another pause. The energy seemed suddenly to drain out of her, and she covered her eyes with one hand. ''But what do I do now? What about Klaus?''

I didn't say anything.

She sighed. ''O'Malley's so upset with me. I am beginning to think he will hate me soon. And how could I manage without O'Malley? How could I live without him?"

"You're never going to have to worry about that, Mama, so don't start thinking about it."

"He doesn't understand."

"Mama, I think he does. I think he understands a whole lot more than you give him credit for sometimes. I wouldn't worry about it."

"I do," she said.

"I can see you do. But don't, Mama. Daddy's not going to give up on you. You know Daddy."

Her expression forlorn, she sighed. "I worry so much," she whispered, and the tears returned to her eyes. "How can O'Malley bear me? I am so dirty. I've let so many evil men touch me. So many filthy pigs. How can it be that I'm not a filthy pig myself? How can O'Malley bear to lie in the same bed with me? How can he love me?"

"Oh, Mama, don't talk like this." I rose up and leaned across the table to hug her. I clutched her head and kissed her hair. "Daddy does love you. You know that. He loves you more than anything else in the world. We all do. What happened before makes absolutely no difference to us. You've got to understand that and believe it, because it's the truth."

She sat back. With one finger she dislodged the tears; she snuffled, then she reached out for the teapot. Pouring another cup of tea, she added milk and stirred it. With the cuff of her nightgown she studiously cleaned away a drop of tea that had spilled on the table. She drank from the mug in gulps.

I glanced at the clock. It was not quite five.

"I always felt so guilty for being Aryan. I was always writing that to Herr Willi. Over and over and over again I had to tell him how guilty it made me feel. So he would forgive me. But it never helped. Now," she said, "when I think about it, I see it isn't simply being Aryan. It's being alive."

She inhaled slowly. "I told Herr Willi that if I'd had to live through that time, I wish I'd been born a Jew. That's the truth. I do. It would have been better to go to your death, innocent. It would have been better to suffer the cruellest evil at other people's hands than to become evil yourself. Then there would have been no shame. Then you would not have to think: The people who love me wish they could stop."

"Please, Mama, please don't think about this any-more. Please? I understand. I do. About József. About the hostel. About Ravensbrück. I understand the things you did and the decisions you made. They're understand-able, Mama."

She looked at me. "You can forgive me then? *Ja?* For what I do, you can forgive me?"

"Oh, yes, Mama. I can forgive you."


The next morning after breakfast when Megan had gone outside to play, I told my father about Mama's rest-less night and the conversation we'd had. He knew about those things. He'd always known, I suppose.

He told me other aspects of those times, about her long, slow recovery from typhus and the aftereffects of the two-and-a-half years in Ravensbrück, where she'd spent most of her time with Polish women like Jadwiga, doing heavy farm labor. He described their harrowing journey back to Lébény and their fruitless, decade-long search for Klaus through the ruins of Germany. That was the real reason, he said, that they'd stayed on in Wales, because it was easier to follow up leads on the Continent from there. A fact I'd never known was that my mother and father had come to the States for a short time immediately after the war and lived with Grandma. However, Mama had been so fretful with worry about the possibility of missing a clue to Klaus's whereabouts that she'd persuaded my father to return to Europe. Yet search as they had, through the orphanages and the Red Cross and all the other agencies set up to reunite families, no substantial evidence about Klaus ever surfaced. All the records from the *Lebensborn* hostel were destroyed and the hostel itself abandoned when invasion by the Allies had seemed imminent. Whoever had taken Klaus either did not know he had been unwillingly given up or else did not come forward. My mother remained tormented. In every crowd of school children she saw him. Every small boy with blond hair and blue eyes might have been him. She could go nowhere without searching the faces of all the children. Every shop, every street, every home with a child in it caught her eye. In the end, my father insisted they leave Europe and return to the U.S. It was 1957, he said, time to get on with their own lives before this thing destroyed them both.

Dad stayed home that Saturday instead of going down to the garage, as he usually did. I had upset him, telling him about the things Mama had said to me in the night. He paced restlessly around the kitchen, washing up the dishes with rough vigor. When I next saw him, he was sitting on the floor beside the couch in the living room, where Mama was still asleep. Gently, gently, he stroked her hair, his face only inches from hers.

Paul was coming over for Saturday lunch. He and Aaron had been out rat shooting the previous evening, so he'd promised to make it up to me on Saturday afternoon. We didn't have much in mind. Just going out to Ladder Creek and being alone.

He arrived about eleven o'clock in a roaring good

mood. He had bet Aaron that he could hit five rats in a
row without missing and had won, so Aaron had had to
buy him three boxes of .22 shells. Gleefully, Paul
brought them in to show me. I told him that his pastime
was disgusting, that it was undoubtedly his least likable
characteristic and that I refused to listen to him glorify it.
But I did volunteer to help him put the guns and the rest
of the shells in the house. I was not going to ride around
with all that crap in the car, I said; it was dangerous. He
agreed wholeheartedly. But I knew all he was worried
about was someone stealing the precious things and
spoiling his main source of entertainment.

After all the trauma in the middle of the night, my
mother, in a way so characteristic of her, was full of rol-
licking good humor when she finally got up. She'd surfaced only slightly ahead of Paul's arrival and was
showering when he came. While we were in the kitchen
cutting up vegetables for a salad for lunch, she wandered
in, her hair still wrapped in a towel.

"Ah, modeling the newest fashions from India," Paul
said when he saw her.

"Where have you found this lout?" she asked me. "In
a dump shooting rats? He has no respect for his elders."
Pulling the makeshift turban off and letting her damp hair
tumble down, Mama flicked the towel at Paul, giving
him a sharp snap on the backside. He jumped, grabbing
the seat of his pants. Both of them were hooting like
chimpanzees.

Lunch was spirited. Mama, rested and relaxed, ban-
tered with everyone. Dad and Paul fell into a serious discussion about the Chicago Cubs. Megan, desperate for
attention, rocked back and forth on the edge of her chair
and inserted non sequiturs into our conversations.

Afterward, Paul and I left. Dad had promised Megs
that he would run her downtown. Megan had gone on ab-

solutely relentlessly in the previous few weeks about getting some shoes she wanted. They were a kind of sneaker that all the other school children were wearing, and Megan seriously believed that her social life would be at an end if she didn't get some too. At first my father had told her that she was just being silly, that we didn't have money to spend for things like that, and that her other shoes were perfectly good enough, especially since they still fit, which was something none of Megan's shoes seemed to do for long. But then Dad received some overtime from the garage, and I guess Megs must have worn him down on the issue. Anyhow, he had promised to run her down to Penney's. Consequently, when Paul and I came through, she was standing barefoot in the hallway because my father had told her to check her socks to make certain they weren't holey or smelly. So there Megan stood, having taken them off completely to have a good look. Dad came blustering in, telling her to hurry up.

"I've got to have those running shoes," Megs was saying to no one in particular. "They cost $10.98 and I got to have them."

My father was muttering under his breath about something else she was going to have to have, if she didn't speed up.

Paul and I went out along Ladder Creek to our familiar spot. I don't know how it came to be that we went there and nowhere else along the creek, but by that point, it was our second home.

We took the blanket from the backseat of the car, brought it down by the water and spread it out over the thin grass. Paul took his shirt off, and we lay down together. I could see little heat waves rising off the plains and looked up to scan the skies. April and May were tornado season and in Kansas, you paid a great deal of attention to what the skies were doing at that time of year. It was clear and cloudless. I wondered how long it would be before the thunderheads formed.

We talked, but not much. The main topic was Paul's going away to school and my going away and the fact that we were going different places. We discussed the survival of our relationship in cool, detached tones, as if it didn't matter too much to either of us if it faded and died, when I knew for a fact that it mattered much. I told Paul I wasn't even certain that I would be going to college, given that I had cashed the bond in. He said he wasn't very sure about Ohio State anymore either. He really did wish he was going to study astronomy, or at least physics. Then he paused. It was easier, he said in a sad tone, when we were kids. Then there never was a worry about things like jobs or money. That comment caused us to digress onto the subject of childhood in general. I said I thought Megan had it a lot easier than I had, that I'd always felt a certain amount of responsibility toward the family that I didn't believe she did. Paul said it was just personalities, in his opinion. That different kids reacted in different ways. He said the same thing was true of him and Aaron. Aaron had no sense of responsibility either. Aaron lived in the here-and-now and had no sense of the future. Basically, he said, Aaron just had no sense, period. The conversation made me think of Megan and her obsession with reading about the war. That had subsided some, but I knew she was still doing it. I couldn't understand where she got it. I said I knew too much already without reading more. I said I did believe that ignorance was bliss in many respects. Paul replied that he thought they got that expression wrong. Innocence, he said, was bliss. But to his way of thinking, ignorance was like standing in a prison cell with an unlocked door and never opening it.

Paul reached over and unbuttoned my blouse. When he lay back down again, I could feel his warm, bare skin. We made love in the hot afternoon stillness. It was much better, easier. I could relax. The heat helped; heavy and soporific, it dulled my thinking, and my body responded effortlessly.

We grew drowsy afterward. Little bugs floated by in clouds, and you could hear their high-pitched, distant buzz, sawing against the silence. We lay, eyes closed, arms around one another, our bodies slippery with sweat. After having been awake in the night, I was tired. I grew sleepy in the warmth and dozed with the steady thumping of Paul's heart against my ear.

A car came along. We heard it on the road. I roused when Paul rose up on one elbow to listen to it. We were down out of sight of the road because of the slope the creek bank created. The car slowed but went on. I fell back onto the blanket. I'd been fully asleep and dreaming. It had been a confused dream, an Alice-down-the-rabbit-hole sort of dream where I had not realized I was actually asleep until I woke. But now, awakened, I was heavy with the desire to return to it. I closed my eyes.

Paul remained poised, up on his elbow, as alert as a jackrabbit. Probably some kid casing out parked cars, he said as the sound diminished. I asked if he had locked the car. Yes, he said. But good thing he'd taken the guns out.

We talked then, lazily, about kids and cars and things like drugs, which were rampant at school if you knew where to look. I asked him if he knew Jennifer Olsen, because I knew for a fact that she was stoned half the time. You could tell too. Paul told me that his mom had caught Aaron with part of a lid not long before, and she'd said that he could just go live with his dad if he felt like doing stuff like that. I asked Paul if he'd ever tried pot. Yeah, he said, once with some of Aaron's friends. He hadn't thought much of it. He hadn't gotten much of a high. What about me? he asked. I said I'd never been anywhere it was offered.

Then we heard the car come back. Paul was sure it was the same car because of the way the engine sounded. He said he was going to check who it was. I wasn't wearing anything. I rolled over and reached for my jeans, just in case we had to make our presence known.

As I was buttoning my blouse, a policeman came over the crest of the embankment. I had a moment's panic, thinking perhaps what Paul and I had obviously been doing was illegal, but it passed. I kept forgetting I was an adult.

"Are you Lesley Elena O'Malley?" the policeman asked.

The panic returned. I was still struggling with the buttons on my blouse. Paul stood halfway between the policeman and me.

"Are you the daughter of Cowan Christopher and Mara Elena O'Malley?" he asked.

"Yes," I said.

"Would you come with me please?"

Numbly, I rose to my feet. The panic had risen to something akin to terror. I had no idea why he wanted me, which made it all the more frightening. I'm listening to Mama's stories too much, I thought. I also thought of running.

"What did I do?" I asked when I found my voice. We were up on the edge of the embankment, nearing the road.

The officer opened the police car door for me. He motioned me in. But when Paul leaned forward to get in with me, the policeman put his arm out. "No, son," he said gently. "Just the young lady."

The officer went around and climbed in the other side. Paul had jumped back down the embankment to get our things. The last I saw of him was when he came struggling back up, the red wool blanket a jumble in his arms. The police car started and we drove off.

Numbness suffuscd my body. I was shaking, but the panic had subsided as abruptly as it came. What replaced it was a disquietingly complete calmness. I felt absurdly clearheaded. "What do you want me for?" I asked.

His eyes were fixed on the rearview mirror, and he did not look at me. "Your mother," he said. "She's just killed three people."

# Twenty-Two

My MAMA HAD WAITED until Paul and I had left and Dad had gone in the car to make the few minutes' run downtown to let Megan off. Then armed with one of Paul's rat-shooting rifles, she went to the Watermans.

Apparently, she killed Toby Waterman first, there in the front yard with his mother, who'd tried to push him inside. Just one shot. Then Mrs. Waterman. Finally, my mother shot Mr. Waterman, reloaded, shot him twice more.

By the time the police arrived, my father was there, trying to get her to give him the gun. But she panicked, seeing the officers with their handguns, and she fired at them. The policeman said he'd had no choice but to shoot back. He fired three times and hit her twice. When she fell, she was still holding the rifle.

During the trip back from Ladder Creek, time took on a bizarre quality, running simultaneously too fast and too slow. Like film in an unreliable movie projector, the scenery flew by the car in jerky, Keystone-Kops fashion. But inside the car, things wound down to slow motion. I saw each movement of the police officer beside me in frame-by-frame detail. He glanced in the rearview mirror, over to the side mirror, looked ahead, rubbed his cheek, signaled, turned the car onto the main highway.

He looked over at me. He smiled politely. His skin was very dark, as if he were of Middle Eastern extraction. His uniform appeared uncomfortable, because he kept scratching at his shirt and pulling the collar out from his neck. Beside him I sat, frozen, all my attention focused acutely outward, every external stimulus from the stubble of his beard to the smell of the police car being registered with permanent, graphic clarity. But inside myself I felt nothing whatsoever. I was empty.

Outside the police station was an enormous crowd of people. There were three police cars and an ambulance, two highway-patrol vehicles and a van marked Channel Seven News. Obliquely, the thought came into my mind of how much excitement my mama had provided for this small Kansas outpost.

"Hello! Hello!" cried a woman as we climbed out of the car. Trailing the cord of a microphone, she ran toward us. The policeman with me grabbed my arm and pulled me to his other side so that he was between the woman and me.

"Are you the daughter?" she shouted. Then a second officer opened the door to the station and tugged me through by the sleeve of my blouse. I turned to look back at the woman. Her question echoed in my head, like words from a foreign language.

My father was there. The police station was little more than just a big room, divided by a wooden partition with a gate in it. The officers' desks were all on the far side. Back behind the big room was a smaller one with a glassed-in office and just one cell. My father was sitting in a wooden chair beside one of the desks near the far wall. He turned when I entered, rose partway up from the chair. Then he stopped, frozen mid-move and gaped at me, as if he were seeing a stranger. He sat back down again.

It was at that moment that the enormity of what had

just happened first hit me. It came as a physical sensation, like scalding heat. The horror was so great, so overwhelming that it wasn't an emotion at all. I felt myself sinking, as if my feet were melting through the floor of the police station. All around me from above came crashing colors of paralyzing, psychedelic brightness. My knees went weak from the weight of them.

Then my father was beside me, his arms around me, supporting my weight, keeping me on my feet. The moment passed; the feeling receded like nausea after vomiting. And it left me with the same sort of foul residue in my mouth.

I hardly recall the rest of the afternoon. For all the minute details etched into my memory about the return from Ladder Creek, almost nothing about the hours spent at the police station registered. I do remember Paul coming in with his mother. It had been his .22 Mama had used. He stood, face pale, hands behind his back. While he talked to the officer, I saw Bo looking over at me and then my father. She stared at us fixedly and did not look away when I turned toward her. Instead, she continued to gaze, as if I were a stranger, or rather, as if I were not quite a person, and so staring did not matter. She was wearing a red silk blouse she had let me try on once. I thought then, as I sat beside my father, that I'd never cared greatly for red anyway. Paul glanced over too, but we were never close enough to speak.

I also remember faces pressed against the glass, almost like a surrealistic painting, when I went out in the hallway on my way to the toilet. But chiefly, I recall the coffee, which they kept giving us in small Styrofoam cups. It was weak and tasted of chemicals from the whitener. What I kept thinking was how, the weekend before, it had made my mother sick to her stomach. I wondered if I too would be ill from drinking it.

The only other clear recollection was of the police sergeant. It had been he whom my father had been talking with when I'd come into the station, whom my father had had to tell all Mama's small secrets to. He was a short, balding man, roly-poly and red cheeked like a Santa Claus. Later, while we were waiting on the long wooden bench in front of the main desk, he came to us and held out his hand to my father. When Dad took it, the sergeant simply continued to hold Dad's hand and did not shake it.

"This is the most tragic thing I've ever heard," he said to my father. "I want you to know I feel so awful. Nobody can hear these things that happened to her and feel anything but the most terrible compassion for your wife."

Not lifting his head, my father nodded. He still held the sergeant's hand.

I remember that.


Sometime in the early evening we were allowed to leave the police station. My father went directly over to the hospital, where Mama was in intensive care. He had the car, so one of the policemen drove me home to avoid the crowd still collected outside the station.

Everything continued to seem unreal to me. As I rode along, I thought about exactly *how* unreal it seemed, and before I was aware of it, I had begun seeing things as they usually were. I could see myself arriving at the front door and opening it. The scent of soup and freshly made bread mingled with the familiar home smell in the darkness of the front hallway. Everything was starkly clear to me. The dusky rose-colored rug on the floor by the front door. Megan's dirty overshoes. The outline of Dad's beloved tall clock in the hallway. The tangle of coats and jackets on the hooks at the bottom of the stairs. That certain kind of darkness that fills a house when only the kitchen is lit. I could smell the soup very distinctly. Lentil. Because it was my father's favorite, Mama made us eat it about once a week. I could hear her voice, first humming, then breaking into song for a line or two, then humming again. It was a song she often sang absently to herself. Neither her voice nor the song was very melodic, and I never even knew what song it was. Upstairs, Megs was playing. I could hear the muted thunk of her sock feet as she ran back and forth in the upstairs hallway. It was all so clear.

Still trapped in imagery, I thanked the officer for the ride and got out. The sights, the sounds, the smells, even the way I always felt emotionally when arriving home, was an illusion so powerful that I was convinced it was real. And this other obscene thing was not. It had just been some awful joke someone had played on me. Elaborate but false. And in bad taste. I knew when I turned the doorknob that there would be the hallway darkness and the light spilling from the kitchen and my mama.

The dream collapsed with sodden suddenness when I opened the door. The house, of course, was empty and unlit. Silence tumbled out on top of me like an armload of books from an overloaded closet. I stood a long minute on the doorstep, feeling bitter and humiliated.

I didn't know what my father had told Megan about the murders. I didn't ask when I finally went to get her from the Reillys' next door. I didn't know how Dad had done it, but Megan certainly knew.

That evening continued to be tainted with a powerful aura of unreality. Megan and I went through the routines of normal living, saying nothing to each other about what had occurred and yet never thinking about anything else. Megan too was doing a great deal of pretending, just to get by. Once, mid-evening, she looked over at me and said, "Really, it's just like Mama's had a bad spell and Daddy's upstairs taking care of her. That's all. And we're down here like usual."

One of Paul's rat rifles was still out in the hall by the coat closet. I had assumed the police would have been over to take it as well, so when I chanced across it, it startled me as much as if it had been a living thing lurking there. I jumped back and cried out in surprise. There too were the boxes of ammunition. I could see they'd been disturbed but I was unable to bring myself to lift up the lids and see which box Mama had taken the shells from. I didn't even want to touch those things, but the fact that they were there unsettled me. It was Megan who resolved to do something about it. She brought out a plastic garbage bag and carefully transferred the boxes of shells into it. We carried the bag and the gun out to the back porch and put them into the cupboard with the vacuum cleaner. Megan shut the door and leaned the dirty-clothes basket against it. Pausing, she regarded the basket pensively before going out to the garage for some rope to run through the door handles, tying the cupboard securely shut.

"There," she said, trying the cupboard to see if it would open. The rope held fast. Thoughtfully, she studied it.

"You don't suppose they'll think we're trying to hide them, do you?" she asked me. "Would they arrest us?"

"No. We're just putting them in a safe place. They'd know that."

We both regarded the cupboard.

"Anyway, they got the other gun down at the police station," I said. "I saw it. They probably don't care about this stuff."

Megan continued to look at the cupboard. Then she turned and went into the kitchen. "Let's lock the door," she said and shut the kitchen door tightly behind me as I came in. She slipped the bolt through.

We ate a supper of cold cuts and bread, food Mama had bought for Sunday lunch. I was hungry and embarrassed by it, since it hardly seemed like a time to feel much like eating.

Around eight my father came home. Mama's condition was not stabilizing the way the people at the hospital had hoped, and they were debating about bringing in a helicopter to fly her down to St. Joseph's in Wichita. She'd had three-and-a-half hours of surgery to remove the bullets and still she continued to hemorrhage. Dad said she had never been conscious the entire time he was there. But then, she was still under the influence of the anaesthetic, so he wasn't too worried. Or at least that's what he said.

After he had a cup of coffee and a sandwich, Dad rang Auntie Caroline in Chicago. Auntie Caroline was his older sister, and she was the only member of my father's family with whom we still had contact.

I grew angry. I didn't want Auntie Caroline to come down. She hardly ever came to visit otherwise, so I didn't want her now. I told my father that. I also told him that every time Auntie Caroline was there she made snide comments about him and Mama and the way we lived. He said he knew that, that it was just Caroline's way. I said I didn't like it and I didn't want Megan to hear that kind of stuff. Especially now. So how could he even suggest it? Moreover, I was upset that he hadn't even bothered to consult Megan and me about the matter. He'd simply gone in the living room and phoned her.

Dad said there wasn't much to consult about. What else could he do? There was no one else to come. He didn't even exchange Christmas cards with Uncle Kip and Uncle Mickey. Aunt Kath was still with the Sisters of Mercy in Colombia. Uncle Colin wouldn't be any help, given the way he drank. And Dad hadn't spoken with Uncle Paddy since that time Mama threw the cranberry juice at Aunt Gretchen. In general, Mama just hadn't made a great impression on Dad's relatives.

I said we didn't need anybody. If I'd been able to cope with things before, I certainly could do it now with just Megs and me. No, he replied in a tone of voice that left no room for argument. If Mama went to Wichita, he would have to go there to stay with her and he didn't want us left alone for days at a time. With Auntie Caroline here, I could return to school and carry on with my ordinary affairs, he said.

Great. Just what I wanted to do, go back to school. After all my agonizing to get back earlier, now I couldn't even bear to contemplate the idea. Given what Mama had just done, the only school I wanted to attend would be in another country. Possibly another planet. I sighed and turned away from my father. That's basically what's wrong with life, I thought morosely. When you want to do something, you can't. When you can, you don't want to.

Afterward, my father went upstairs, showered, shaved and put on a clean shirt. Then he kissed both of us and went back to the hospital to spend the night with Mama. That left Megan and me alone once again.

Since the murders had occurred, there had been an almost constant barrage of people from the media. The police had put a van outside our house to discourage them from bothering Megan and me. They also told us to keep the phone off the hook. But Dad, without thinking, had replaced the receiver after talking to Auntie Caroline. About fifteen minutes after he'd gone back to the hospital, the phone rang.

It was a quarter to ten. I remember looking at the clock and wondering who would be calling so late before it occurred to me that we shouldn't answer it. Megan already had.

By the baffled expression she had on her face, it was clear that the caller was someone we did not know. Cupping the receiver in both hands, she was listening intently to what the person was saying.

He must have known he had a child, someone who didn't know how to put him off, because whoever it was, he was talking a great deal. I could hear the faint buzz of his voice. I gestured for Megan to hang up.

"Who is it?" I mouthed when she continued to listen.

She shook her head slightly, still intent on what the caller was saying.

I stood just outside the small circle of light thrown out from the table lamp. Megan, bathed in incandescent gold, began to cry. The tears welled up around the corners of her eyes; they glittered in the lamplight.

Reaching over, I removed the phone from her hands. The man's voice was still audible as I gently laid the receiver down in the cradle. Giving the line a few minutes to clear, I then lifted the receiver and laid it alongside the telephone.

"Don't put it back," I said. "Just leave it there, Meggie. And if it gets put back accidentally, I don't want you to answer the phone. Understand?"

With the tip of one finger she was flicking back traces of tears, hoping, I think, that I hadn't noticed them. "Has Mama accepted Jesus, Les?"

"Is that what he was on about? Look, Megs, don't pay any attention to that."

"But has she? He said Mama had the Devil in her. That the Devil made her go out and kill innocent people. That God was trying her and she needed to accept Jesus."

"Megan, forget it. We believe differently than that man does. Don't pay any attention to what he was saying."

Her face remained puckered with concern. "But he said Mama'd go to Hell. He said she'd die and go to Hell and burn forever for what she did. He said I had to go over to the hospital right away and tell her to accept Jesus as her savior quick, in case she died, so she'd be saved from Hell.''

I knelt and put my arms around her. "Meggie, that's what that man believes. It's not what we believe. Mama's innocent, Megan. Even if she did do it, she didn't mean to. She just got things confused. But she didn't mean to. She's not going to Hell. Mama's not even dying. So just forget what he said. Don't worry about it.''

She was having a difficult time keeping up with the tears. They never fell but they continually puddled up. As soon as she wiped them away, they were back. "But I think he might be right, Les. It's a sin. It's against the Ten Commandments to kill someone. I don't think Jesus would be very pleased, even if it was just one of Mama's things. You're not supposed to kill people for any reason.''

The telephone call upset us both. Megan had a nearly impossible time getting it out of her head. It was late anyhow, well past her normal bedtime, and both of us were extended far beyond our ability to judge things rationally. For me it was upsetting because it made me suddenly feel very vulnerable there in the house alone. Maybe having Auntie Caroline wasn't such a bad idea after all. Before going to bed I went through the house and made sure all the windows and doors were locked and the curtains were closed. Although a police van with two officers remained outside on the street, for some reason I was not comforted. While upstairs brushing my teeth, I glanced over at Megan, who was changing her clothes. Without speaking, we went downstairs afterward and put chairs under all the doorknobs.

We slept together. First we planned to sleep in her bed. Then in mine. Finally, we ended up in our parents' bed. What if Daddy comes home? Megan asked hopefully. I said I didn't think he was planning to. But if he did, there was enough room in there for him too.

The three of us, Megan, me and Big Cattie, lay clutched together in the dark. All the windows were closed against the balmy, scented spring night; all the curtains were pulled. Megan's hair, long and dark, spilled over us like an extra covering. She smelled good. Being close to her, my nose was filled with her warm, familiar child's scent, and for an instant, it seemed perhaps the possibility still existed that this was just a nightmare and we might soon waken.

I couldn't sleep. I lay perfectly motionless with Megan and the stuffed cat still in my arms but I did not even close my eyes. Megan too lay without moving. A long time after I had assumed she was asleep, she spoke.

"Are you awake, Lessie?"

"Yes."

"I'm scared."

I drew her even closer to me.

"Are you scared?" she asked.

"A little."

Silence.

"They're dead."

"What?"

"I said, they're dead. I keep seeing them. You know, that little boy, that little Toby Waterman. I remember the first day when I was with Mama and we saw him. I can see him clear as anything. Like he's right in front of my eyes. And then I see him shot dead. Right out there in the bushes by the creek. I know that isn't how it happened, but that's what I keep seeing. And he looks like Mrs. Beckerman's cat looked when it got run over. All squashed out."

"Megan, don't think of such things."

Silence.

"Lessie, that gun's down there. In the cupboard. We should have made Daddy take it away."

"Megs, that's not the gun. Don't think about it. Just forget it."

Silence.

More silence.

"Can you forget about it, Lessie?"

Silence.

"Can you, Les?"

"No."

# Twenty-Three

THE MATTRESS in my parents' bed sagged in the middle, and it was nearly impossible to sleep without rolling on top of Megan. Megan, restive in her sleep anyway, continually hit against me. Underneath us was the muted plastic crunch of the waterproof sheet Megan had put on in case she wet the bed. So I awoke very early, feeling as if I had never been asleep. Megan, whose relaxed body was flung out in abandon across the big bed, stirred when I climbed over her, because moving on the bed without jostling her was out of the question. Disoriented a moment, she rose up on her elbows and looked at me. But before I could tell her to go back to sleep, she already had.

It was not quite six-fifteen, and everything was bathed in morning quiet. The day had dawned peerlessly clear and cool, the sun so bright that it shimmered on the dewy grass. Without thinking, I went to get the Sunday paper off the front step. Wearing only one of Dad's T-shirts and my underpants, I was startled to find one of the two officers in the police van watching me as I opened the door. He waved when I looked up, paper in hand. Embarrassed, I pulled back inside and slammed the door.

In the kitchen, I got myself a glass of apple juice and sat down at the table to unroll the paper. There, right

across the top, as I unfolded it, were banner headlines.
LOCAL WOMAN HELD ON TRIPLE MURDER CHARGE.

There was a large photograph of Mama beside the article. The first thing to occur to me was to wonder who
supplied them with that picture. It was from a family
snapshot taken the previous summer during a picnic
at Scott Reservoir. Mama was wearing her old red-
checkered shirt, the one with the collar that curled up regardless of how often she smacked it with the iron.
Mama was smiling in that casual, off-handed way she
had sometimes. Her long hair was pulled back. The sun
had been behind her, so it created a halo all around her
head in the photograph, causing her hair to appear even
blonder than it actually was. The lighting also made her
look a little more foreign, a little more exotic with her
high cheekbones and her wide-set eyes, squeezed into
slits by her smile. Yet, it remained a disarmingly friendly
picture, the kind that made you believe you really could
trust her to recommend the best brand of laundry deter-
gent or panty hose or sausages, not that she had just murdered three people.

Missing Mama had already grown into an identifiable
ache. My father was always coming and going anyway,
so the fact that he was absent from the house was noticeable but acceptable. However, Mama was never gone. I
was brutally conscious of the fact that it was morning and
my mother was not at home. She was no longer distanced
from me and my thoughts, the way she had been the previous afternoon. Now I was aware of only two things:
she was my mama and she was conspicuously absent.

It was that feeling, I suppose, that made reading the article in the newspaper so much more difficult than I had
anticipated, because in it the woman they talked about
was simultaneously my mama and a stranger.

The article was long but rather vague. They had her
birthday wrong. They muddled up the fact that she was

Hungarian, saying that she was German. There were brief, relatively accurate details about the concentration-camp experiences, but they said nothing about the breeding hostel. And they made no mention of the connection between those years and the Watermans. The killings appeared senseless.

Only the description of the murders was given in detail. Even then, reading about them in the newspaper, they seemed unreal, as if the Watermans were people in a television show, whose lives and deaths did not matter. Intellectually, I knew I shouldn't think like that. They were real people and they had been murdered. And my mother had done it. She had taken a rifle and deliberately shot them all dead. All the blood and gore faked on the screen was, for that instant in that small Kansas farmhouse, a reality.

I tried to make myself think of it. I tried to see Mrs. Waterman crouched helplessly over her son, the way the article described. I tried to picture their bodies, the blood pooled and red in the same hot sunlight under which Paul and I had been making love. I tried to conjure up the other Waterman children, terrified, huddled together in a back-room closet. But I could not. They stayed dream people, like the memory of something once imagined.

Sitting at the kitchen table with a glass of apple juice and the Sunday paper spread out, I could only call up the image of Toby Waterman the day that I was home from the dentist's. There across from me was the chair he had been sitting in. He had been such a horrid child, with his mucky hair and his odd eyes, and so cocky and confident about his right to a relationship with my mother. He had scared me. Right from the very first moment out by the tree trunk. He had believed so easily what my mama had told him.

And now he was dead. As simple as that. Never to grow up and be a man. Never to go to school and know the guileless tedium of learning. Never even to know what this brilliant spring morning looked like, when the morning before he had woken up just like I had. How could you really understand a thing like that?

Auntie Caroline's bus arrived at half-past eleven. Before then, my father had come home for a brief while. He'd shaved again and changed his shirt again, so I knew Megan and I were going to have to put on better clothes too. But we stayed home and let Dad go to the bus depot alone. I had seen the reporters run up to my father's car as he had turned off Bailey Street when he came home from the hospital. It seemed judicious for Megan and me to avoid them, if possible.

By the time Auntie Caroline and my father reached the front door they were already in an argument. Dad had her suitcase in one hand and a flight bag in the other.

"Cowan, you ought to have told me Mara was like this. It does no good to pretend about such things. Not with family, at least. You just ought to have said something earlier," Auntie Caroline was saying to him as he came in the door. Dad put the suitcase down by the foot of the stairs and balanced the flight bag on top.

"The thing is, Caroline," he said, "Mara *wasn't* like this. I've told you that." His voice was tight with restraint. They must have been arguing for some time. He marched past Megan and me and went into the kitchen. Filling up the teakettle with water, he slammed it onto the stove.

"She always has been highly strung, Cowan. Ever since the beginning. Ever since that first time you brought her home. Remember that? Remember how she kept carrying on with Mother?"

"Caroline, *anybody*'d carry on with Mother. Besides, for God's sake, she was still sick. She was still recovering from all that. Honestly, what did you expect out of her?''

"She certainly was full of her opinions though. And she was so highly strung. Every little word and she was upset.''

"Well, did Mother have to keep going on at her? Did Mother have to harp constantly about religion all the time?''

"Yes, Cowan, but did Mara have to keep saying what rubbish it all was? She could tell how Mother felt about it.''

"And Mother could damned well tell how she felt too. Honestly, Caroline, there she was, a guest in our house, a stranger in a foreign land, still sick, still half-starved, just having gone through experiences you and I would never survive. Did Mother have to say all those things to her?'' He paused, looked down at the floor and then back. "I married her, Caroline. She was my wife and I loved her. It was as big a slam to me, Mother saying all those things, as it ever was to Mara.''

Auntie Caroline just shook her head.

"It was, Caroline. It was just Mother trying to make me look like a failure one more time.''

Caroline turned. "You're too sensitive, Cowan. You always have been.'' It was then she saw Megan and me, standing just outside the kitchen doorway.

She smiled suddenly, disarmingly. Her arms opened and we were both wrapped up in a hug together.

My father returned to the hospital immediately, not even stopping to have lunch with us. That left Megan and me to help Auntie Caroline settle in. She had to sleep in the study on the bed that pulled out from the couch. So Megan and I carried her things up, pulled the bed out and put sheets on it. Auntie Caroline stayed downstairs and prepared a meal for us.

She did a good job with what was around the house.

No one had done the weekly shopping, so there wasn't much choice. Mama's constant craving for starchy things ensured that, while we might be running out of other food, you could count on there being plenty of bread and pasta and potatoes. So there was Auntie Caroline amid our vast collection of Rice-A-Roni and boxed macaroni and cheese, trying to make a Sunday dinner.

My aunt had a life-style considerably different from ours. Her husband, our Uncle Roger, was a dentist in Winnetka, and they had lived for thirty-four years in the same house on the same street. Their children were all raised there and had all grown up and married and had families of their own. Auntie Caroline devoted most of her time to playing bridge. The rest she spent at church or at Weight Watchers. Unlike all the men in Dad's family, both Aunt Kath and Auntie Caroline had figures that were 40-40-40. Auntie Caroline must have been a founding member of her Weight Watchers group, because she'd been going to the meetings for as long as I could remember. And she was still overweight. When she had come to visit us, she would always give Mama heck for her carbohydrate fetish. The two of them were like Jack Sprat and his wife, one unable to gain, one unable to lose, and both not-so-covertly envious of the other.

Auntie Caroline used to visit us quite frequently, although Uncle Roger seldom accompanied her. Caroline said it was because of his practice, but I suspect it was more because of Mama. Mama loathed dentists. She had had several courses of experimental dental work, without anaesthetic, while she was in Ravensbrück and after that, I don't think she was ever fully relieved of the belief that all dentists were in cahoots with the SS. She could argue this logic in a sophisticated, virtually flawless fashion, the way she could so many of her convictions, which made countering her points almost impossible. And she never let the argument drop. Repeatedly, she would corner Uncle Roger and tell him that there had to be something sadistic in the psychological makeup of an individual who chose a profession that caused most people to be terrified of him and allowed him to legally hurt them. Understandably, this point of view did not endear Mama to Uncle Roger, who was a rather soft-spoken, unobtrusive man. I remember once, when Mama had pursued Uncle Roger into the kitchen to continue the discussion, his saying to her in his quiet, patient voice, that dentists were there to *stop* people's pain and that they didn't really want to make people afraid of them. And Mama laughed. She threw her head back and howled like a hyena. Uncle Roger never came again, after that.

At lunch that Sunday, I could not eat. I came into the kitchen, sat down, took my serving of Auntie Caroline's casserole and then sat there, knowing that if I ate, I would be sick all over the table. Auntie Caroline sat, eyeing me from my mother's chair across the table.

"I haven't got much of an appetite, I'm afraid," I said finally. It was reaching the point that even the smell of food was making me nauseated.

"I think you ought to try," she replied. "You look like a walking skeleton, Lesley. Have you looked at yourself in the mirror lately? You can't have been eating right."

"I've been eating fine. I'm just not hungry now."

Auntie Caroline sighed.

"I'm sorry," I said. "It's not the food or anything. It's just me."

"You look anorectic, if you ask me," she said. She lifted an eyebrow. "Are you?"

"What's anorectic, Auntie?" Megan asked.

"Anorexia nervosa," replied Auntie Caroline.

"Oh," said Megan, still perplexed. She mulled the information over for a few moments. "Does that mean nerves? Bad nerves? Nervosa?"

"Something like that," Aunt Caroline said.

"Yeah, I think Lesley's got bad nerves too."

I pushed the food around.

"You just better watch out, that's all I can say," Auntie Caroline said to me. "Or you'll end up just like your mother."

About 5:30 my father returned. The doctors at the hospital had decided they would transfer Mama to Wichita. He was going to drive the car over so that he would be there when the helicopter arrived. If I wanted, he said, I could go down to the hospital to see her for a little while before she was moved.

Megan, sitting beside me, leaped up, saying she wanted to go too. She broke into tears before my father even had a chance to tell her no. You're not quite old enough, sweetheart, he said to her, pushing her hair back from her face. When she continued to cry, he sat down and lifted her into his lap. We'll go another day when Mama's feeling better, he said to her. Auntie Caroline can bring you down to Wichita on the bus.

The hospital was quiet. It was too late for regular visitors, so I was all alone in the corridor. My footsteps echoed far ahead of me as I walked. The hospital was so small that there seemed to be no activity anywhere.

The intensive-care unit consisted of only two tiny rooms separated from one another by a nursing desk and the medical monitors. Only Mama's room was occupied. The other care unit was empty. At the desk, two nurses were absorbed in writing. One looked up, smiled and said I could only have ten minutes.

Mama was all alone in the room. It was a small place, barely large enough for the bed. It faced west and all was bathed in a deep, murky twilight when I entered. There were no lights on, and what came back to me in that quirky, leapfrogging manner memories have of returning at odd moments, was the previous weekend when I had opened the door to my parents' bedroom and had seen her asleep in my daddy's arms. She was asleep now, or comatose, I didn't know which. My father said she'd been conscious on and off through the day. But now she lay in the bed, silent and still, like Snow White in her glass coffin.

All around one side of the room were traces of my father's lengthy vigil. Newspapers, a soft-drink can, numerous empty coffee cups, a paperback book with its cover bent, half a dozen cellophane salted-peanut bags wadded into balls, a crumpled, half-eaten packet of jelly beans. His watch was there too, apparently taken off at some random moment, set on the bedside table and forgotten.

When I came close to Mama, I saw the tangle of modern technology spilling out the far side of the bed, like spaghetti. She had a tube in her nose. It was connected to a bottle on the table that frothed and foamed with the private workings of her stomach. A bag of blood hung above the bed on my side. Across from it were two other bags filled with clear solutions. The wires of the heart monitor went down through the sheet and out by the railing on the far side of the bed.

Cautiously, I put my hand into the snarl of tubes and wires to touch her face. She was flushed, and when I touched her skin, I could feel the fever. Looking around the room to see if there was a cloth somewhere that I might be able to dampen with cool water, I saw none. I was afraid to go out and ask the nurse for one, in case she wouldn't let me come back in. So, instead, I dipped my fingers into the pitcher of icy water on the bedside table and wiped the perspiration away from her hairline with my fingers.

"Mama? Can you hear me, Mama? It's Lesley. Can you hear me?" My fear was that locked within an inert body, she might be aware. She would be terrified by all this, to be here alone and in pain and without us and her familiar things around her. I knew Daddy had that concern as well, because he'd been so adamant about being allowed to stay with her, even in intensive care. I was overwhelmed with an urge to get into the bed with her and put my arms around her. Instead, I leaned over and kissed her. On the forehead. On the cheek. I wanted to kiss her on the lips, but with the gastric tube, I couldn't. Then I sat down in the chair beside the bed.

She moved. In a slow, ponderous motion, she turned her head and opened her eyes. She tried to speak but no sound came out.

"Do you want a drink, Mama?" I asked. I looked for a glass but there was none. Only the pitcher. Then it occurred to me that with the tube she couldn't drink anyway and the water must have been for my father. Her lips were cracked with fever, and I thought perhaps the coolness might make her feel better. So I fished a piece of ice from the pitcher with my fingers and put it in her mouth. The suction jar made a loud, obscene gurgle next to me. Startled, I jumped. Mama smiled.

There were a hundred million things I wanted to say to her. I stood over her, watching her, putting small bits of ice between her lips, and I was desperate to talk. I wanted her to know that it didn't matter to me what she had done. I loved her. I didn't care about the horrible things people were saying. Nothing mattered at all except that she get better and come home to Daddy and Meggie and me. I wanted her to be assured that I hadn't really minded all those days of staying home from school with her. I hadn't minded any of the things I had complained about. Not really. They were nothing. She was everything.

The problem was, I couldn't speak. There was the fear far back in my mind that I would be making peace with her, and if I did that, she could die. But if I didn't, somehow she would have to survive so I could tell her later.

The bigger problem was that I just could not get the words into my mouth or my mouth open. So I stood, mute.

"Where's O'Malley?" she whispered.

"He's at home right now, Mama. With Meggie. They're going to take you to St. Joseph's. To Wichita. So you'll get better faster. You're going in a helicopter, and Daddy wants to take the car over so that he will be there when you arrive." I managed to smile. "Have you ever ridden in a helicopter before? I haven't. It sounds exciting, doesn't it?"

"I'm tired," she said and closed her eyes.

"You can sleep, if you want, Mama. I'll stay with you. And you can sleep. I'm here."

She struggled against the tube for a deeper breath. Reaching through the rail to take her hand, I realized I was shaking. Afraid she would notice too, I pushed my other hand through to keep the first steady. But she noticed nonetheless, turned her head and looked at me.

"I've got to admit, you've sort of scared me, Mama, getting hurt like this," I said. "I don't want anything to happen to you. I love you."

*"O Liebes,"* she said. "Come down here, baby, and let me touch you."

I put the railing down and sat in the chair beside the bed, my head on the sheet. She lifted her hand into my hair, and the tubing from the IV dropped across my face. Silence too lay down upon us like a comforter, and we did not speak for a very long time. I simply lay with my head against her, the familiar weight of her hand over my ear and through my hair.

"Can you see now, baby?" she whispered to me.

I didn't know what she was referring to. I was too overpowered by emotion at that moment to be able to ask, and when I finally moved to see her face, I saw she had slipped back into the sleeplike state.

My memory pulled me back just then to that very long ago time in West Texas when I was lost in the sunflower forest, when she had crashed in among the stalks and saved me and lifted me high up onto her shoulders so that I could see beyond the flowers.

I don't suppose that's what she meant when she spoke. I don't really know. But as I sat in thick and grainy April twilight, those were the thoughts I had.

# Twenty-Four

THE NEXT MORNING I came into the kitchen to find Auntie Caroline making oatmeal for breakfast. No one in the family liked it except Mama. The oatmeal was hers. None of the rest of us ate it and Megan in particular loathed it.

I watched Auntie Caroline for a few moments. She still was wearing her bathrobe and she bustled around the kitchen like she'd been in it for years.

"Megan doesn't really like oatmeal," I said.

"No wonder everyone in this house looks like sticks," Auntie Caroline replied.

"I could scramble her an egg or something," I offered. I was not up to the scene Megan would create if she got nothing for breakfast but oatmeal. Megan wasn't given to scenes about food, but on top of everything else, I knew she wouldn't tolerate this.

Neither would Auntie Caroline. "I've put raisins in it. I'm sure she's never had it with raisins and she'll like it just fine."

"I don't think so," I said.

"Well, if she doesn't, she can just go hungry."

Hands in the pockets of my jeans, I stood there. Neither Megan nor I was going to school and suddenly the day seemed to stretch out forever.

"Auntie Caroline, may I ask you something?"

She turned. One of the curlers in her hair sagged over her left ear.

"How come you came? I mean, if you don't like being with us, how come you came in the first place?"

She smiled. It was a soft smile, disarming in its suddenness. "I do like being here, Lesley. And I came because your father asked me. Because we're family, no matter what, and this is what families are for. But I'm not going to treat you special, if that's what you mean. I'm planning to treat you just the way I'd treat my own children. Just because your mother did what she did, that's no excuse to feel sorry for yourselves. She did that because of her particular problems. You have your own lives to get on with."

I turned away and went to the table to sit down. A wave of depression overtook me. "I wasn't asking for special treatment, Aunt Caroline. I just wanted eggs instead of oatmeal. We don't like oatmeal. Nobody does. Except Mama. It's Mama's oatmeal and not ours. It's for her."

Auntie Caroline rerolled the loose curler and put the pin back into it. Then she sighed and looked over at the stove. There was a long minute's pause. "Well, I suppose just this once. It's good for you; mind you, you should be eating it. Skinny as pencils, every one of you. Cowan worse than anybody. Probably anemic. But I suppose just this once we could skip it."

The day was intolerable. With nowhere to go and nothing to do, both Megan and I were soon miserably bored. Neither of us could concentrate for long. Twice we got out board games and started them. Twice we had to put them away unfinished. We turned the television on but were too restless to watch.

About eleven Auntie Caroline and I heard a terrific clatter from overhead and went upstairs to discover Megan in the hallway with the sewing machine. She had spools of thread and cloth and patterns strewn all over the floor of the hallway and down into her room.

"What on earth are you doing?" I asked. "Look at the mess you've made."

"I was going to set up the sewing machine. Mama said she'd make me a stuffed dog from this pattern, remember? I was just going to cut out the material for her."

Hands on hips, Auntie Caroline shook her head, then went to relieve Megan of the machine. Megan would not give it to her.

"Your mother is not going to be in any position to be sewing, Megan. Now, let's just put this away for the time being."

"I want to cut the pattern out."

"You can do that downstairs. We'll get you the scissors and the pins and you can take the material down to the kitchen table. Now, let's put all the rest of this away." Auntie Caroline was still trying to wrest the handle from her.

"Oh Megan," I said, "Mama wasn't even going to do it for you. You know that. She said maybe. And when's the last time you saw Mama sewing?"

"She made one of those dogs for you, Lesley."

"Cripes, that was years ago. Geez, like 1965 or something."

"Well, if she made one for you, then I want her to make me one too." She still clung tenaciously to the sewing machine, her face set in a petulant expression. Auntie Caroline gave up and went past her to pick up all the paraphernalia Megan had strewn about.

"Megan, I was littler than you are when Mama made me that dog."

"So?"

"So, grow up, Megs. You're nearly ten. You don't need to bug Mama about making you some stupid stuffed toy."

"But I want one. You got all the things done for you when you were little. Mama never does those things for me."

"Oh Megan, for pity's sake. Mama isn't even here."

"But when she comes back, I want her to make me a dog. To go with Big Cattie. You know. So I'll have a cat and a dog. Mama said she would."

"She said she *might*," I replied. "That's hardly the same thing."

"Girls, girls," Auntie Caroline said, returning to us with her arms full. She put everything back into the hall closet. "Don't argue."

With rude loudness Megan broke into tears.

"Megan Mary! I'm surprised at you," Auntie Caroline said.

"Come off it, Megs. What are you crying for? Some stupid dog pattern? Jesus Christ, Megan, Mama is a hundred and fifty miles away in the hospital and not about to make you some stupid stuffed animal now anyway. Don't be such a big baby."

Her bawling escalated. Dropping the handle of the sewing machine, she kicked it savagely.

"Megan Mary O'Malley!" cried Auntie Caroline in horror. "You stop that this instant."

Still screaming, Megan plunked down right in the middle of the hall floor.

"Well, I never," Aunt Caroline said. "Look at you. A great big girl like you having a tantrum."

"I *want* a tantrum!" Megan screamed back.

At lunch Auntie Caroline suggested that perhaps Megan and I ought to go back to school. We were so restive and disordered that she thought school might help. Besides, she said, it would better to get it over with, to face the music, as she put it.

I couldn't bear even to consider it. I just could not imagine sitting in German and answering Mr. Tennant's

perennial Monday afternoon question, "And what did
*you* do this weekend?"

Megan responded to Caroline's suggestion by getting
sick all over the kitchen floor.

As the afternoon wore on, my thoughts grew increasingly troubled. The numbness that had initially protected
me from the horror of what my mother had done began to
erode. Gruesome reality was beneath it. Images of Toby
Waterman with his blind-dog eyes and his brash, vaguely
sinister innocence kept forming. Thoughts of the murders
themselves had dogged me for some time. They skulked
quietly in the back of my mind until I was off my guard
and then they returned, the way thoughts of owed money
do, dragging with them that weary, inescapable burden
of being true.

I could picture the physical minutiae of the killings
quite vividly. Pieced together from what I'd read in the
newspapers, from my own knowledge of the Waterman
place, and from my imagination, I could create a very
realistic-seeming scenario. Mainly, it was Toby that I
saw. In my visions he was always already dead, his colorless eyes open, his face covered with blood, like Sissy
Spacek's in *Carrie*. Intellectually, I knew that, in spite of
how realistic these impressions were, they probably
weren't very accurate. But that didn't seem to matter.
Like film in a broken projector, over and over the
thoughts played in my mind.

Bizarrely yoked with these horrific visions was an
ever-increasing anxiety about what was going to happen
to my mama. I was sitting in the living room, watching
out the window that afternoon, and the longer I sat, the
more upset I felt. What would they do to her? Where
would they take her? Even if they realized she was as
much a victim of what had happened as the Watermans,
the authorities weren't going to simply forgive and forget. Not for something like this. Finally, I asked Auntie

Caroline as she passed through the room on her way up to see Megan. What did she reckon would become of Mama? I asked. Would they send her to prison or to the state hospital? I asked her which she thought would be a better place to go. Auntie Caroline froze mid-step, her mouth dropped open in shocked expression, and she said to me, what a coldhearted child I was to think of things like that so analytically. I started to cry. Auntie Caroline's features softened in sympathy and she came and put her arms around my shoulders. She told me not to brood about it. She said, we didn't know, did we? So there was no point in worrying before we had to.

I worried anyway. I was nibbled, gnawed and devoured by worry. All afternoon I could think of nothing else.

Two matters kept surfacing. One was that this was going to be the second time my mother had lost her liberty. There seemed something cruelly unjust about that to me, because if there hadn't been a first time, there probably wouldn't have been a second. The other was my awareness of Mama's intense pleasure in mundane things. Mama was constantly conscious of the difference between her life with us and her life during the war. Of all the knowledge that she'd passed on to Megan and me, nothing was more important to her than that we realize what a very special gift an ordinary day was. And Mama so cherished her little freedoms. The big ones didn't matter as much to her. I reckoned she could survive being confined to a building or grounds somewhere. But she would be tormented by not having the liberty to make a cup of coffee when she wanted one or to wash her hair or otherwise order the small details of her day.

My thoughts were tortured by the innocent cruelty of the system. Her preferences, her pleasures, her feelings would not carry any weight in an institution. She'd be nothing more than just another middle-aged woman to

the staff working there. She would be treated much like
the ladies I had worked with in the nursing home. Gotten
up in the mornings, hurried through the day to someone
else's schedule, fed, prodded, taken to the toilet,
watched like a distrusted pet. We laughed at them behind
their backs, at their silly, senile ways. Not to make fun of
them but simply because they were funny and we didn't
love any of them. They had no dignity in our eyes. They
were our work. We treated them well but indifferently,
even the best of the girls did.

My father didn't come home at all that day. Instead, he
remained in Wichita with Mama. He phoned to tell us he
planned to return in the morning. Then he'd take Megan
and me back with him to see Mama. We could stay overnight and come home on the bus. I asked him how Mama
was. Better, he said. She was conscious most of the time
now. Was she scared? I asked. He said no, he didn't
think so. Then he laughed self-consciously, saying
Mama was being stronger about this than he was. Which
was probably true.

Auntie Caroline talked with him. She told him about
the two news reporters who'd knocked on the door after
supper, and about Megan, who had been vomiting all afternoon. It still sounded peculiar to me to hear someone
call my father Cowan.

When night came again I was unable to sleep. I was
tired enough. In fact, I felt crawlly with nervous exhaustion. But long after getting into bed, I was still awake.

Megan continued to be very sick, which made sleeping
even more difficult because I could hear her every time
she went into the bathroom. Auntie Caroline was up with
her once, and they stood in the hallway outside my bedroom and talked. Megan was bawling again, afraid she
wasn't going to be allowed to go to Wichita with Dad in
the morning because she was so sick. Auntie Caroline in

a gentle, motherly voice, was telling her not to worry about things that hadn't happened yet and no doubt, come morning, she'd feel fine. Megan obviously was not believing her.

Long after Auntie Caroline had returned to her bed in the study, I could hear Megan still crying in her room. The study was at the opposite end of the hallway, so Caroline probably was not aware of how upset Megan was. Finally, after listening to her get up and vomit again and then go snuffling back by my doorway, I rose to go see about her myself.

I sat down on the bed next to her. "Do you want me to get you some ginger tea or something, Meggie? Some Seven-Up?"

She shook her head.

"Here roll over. I'll rub your back. That'll make you feel better."

"No."

"That's what Mama would do." I reached out to stroke her hair. "Come on. Roll over."

Reluctantly, Megan complied. She had Big Cattie with her, its furry ears pressed against her cheek.

"You know what?" she said to me as I rubbed her back.

"What's that?"

"It's my fault."

"What is?"

She shifted away from me and pulled the covers up. "That Mama did that. That she went out and shot the Watermans."

"Oh Megan, it's not. How did you get such an idea?"

"I made Daddy take me downtown, remember? He was just going to drop me off and go right home, but I made him come in. I said, you got to come with me, because really what I wanted was for him to see the sandals they had too. I wanted him to buy those and the running shoes both.''

"Megan, that doesn't have anything to do with what Mama did.''

"Yes sir. If I hadn't done that, he would only have been gone a teeny-weeny bit of time, like he intended. He would have got back before she could have gone out there. He would have caught her. If I hadn't made him stay.''

"Megs, that still doesn't make it your fault.''

"But if I hadn't done that, it wouldn't have happened. We'd be like always, except that I was so selfish.''

"Don't think of it that way, Meggie. Mama probably would have done it anyway. She was kind of desperate, Megs. Don't go blaming yourself, because I think maybe it would have happened anyway. It wasn't your fault.''

Wearily, Megan rubbed her eyes. She was exhausted. Pressing the tiger cat over her face, she closed her eyes for a moment. Then she opened them again. "Maybe it's going to be me who'll go to Hell. For being selfish and making it so Mama could go kill all those people.''

"Megan, it's not your fault.''

"You don't know how God feels," she said quietly. "You just never really know about those things.''


Mama died.

At 5:35 in the morning, which was the first day of May, my mother died quietly in her sleep. She had been awake most of the night before, talking to my father about ordinary things, about how Megan was doing at school, which wasn't very good, about the weather, which was humid in Wichita for that time of year, and about Dad, who was getting a rash from the socks he had on. Her throat was sore from the gastric tube, and he was feeding her hard candies to ease the roughness. The fluid in the suction jar had turned the color of cherry Life

Savers. Then sometime in the wee hours, Mama went to sleep.

My father had believed that she was improving. She was so alert, so talkative, that he'd assumed the worst was behind them. When he reached over to pull up the blankets about five, she felt cold to him, but he didn't think much about it. The night was chilly. So, instead of calling a nurse, he'd pulled back the covers to steal a few moments in bed with her. I suppose it was the best way for her to die, in the warmth of my father's arms.

After such a fiery life, she died so quietly that, had there not been a monitor on, they would not have realized what was happening. She was never conscious again; she never stirred; she never spoke. That was my father's single greatest regret, that Mama's last words to him had been in conversation about a rash on his feet. But maybe that too was best, that my mother at least could die surrounded by only small, mundane concerns.

My father came weeping into our house the next morning. Walking through the hall and into the kitchen, he dropped into his chair at the table. He wept not in the way I'd thought a man would cry, but in tiny, high-pitched sobs. His shoulders shook, and none of us could comfort him.

While Megan and my Aunt Caroline joined Dad in the kitchen, I walked first into the living room and then eventually outside onto the front steps. Sitting down on the top step, I braced my chin in my hands and looked out across the street. They were all crying, all three of them, including my Auntie Caroline, who probably had never loved my mother a day in her life. I sat outside on the step, empty. I remained there, conscious and breathing, and was without any life whatsoever inside myself.

I sat and wondered where things went now, without my mother. I wondered where I would be in the summer or the next year or in ten years. I wondered how things would ever become ordinary again when it seemed suddenly possible that they never could be. And in a small corner of my mind, I wondered about Mama, about where her irreligious soul had gone. Hell? Did you really go to Hell for not believing in Jesus? For killing people? If you went for anything, it would undoubtedly be for that. I tried to picture her, cold and still. I had seen corpses at the nursing home, old men and women, their mouths gone slack in death. But not my mama.

I thought too about Klaus who had caused it all and had escaped everything, even the sweet agony of loving Mama. It could so easily have been me, if I had simply been born first instead of third. It could have been me, spirited away, living, and loving other people and never realizing the anguish my existence had caused, never knowing people had died for me.

# Twenty-Five

MY FATHER AND I got into an argument the evening of the same day Mama died. It started off over something entirely irrelevant to the events surrounding us. Megan had a dental appointment on Friday. It was Tuesday evening, and I said I didn't think she should have to go. We still weren't certain when Mama's funeral was going to be, and what with all the brouhaha over the murders and all, I told Dad I didn't think we needed to subject Megs to a trip to the dentist's on top of everything. My father refused to consider having her miss it. She was just going to have her teeth cleaned and fluoridated, he said, nothing unpleasant, and as hard as that dentist's office was to get into, he wasn't about to cancel for no reason at all.

It was that statement which triggered the argument, when he said, for no reason at all. Did he really think that what had happened to us was no reason at all to cancel a dental appointment? I asked, my voice too loud. Then I said he never could get his priorities right anyway. He yelled back that I was too young to understand, and besides, since when had he been obliged to check with me about Megan's teeth? What business was it of mine? That was when Auntie Caroline, hearing all the noise, came to the door of the study. She told us to shut up, in the name of God. Poor Mara, she said, she was hardly dead and here we were screeching like gulls over garbage about a checkup at the dentist's. That caused us both to yell at her. I'm not sure why. Perhaps just because she said Mama was dead. Saying it outright sounded obscene to me. But we broke the argument off, Dad and I, although the anger remained unspent.

Paul came over the next morning. Since it was a Wednesday, I knew he'd cut school. We sat down on the front step.

"I wanted to come over before this," he said to me, "but my mom wouldn't let me. I wanted to come over and say how sorry I was."

I crossed my arms over my knees and rested my chin on them. On the other side of the street, Mrs. Beckerman was washing her windows. There were red tulips blooming in her flower bed, and she was being careful to move the stepladder so as to avoid hitting them. She was fat, so it seemed a ludicrous scene to me. "Tiptoe Through the Tulips," was running through my mind.

"I guess sorry is what you say," Paul added. "I wasn't exactly sure. I've been sitting at home thinking about it. God, Les, you can't imagine how I've been thinking about it."

"I can imagine," I said.

"Yes," he replied after a pause, "I suppose you can."

Silence. I was surprised how easy it was to lose myself in something as tedious as watching Mrs. Beckerman wash her windows. But I could. I could watch her and think of absolutely nothing else at all.

"But I *am* sorry, Les."

I nodded.

Silence again. The postman was coming down the street on the other side. I transferred my attention to him as he went from house to house. Would someone think to send us sympathy cards for Mama's death? Did you do that when a person was killed by the police?

"Did you know Mama died?" I asked Paul.

"Yes, I read it in the paper."

The postman was whistling, "I've Been Working on the Railroad."

"I feel terrible, Lesley," Paul said. "I loved your mother. I really did. She was super. I thought she was one of the greatest people I'd ever met in my entire life."

"Toby Waterman thought so too."

Paul said nothing else. The postman reached the Beckermans. Mrs. Beckerman climbed laboriously down off her ladder, stepped carefully through the tulips and waddled over to the front gate. Good Morning! Nice day! the postman was saying cheerfully. I think they were both aware of us sitting over on the step and, while dying to exchange the latest gossip about what was going on over here, didn't dare to. I saw them glance in our direction before turning their heads away. Their voices dropped. How amazingly cruel people could be without ever intending it.

"I understand," Paul said.

"Understand what?" I saw the postman flip through his letters for Mrs. Beckerman.

"Understand why your mother did it. I mean, I can see what happened. I can see how she came to feel that way."

Mrs. Beckerman was holding up one of the letters to see through the envelope. It was probably a letter from her son, Sidney. She used to tell Mama that Sidney was always taking up with the wrong girls. She never knew how a nice boy like Sidney could have such lousy taste.

"It's not a crime really, I think," Paul said. "Not the way robbing a 7-Eleven and then gunning down the cashier is. What your mother did was different."

"You couldn't tell a policeman that."

"But it *was* different. She had a reason."

"So does the guy sticking up the 7-Eleven."

"No, Les, this is different. What she did, well, in its own way it was sort of honorable. You know what I mean? It was like she was going out there and saving him. She wasn't going to let him be raised a Nazi, to grow up in that kind of world. It's almost, well, noble."

"There's nothing noble about murdering people, Paul. She *killed* the Watermans. They're dead. It isn't some show on TV."

"But she believed in what she was doing. She thought he was her son. She *believed* they were Nazis. She just thought death was better for him. And that's noble, if you really think about it." He shrugged. "Wrong maybe, but still noble."

Sitting back, I glanced over at him, wondering how the conversation had gotten to where it had without my noticing it. How had we come to the point where Paul was defending my mother and I was on the opposite side?

"You don't know anything about it, Paul."

"Well, I mean, I was just thinking about it."

"Paul, I said you don't know anything about it. You don't know what my mother was like. You don't know anything about living with her. About what she went through in the war and how all these years afterward, we're still suffering from it. Even me and Megs, who had nothing to do with it. You live over on Cedar Street in a great big lawyer's house. You've got two cars and your brother's got his own stereo set right in his room. And you've got dogs. We couldn't ever have a dog after Piffi. After Piffi got run over. By a garbage truck, of all things. Great big hulking monster and he gets himself run over by a shitty garbage truck. And my mama was so upset that Dad wouldn't let us ever have a dog again. You know how bad I've wanted a dog all this time? Do you know? I was only twelve years old when Piffi got hit, and Dad wouldn't let us get another dog. He said it upset Mama too much to lose things. I was twelve and I've been wanting a goddamned dog every day of my life for the last six years. But we couldn't have one. And you have two.''

"Oh Les," he said gently and reached an arm out to put around my shoulder.

I jerked back. "So how can you know anything? You don't. You don't have the faintest clue."

*"Lesley."*

"It's my stupid father's fault. He never stopped to think about us. He never did anything in his whole life but worry about Mama. And then all he did was worry. He never *did* anything. He could have stopped this. He could have taken her somewhere or moved us or got her some help. Cripes, even having her locked up is better than having her dead. He could have changed things. He could have stopped her somehow, and then she would have been alive.''

Paul was still trying to put his arm around me. I was shouting. I knew I was. I knew Mrs. Beckerman had paused from her window cleaning. Probably the postman had stopped too. But what the hell? They already assumed we were all nuts over here anyway. We might as well give them the show they expected.

"He should have done something. He just wouldn't because *he* didn't want to get hurt. Not because of Mama. Mama was strong. Things hurt her but she survived. It was *him*. He couldn't bear to see her unhappy. Even when something made her really happy first, he couldn't stand it if she got unhappy from it afterward. She would have loved another dog. She wouldn't have needed to go find some strange kid to dream up as a son. But Daddy refused. No matter how many times I asked him for a dog, he said no. And Mama wanted one too. She knew things died. Jesus Christ, she knew that better than any of us. He could have given her a dog. Or at least he could have given me one.''

"Look, Les, I am sorry," Paul replied. He had given up trying to touch me and sat apart on the other side of the step.

"Go away," I said. "You don't understand."

"I'm sorry."

"Just go away and leave me alone."

"Okay," he said, rising. "I have to get back anyway. I skipped history." Reaching down, he touched the top of my head. "I'll see you later, all right? When you're feeling better."

"Just go away."

That afternoon I was lying across my bed and reading when Megan came to the door. She still had her virus or whatever it was, so she'd slouched around the house most of the day in her pajamas. I was neither in a more benevolent mood than earlier nor ecstatically happy to see her in my room, because she never seemed to have much warning before she vomited. If she got sick in my room, I told her, I was going to make her clean it up herself.

She came in anyway and sat down on the bed with me. She leaned back against the wall. "Where's Mama's recording of *The Lark Ascending?*"

"Probably in the record cabinet," I said without looking up from the book. I didn't bother to stop reading.

"No, it's not. I've already looked. It's not in there, and Auntie Caroline doesn't know where it is either. I asked her."

"Well, neither do I."

"Where do you think it might be?"

"Megs, believe it or not, I'm trying to read. I don't want to talk. So beat it, all right?"

She scooted around and leaned back against my pillow. This put her feet nearly into my face, and they smelled. Megan was at that age when she wouldn't bath for a month, if no one made her. I thumped her ankles. This caused her to flex her knees and pull her feet away.

"My stomach still hurts," she said pensively and stared up at the ceiling. "I wonder if it's going to get better."

"Probably not," I said, keeping a finger under the line I was reading in an attempt to cope with the distraction.

"Lesley, that's not a funny thing to say."

I kept reading.

"What's the matter with you anyway?"

"You, mostly. Because you keep annoying me. I said I wanted to read, not talk."

"Oh," she replied, as if it were a new idea. She lay a few minutes in silence. "Les, you want to know what I was thinking?"

"Hardly."

"Well, I was looking for *The Lark Ascending* so that we could give it to the mortuary man when he comes over. I want them to play it at Mama's funeral."

I looked up. "Megan, it's too long. Besides, they don't play music like that at people's funerals."

"Why not? It's Mama's favorite piece. She liked that better than any other music there is. So I think they ought to. It would make Mama happy."

"Mama's hardly going to care now, Megs."

Abruptly, she sat up. "I just can't figure you out lately. You're being horrible to everybody. I just can't understand what's the matter with you."

It was *The Lark Ascending* that got us into trouble again that evening at the dinner table. For the first time since Monday lunch Megan had rejoined us for a meal. Her illness hadn't seriously affected her appetite, which made me feel that she was doing it all for sympathy. I grew angry because no one seemed to care that she was just making it up for attention. Then she started in on *The Lark Ascending* issue again.

"Can we have it, Daddy?" she asked him.

"That's not the kind of music they play at funerals, dumbhead," I said. "I've already told you that."

"I'm asking Daddy, Lesley. Not you."

"You can't let her, Dad."

"I found the record," Megan added. "It was down behind the record player. So, I thought when the man from the funeral home comes over, Daddy, that I could give it to him and he could listen to it. And if it's too long, he could use part of it."

"Oh, honestly, Megan," I said. "What a stupid idea. You are such an idiot. No wonder you flunked first grade."

"It is *not* a stupid idea!" Megan shouted. She rose up in her chair and waved her fork menacingly at me. "You're the one who's stupid, because that's Mama's favorite piece of music. I want her to hear it one last time. And it's a *good* idea." She turned to my father. "Tell her, Dad. Tell her it isn't a stupid idea, because it isn't."

Both my father and Auntie Caroline sat with stunned expressions on their faces. Our argument had escalated into a shouting match before either of them had caught up with what was happening.

Then Dad brought his hand down on the table in one loud crash. The dishes all clattered. Gravy spilled onto the tablecloth. Without saying a word, he looked in my direction and pointed to the door. There was a long, loud, deafening silence as I sat and debated whether or not to challenge him. But I decided against it. Throwing my fork down in disgust, I rose and stormed out.

I didn't go upstairs, which is where my father intended me to go. Instead, I went to the front door. Hands in my pockets, I gazed through the screen door at the street and Mrs. Beckerman's red tulips.

I didn't know why I was so mad. It was like the earlier conversation with Paul about dogs. I hadn't meant that to happen either. I didn't think I really cared so passionately about not having a dog. If I did, most of the time I hadn't been aware of it. But at just that instant, when talking with Paul, the dog I'd never gotten seemed at the root of all life's problems. It was the same way now. *The Lark Ascending* wasn't such an illogical choice. It had been Mama's favorite music. No denying that.

But I didn't want it played.

That music made me see Lébény and the gardens of the estate and the mill pond and the gazebo. One section sounded almost like a folk dance, and when I heard it, I always visualized shadowy, faceless men and women wearing white suits and flowered dresses, like the rich people in *The Great Gatsby*. They were beautiful and golden dream people, the way I pictured Mama to be in her childhood, before *Lebensborn* and Ravensbrück and the war. I could not bear the thought of losing those images and remembering *The Lark Ascending* only as music from my mother's funeral.

But there was another part of the piece also, the first part, which I suspect was what Elek was always playing. The later, folksy interlude was orchestrated, but this first part was for violin only. It was a heartbreakingly beautiful solo, the musical ascent of the lark, haunted and lonely, before the verdant tones of the other instruments joined in. Listening to it as a child, I had always counted the seconds, like sheep, waiting for the desolate courage of the violin to be swallowed up by friendlier sounds. Even more than losing the imagery of the graceful dancers, I could not bear to have Mama leave me in the company of that violin.

But I found no way to explain to my father or my sister what the music did to me. I was without words for it. So, hands in my pockets, I stood alone and stared out the front door.

# Twenty-Six

THE FUNERAL WAS on Friday morning. So Megan did not go to the dentist's after all. As I was sitting on my bed that morning and putting on my panty hose, I wondered if Dad had remembered to phone Dr. Thompson and tell him Megan wasn't coming; then I was horrified to find myself thinking about such a stupid thing on the morning we were burying my mother.

We rode to the funeral home in a black limousine, my first ride in such a car. I touched the supple leather by the door and watched the scenery pass by, reflected in the chrome.

Once there, Auntie Caroline, Dad, Megan and I sat apart from the main room in a small alcove. I had to lean forward to see the other mourners.

There weren't many people. Mr. Hughson and several of the men from the garage were there. Mr. Hughson had on a suit and tie, and his dark hair was slicked straight back; I almost didn't recognize him, he looked so different. I couldn't remember the names of most of the men with him. I had only met them a few times. But I saw Bobby was there. Bobby was Mr. Hughson's nephew. He was slightly retarded and had a sweet, anxious face, the sort you see so commonly on people who know they are superfluous. He helped Daddy under the cars sometimes, but mostly he ran errands and made coffee for the other men. I saw Mr. and Mrs. Reilly, our next-door neighbors, in the second row. Farther back was the checkout lady from the supermarket. Sitting alone way in the back was Paul. I thought at first he must have skipped history again but then, noticing that he was wearing a suit, I realized he must have skipped the whole morning. The only other person there was the police sergeant, the one with the terrible compassion. He saw me looking, and he smiled. Not knowing what else to do, I smiled back.

What Mama would have thought of the funeral, I couldn't imagine. I don't think she would have wanted a service at all, if she'd been given a say in the matter. Mama wasn't one for ceremonies.

The funeral director had chosen to use *The Lark Ascending* and, as I feared, he chose the violin solo. The man who played it I had never seen before. He stood at the front of the room and coaxed the music from the violin very slowly, his eyes closed. He was small and thin and looked foreign to me, like someone from Southern Europe. Or maybe he was Jewish. I hoped he was; that would have made Mama happy. With a lover's touch he drew the notes from the instrument and, trapped in that small room, the thin sound grew achingly sad. I expected to cry then. Megan and Caroline and my father were crying. But I sat, separate and dry eyed and desperately lonesome for Mama, who had left me here and gone away.

Although my father had tried to keep religion out of the ceremony, he hadn't been entirely successful. *The Lark Ascending* had replaced the hymn. A reading from William Shakespeare's *The Tempest* had replaced Bible verses. But the man who conducted the service still invoked the name of God. As I listened to him, I wondered what Mama's real beliefs had been. I don't know. It was religion she held in such contempt, but whether or not

she thought there was still something or someone responsible for ordering the universe is hard to say. My mother
tended to be very vocal about a few things, and it made
you believe she was saying a lot, which, I suspect, was
what she wanted. But in fact, I think most of her thoughts
she kept to herself.

The worst part for me was discovering the casket was
open. Dad hadn't told me it would be, and I was repulsed
by the sight of it. Why would people want to look at
Mama when she was dead? Besides, it didn't even look
like Mama. It looked like one of those figures in a wax
museum, exceptionally lifelike, but sterile and inanimate, nonetheless. Megan kissed her on the lips and
placed a branch of lilacs beside her. I didn't touch her.

When we returned home, I got out of the car, went into
the house, straight through it and out the back door into
the yard. I walked to the other end of the backyard, to the
fence beside the lilac bushes that marked the end of our
property. I had no reason in mind for going there other
than to escape Megan and my father's inane conversation. I wanted to be alone. There weren't many places
around our house for doing that.

I was still dressed up, teetering uncertainly in a pair of
Auntie Caroline's high heels because I didn't own a pair
myself. Over my dress I had the turquoise shawl Mama
had given me, the only time I had ever worn it. It'd been
the single bright color amid blacks and browns and grays.
But I reckon Mama would have wanted me to wear it, so
I didn't care what Auntie Caroline said to Dad about it.

There wasn't much to look at from where I was standing. Just the chain-link fence, the alley and the back of
the Nelsons' house on the other side. Distantly, between
farther houses I could see the plains encroaching, their
emptiness never quite arrested, even in the town.

Easing out of the heels, I stood in my stockings and
felt the damp coolness of grass on the soles of my feet.

The air was heady with the smell of lilacs. It made me think of Mama's stories of Lébény, about her sister, Johanna, who had died of scarlet fever while my mother waited downstairs in the great hall, surrounded by the scent of lilacs. I wondered if Mama ever stopped to think that she too might die when the lilacs were in bloom. Sad, I thought, that she should have died in springtime when all the flowers she had missed so much in winter were finally alive. But in the end I supposed it was best that way, to die in spring and never know another winter.

Time passed and I remained, fingering the chain-link fence.

"Lesley, why don't you come into the house?" It was Auntie Caroline.

"I don't want to," I said. "I'd rather be alone."

"No, come on, honey," she replied and put her hand on my shoulder. "I know how hard it must be for you."

"Please, just leave me alone. I want to stay here."

"I've made sandwiches," she said.

"I'm not hungry."

I could hear her standing there, although she was doing no more than standing. I didn't turn to look at her.

"It's no one's fault, what happened."

I did not answer.

"It's easy to want to blame someone or something or yourself when a truly terrible thing happens. That's natural. But you mustn't do it. Don't do it, Lesley. Don't be angry now. This is devastating your father. Please don't make it worse for him."

Absently, I ran my hand back and forth along the cool metal in the fence.

"Your mother was a very hard person to live with, Lesley. I know you loved her dearly. I know you all did. Cowan most of all. But she was a difficult person."

"Leave me alone, all right?" I still had my back to her.

"Maybe she was a difficult person all her life. Maybe even in Hungary when she was a girl. Who knows. But she certainly was after the war. A brilliant, gifted, sensitive woman, yes, but so difficult."

"I don't need you to tell me about my mother, Auntie Caroline. I know all about my mother. I don't need you to tell me."

"Someone needs to, Lesley. You're no longer a child."

"I know all I need to know, thank you."

"But this isn't your father's fault. I don't want to see you blame him for it, because he wasn't responsible. If he's to blame for anything, it's simply for having loved someone a little more imperfect than the rest of us."

I shut myself in my room. After changing my clothes, I took out the book I had been reading, curled up on my bed and opened it. It was a good book. It must have been, because I found it so engrossing.

Megan came to my door to say that supper was on. I told her I didn't want any, that I wasn't coming down. When she tried to open my door, I leaped up and slammed it shut on her, hitting her soundly in the head with it. I could hear her in the hallway, gasping from the pain but determined not to give me the satisfaction of hearing her cry. Finally, she went back downstairs to the kitchen.

Sometime mid-evening my father came up. He didn't bother to knock; he simply let himself in and closed the door firmly behind him. Crossing the room, he grabbed the chair from my desk, put it alongside the bed and sat down.

"Somehow," he said, "I get the feeling you're awfully upset with me."

"Not especially."

I continued to read.

"This is a difficult time for us, Lessie."

Not only was I able to continue reading but I was also able to continue concentrating on the gist of the story.

"This has been nearly unbearable."

It was as if he were not there.

"And I must confess, this just isn't the time I need you to do this to me, Lesley."

"I'm not doing anything," I said and kept reading.

For several seconds my father watched me. I could feel him watching me. Then he leaned over and put his hand across the page of the book. I looked up. He was only inches from my face.

"If you really must know," I said, "I do think if you'd wanted to, you could have saved her."

He flinched. Not in his body, but in his eyes. His pupils contracted and then dilated again. He shook his head.

"You could have," I said.

"No."

"Yes sir. Yes, you could have. If you'd really wanted to. If you'd ever really tried."

Again he shook his head.

"You could have moved us, Dad. Like we were thinking about in the winter anyhow. We could have gone to New Mexico or Florida or somewhere and gotten away from the Watermans."

He was still shaking his head. "No. She wouldn't have gone."

"You could have made her. Or you could have gotten her to go to a psychiatrist earlier. Why didn't you do that? Remember, clear back in March I was saying maybe she ought to see a doctor. Remember? You could have made her go."

He looked down.

"Geez, Dad, it would have been better if she'd been put in a hospital or something. I know she was scared. But she could have gone in the hospital for a little while and gotten over this, and we could have had her back. If you love somebody, sometimes you got to do things they don't want you to. Anything would have been better than what happened. You should have done something.''

"Lesley, I couldn't ever have made your mother do what she didn't want to do. Never. No one could.''

"You could have *tried!* You could have stood up to her. Just for once. You could have made her see the truth about things. She would have believed you. Not me or Megan or some doctor, but she would have believed you. Of course she was scared of psychiatrists and policemen and being locked up. I *know* she was. And I know perfectly well how come. But someone needed to force her to understand that you can't do what she was doing, that even in America they'd come and get you, if you acted like that. You never explained things clearly enough to her. And she would have listened to you.''

"And you think I didn't try? You really believe that?''

Silence fell between us. I'd made him angry. It flared up and then died down all within the space of that silence. At last he lowered his head, put the end of one fist to his mouth and blew out a long breath. Wearily, he shook his head.

"Lesley, you've got to understand how much I loved your mother. She was all the world to me. From the moment I met her. I loved her more than I ever thought it was possible to love another person. She was such an incredible individual. So unusual. So vibrant. Lesley, I'm not like that. I'm very ordinary. Loving her was the only exceptional thing I've ever accomplished with my life.''

A moment's stillness followed.

"But, honey, your mama was very much her own person. She controlled her own life. She always did. I never possessed her and I don't think anyone could.''

He raised his eyes to me. "I took her away from all those things that happened. That was all I could do for her. I took her away and I tried to keep her as safe as I could. I've spent all my life keeping her safe. I don't regret it, but it has been my whole adult life.'' There was another small pause. "So, do you think I haven't asked myself all those questions already? Do you think I don't feel bad enough about what happened without your help?''

I picked up a bit of lint off the bedspread.

Finally, I shrugged. "I'm just saying that I think you should have done more than you did, that's all. You didn't face up to things, and they were obvious. I kept saying we needed to do something. I kept trying to make you see that we couldn't just let her go on doing whatever she wanted.''

"Hindsight's 20/20, Les. But what's in front of us at the time, we don't have a script for. I was doing the best I could.''

"You were *doing* nothing.''

He sighed very deeply and turned his head away toward the window. I could tell he was being consumed by the same sort of taut, desperate anger as I was. I wished suddenly that he would shout at me, that he would scream at me and I could scream back. But he didn't and the anger stayed cold and restless between us.

"You have to understand that your mother did have some serious problems.''

"I don't need to hear about Mama's problems. Auntie Caroline's already told me all I want to know about Mama's problems today.''

"What I'm trying to say, Lesley, is that I've lived with your mother for over thirty years, and that's a long, long time to get to know someone in. And in those years I saw her in so many ups and downs, in so many good moods and bad, in what I thought was every conceivable situation—including all the other traumas over Klaus that we had. But Les, I still was not her. I still was not inside her head, thinking her thoughts, feeling her emotions. She did have some real problems; you cannot deny that. And she had some difficulties that you just couldn't work your way around. But she was a good woman. For all her troubles, she was a good person. And there was never one thing in her character that had ever made me believe she'd go out and do what she did. Holy God, Lesley, of *course* I would have done more, if I had thought that, if I'd even had the slightest inkling of it. Of course, I would have. But the thing is, I never even dreamed of it.''

I sighed and looked down at my book.

"She was a very complex woman. I did my best by her. I probably made plenty of mistakes along the way. And no doubt through the years there were a lot of things I could have done better. But, Les, I always did the best I could.''

With one fingernail I riffled along the edges of the pages in the book. Weary depression was superseding the anger in me. I felt tired. Too tired to keep on with the conversation. Too tired to cry. Too tired to even care.

My father remained sitting on the chair next to my bed, his hands in his lap.

"Why did it happen, Dad?"

He looked over.

"She *was* a good person. Why did she have to suffer through all those atrocious things? They ruined her life. They've nearly ruined ours. Why did this happen to us?''

He shook his head. "I don't know.''

"I keep wondering what the point of it is. I keep trying to figure out why we deserved this.''

He shrugged. It was a slight movement, just a twitch of his shoulders. "I don't know,'' he said. "I think it just happened.''

"There've got to be reasons," I said.

He didn't reply.

"There've got to be answers.''

"No,'' he said. "I'm not sure there do. Or at least I'm not sure we ever necessarily know them.''

I lowered my head. "I can accept this happening. If I know why, I think I can accept it, but I do need to know the answers.''

And all my father did was sigh.

# Twenty-Seven

OUTWARDLY, a semblance of normalcy returned. On Wednesday of the following week, Auntie Caroline went back to Winnetka, leaving Dad, Megs and me to try life without Mama on our own. On Thursday Dad decided that it was time for Megan and me to go back to school. It had to be faced sooner or later, he said, and the sooner the better, especially in my sister's case, because her work had suffered disastrously during the weeks leading up to the murders. My father took Megan back the following morning, so that he could have a word with her teacher and the principal. I returned to the high school by myself.

Inwardly, however, for me at least, not even a semblance of normalcy showed itself. The thing I had not counted on was the almost palpable way I missed Mama. It was the sense of absence that destroyed me. I woke with it, a curiously flat emotion, and lay in bed, listening for my father to get up first. I couldn't bear going by his bedroom, seeing him curled up alone in the big bed, still scrupulously keeping to his side, leaving the other half undisturbed. So I would wait. Even on the weekends when I generally got up first, I would wake and wait. The worst time of day, however, was late afternoon. I would always arrive home from school, expecting Mama to be there. Long after I consciously had given up expecting it,

317

some small part of me would tense with anticipation when I opened the door. Then I would see only Megan, sitting alone at the kitchen table, and the flatness would return. The house was soaked in incompleteness. My days were all stained gray.

I felt weighted down. The weeks were warm and scented with lilacs and hawthorn, and each day that passed seemed to add another weight. Day by day, the burden grew heavier, and my shoulders ached with a physical pain and my back hurt so much that standing became an agony. I told Dad about it, and he made me hot compresses and rubbed my shoulders. When that didn't help, he made an appointment with the doctor for me. But it was the passing days that were so heavy. I said this to the doctor, and he nodded and gave me a prescription for Valium.

The only way to make my back and shoulders stop hurting was to lie flat on my bed. That helped. More and more of my free time was spent in my room on the bed. If I lay perfectly still and did not move, I felt okay. But I had to keep the door shut to prevent Megan from bothering me, because I discovered talking to Megan made me move too much. And after a while I found talking to Paul or Brianna or Dad hurt too much too. So I locked the door.

Most of the time in the bedroom I did nothing. I just lay there, stared at the crack in the ceiling over my bed and didn't dare to move for the pain. And I thought. At first it was just about Mama. My ability to create images of things in my head had always been good, and I could visualize her with intense clarity: the tilt of her head, the hang of her clothes, the spirited quickness of her movements. I could hear her too. She'd had a very distinctive laugh. When she was really pleased, her laugh would go way up the scale to a high note and burst into cackles.

Her heavy accent had always dominated her speaking voice and made it very easy to recollect. Her *r*'s especially had sounded foreign, pronounced in a rolled, throaty way that made them nearly lisped. And she had been capable of absolutely fracturing English on occasion, either by using German sentence structure that kept us all waiting breathlessly for the verb, or by committing hilarious malapropisms, like the time she told Megan's second-grade teacher that Megs was suffering from conjugal bliss when she meant conjunctivitis. Mama had never been wholly at home in English. It had always been a troublesome language for her that she littered with not-quite words, like "quietful" and "longly," and retreated from whenever it became too inconvenient. As a child I had been annoyed by her accent, her unwillingness to accept English, her persistent foreignness. Now these things drenched my memories with tender affection.

I wondered about Mama as a little girl. I tried to create a picture of her with pigtails and knock-knees, full of childhood's eager clumsiness and innocence. The sweeping panoramas of Lébény and of Dresden with Tante Elfie unfolded themselves with willing familiarity, but I realized abruptly that I had never been quite able to formulate an ordinary girl to go with them. All I could ever conjure up was a survivor, someone who lived only in extremes, where everything had always been loyalty or betrayal, trust or treachery, life or death. Childish concerns were impossible to measure on such an heroic scale. What did girlish rivalries with school friends, fights at home for the biggest piece of cake, desperation at being left out of a list of invitations to a party, weigh in comparison? Thus, the only girl I had ever brought to mind had bold Aryan features and the veiled, uneasy acumen so common to the very bright. But she never had innocence.

I wondered, when I couldn't re-create the girl from before the war, what she must have been like right afterward. I couldn't picture Mama then either, with less than a hundred pounds on her tall, rangy frame. I couldn't imagine her with short hair. Dad, during that era, came to me more clearly. I saw him the way he looked in the photograph we had of Uncle Kip's wedding. Dad had been best man. Slight and slim in his dress uniform, he'd stood beside Kip on the steps outside the church. His cheeks had been round and red as autumn apples, his eyes completely obscured by the shadow of the visor on his hat. But how had he looked to Mama in that hospital in Germany? She, with her love of classical music and ballet, with her sophisticated knowledge of upperclass European life, with her restless, undisciplined intelligence. How had he beguiled her to want a pimply-faced farm boy from Illinois? What kind of magic did he use to make her choose a life of wearing secondhand denim and scrubbing her own floors and wandering from one backwater community to another with a man whose only accomplishment was loving her? I could create images but I could never give life to the young man and woman they must have been.

On other occasions I contemplated Klaus. Where did he live? What did he look like? Did he resemble Mama? She had a very distinctive mouth, wide and supple, and both Megan and I had inherited it. Had he? And what was he doing that precise moment I was thinking of him? One afternoon I counted out the time zones in the Atlas. Seven hours difference between Kansas and Germany. After that I could never look at the clock without doing quick calculations regarding Klaus. Four-fifteen, I'd think, and it is 11:15 at night there. Is Klaus asleep? Is he taking a bath or finding a book to read or doing any of the other countless little things one does before bed? Does he have children now? Maybe he has a boy or a girl of his own. Is he kissing them good night?

Perhaps the most bewitching aspect of reflecting on Klaus and József was the eerie knowledge that Mama had been willing to kill them both. My skin would crawl when I really thought about that. To be the child of a mother capable of murdering her own children was a concept that was almost paralytic when I fully considered it; yet, because I was in no danger, I could regard it with fascinated horror. The odd part was that the woman capable of such an act stayed as distant from my mama, to me, as did Klaus and József.

What eventually grew out of my thoughts was an uncontrollable desire to pursue the past. I was transfixed not only by the power of Mama's stories and the events that came of them, but also by Mama, herself. The magic of our bond was irrefutable. She *made* me, I'd think, she carried me inside her own body, just as she had Klaus and József. I was part of her before I was myself. I had a right to her world and her dreams and her memories. With incredible clarity, I would think: *They're mine.* They *are* my memories.

I thought of going to Hungary and visiting Lébény. I thought of tracing Mama and Daddy's trek from northern Germany, where they had met, down through Austria and Czechoslovakia. I thought of going to see the location of Ravensbrück. I thought of searching for Klaus myself. And perhaps most of all I thought of going to Forest of Flowers where my mother's resurrection took place. Wherever, I realized I had to go.

The first few days back at school were a crash course in human behavior for me. I learned quickly to recognize all the little signs: the looks, the avoidance of looks, the instant exit, the intense discomfort I could provoke simply by being present. I also became acutely aware of the countless, casual phrases regarding murder and insanity that littered everyday speech and that took on a brave new meaning when I was in the room.

During the week following my return, I stopped by the French language lab after school to ask Miss Conway if I could get back to working on the French tapes in my free time. Desperate for something to take my mind off things, I thought maybe this would help. I was also nursing the secret hope that she might still invite me over to her apartment to see her slides of Paris as she had promised. In fact, I dreamed about that shamelessly, thinking perhaps we could be friends. She was only twenty-three. I knew that because Brianna, who worked in the front office at school, had looked it up for me, and I thought now that I was an adult and nearly graduated, if she saw me out of school and we talked French together, maybe she would forget I was just a student.

It was after four in the afternoon when I went in to see her, and the school was dead silent. Miss Conway was methodically putting assignments into folders, one after another, and the room was so quiet I could hear her fingernails against the folders.

"You do well enough in French," she said to me when I asked about the tapes. "Why don't you go see Mr. Tennant, Lesley? I think you'd be better off exploring advanced German. With your background . . ."

She didn't finish the sentence. She didn't need to because I knew what came next. It was no secret to anyone now where my expertise in German came from. If you read the newspapers, you knew.

"I'm really a lot more interested in French," I replied. "And I need more practice."

For several moments she did not say anything but continued putting the assignments away. I watched her. She was a tiny person, maybe four feet ten or eleven, and I towered over her. I felt clumsy beside her.

She looked up. "I really am sorry, Lesley. But I just don't have the time anymore to do those tapes with you. You understand. With the end of school and everything . . ." She smiled. It was a polite smile, impeccably so. You almost couldn't tell it wasn't friendliness.

I fiddled with a button on my blouse. "I could do them on my own. If you don't mind. You know, like I did in March. I could just do them in here on my own." There was suddenly an intense urge to cry. I wanted her to know how much I was suffering, how much I needed something to divert my attention, how important French was to me, just because it *wasn't* connected to my mother. Perhaps even more, I wanted her to feel sorry for me, to put her arms around me and tell me she understood. The tears rose in my eyes but didn't fall. However, I did not try to hide them from her.

If she saw my tears, she gave no indication of it. Instead, she turned and went over to the file cabinet. "No," she said, "the lab has to be locked when I'm not in it. There has to be a teacher supervising. You understand. Those are the school rules."

I studied her face. I had thought she was beautiful. Indeed, I still did. She had very dark hair and large eyes that intimated a Latin American heritage. Her features had the delicate sharpness of a bisque doll's.

"You do understand, don't you?" she asked again when I hadn't responded. "Why don't you go and see Mr. Tennant? I think he usually stays late on Wednesdays and Fridays. You could do German tapes then."

"I've been alone in the lab before, Miss Conway. All

those other times I worked on my own and you weren't there."

"No," she said and it was final.

At home that evening Dad and I sat together in the kitchen. Dad had made a pot of Mama's strong European coffee after supper, and he even allowed Megan to drink some. Then she wandered off to' some other part of the house, leaving us alone with the rest of the pot.

It was a very hot night. All the' windows and the back door were open, and Dad had the fan on the kitchen counter. It whirred back and forth, blowing my hair across my face as it passed. The two of us sat, sweat beaded on our foreheads, and drank cup after cup of steaming coffee.

"You know, I'm thinking," I said, "that maybe when school's out, I'll go away for a while."

He looked up abruptly. He had been carefully measuring sugar into his mug, stirring it, staring into it, measuring a wee bit more. Mama never took sugar, just cream, but my father had never adjusted to the thick, powerful taste. But now he stopped, holding the spoon, sugar and all, poised over the mug.

"You mean college?" he asked with suspicion in his voice. I knew he knew I didn't mean college.

I shook my head. "No. Just away."

"Where?"

I shrugged. "I don't know. I just need to get away."

Brow puckered, he lowered the spoon into the coffee and stirred it. "I don't want to hear this kind of talk right now, Les. There's been too much happening over the past few weeks. We all need to settle down again. Let's not think of doing wild things."

"It's not wild. I just want to go away for a while. I need to get out. I need to think. I feel like a boulder is sitting on me."

He said nothing.

"I can't stand it here anymore."

He looked up. "What can't you stand?"

I gazed off across the kitchen. The counter was littered with the aftermath of supper preparation: dirty utensils, half an onion, potato peelings on the drainboard. I wondered what, in ten or twenty years' time, I would remember of this kitchen. I wondered which of the million moments I had spent here would stay with me.

"What can't you stand?" he repeated.

I turned back. "You remember Miss Conway? My French teacher. You know." I looked at him. "Remember how she used to let me listen to those tapes all the time in the language lab after school? Remember me doing that in March?"

He nodded.

"Well, I asked her if I could start back on them. I was thinking if I could get involved in something that, well . . . well, maybe it'd take my mind off . . . Anyway, I asked her and you know what she said? No. Just like that. Not maybe. Not wait a little, it's inconvenient. Just no. She said she couldn't leave me alone in there any longer. That she didn't want to stay herself. That she had to keep the lab locked. And cripes, Dad, she let me work in there alone a thousand times before."

I frowned into my mug. "You know how that makes me feel?"

"Yes," he said.

"I can't stand it. It's bad enough having everyone always looking at me, always whispering there goes the daughter of Mara O'Malley. But now not only does Miss Conway not want to be alone with me in the lab, she doesn't even trust me with her stupid tapes."

He lifted one shoulder in an expressive little gesture of

understanding. "It'll get better. We have to give it time."

"It's humiliating."

"Yes, it is. But there's not much we can do about it except live through it and prove them all wrong."

I grimaced. The room was sweltering, and I became abruptly aware of how uncomfortably sweaty I was. Why the hell was I drinking coffee? I pushed the mug away.

"I liked her," I said. "And I thought she liked me. I was the best student in the whole class. I killed myself to be best. Just because I knew French mattered to her and I liked her. I could have done that well in German without even bothering to bring home the book. I could have had it a lot easier."

Dad wiped his forehead with the heel of his palm. He sighed. "So, you want to run away."

"No. Not run away. That's not what I said, was it? That's not what I'm talking about. I said I just wanted to get out of here and pull myself together."

"You'll be leaving in the fall anyway, Lesley. When you go to Kansas City."

I shook my head. "That's not what I want."

There followed a poignant moment when neither of us spoke. The intensity of my desperation swelled in the silence, and I think he was as aware of it as I was. He sighed.

"It's *not* running away, Dad. It isn't the same thing."

"When you get out because someone humiliates you at school, Lesley, that's running away."

I released a long breath and let my shoulders sag. "That's not what I mean. Not really. It only looks like that, but it's not the reason."

"Then what is?"

I fingered the tablecloth.

"This is a good family, Lessie. We've been through some bad times, but it's still a good family."

"I know it. But I just need to be outside it for a while. Can't you understand that? Can't you see what I mean?"

He turned around and lifted the coffeepot from the stove. First the coffee went into his mug, then the sugar, slowly, in measured spoonfuls, then the milk. He stirred it and then finally raised his head to look at me. When he saw that I was still watching him, he looked back down, paused with the teaspoon in his hand. "No," he said, "I'm afraid I can't."

# Twenty-Eight

MAMA HAD LET ME SLEEP with her when I was very young. My father, snoring softly, had formed the mountainous horizon of those nights, but it was with Mama that I slept, nuzzling into the thickness of her hair, protected by the tired bulk of her body. My memories of those nights were mostly of darkness, blissfully satiating after the autonomy of the day. I would drowse against her breasts and be enveloped in her deep, familiar smell. I didn't have my own bed until I was more than three, until we moved to West Texas.

Megan too had slept with Mama and Daddy. I was old enough by then to remember them together clearly. Megan never had a real crib. Just a laundry basket with a gingham lining that Mama would carry from room to room in the daytime. At night, even as a newborn, Meggie was snuggled down between Mama and Daddy in the big bed. I recall once coming in during the night. I had been sick to my stomach and had come for comforting. Megan was maybe two then, her hair already long and straight, like Mama's, and there they were together. Mama, free of the restless energy that dominated her waking hours, was deeply asleep, her breathing soft and even. And Megan, like a little dormouse, was curled snugly into the small hollow beneath Mama's arm. Even in the blackness I could see their hair mingled together,

328

light and dark, and I could see the slack peace of their dreams. It was my father who'd awakened, not Mama, and although he'd let me into the big bed with them and had held me in his arms, I remember crying just a little because neither Megan nor Mama had stirred.

During the course of that May following the murders, the memories of those nights returned persistently to me. I couldn't sleep very well, and while I lay awake in bed, I found it curiously easy to evoke the darkness that had surrounded me in infancy, to recall the unconditional safeness of those nights. Yet, I could bring back only the dim, snuggly emotions and not the actual heavy warmth itself. Thus, the memories always left me longing.

Deep into one night I actually got up, my head full of hazy, unformed thoughts about sleeping with Megan. It was then that I chanced across my father. He was in his nightclothes, tissues clutched in one hand.

"What are you doing, Dad?" I asked. The house was dark.

He shook his head.

I was only half awake myself. It was like seeing an apparition. When he didn't answer, I turned, bewildered, and went back to my bed, having forgotten what I'd gotten up to do.

That was the first time I noticed. But soon I discovered he paced every night after Megan and I were in bed. Like a forsaken, forgotten ghost, he wandered through the house. Things seemed so normal with him during the day. He said virtually nothing to us about his grief. But then he didn't need to. Hearing his footsteps as he searched from room to room in the darkness was enough.

"You want to know a secret?" Megan asked me one afternoon. It was after school, and we were alone in the house. I was lying on my bed because my back hurt, and Megan had come to stand in the doorway and swing back and forth with her hands on the frame. I'd told her to go away because I was sick of her always hanging around me after school, but she stayed, swaying in and out of the doorway.

"What secret's that?" I asked.

"You want to know it?"

"Okay," I said.

"I know where Mama is."

I didn't respond. I didn't know exactly what to say. She continued her motion in the doorway, and her long hair flowed rhythmically around her.

"You want to know?"

I nodded.

Letting go of the door frame, she straightened up. "Come with me. I'll show you."

I rose from the bed and followed her. She walked down the hallway to the linen closet. "Okay, Les. Now, you got to close your eyes."

"What stupid joke is this, Megs?"

"Just do it, okay? Just close your eyes for a sec."

Feeling dumb, I closed my eyes, and I could hear Megan opening the door to the linen closet. She took hold of my arm and pulled me inside.

"Okay, now smell, Les. Keep your eyes closed and smell in here."

I inhaled deeply. It stank of stale cigarette smoke, an ugly ashtray odor that I had always hated. Mama had been inclined to iron everything. She'd iron the sheets and the pillowcases, the towels and even the washcloths. If we didn't get them off the line in time, she'd iron Megs's and my underwear. And all the while she was working, she would smoke, and the smell of her cigarettes would permeate the cloth with the steam and the heat of the iron.

I had yelled at her about it. In seventh grade when we were studying the effects of smoking in hygiene class, I had come home every night and screamed at her to stop. I'd cried and pleaded and brought her pictures of cancerous lungs and addicted monkeys. In the end I'd told her never to kiss me because she stank, and that had made her cry.

Now, I stood in the gloom of the linen closet and breathed in the odor deeply.

"Sometimes I come in here after school before you get home," Megan said. "I just stand here with my eyes closed and smell. It makes it like Mama's just exactly right here, doesn't it? Like she's standing nearby."

I turned toward her. Megan had a sheet down and pressed close against her face. Like someone snorting cocaine, she was inhaling in deep, measured breaths. Then slowly, she lowered the sheet, returned it to the shelf and smoothed the ironed surface. We said nothing to one another but remained standing in the small, dark closet.

Megan looked up. She searched my face. "How come this happened? How come Mama died, Les?"

I regarded her. What I noticed was what a little kid she still was. She was wearing hot-pink terry-cloth shorts and a T-shirt she was growing too big for. Her stomach was still rounded, giving her that swaybacked, potbellied profile young children have. There were no signs of the softening curves of preadolescence in her.

"Do you think maybe if we hadn't been so much trouble to her, she might have been happy with us?" Megan asked. "You know. And not needed to go find that little boy."

I shook my head.

"Maybe if we'd been better. If I could have done better at school. Mama worried because I didn't do my schoolwork. She said that to me once. That I had to do my work so I could go to university when I got big. And you know what? I told her I didn't ever want to go to university." There was a pause and Megan reached a hand out to stroke the sheet on the shelf. "I shouldn't have said that. If I'd done better at school, maybe she wouldn't have had to do what she did."

"Megs, Mama was sick. Just as if she'd had cancer or something. You know that. That's what Daddy was explaining to you the other night."

"Then how come I couldn't tell it? She didn't act sick to me."

"But she was. Inside where you couldn't see it. And just like cancer makes people die sometimes, this made Mama die. That's what happened. It wasn't anything else."

Wearily, Megan looked away. With the toe of one foot, she nudged the base of the shelves. "Is that what you believe?"

"Yes," I said.

"I don't know," she said doubtfully. "Maybe so. Maybe not."

Then one night I dreamed of Klaus. I dreamed I saw him in a field of sunflowers. He was a baby still, abandoned in a laundry basket. He was some distance away among the stalks. Although I could see him, I was terrified of going in among the sunflowers to get him. Yet, the urge to rescue Klaus and be the one to bring him to my mother was so strong that I managed to plunge in anyway. At least I kept trying to. It was one of those frustrating dreams where everything I did was of no use, and I could hardly get through the stalks. By the time I finally reached the basket, I discovered it was no longer Klaus in there but rather, Megan's stuffed tiger cat.

I woke up crying. It was sometime after three in the morning, and I woke, choked with tears. Sitting up, I turned on the bedside lamp to dispel the dream, but it clung to me, seeming very real. Amid my rumpled bedclothes, I sat and wept.

Rubbing his eyes, my father appeared in the doorway.

His hair was wildly tousled. He was bare chested, wearing only the bottoms to his blue-striped pajamas, the ones that were too long for him and hung down over the tops of his feet.

"What's wrong, sweetheart?" he asked, shuffling into the brightness of my little lamp. He reached down to touch my hair. "Did you have a bad dream or something? What's happened?"

I couldn't answer.

"Hey now," he whispered and sat down on the bed. Putting his arms around me, he pulled me close against the crinkly hair on his chest.

I tried to explain. I tried to tell him about the dream, about how I found Klaus, about *wanting* to go among the sunflowers to get him. And then when I did, it wasn't Klaus, and the bitter disappointment had awakened me. Daddy kept his hand against my face and whispered softly into my hair. He kissed me. But I could not stop crying. It wasn't the disappointment that had shattered me so much. What had was the brutal realization when I woke that, even if I had found Klaus, Mama was no longer there to bring him back to.

I could see I had to leave. Again and again I tried to explain to my father what I meant, why I felt getting away was so necessary. I couldn't see how he'd fail to understand what it was like for me in this family, to be smothered by things, great, glorious and extending back before memory. But I was apparently not finding the right words, because every time I tried, he would simply frown and turn away.

What are you searching for? he would ask. Why are you running away? What do you want to escape?

I could no more answer his questions than he could answer mine.

* * *

"Where are you thinking of going?" Dad asked me one evening while we were doing the supper dishes together.

I shrugged.

"Would you like to go spend some time with Caroline and Roger? I got a letter from Caroline today. She says you can spend the summer with them, if you'd like. I was telling her about things, you know, and she says they'd be more than glad to have you. Roger says he might be able to give you work in his office. Not much, maybe some filing and phone answering. But it'd be pocket money."

"No."

My father looked over. He had his shirt sleeves rolled up and his hands plunged into the dishwater. There were suds clear up to his elbows.

"Dad, I need to get away. Not go visiting Auntie Caroline and Uncle Roger. You see what I mean?"

"Not really, Lesley, I must admit."

I scratched the side of my face, I turned away, then back. Picking up a glass from the counter, I dried it and then held it up to the light to see if I'd gotten all the spots. "What I think," I said, more to the glass than my father, "is that I want to go see the places Mama was. After the war."

"Like where?"

I shrugged. "Hungary, maybe. Germany. Or Wales."

"Oh surely not clear over there. You don't need to go that far. I don't want you gallivanting all over creation on your own."

"I'm eighteen."

"I'm well aware of that. And in many ways you're very mature and responsible. But we've never vacationed much, Lesley, and you're not very informed about things like that. Those are foreign countries you're talking about."

"I can manage."

I took up a pot and dried it with intense thoroughness. Then I dried the plates and took them to the cupboard.

"It would be nice to work in Uncle Roger's office, I'd think," my father said at last. His voice was soft but hopeful. "And you could stay with them in their house. You've always liked their house. Remember that big porch swing? And Caroline says she'll take you shopping in Chicago. Maybe you can get some new things for college. Caroline could help you. She's very good with that sort of thing, you know. She was always the best of all the girls when it came to looking nice. And Betsy and Carl are over all the time with the grandkids. You'd be the first to see Betsy's new baby. You'd like that, wouldn't you?"

"No."

"You could think about it. I'll tell Caroline that you're considering it."

"No, Dad. I'm not considering it."

He drained the dishpan into the sink. There was distance between us. It might as well have been a mile instead of a few feet. Or a month instead of a few moments. With the sprayer he rinsed the sink out, swirling the water around with the dishrag.

"So, just what exactly do you think you're going to do, going to those places?"

I shrugged. "Just go there. I was thinking mostly about Forest of Flowers. We still have the tickets anyhow. I thought I could go and see what it was like."

He turned on the tap.

"Or I thought I might go to Germany. I'd like to see some of those places, those camps and stuff, where all those things took place. They've had such an influence on my life that I'd just like to know what they look like."

He squeezed out the dishrag. There was silence, faint and ill-defined by the sounds of the faucet. I dried my hands on the dish towel and then pressed it to my cheek. It was damp and felt good in the humid heat of the kitchen.

"Actually," I said, "I was thinking that if I went to Germany, maybe I would look for Klaus."

My father's activity at the sink halted abruptly. Frozen for a moment, he made no sound. The color drained away from his cheeks and left his face an ashen hue.

"No," he said sharply.

"Dad, Klaus is my brother, my half brother. He's my flesh and blood. After all that's happened, I really would like to see him. I keep thinking about him all the time, about who he is and what he's like. I dream about him. I just cannot get him out of my mind."

"No," he said flatly. "Holy God in heaven, Lesley, I am not going to let this happen to you too. If you want to go off on some cockeyed trip, if you feel your life is so blighted that you can't exist without that and you have to go, that's one thing. In the end I can probably accept that. But not this. Not Germany. Germany I forbid. Klaus is not going to get you too."

"It's different for me than for Mama, Dad."

"No. It isn't. And he's not having you. I mean it. You don't go there."

The expression on his face left no room for argument. Sighing, I turned away and hung up the dish towel. It seemed hopeless, this conversation. We'd already had it in so many other forms. "Don't you understand, Dad?"

"No," he said. "I don't. I guess that's the whole problem between you and me."

"I carry Klaus and Germany and Lébény and Wales and all the other places around inside of me, like that stuff happened to me instead of you and Mama. I've got your worlds in my head. And I need to make my own world. It's time for me to grow up and have some experiences of my own. Not just secondhand ones."

Slowly he turned and leaned back against the counter. He regarded me for several moments. "To me," he said at last, "it doesn't sound like you know what you do want, Lesley. On one hand, all you talk about is escaping, getting new experiences, getting away from the burden this family suddenly seems to have become for you. And on the other hand, where is it that you want to go? Back to these very same places Mama told you about. Back to Mama's stories. Back to Klaus, after all he's done to us. I guess I could understand it, if you wanted to go somewhere completely foreign, to Spain or Norway or Argentina, but the places you're talking about are no escape. And it just doesn't make sense to me."

Frustrated, I stood without replying. I didn't know what to say to him to make him understand what I meant.

"You're not going to find any answers over there. I can tell you that right now, Lesley."

"Well," I replied, "if I can't find the answers, then at least I need to find the questions."

# Twenty-Nine

I DECIDED ON WALES. It was the least volatile of my options, and moreover, the travel arrangements were already sorted out. Dad suggested that I write a letter to the farmer who owned Forest of Flowers and see if he minded if I visited and if he could tell me where to stay while I was there.

The son of the farmer wrote back to me. His father died in 1968 and he was owner of the farm and of Forest of Flowers. I was most welcome to come and see the cottage, he wrote. I could stay at the farm, if I wanted.

Resigned to the notion of the trip, my father sat down one evening and helped me with the impossible-looking Welsh place-names. Not a language for foreigners, all the words had too many consonants and sometimes no vowels at all. Carefully, my father pronounced them for me, and they sounded strange coming from his mouth. All those years Mama had chattered away, first in one language and then another, often in the same breath. However, never in all that time had I heard my father utter anything but English. He never answered her the way Megan and I had, saying *ja ja* Mama, until we, like she, said *ja* all the time, instead of yes, and got into trouble for it at school because our teachers believed we were lazily saying yeah. He never spoke back to her in the language she was using, as we did, so that at night when Mama

338

was tired, you could hear a completely bilingual conversation between them, Mama in German, Dad in English, back and forth, as if it were one language. So it sounded odd to hear him say the convoluted Welsh place-names so easily. Llanymawddwy. Cwmystradllyn. Bwlch-llwyd-ddu. He wrote out the phonetic pronunciations of the words beside each one for me: Coed-y-Bleiddiau (coyd-uh-BLAITHE-ee-aye), the Welsh name for Forest of Flowers.

Somehow, we did survive that May. And finally it was June, the month all the high-school seniors were waiting for. So immersed in these other things was I that I almost forgot graduation was imminent. It had lost its importance for me, other than marking an end. The senior prom, the graduation dinner, the baccalaureate service all went by without my caring. However, my father insisted that I go through the graduation ceremony itself.

The house was in chaos the night of graduation. Megan, wearing nothing but her underpants, was standing at the bottom of the stairs. "Dad? Daddy?" she was bellowing up, "you got to iron this for me."

I was in my room and could hear my father come out of his. He went to the head of the stairway. "Megan, you can't wear that," he called down to her. "That's too small for you. Wear the pink dress in your room. The one with the bows on it. It's already ironed."

"Noooo," Megan moaned. "I want to wear this. But I don't know how to iron the little thingies. Do it for me okay?"

"Wear the other dress, I said. That one you have there is too small for you."

"No, it isn't. Please, Dad? I want to wear this one. *Please?*"

I was standing in front of my mirror. I was already dressed and had pulled on the gown to see how it'd look.

The cap, I noticed, was slightly too large and the point in the front came down between my eyebrows. In the mirror I saw Dad go by, returning to his room. He was struggling to get the cuff links into his shirt. Megan had been left standing at the bottom of the stairs. I could hear her begin to cry.

*"Daddy!"* she wailed. There was no response from his end of the hall.

I stared at myself in the mirror. Thirteen whole years of my life, I thought, if I counted kindergarten. All those Halloween parties and Valentine cards and Christmas plays. All the arithmetic papers and flash cards and papier-mâché maps for social studies. I could very clearly remember learning to read, Mrs. Johnson printing the letters carefully on the chalkboard, keeping me after school because I kept forgetting what came after *R* in the alphabet. I remembered throwing up in the garbage can in second grade, and my teacher telling me what a good girl I was for not throwing up on the floor. I remembered Mama clapping so loudly at the Mother's Day pageant when I was ten that I told the girl next to me I didn't know who she was.

And now it was over. Somehow, I'd thought graduation would mean more to me than it did. I felt nothing.

Megan was in the doorway. Eyes teary, she clutched the dress to her chest. It was the blue gingham cotton one with the eyelet pinafore that Mama had bought her for Easter the year before. Megan had been into her overalls-and-turtlenecks stage then and had gotten invited to Easter dinner with her friend Katie, so Mama had had to take her out to get something presentable.

"Will you iron it for me, Lessie?" she asked with a snuffle.

"Megs, it really is too small for you."

"No, it isn't."

"Meggie, it's going to show your underpants when

you bend down. Now, you don't want all the boys to see your panties, do you?''

Tears over her checks again, she just stood, staring at it. Her mouth dragged down into an unhappy grimace. ''I won't bend down, okay?''

''Wear the pink one that Daddy did for you already. You look really pretty in that one. You do. It looks nice with your hair.''

''It's these,'' she said sorrowfully and fingered around the tucks in the front of the pinafore. ''I don't know how to iron them so they look nice. Please, Les, won't you do it for me?''

Then my father was there. With one hand, he tugged his tie into place. ''Megan, I thought I told you to put on that other dress. Now I mean it. Put this one away and get going. We'll be late.''

Once again she was crying in earnest.

Dad sighed, eyes rolling heavenward.

''Mama would have ironed it for me,'' Megan sobbed. ''If Mama was here, it wouldn't be like this.''

''Even your mama couldn't have stopped you from growing, sweetheart, and that's all that's happened to that dress. Nothing else. Now get down to your room and get changed.''

I watched the whole transaction in my mirror. Still clothed in my cap and gown, I kept my back to the door-way.

''Are you ready?'' Dad asked me. ''I want you to come downstairs so we can take some pictures.''

I regarded him.

''Outside by the spruce tree, I think. That would be a good contrast to your gown.''

''I don't want to, Dad.''

''Are you worrying about Megs? She'll be all right. You know how she's been. Don't worry.''

''She's going to be all snotty nosed from crying.''

"She'll be okay."

I continued looking at his image in the mirror. Even from where I was, I could smell his after-shave. It was something with a dreadfully erotic name that Megs had bought him for his birthday. The smell was musky but cloying.

"I don't really want to do this," I said.

"What? Take pictures?"

"No. This. All of it. You know what I mean." I pulled out the gown.

"Once you get going, you'll be all right. It's just nerves."

I shook my head. There was a pause and it grew long and apparent.

"I don't feel anything, Dad. Nothing whatsoever. I stand here and I look at myself and it's like I'm dressed up for Halloween. I just don't want to go. It's make-believe. After everything that's happened, to pretend this is important is just make-believe."

He shook his head.

"I don't want to go."

"If you don't, you'll regret it," he replied. "In years to come, when things are different, you'll regret missing this a lot, if you don't go through with it."

I stared at him in the mirror. I couldn't imagine when things would ever be different.

Three days after graduation I went with Paul to the park at Third and Elm to walk his dogs. The day was a very warm one. He'd let the dogs off their leashes to run while we sat on a park bench near the playground. The two dogs galloped from spot to spot around the park, sniffing urgently, reading dog messages, leaving them. With my eyes I followed them as they moved, their black tails held jauntily as they went about their business.

"I got into that course," Paul said to me. He was

scraping dirt out from under one of his fingernails with a twig. "That course that runs first summer term up at Fort Hays."

"The one on computers?"

"Yeah," he said. "I didn't think I was going to get in. Rob Thurman's going on it too and he's a lot better at that kind of stuff than I am. He's going into some kind of computer programming or something at Cal Tech in the fall. Did you know that?"

I shook my head.

"Anyway, I'm really relieved about this course. I need computing. I mean, you can't get anywhere in an area like statistics, if you can't use a computer."

I wiped perspiration from my temple. Lowering my hand, I regarded the moisture. It made my fingertip glisten in the sunlight.

"Hey, did I tell you," Paul said, "I managed to sell my telescope the other day? I got a really good price for it. Almost five hundred dollars. A guy from Dodge City bought it."

"Geez."

"It was worth more. I paid eight hundred, and that was almost five years ago. And a telescope's not going to wear out, is it? But even so, that's more money than I thought I'd get."

There was a small pause. I looked over at him. "What about the other one?"

He turned his head in my direction. "What other one?"

"You know. The one you and I were going to build. Before everything happened."

"Oh, that one." He shrugged. "We never did get very far. All we had really were the mirrors and lenses."

"What did you do with them?"

"They're in a box under my bed."

Again, a pause. Paul picked up one of the dog leashes and swung it around.

"I dunno," he said: "I'm thinking maybe I'll sell those too. I told that guy from Dodge City that I had them, and he sounded sort of interested. I might as well. They're just taking up room. And I can always use the money."

"But if we don't build that telescope and you've sold the other one, you won't have any," I replied, thinking not only of the hours of fun we had had together stargazing but also of all the volumes of notes and observations Paul had made over the years. He had started watching the skies when he was twelve and had charted the stars on almost every clear night since. "You're going to lose track of where everything is in the sky, if you quit watching."

Still swinging the leash, he studied its motion. Finally, he let it drop between his hands. "Yeah, but . . . I mean, I couldn't have done it at college anyway, could I? There wouldn't have been the time. And they wouldn't let you set up a telescope anyplace interesting. Besides, somebody'd probably just rip it off, and then where would I be? A lot of bucks poorer." He picked up the leash, coiled it and put it between us on the bench. "What the hell. It was just kid stuff anyhow."

We were only yards away from the playground part of the park, and there was a little girl climbing up the slide. She was very young, hardly more than a toddler, and when she got to the top of the slide, she was afraid to come down. The grandfatherly man who was with her stood at the bottom of the slide and attempted to talk her into trying. His voice was coaxing but embroidered with impatience.

Paul and I sat without talking. Minutes went by. Paul whistled one of the dogs back from the edge of the road.

"What are you going to do with all that money from the telescope?" I asked.

"I don't know."

One of the dogs came running over to us. Even though it was fully grown, it had a floppy-puppy gait, and that goofy, gleeful expression of joy that is so endearing in Labradors.

"You want to come with me?" I asked. "If you sold the lenses and mirrors too that'd probably be enough money."

"What do you mean? To Wales?"

"Yeah," I said and grinned. "It'd be a blast. We could have a really good time, the two of us, just bumming around."

There was a slight smile on his lips, and I knew he was considering it. The smile never quite faded. He lay his hand on my thigh.

"Why don't you?" I urged.

Finally, a sigh, and he shook his head. "I can't."

"Why not? Your folks wouldn't care."

"They would. My dad would. He'd think I was screwing around with his money."

"But it's your money."

"Well, so he'd think I was screwing around with my money then. Same thing. Just as bad. Actually, probably worse, because it'd make him believe he was right about me and the way I do things. Besides," he said, "I have that computer course in Fort Hays, remember?"

"Stick the stupid computer course, Paul. You can do that some other time."

He didn't respond immediately. The one dog remained near us, and Paul rumpled the fur around its collar with his hand. Looking over to see what had become of the little girl and the man, I noticed them by the swings. I wondered how the conflict on the slide had been resolved. I hadn't been watching.

"The thing is," Paul said, "I really need that course. Like I was saying, I got to know computing to be any good at statistics, and this is my chance to get a head start."

"You're really getting serious about this statistics stuff, aren't you?"

He shrugged. "Well, you got to get serious some time, don't you? There's about ten million other people out there trying to get good jobs, and the only way I'm going to make it is to not goof around and wreck my chances."

I looked away.

He sighed. Kicking the dirt under the bench with the toe of his shoes, he sighed again. "Things change, Les," he said softly. "I'm beginning to understand that. Things got to change. You got to grow up. I couldn't keep playing *Star Wars* forever. If I learned anything this spring, it's been that. The telescope and stuff, they were good fun, but they weren't the real world. The stars are still going to be up there. They don't need me watching them to keep them in their places. They'll go on without me."

As he spoke, I sat motionless beside him. The sunlight was very, very warm. On my hair, on my shoulders, on my legs. Perspiration soaked into my shirt under my arms. I stared at the ground and lost awareness of what else was going on around us in the park.

Paul was still talking, but even he faded. What overtook my thoughts was his reference to *Star Wars*. It pulled me unexpectedly back to that very first night we dated, when he took me out to Ladder Creek. I was walking through the barren landscape, through the bitter, cold January darkness while he told me that he shot rats on the creek bank and pretended that he was Luke Skywalker, trying to save the freedom of the universe by hitting the Death Star. And I remember thinking, what kind of first-rate idiot have I uncovered here?

I turned my head to look at him. He was a very ordinary-looking person. Brown hair, hazel eyes, T-shirt, jeans, running shoes. He had his hands clasped, elbows resting on his knees. He was studying his knuckles. Suddenly, I wanted to touch him. I wanted to reach over and touch him and bring him back to the way we had been that first night on Ladder Creek. Or in the wayside park in Eads, Colorado, when we had fumbled in the dark. We didn't fumble anymore, and as I sat there in the sunlight, I wished sadly that we still did.

"What I'll do is give you my mom's new address," he was saying, "and then as soon as I know where I'm staying in Fort Hays, I'll write her. And then you write from Wales when you know where you'll be at. And then when I get to Ohio State, I'll write and tell you what my new address is there."

I didn't speak. I couldn't speak. I was still half-trapped in January darkness, and what was in my mind was that for all his trying, Paul had failed to hit the Death Star.

Then came the last night. My backpack was full and settled by the front door. My traveling clothes were ironed and waiting to be put on first thing in the morning. The airline tickets lay ready on the table in the kitchen.

After supper that evening my father and I sat together on the front step. He was still wearing his work shirt and had rolled the sleeves up. When he came home from work, he seldom showered and changed as he had before, so there was always about him a smell of oil and sweat. It was an odor evocative of hard, masculine work, not unpleasant but different from the friendly smells of Lifebuoy soap and flannel shirts I had been used to.

"You will be careful, won't you?" he said to me. I was running a finger over the rough surface of the concrete step. "It is a foreign country. Just because they speak English there, don't forget. It is a foreign country.''

"You keep telling me.''

"Well, I want you to be careful.''

"I will. I said I would be and I will.''

"Well . . .'' he said.

There was silence then, pregnant with unsaid things. I rested my elbows on my knees and my chin on my hands and gazed out over the street. The neighborhood was alive with the noise of summer, sound after sound layered on top of one another. In the street was one of Mrs. Beckerman's cats, rolling in the dust. It was black and white and a lot skinnier than she was. I watched it and had to restrain myself from going over to pet it.

"I hope you understand,'' my father said, "that no matter where you go, no matter how far away, you're always going to wake up in the morning and find you're still Lesley O'Malley. You'll never change that fact.''

"I'm not trying to change it, Dad. I already know that.''

"Knowing it and understanding it are two different things.''

Again the silence. My father was also watching the cat. I felt crawlly with excitement about leaving in the morning, and yet I was thinking back in some nearly obscured part of my mind that if he told me not to go, I wouldn't.

Megan materialized and sat down on my father's other side. She was barefoot. She looked like some wild thing you see in those illustrated fantasy books, with her long, long straight hair and her thin, rangy limbs. Her knees were scabbed over. Her legs were already turning brown in the late spring heat. Without looking at her I could still see her in my peripheral vision, and I was struck then by that untamed, atavistic quality she always had about her.

I'd never been that way, never in all my life. I'd always been the tame one, responsible and ordinary.

"I'm sorry," Dad said to me. "I'm sorry things turned out like they have for you, Lessie. I'm sorry whatever it was, the burden or the expectations or whatever, has been so heavy. I wish we could have been a better family."

"Dad, let's not talk about it, okay?"

There was movement in his body as he readjusted himself on the step.

Chin on my hands still, I watched the cat, which continued to roll languidly in the warm dust. The roar of canned laughter wafted through the Beckermans' open window, and I raised my head to see the flicker of their television set. Somewhere, children were shouting. Megan reached down and scratched her leg.

Mr. Reilly next door started up his lawn mower in the back of the house. Megan picked up a blade of grass from beside the step. She put it between her thumbs and tried to make it whistle. She couldn't. She tried again. My father reached a hand over to stop her. She dropped the blade, and I saw the concrete go damp around it from her saliva.

The cat rose up and, with a shimmy of its coat, shook the loose dust off.

"I ran away once," my father said softly. "Did I ever tell you about that?"

"I'm not running away, Dad."

"He wanted me to be a priest." Elbows on his knees, he clasped his hands together. "It's the way they did things in those days. The way they did them in Ireland, I guess. He remembered Ireland sometimes. At least he thought he did. Anyway, according to him, the first son became the heir. The second son became a priest."

There was a pause. I turned my head slightly to see his face without looking directly at him.

"I used to read to him from the Bible. His eyes were going. Even then, he couldn't really see to read. Or maybe he just couldn't read very well. I don't know. I never did. So, I read to him. From Psalms. Always Psalms. He never wanted to hear anything else."

Megan slid closer to him. She lay her head against his arm, and he touched her hair. With one hand he worked his fingers into it and pulled the strands out, the way he used to do with Mama's hair when she'd put her head in his lap.

"I remember them bringing him in that day," my father was saying, "Mother had gone down to Marconis'. I was out in the cabbages, hoeing. And keeping an eye on Mickey. Mick was maybe two or three then. The two men from up at Oak Grange brought him in. Bill and Tupper, I think their names were. Or maybe it was Tucker. Bill and Tucker. They were carrying my father between them. His arm . . . it was hanging like this. Loose, you know, hanging down, and all I saw was the blood on his shirt. And they took him into the parlor.

"I told them not to. Mother always kept the parlor done up nice. For when Father MacCauley came around. Or Mrs. Mavis Jones. I told Bill and Tucker that and that Mother'd whip me if I let them get blood on the parlor floor."

My father paused. He had Megan clasped tenderly against him, his hand still entwined in her hair. She sat, examining her thumbnail, her expression far away.

"He slapped me, Bill did, across the mouth with the back of his hand. Hard enough to hurt. He said, 'Boy, now we can't get him up the stairs like this. We can't take him up to the bedroom, so we're leaving him here.' And they laid him on the settee in the parlor and he dripped blood all over Mother's Persian rug.

"They left then. I guess. I can't remember exactly. Maybe they went to get the doctor. We didn't have a phone in those days, and I guess Bill and Tucker must have gone for him.

"I remember thinking Father was dying. I knew that. I remember Mickey was crying, and I didn't know what to do. I just stood and watched the blood spread on the rug. It seemed like hours." He shook his head. "It's funny. What I remember most was that the house was cool. I was barefoot and my feet were cold. It was the middle of July. They'd been haying, and it was terribly hot down in the pasture. But the parlor was cold. I remember that, remember thinking that while I was watching him.

"And he said to me, 'You are a useless boy, standing there.' So I went to get the Bible for him. To read to him. I sat down on the rug beside him and started to read the 23rd Psalm and he said, no, to read Psalm 103. 'As for a man, his days are as grass: as a flower of the field, so he flourisheth. For the wind passeth over it, and it is gone; and the place thereof shall know it no more.' That's what he wanted to hear. And when I was done reading, he said to me, 'You will go into the priesthood. You belong to the Church.'

"I said I would. I was scared to bits. I was thirteen and I knew he was going to die there on the settee in the parlor. So I said yes, I'd become a priest. And he said, 'Promise me that. Put your hand on the Bible and promise me.' And I did. Of course, I did. He was my father."

Silence. Megan, still against him, was chewing her fingernails. In spite of all the sounds around us, I could hear the almost rhythmic clipping of her teeth against her nail.

I raised my head and looked out across the street. We were surrounded in a deep, summer warmth. It was not the kind of heat to make you sweat, but dry and soothing, like a well-heated room in winter.

Megan shifted her weight. "Is that when you ran away, Daddy? When your father died?"

He shook his head. "No. No, actually I didn't run away for a long time after that. But it was because of that. Because I had promised him and your grandmother and I knew I never could be a priest."

Megan looked up.

"I ran away when I was eighteen. The day I turned eighteen. That's how old you had to be to join the army without your parents' consent. So, the day I turned eighteen, I simply left the farm and joined up."

"But your birthday's in January," I said. "I thought you graduated from high school first."

"No."

That was news to me. I glanced over at him.

"No," he said again. "I got a diploma eventually. An equivalency diploma after the war. But I never finished high school. All they cared about in the army was that you were old enough. So when I was, I signed up."

Chin on his knuckles, he gazed at the street. The black-and-white cat was perched on the curb, washing itself.

"I loved the Church," he said, his voice soft. "That's what Mother could never understand, how I was able to love the Church so much and then leave it. I never could explain it to her, so that she'd understand."

He smiled over at me. "Then I met your mama and that's all there was to it. First your mama, then you, then Meggie. And I never looked back."

"Did you ever regret it?" I asked. "Not being a priest, I mean. Did you ever regret marrying Mama instead?"

"No."

I sat. Slightly apart from my father and my sister, I kept my knees drawn up, my arms resting on them. The air around us was heavy with the smell of cut grass from the Reillys' yard. A variety-show host's voice droned from the television across the street. But the road itself was empty. Even the cat had gone. Absently, I wondered what had happened to all those street games kids used to play on summer evenings when I was little.

Beyond the Beckermans' house, beyond the house behind theirs, the plains were visible. They stretched away into the blackness of an approaching thunderstorm, but the storm was so distant that all I could see of it was the occasional arc of lightning. The thunder was still inaudible, and the clouds had so far failed to deepen the twilight.

"If that happened to you," I said, "then you must be able to understand why I have to go."

"I suppose I can," my father replied. "But what I really understand now is how my mother must have felt."

# Thirty

When I awoke there was a girl sitting on the seat opposite. She was holding a fat baby of indeterminate age and sex. While the train was crossing the flat, industrialized heart of England, I'd fallen asleep, and except for an occasional prod from the conductor to show my ticket, nothing had disturbed my dreamless, almost drugged, slumber. The train had gone far over the border into Wales before I woke. When and where the girl with the baby had boarded, I didn't know.

Blearily, I sat up, rubbed my eyes and peered out the window. All was gray. Mountains rose up on the left-hand side of the train. They were bulky and lumpish looking, like defeated prizefighters in poorly knit sweaters. Swollen by the mist, they clumped off into the distance until they blended with the clouds. On the other side of the train was the Irish Sea, only a matter of yards from the track. Troubled and restless, it too stretched as far as the eye could see until there was no distinction between sea and sky.

"On holiday then?" the girl asked me.

I had intended to go back to sleep. The traveling, the time-zone changes, the sudden foreignness were all taking their toll. I was starting to drop off to sleep every time I had a few spare moments. But I'd had to sit up and shift the backpack so that I could stretch out my legs. This movement she apparently interpreted as consciousness on my part.

"Where from then?" she persisted when I didn't answer immediately. On one knee she dandled the baby in a casual, almost careless fashion. It had a face round as a globe and was dressed in a navy blue and red sweater, covered with pill-balls. "Are you from America?"

Disconcerted to be so recognizable, I nodded.

"I thought so. I heard you when you spoke to the ticket taker."

Rubbing a hand over my face, I turned and glanced out the window again. What Mama must have gone through, I thought, to have been identified as a foreigner every time she opened her mouth. I remembered her saying to my father how much it bothered her not to be able to sound like the other midwesterners. I'd always been amused by the funny way she said some words. (It's a joke, Mama. A funny joke. And yolk. Yolk of an egg. Not the joke of an egg. And we don't laugh at yolks.) But now, for the first time, I understood. It was a surprisingly powerful enlightenment because before it had always seemed like such a minor thing. But now, here, understood.

"What part of America are you from?" the girl asked. The baby began to fuss, and she bounced it more spiritedly.

"Kansas," I said.

Her brow wrinkled. "Where's that?"

"Do you know where Denver is?" I asked.

She shook her head.

"It's in Colorado. A big city. You know Colorado?"

Another shake. "I know where Miami is."

"It isn't near Miami."

"Is it near Hollywood?" she asked.

I considered. "Closer to Hollywood than Miami."

Then the light bulb switched on, and she smiled

brightly. "Kansas! Where Judy Garland was in *The Wizard of Oz!*" Then, abruptly, a look of bewilderment. "Is it real? A *real* place, I mean?" she asked, as if I had said I came from never-never land.

I nodded. Turning my head I gazed out the window. Vague depression settled over me.

This was not the place my dreams were made of. I'd had Mama's stories so well imagined, the landscape so familiarly visualized that I had believed I knew it. But this sure wasn't it. The train clung to a narrow ledge suspended between sheer rock on one side and the sea on the other. We were into the foothills of the mountains; they were no more than solid gray rock covered with scrubby brush. The mountains themselves were beyond, their lower slopes obscured by the immediate hills, their peaks cloaked in clouds. They were not huge mountains, like the Rockies, nor distant, but instead they hulked up in the grayness, sullen and unwelcoming. Beside the track, the rocky hills were sectioned irregularly by crumbling stone walls that often ran straight up the inclines. Everywhere the land was overrun by grimy, shaggy-haired sheep that scattered blindly away from the sound of the train. I was filled with a sudden longing for Kansas just then, as I watched the sheep. I was overcome with homesickness for the sunny, wide and familiar plains.

The girl opposite refused to stop talking. Whether I answered or not, she continued to chat. I never learned her name, but the baby was called Christopher. She was nineteen and he was her son. She'd been on a day trip to Rhyl, she said, because her mother lived there. But now she was returning to the Lleyn Peninsula where she lived with her husband, who was a butcher, and his parents.

When she asked me where I was going, I said the Dark Gray Pass. Her expression was quizzical, so I said it again, assuming she didn't know where the village was.

Digging out the paper with my father's list of names on it, I showed her the Welsh name. Oh, Bwlch-llwyd-ddu! she exclaimed. And laughed.

It wasn't like my mama said. Or maybe my mama never said it. Maybe I just interpreted what she did say wrongly. Mama had always called so many Welsh place-names by their English translations. They have such a way with names, the Welsh, she'd always say. They were such lyrically descriptive names that she wanted Megan and me to appreciate them. Forest of Flowers, Wall of Mists, River That Lies in the Eye of the Sun. I had assumed that since all the Welsh were bilingual anyway, they'd use the English names too. Or at least recognize them. But much to my dismay, I discovered, that if you wanted a place with a name like Bwlch-llwyd-ddu, you could not translate it as my mother had always done. You had to say Bwlch-llwyd-ddu, no matter how badly you massacred it. The Dark Gray Pass? Delightedly and unashamedly, the girl was still laughing at me, at my ignorance, her head thrown back so I could see all her teeth.

I felt suddenly stupid in the presence of this plain-looking girl who thought Kansas was part of a fairy tale. I didn't tell her that I'd always called Coed-y-Bleiddiau simply Forest of Flowers. How ridiculous to come six thousand miles to see a place whose name you couldn't even pronounce correctly.

She could tell she'd hurt my feelings. Give me the paper, she said, extending her hand, and I'll help you with the pronunciations. As she glanced down the list, she said with that peculiar kind of pride people have for their homeland, that even though Wales had been a conquered country for nearly seven hundred years, the Welsh had never forgotten their heritage and, though weakened, their ancient language persisted tenaciously in the shadow of world-dominating English. With words like these, I said to her, I could understand that. It was purely an insider's language.

We talked of other things too. She wanted to know about the United States. Had I ever been to Hollywood? Did I ever see any movie stars? She clearly thought Kansas was just down the road from L.A., a day trip, like going to see your mama in Rhyl. She was having a holiday in the States someday, she said. She'd go see the movie stars for herself. Hollywood. And then Florida. To lie on a warm beach and get a good tan. The beach at Rhyl wasn't always very warm, she said, not in June it wasn't. Not necessarily even in August. But someday she'd go to Florida where it was always sunny.

America was wonderful to her sitting there in the dusty, dirty second-class compartment with her fat baby. She had the same dreamy-eyed expression that my mama would get when she talked about places she had never been, places she knew were better than the place we already lived in. I tried to dissuade the girl. I told her there was terrible crime in Florida, a lot worse than in Wales. People were getting murdered right, left and center in Florida. And all over the U.S. There were people getting murdered and mugged, people not able to afford to go to hospitals when they were sick, people not wanting to help take care of other people, if there was no money in it for them. Money, I said, that was it. Everything was money there. The girl looked nonplussed. She lifted her shoulders in a casual shrug. Someday, she said, I want a suntan like you get in Florida.

The baby fussed and the girl took crackers out of her handbag and fed them to him. Holding him against her breast, she crooned to him in Welsh, her voice soft and high pitched and full of love. Lulled by the motion of the train, I gazed at the sheep in their rocky pastures, at the gray stone walls, at the sea. Mama certainly had been right about one thing. All of Wales was gray and green.

The girl did not speak to me again. She became too involved with the baby, jiggling him, tickling him, trying to coerce a smile. From the smell, it was obvious he had filled his diaper, but she didn't seem to take notice. Although I wasn't watching her, I couldn't help but listen to the gentle, foreign patter. What I began thinking about was the fact that she was married and a mother and so nearly my age. She seemed immature to me with her silly dreams of movie stars and Hollywood. Yet, inexplicably, I felt inferior, sitting there with my backpack and my freedom. *Was this how it was for you, Mama? A woman at nineteen while I am only a child?*

My journey on the train terminated at Bangor in North Wales. From there I had to catch a bus to the village of Bwlch-llwyd-ddu. After getting off the train, I bought a can of lukewarm Coca-Cola at the kiosk on the station platform and put it into my pack with the intention of drinking it on the bus. Then lofting the pack onto my back, I worked my way across town to the bus stop.

The bus itself was old and green and battered. It lurched off into the Welsh countryside with a bone-rattling rumble. At first we followed an ordinary highway, but after a half an hour or so, the sea plain was left behind and the bus climbed into the mountains. The road was unbelievable. In many places it was so narrow that there was no way for oncoming cars to pass us. So then the bus driver would back up into the nearest farm drive to let the car squeeze by before we struggled upward again. We careened around sharp corners and up steep inclines through tiny hamlets.

I took out my can of pop. The first portion spilled into my lap when the bus hit an unexpected curve while I was opening it. I took a gulp to prevent more spillage, and bubbles foamed up into my nose. Even though I was very thirsty, I found it a nasty drink unchilled. tasting mostly of sweet syrup. Slowly, the motion of the bus itself, combined with thick cigarette smoke and the fizzy Coke, began to make me feel carsick. So I held the half-full can and waited for the interminably slow journey to be over.

I walked the last four miles up to Bwlch-llwyd-ddu. The bus I'd been riding went through a village at the bottom of the valley, but if I wanted to get to Bwlch-llwyd-ddu, I had to wait for a connecting bus due in ninety minutes. Since it was only four miles and I was still feeling sick, I decided to walk, hoping perhaps I could hitch a ride along the way.

I couldn't. Only two cars passed, both going the opposite direction.

Wearily, I climbed the last long stretch of road and crested the hill to see the village. I paused, took off my pack, lay it atop the stone wall adjoining the road, and leaned heavily against it to catch my breath.

Was this it? Mama used to tell Megs and me about the village, about how she walked the three-and-a-half miles down from Forest of Flowers. She made such a fun-sounding adventure out of it, about how she had to dodge the Jones's sheep dog, who would nip at her heels, about how she waded the stream by the cottage because she feared she might slip on the wet footbridge and spill her precious load of still-rationed food, about how she would sometimes sit with old Mrs. Evans in front of the post office and help her card wool.

Was this it? Was this where she was coming? Did this narrow street between gray, lichen-covered buildings lead home for her and Daddy?

I remained leaning against the wall at the crest of the hill and looked at the place. Bwlch-llwyd-ddu wasn't even a hamlet. In Kansas they would never have bothered to dignify it with its own name. It was just a cluster of stone houses built of the local dark gray slate. There was a shop with wooden boxes of green cabbages and oranges sitting outside, newspapers stuffed into a rack attached to

the door frame and a red-and-gold post-office sign above.
But that and the handful of houses was all there was to
Bwlch-llwyd-ddu. Nothing more.

The clouds were coming down. All day it had been
overcast, but closer to sea level it hadn't been particularly
pervasive. However, up here at the higher end of the valley, I could see the mists that shrouded the mountains on
either side were simply low clouds, and now, down the
narrow road and in around the slate-built houses they
rolled, moist and surprisingly warm, like cow's breath.

Two sheep strolled down the street in front of me,
glanced up, parted around me and walked on by. There
were sheep *everywhere*. They clearly outnumbered the
human inhabitants in this part of Wales, and the land was
theirs. With casual confidence, they meandered down
village streets, dozed on front porches and munched their
way through curbside weeds.

I stopped in the village shop to get directions up to the
farm. The shopkeeper, an older woman, perhaps in her
sixties, looked at the address for Owen Jones, the farmer
who owned Forest of Flowers. Go up the road, she said,
and then keep right. Stay with it. Then second turning on
the left. You'll see a big oak. She went on and on with
her directions, taking right turns and left turns, veering
around trees and derelict cottages, going over cattle
guards and through gates until she made the Jones farm
sound halfway back to England. I scribbled hastily. Her
English had the lilting intonation of Welsh, and I
couldn't understand her well. How far? I asked. Two
miles.

Just beyond the clutch of houses, the main street dwin-
dled to a narrow, single-track lane, walled in on either
side by slate, dry-walled in an intricate jigsaw pattern,
covered with green and yellow lichen. The mist remained
down so that I couldn't see the mountains I was walking
into. The lane simply continued to disappear upward into

the grayness. So I kept my eyes on the pastures to either side of me, on the stone walls and holly trees that grew along the lane in places.

It was a beautiful country. Even through my weariness, I was beginning to realize that. But it was a very, very different kind of beauty than I had imagined. I'd seen a Walt Disney world in my head, bright and gay and unblemished. This place was ancient and anguished, crumbling in the mist, overran by the slowest of things: slugs and snails and lichen. Yet it had a beauty about it so plain I could not miss it and so achingly primal that it bordered on pain.

The lane terminated right in the yard of the Jones's farmhouse. The house was unimposing, and like everything else, was made of slate. I paused a moment. Then I went up and knocked.

A woman answered.

"My name is Lesley O'Malley. I wrote from America in May. About coming up to see a cottage on the farm. My parents used to live here after the war. In Coed-y-Bleiddiau."

From her expression I could tell I had crucified the pronunciation. So I dug out the paper and showed it to her.

She smiled. "You'll be wanting my husband then," she said. "I remember you now. I remember your letter. Come on in."

I followed her through latch-handled wooden doors and low-ceilinged rooms with heavy black beams until we came into the kitchen at the back of the house. It was a small room, dark in spite of white walls, and made hellishly hot by a coal-burning cookstove set into the recess of a gigantic old fireplace. Even though the weather was overcast and misty, the day was still reasonably warm, so the stove made the temperature in the kitchen about eighty-five degrees. Two very young boys were playing on the floor. They paused when they saw me enter and stared at me before they fell back into conversation with one another.

I couldn't guess the woman's age. She might have been twenty-five or thirty or forty. Her hair was dark; her features unremarkable. Owen Jones, she told me as she prepared a pot of tea, was up in the high pasture with the sheep. He'd be down for his tea break soon enough, she said, so if I wanted, I could make myself comfortable and wait. You'll have a cup of tea too, won't you? she asked as I slipped off my pack and leaned it against the wall. I sat down at a very long, well-scrubbed pine table. The tea had already been set down, steaming in a cup.

The foreignness of this place was overwhelming. It was as if I had stepped onto a movie set, half in another country, half in another age. There was nothing about it that was even faintly reminiscent of what I'd left in America. Sitting over the cup, I watched the tea leaves swirl and settle into the darkness before I added milk and stirred them to life again. I was awash with homesickness. All I wanted at just that moment was to be teleported back to Kansas.

The older of the two children rose from the floor and came over to accept a cup of milky tea from his mother. He was perhaps three or four, dressed in shorts and sandals that looked like little girl's shoes to me. He paused beside me at the table.

"Please, Miss," he said, looking me in the eyes, "what's your name?"

"Lesley," I said. "What's yours?"

"Eirian Wyn Jones," he replied. His gaze was steady. "Please, Miss, are you going to stay with us?"

I smiled.

Owen Jones, like my father, was short and dark and wiry. He had masses of curly hair shoved under a tweed flat cap and the same not-quite-blue eyes as everyone else in this valley seemed to have. He wore a pair of baggy, blue twill overalls, belted around the middle, and a red-plaid flannel shirt. Over it, incongruously, he wore what looked to me like a tweed sports jacket.

His wife explained to him who I was as he stood by the coal-burning stove and poured tea into an orange enameled mug. She buttered slices of freshly cut bread and put them on the table. The two children scrambled up beside me on the bench.

"So, you're The Lady's daughter, are you?" he said, coming over to the table and sitting down opposite. "I can see a bit of her in you. You've her coloring, haven't you? Yes, you've the look of The Lady about you, all right." He smiled.

*"Duw,"* he said and took a slice of bread, "the things your letter called up. I hadn't thought about The Lady in years. And now here you are."

Memory glazed his expression, and he stirred his tea without attending to it. A smile touched the corners of his lips. "I was just a lad when they came. Seven, I was, I think. Just a little lad. But I remember the very day they came, your dad and mam. She was so beautiful, your mam. With that yellow hair."

Owen Jones's smile turned inward. He ate his slice of bread, chewing thoughtfully, still smiling, staring off somewhere beyond my shoulder.

"My dad gave them the old cottage. It was derelict. Overrun by the sheep. There wasn't even any glass left in the windows when they came. Your father brought up cardboard from the shop that first winter. Always with his hammer, your dad, always trying to do it up nice."

He paused. "Ah, but your mam . . ." He smiled directly at me. "There were three of us little lads. Me and my two brothers. Emyr, he was the oldest. He would have been about twelve that year. And Dai was the baby. And that day they came, Dai, he says to Emyr and me, that she looked like the Lady Guinevere, you know, King Arthur's queen. We always called her that, The Lady. It seemed respectful because she was so beautiful.'' He laughed. ''At least it did to us as lads.''

I smiled too, amused at the thought of Mama beguiling this man as a boy.

''You do have her look about you,'' he said. ''I could tell you were The Lady's daughter even before Angharad said.''

Embarrassed by the implied compliment, I ducked my head.

Owen Jones reached for another slice of bread. ''So then, how are they, your parents? Where are they living now?''

Silence.

I stared into my tea. Taking up the spoon, I stirred it again. There was nothing left but a bit in the bottom of the cup that couldn't be drunk without drinking in tea leaves as well. I stirred and watched the leaves rise and fall in the murky liquid and wondered what it took to be able to read them.

''My mother's just died,'' I said. ''In May.''

''She hasn't!'' he replied in shocked tones. A lengthy, expectant pause followed, meant to be filled, I suspect, with the cause of death. But I didn't say and he was too polite to ask.

''My father's still back in America. I have a little sister too, who's nine. So he's home taking care of her.''

''*Duw,*'' said Owen Jones under his breath. ''The Lady's died. Do you hear, Angharad?'' he said, turning toward his wife. ''The Lady's died.''

''I guess it's sort of why I came over,'' I said. ''My mama loved it here so much. She was always telling me and my sister about it. All these really wonderful stories. I guess I sort of wanted to know for myself what it was like here. I wanted to see it.''

For a moment I thought he was going to hug me. He had that sort of aching sympathy in his eyes that made it conceivable to picture this middle-aged Welsh farmer reaching across the table to put his arms around me. But the expression subsided.

He sighed. *"Duw, Duw,* it does make you feel old.*"* There was a lonely silence and then slowly the reflexive smile returned to his lips. "She was a good woman, your mam. My brother Dai, he was walleyed. The other lads, they were always at him. Merciless, they were. And The Lady, she'd come find him crying by the wall. Pay them no mind, Dai, she'd always say to him. Come up to the cottage with me and I'll give you buttered bread with sugar on it, she'd say. There's a good lad, Dai, come up and I'll tell you a story. Soon enough, we were all wishing for walleyes too." He grinned.

Then stillness engulfed us. Owen Jones's wife was cutting green spring cabbage into a pot on the cookstove. The two little boys were back on the floor, murmuring to one another. I listened carefully to them, trying to ascertain if they were speaking in Welsh or simply in oddly intonated English. Through the small, four-paned window beside the bench I was sitting on, I could see into the farmyard and beyond to the pastures, vibrantly green in the mist. Green and gray.

Even more apparent than the dichromatic sameness was the antiquity of the land. I reckoned time had never meant much here. Twenty or thirty years was nothing to the thin-soiled fields or the clouded mountains. My parents could have been sitting in this kitchen an eye blink earlier.

"They were in the war, weren't they?" Owen Jones asked. "I remember that now. I was trying to recall what brought them here in the first place. But it was the war, wasn't it? Your father was stationed somewhere in Suffolk, I think."

I nodded.

"And The Lady . . ." He let the words drift off as he thoughtfully stirred a second mug of tea.

"She was in the war too," I said.

"I don't remember a whole lot about when they very first came. She was poorly. I recall that. My mam used to send me up to the cottage with butter off the first churning in hopes it'd make her stronger. My mam was forever fretting about The Lady. She was so thin. So slow to improve, to my mam's way of thinking. I remember Mam talking about it with my dad. I remember her bringing up The Lady's name for prayer in chapel. And The Lady's hair was short. Like a boy's almost, when they first came. But she let it grow very long. I don't think she ever cut it. But it was yellow even when it was short. Dai and me and Emyr, we were fascinated."

Pensively, he ran a finger along his lower lip. "I remember one incident. It wasn't very long after they came. The first summer, I think. I went up to the cottage, and she was out in the garden with the flowers. And I thought, I would surprise her, like. So I hid behind the wall. When she stood up; I jumped out." He ruminated over the tea. "I scared her. *Duw.* She screamed. *Arglwydd mawr,* did she scream. It frightened me so much I took off and ran all the way back down to the farm." He smiled at me. "But you see, it was the war, wasn't it? It was surprising her and her having been in the war. I didn't understand then. I thought it was me she was screaming at."

Another long, thoughtful pause. Owen Jones was playing with a crumb of bread, pushing it back and forth across the tabletop with his finger. "They lost a son in the war, didn't they?" he asked, and then before I could respond, went on. "I remember The Lady talking about it. About losing him. It must have been frightful. Even then I knew that. He would have been a year younger than me. How many times she would tell me that. That her little boy and I would have been almost the same age.''

Abruptly, he grinned. ''When Mam would get mad at me, if I'd been stroppy and she'd smacked me, I remember saying to her sometimes, 'I'm going to live with The Lady now, Mam,' and head for the door. *Duw*, that would make my mam mad! But it was a dream with me, to belong to The Lady Guinevere. To be her lost son.''

The smile drifted into sadness. ''The truth said though, now that I look back on it with years behind me and little lads of my own, I think how your mam must have been suffering over it. I was too young to understand what was wrong, but even then, I knew it broke her heart to have lost that little boy.''

I nodded. ''Yes, it did. She never really got over it.''

# Thirty-One

BEFORE SUPPER Angharad, Owen Jones's wife, took me upstairs to the room where I would sleep. It was a small room wallpapered in a pattern that had huge pink and lavender flowers, and there was a tiny sink in the corner. The bed was soft and bouncy and hidden under a wildly colored tapestry bedspread. Angharad explained that this was one of two guest rooms. She earned pin money in the summers by letting out the two bedrooms as B&B's, meaning that people passing through the area could drive up and pay to spend the night and have breakfast in the morning.

I ate the evening meal with the Joneses. They called it tea; I called it supper. It wasn't part of the original arrangement for my staying there, but Angharad invited me, and it seemed the right thing to do. We were like distant relatives, not knowing one another and yet connected. Owen Jones promised to take me up to Coed-y-Bleiddiau after we finished.

While we were eating, the sun broke through, and long, golden shafts of light knifed across the warm kitchen. It was an eerie light, thick and very yellow. The two little boys, Eirian and Siôn Twm, were sitting directly in the sun's path, and their faces took on a pale hue, like those of saints on painted icons. Outside, the gray mist was pulling apart on the mountainsides. The grass, the stones, the walls, even the sheep were gilded in the evening light.

After supper Owen Jones backed his Land Rover out of the barn. A pair of black-and-white sheep dogs exploded from the doorway of one of the sheds and raced across the yard toward him. He climbed out and opened the back of the vehicle for the dogs. ''Jump in,'' he said to me.

The road we left the farm on was no more than a dirt track between two stone walls. The Land Rover, ancient and battered, lurched along steep inclines. The land beyond the walls was what Owen Jones termed open moorland—bare, boggy and covered with dense heather and bracken.

Then the stone walls turned away from us, leaving us on a broad plateau. The road disappeared into ruts in the grass. Soon the incline pitched abruptly upward, and Owen Jones geared down. The Land Rover shuddered, coughed and then on up we went.

The view was spectacular. After seeing nothing of Wales all day except clouds and mist, I was startled by its brutal, rocky splendor in the sunlight. We could see clear to the Irish Sea, more than ten miles to the west, as the mountains gave way to the valley and the valley gave way to the sea. On the valley floor, a broad river wound out to the estuary, like a gold-paved road.

From our increasing height I realized what an astonishingly small country Wales actually was. The Irish Sea was visible not only in the west but also in the north as well. A full third of Wales was viewable from where we were. And all of it was mountains, from sea to sea.

Over there, Owen Jones said, pointing, sleeps the Old Man. He let the Land Rover slow to a crawl. Still hidden in a cloud bank beyond us was the Snowdon massif, the highest mountain in Wales. Yr Wyddfa is its name in the old language, Owen Jones said, which means The Tomb.

On our right, forest appeared.

"This is it," he said. "It's a walk from here." He brought the vehicle to a halt.

There was a moment's silence, and Owen Jones leaned forward on the steering wheel. He had his tweed cap pulled down almost to touch his eyebrows. With one hand, he adjusted the brim. "You'll be wanting to go on alone, I reckon."

I nodded. "Yes, I'd like to."

"Can you see the path there? To the left of the oaks?"

I squinted. In my opinion one tree looked very much like another from this distance. "Yes. I think so."

"Follow that. Mind you don't get off it when it comes out of the forest, the other side. Stay to the right or you'll end up on the ridge."

"Okay."

"I'll be back here for you about nine. All right?"

I nodded.

There was a small, expectant pause as he remained leaning against the steering wheel. One of the dogs in back pushed its head over the seat.

"There's not much there, you know. It's been abandoned, like, for a long, long time. No one's been living there. Just sheep. I hope you aren't expecting much."

"I'm not," I said. "But thanks."

The beauty of the forest contrasted sharply with the rocky hillside. It was an oak forest. The trees were ancient and gnarled. Massive Tolkienian roots rose up out of the forest floor. But among them everywhere in the murky greenness sprang rhododendrons. They were nearly all past blooming at that point in June. But not quite. Huge masses of blossoms hung from bushes so tall that they created a forest within a forest.

I'd never seen rhododendrons like that. My only experience had been with small, cosseted bushes we had tried to coax through a dry winter in Yakima. Here they grew, most of them, taller than I was, and littered the forest ankle-deep with purple blossoms. In awe I stopped and gazed around me. No wonder the cottage was called Forest of Flowers.

The path was hard to follow, partly because of the leaves and blossoms on the forest floor, but mainly because there just wasn't much of a path. The sun continued to shine, slanting in almost horizontally, so it illuminated very little of the forest. I picked my way along carefully but not very speedily. Then without warning the trail broke into the open and I was standing on the crest of a hill which overlooked a different, steep-sided valley than the one that led to the sea. I could see clearly the path to the left that continued up over the top of the hill. The other ran across the hillside, over a small footbridge and to the cottage.

Owen Jones was right. There wasn't much there. Built of slate with coats and coats of whitewash crumbling from the stones, it stood empty and forlorn in a small dip on the hillside. It was utterly alone, hidden even from the forest by a small stony outcropping. I'd always assumed from the name that it was in the forest proper, but it wasn't. There were no trees around it whatsoever. It stood completely on its own on barren land. Only a few rhododendrons had begun to bridge the distance from the forest.

There was a low wall surrounding the place, and I paused there a moment to try and reconcile what I'd carried around in my head all these years with what I was

seeing. While the forest had been beautiful beyond anything I could have dreamed of, the cottage fell pretty far
short of even my scaled-down ideas. It was not the ruined
appearance as much as the utter isolation, the loneliness
of the treeless hillside. And the cottage itself just wasn't
much. They had lived very simply in those days. It was
only two rooms. Two tiny rooms. The whole of the cottage would have fit into the space of Megan's and my
rooms at home. The floors, I discovered, when I went inside, were nothing but flat slates over dirt. The toilet was
in a stone shanty out back. Running water must have
meant the small but vigorous stream under the footbridge.

I guess I should have realized those things. Even if
Mama never mentioned them, I should have put that
much together for myself. You would hardly expect a
farmer you didn't know to give you a castle rent free.
And you would probably conclude that something that
did not even have a road to it was not the Taj Mahal. Yet,
as I stood, gaping at it, I knew I had expected more. The
way Mama always talked about it, the *joy* of those wonderful happy stories, I guess made me want more for her
and Daddy than this.

Inside, I paced the length of one of the rooms. Then
the other. Both were about nine by fifteen feet. The main
room, where the outside door entered, also had a gigantic
fireplace that extended the entire length of the end wall.
It was more than four feet deep, and a massive, dark
beam arched over it. There were still old, rusted nails and
hooks sticking out of the beam.

With the toe of my shoe I pushed sheep droppings
aside. Then I sat on the floor, because there was no place
else to sit, and looked around me. The cottage had a
dank, although not unpleasant, smell—rather woodsy,
like moss and wet, decaying logs. The slate floor was

very cold, and I could feel it through the seat of my pants. Hardly any light came in through the small, low windows.

On my hands and knees I crawled around the perimeter of the room, inspecting the stones in the walls, the slate windowsills and the deep recesses to the windows themselves, with their moldering, glassless frames. Standing, I ran my hand along the ancient beam above the fireplace. I stepped into the fireplace cavity and looked up through the chimney, black with centuries of fires. The sky was visible. Carefully, thoroughly, I searched the entire cottage for some message, some sign reaching out across the years to comfort me. Of course, I found nothing.

There seemed to be as many spiders in this part of Wales as there were sheep, and they were nearly as big. While leaning against a windowsill, I watched one that must have measured at least two inches across from leg to leg. It scurried out of the wall when I disturbed it, ran into the middle of the room. It paused there and waited, then when I didn't move again, it cautiously started back. I meant to step on it but didn't. It came right back to where I stood, past my shoe and into another crevice in the wall.

Outside, I walked through the erstwhile garden. Although you couldn't see the forest from the house, over the ridge of the hill came the rhododendrons, like advancing troops. A few more years and they would reach the wall around the garden and breach it. The sheep had already been throughout the garden and had closely grazed it. A few straggling holly bushes from the old hedge were on the far side of the house, but otherwise, it was impossible to tell where things had grown. The only sign of flowers were the masses of daffodil leaves everywhere, with seed pods swollen from spring blooming.

I stopped where the garden arch must have been, the one with the honeysuckle over it that Mama had braided into wreaths to make the cottage smell good. Now there was only the skeleton of the archway, arcing up at a curious angle. If there had been any honeysuckle left, the sheep must have dispensed with it.

The view there from the garden arch was in its own way more boundless than the plains were at home. Below was the vast drop into the valley. Beyond, you could see range after range of mountains, all hazy gold in the setting sun. It was a view of such staggering proportions that the beauty of it was overfilling. Transfixed, I leaned against the garden wall and gazed at it. Yet it left me feeling lonely. Such immense splendor only dwarfed the cottage, huddled on its barren hillside, even further.

Lifting myself up, I sat on the garden wall. Now what?

Owen Jones was singing. His voice, deep and full bodied, swelled through the forest, so that I heard him long before I emerged from the trees. The song was solemn as a hymn, but he sang it lustily as he loaded three sheep into the back of the Land Rover. The sun was resting low on the distant sea when I came out of the trees. He waved. His dogs leaped wildly around him.

"Well, have you seen your cottage then?" he asked as I approached. I was carrying a bouquet of rhododendrons, but they were so far past their prime that even as I held them, the blossoms fell.

I smiled and nodded.

"What did you think?" he asked.

Opening the door of the Land Rover, I climbed up onto

the seat. I grinned. "I don't know what I'd been expecting," I said, "but I must admit, it wasn't precisely that."

He laughed. "Ay, I reckoned as much."

We bumped down the rutted track, the three sheep bleating mournfully against my shoulder, the two dogs struggling to keep their footing on the vinyl seat between Owen Jones and me. Owen Jones was humming the same song he'd been singing before.

"Did you know my father very well?" I asked.

He turned his head in my direction.

"I mean, you have such a clear recollection of my mother. Do you remember very much about my father?"

Pensive silence. The Land Rover jolted forward over a rock, and one of the dogs slid off the seat. I scooted aside to let it up again. A sheep with its nose against my left ear let out a mighty bleat.

"He was very handy with his hands. More than my dad was. Always doing up, was your dad. I don't remember much because of it. He was always working. Your mam, of course, she was in the cottage, so we saw a lot of her. But your dad was usually out on the farm. Always with my dad. Always helping. I remember Dad saying something once about it. Saying how reliable he was. How he worked harder than the cottage was worth."

We bounced on down the hillside. Owen Jones was driving faster than he had when we'd come up, and we were literally bouncing up and down, us, the two dogs, the three sheep.

"Once I remember he made us this little car. A little wooden box on wheels for me and Dai to roll down the lane in front of the house. Right posh it was too, with paint on it and everything. Ay, he was a good one, your dad, for doing things. And patient too. Never one for minding us helping him. My dad wasn't that way. Couldn't stand us lads under his feet when he was working. But not your dad. He never minded that Dai got things wrong. Dai, you see, he was very fond of your dad. Liked to help out, did our Dai, but he couldn't see properly with his eye. Always making a mess. And your dad was ever so patient with him. Never yelled.''

"Anything else you can remember?''

Again the thinking silence. Then there was the upward quirk of his lips, and he chuckled. "Ay. Ay, but it sounds daft to say now. You see, we were a little jealous of him, Emyr and me.'' Owen Jones paused, and the grin went inward. He rubbed his chin. "Me, at least, I was. Maybe not Emry. Maybe just me.

"I remember once when I was eight. I asked your mam to marry me. Right daft about her, I was. But I said that if she'd wait until I was a man, then I'd marry her and she could come down to live in the big house.'' Owen Jones looked over at me and smiled. "It sounds a laugh, doesn't it? To remember the things you said as a child. But, ay, I was daft as could be about her. And she says to me, "Owen *bach*, I have a husband already.' And you see, she would always send us home. We would be there at the cottage, and when he would come up the path, she would say very excitedly, 'Here comes O'Malley!' You could hear how happy she was about that. She'd say, 'Here comes O'Malley. You have to go now.' And once I asked her why I had to leave. Why couldn't I stay? And she said, 'I want to be with him now. I am his wife.' '' Owen Jones nodded. "Ay, I was jealous. I didn't like always having to go home when O'Malley came.'' Another nod. "So that's what I remember most about your dad. That he was always coming home!'' And he laughed.

We drove into the farmyard. Once out, I helped hold the back door of the vehicle open while Owen Jones pried out the sheep. He shooed them into a pen inside the barn. I followed him into the gloomy darkness.

"Would you mind if I stayed there a little while?" I asked.

"Stayed where?"

"Up at the cottage. I've got my sleeping bag and stuff. Would you care if I camped there for a few days?"

"We've plenty of room down here at the farm. You needn't stay up there."

"I was thinking I'd like to. If you wouldn't mind. Just a day or two or something."

"There's nothing there, you know," he said. "No lights. No plumbing. Nothing." He removed his cap and ran his fingers through his hair.

"I just think I'd like to be up there, that's all. If you wouldn't mind. I could pay you the same as I was going to for staying here."

He snorted and flapped a hand in my direction. *"Duw,* wouldn't think of it. It's all yours. No one else uses it, excepting the sheep."

When we came into the kitchen, Angharad was sitting in a rocking chair beside the coal-burning stove. She held the younger boy, Siôn Twm, in her arms. He was asleep, his head flopped back over her arm, his lips parted, his dark hair plastered to his forehead by the raging heat of the stove. She smiled at us and rose to put the boy, still sleeping, down onto one of the benches at the table. To Owen Jones she said something in Welsh, and he laughed. He went and leaned over the child, smoothing back the boy's curly hair with his fingertips.

"A right Winnie-the-Pooh is our Siôn Twm," he

said to me. "Cleaned out the honey pot again." He bent and kissed the small boy's head.

Angharad made a pot of tea. She brought down a big tin box filled with plain cookies and handed it to me, then the mugs, the small plates, the teaspoons. Unexpectedly, I was reminded of the countless times Megan and I had set the table together at home. I glanced at the clock. It would be just after lunch in Kansas. I wondered what Megs and Daddy were doing. I wondered if they ever thought of me in this way, reminded by small, incidental things. And eventually, as all things seemed to affect me then, I was reminded of Mama.

"Do you remember the sunflowers?" I asked Owen Jones. He was sitting on the bench beside the sleeping child. Having opened the box of cookies, he was engrossed in selecting and eating them, one by one. "Up at the cottage," I said. "My Mama always used to talk about the sunflowers. They were growing wild when she and my father came."

Lost in memory for a few moments, Owen Jones contemplated one of the cookies. Angharad poured the tea. She had a strainer this time to catch the tea leaves. Adding milk to her husband's mug, she handed it to him. He was still thinking.

Then he shook his head. "No, I don't. But then I'm not a gardener. Could have been anything growing up there and they'd all be just flowers to me."

Angharad laughed in agreement. Owen Jones grinned at her.

I smiled too. It was hard not to around Owen Jones. He had a very contagious sort of happiness about him.

"It's just that my mother was always telling me about them. Great wonderful stories. She loved flowers, and those sunflowers meant so much to her. She'd been in a camp during the war, you know, a concentration camp . . .''

I looked down at the tea mug. The tea steamed. I blew on the surface and circles formed. Then I lifted the mug and drank. It was too hot and burned my tongue. I added more of the rich milk from the creamer.

"Anyway, when she and Dad came here, there were sunflowers growing wild at Coed-y-Bleiddiau. That was what made her fall in love with the place right off. Those sunflowers made her so happy."

"Ay," said Owen Jones, "I remember her with her flowers. She was always in the garden. And beautiful things she'd grow. She'd bring them down to the house sometimes. My old *nain* was alive then, and The Lady would bring her flowers from the cottage garden to set in the parlor." He turned to his wife. "Remember that, Angharad, those photographs of Nain? Remember those flowers in the vase? Those was The Lady's flowers."

"I looked for the sunflowers. I looked especially for them," I said. "But the sheep must have got them. They seem to have eaten everything but the daffodils. So I guess I was just wondering if you remembered where they'd grown."

"No," replied Owen Jones. "I'm afraid I'm no help to you there. And it was a long time ago."

The small boy stirred. He was between Owen Jones and his wife on the high-backed bench, and both of them turned to the child when he moved. Owen Jones bent low over him and covered the boy's face almost entirely with one hand, leathery and calloused against the child's translucent skin. He whispered to him. The child shifted but still slept.

I wondered why the boy was here and not in his bed. Had Angharad thought he would be sick from eating all that honey? Or perhaps she had punished him for it and was sorry for it now. Or reluctant to let him go to sleep crying.

Finally, Angharad lifted her head and turned her attention from the child. She reached over and put the lid back on the metal box containing the cookies. She picked up the tea strainer and put it on her plate. It had left a small puddle of tea on the tabletop. Owen Jones noticed it, took out his handkerchief and wiped it away. All around us was a soft, end-of-day silence.

"I've never seen anything like those rhododenrons. When I thought of a forest of flowers here, I never imagined rhododendrons. They're gorgeous."

Owen Jones looked over. He snorted derisively.

"Don't you like them?"

"Bloody nuisance is what they are. They're overrunning us up here."

Surprised by his animosity, I shook my head. "People in America grow them in their gardens."

"Ay. And some bloody fool did that here too, and look what's happened. The rhodos all but own the place now."

"But they're valuable. In America they'd be worth a fortune, growing big like that. In America we'd have made a park out of that forest."

"Ay, no doubt. And I'll sell you these any time you want them. Can't get rid of them. Hack and hack and hack, I do. But you can't kill the bleeding things. Come up in a million places then. Just like bloody starfish, they are. The more you cut them down, the more you've got. Even the sheep can't eat them."

I paused, thoughtful, and drained my mug. The deep, nighttime silence came back around us, and I felt my tiredness. Angharad bent and picked up the small boy in her arms. She leaned back against the wall and cuddled him.

"They're beautiful though," I said. "With all those flowers, they are beautiful."

"Ay, they're that," Owen Jones replied. "But it doesn't make them good."

# Thirty-Two

I STAYED ON. Not for one day or two days or a week but
instead for all of June and July and into August. Most of
the time I was up at Coed-y-Bleiddiau, but sometimes I
stayed down at the farm. I drifted into an informal arrangement with the Joneses, trading help with the children, the garden or the farm work for the privilege of the
cottage and for some of the more basic amenities, such as
baths.

Most of June I spent making the cottage habitable. I
scrubbed the stone floors, dusted out the majority of the
spiders, swept down the fireplace, which was so large
that it contained internal steps to allow the child chimney
sweeps of centuries past to climb up inside and clean it.

Angharad helped me put up sheets of clear plastic over
the windows and Owen Jones came up one Saturday and
covered the worst of the broken slates in the roof over the
main room. Even then the cottage provided only the
barest form of shelter, and my stay was never really ele-
vated above camping out. But on the other hand, it was
free and it kept me safely in the damp, green Welsh
mountains, which was where I wanted to stay.

I learned to survive on the surplus of eggs and milk and
butter from the farm, to build fires from green rhododen-
dron wood and to cook over the open grate. I tolerated the
drafts, the rain down the chimney and the outhouse in

back of the cottage, which while primitive and full of spiders, was functional. Perhaps most of all, I learned to make myself indispensable to the Joneses by working harder and longer than I ever had in my life. If they questioned my sudden appearance in their lives, they never said. Mostly, I suspect they didn't. Hospitality was a tradable commodity up here on the isolated farms, and I think they realized they were getting a good rate of exchange.

Initially, I had been frightened of Angharad Jones. She was a very silent woman in a way I had never encountered in America. Not knowing what caused it, I was afraid that she didn't like me, that she found my presence a troublesome intrusion or perhaps that she felt excluded from the animated discussions Owen Jones and I had about people she had never known. But as the summer passed, I grew accustomed to her silence and saw it as unrelated to me. She was simply a woman of few words. In fact, beneath the silence was a casual, down-to-earth sort of friendliness. Angharad accepted me, I suspect, with the same unaffected regard she had for the rejected lambs during lambing season, which Owen Jones brought down for her to put in cardboard boxes and keep warm in the open oven of the cookstove.

I knew Angharad was grateful for the extra pair of hands around the house because she often did say that to me. And I came to believe that she also appreciated my company, because whenever I mentioned its being time for me to go back up to the cottage, she always offered one more cup of tea or suggested one more thing that needed doing there in the house. But she was never talkative. She never inquired about me personally, about my family, about my life before. Nor did she ever tell me about herself or her existence before I entered it. In a way it was comforting to be padded with that silence. For the first time in ages I found myself able to loosen my guard and relax, knowing there'd never be any questions. And that relief was tremendous. Eventually, I was completely comfortable with the peace in the house and seldom spoke either. When we did talk, it was only of things having to do directly with the farm. Our days revolved around food and fuel, the children, the weather, the sheep and the dogs. Those were the only things that had importance here. Angharad accepted me as part of that, taught me how to survive in such a world and never questioned why I should want to know it.

Garrulous and good-humored, Owen Jones had his head as full of stories as did my mama. We talked constantly about my parents. Often I would keep him company when he moved the flocks of sheep from one pasture to another. It was then he was most likely to spin out the long, rambling tales of his boyhood, growing up here on the farm with his two brothers. He never needed much of an audience when he talked. Mama would want you to hang on every word, to urge her on to tell what came next, to participate so fully that in the end the story was as much your own as hers. But not Owen Jones. Once started, he rolled onward with his tale without any prompting to continue. Sometimes I had to run to keep up with him, as he walked on the hillsides, to avoid missing out on the things he said. But otherwise, I never had to do more than listen. Perhaps because of that, there was a remoteness to the stories. My parents evolved into people I was familiar with, like characters from an often-watched television show, but whom I no longer knew

In many ways Owen Jones stood in stark contrast to my mother. Despite his head for stories, he was no dreamer. He was an unsentimental, almost cold-bloodedly realistic man. Contriving a livelihood out of thin soil over solid rock was a kind of skilled warfare for him, and

it left him with few romantic notions about his or anybody else's way of life. Yet, at the same time he had a
profound relationship with his environment. Its magic
was already there for him; he did not create it.

We were up in the high pasture one day. It was drizzly,
and the clouds were so low that you could see nothing beyond the curvature of the mountainside. I'd come along
to help Owen Jones fit stones back into a wall where it
had tumbled down in one place. Wearing both the trousers and jacket to my waterproofs, I was as wet with perspiration from heaving up the stones for him to replace in
the wall as if I had never worn any protection from the
rain at all.

We took a breather. I was on one side of the wall; he
was on the other. Unzipping his jacket, he flapped it open
to let in air, then turned with his back to me and leaned
against the wall.

"Look at those daft sheep," he said and pointed across
the pasture to where a small flock of ewes was grazing
through boggy heather. "Standing right in the water.
They'll have foot rot, sure as anything. Look at them.
Right in the bog. Daft, bloody daft sheep."

I wasn't looking at them. Trying to rest my arms between the top slates set upright in the wall to form a spiky
barrier, I was staring across the pasture to the shrouded
hillside. From this vantage point you could see the edge
of the forest rising up over the crest of the hill but because
of the clouds, it was no more than a vague rib of darkness
fading into gray. The thing I was thinking about was how
drab and ordinary this landscape was in sunlight. It
wasn't an area meant to be seen clearly, because then, all
that was visible were the faults. You saw dilapidated
farms huddling on hillsides that looked equally worn.
You saw scars of a century's slate mining and the abandoned skeletons of Victorian industry. The mountains

themselves were reduced to smallish, barren slopes. But when the clouds dropped and the mists rolled in, the landscape renewed itself. It became a vibrant contrast of shiny greens and grays and blacks in the rain. The mists seemed full of haunting promise and the mountains grew huge and mysterious behind their shrouds. Most remarkable of all was the sense of timelessness. You didn't need books to tell you how old this area was; you *felt* it. And you felt that if the thin film separating past from present might be torn anywhere, it would be here.

Owen Jones was still talking about the sheep. He was worrying because he wanted to go down to Dolgellau to the sheep-dog trials which meant he would be gone from the farm for two days. There was so much to be done, so many of the sheep were unhealthy this year, he was saying. A wet summer always meant more work.

"Have you ever lived anywhere else?" I asked him.

"Huh?" He turned his head.

"I said have you ever lived anywhere other than on the farm? Like when you were younger."

"No."

The rain strengthened. Owen Jones zipped his jacket but made no effort to resume work on the wall. Beyond us in the pasture a ewe bleated. Once, twice. She looked over at us. A lamb answered.

"Went to Liverpool once," he said. "When I was about fifteen. My father went to get two shire horses and I went along to help him." He gave a long, low whistle and shook his head. "Never again. Never. Too many people. The crowds made me nervous. I got a sick stomach from it."

"What I mean is, did you ever *live* anywhere else but here?" I was trying to imagine what it must feel like to be Owen Jones, living all your life in the place you were born. After all the years of wandering after Mama, I couldn't really conceive of what that kind of familiarity with a place would be like. "Did you ever want to?"

"No."

The same ewe was still bleating, standing up to her ankles in the bog and crying. It was a melancholy sound, startlingly human in its timbre.

We were watching her, and she was watching us.

"No," Owen Jones said again. "That trip to Liverpool, that's the only time I've been out of Wales. And that was enough."

I fell silent. There was lichen on the rocks in the wall between us. I scraped at it with my fingernail.

"You've not even been to London?" I asked.

"No." Pursing his lips, he ruminated a few moments. "Once," he said, "a friend of mine, Gareth was his name, he asked me to go. To go down to London with him for a weekend. He meant for a good time, you know. To go to those places, you know. Where lads go when they're in their twenties. Anyway, he asked me. It was a long time ago now. 1962, maybe. Or 1963. I don't remember. Anyway, he asked me and it was summer. And I said, 'No, Gareth, not in summer.' It'd be hot and miserable in London in the summer, while it was cool here. I didn't want to go. So time went by. And Gareth came again and he says, 'Owen, do you fancy going with me to London for a weekend?' By then it was autumn. And I thought to myself, I can't go in autumn. There's too much to be done on the farm in autumn. And so I said, 'No, Gareth, not this time.' I didn't want to go. So, time goes by again. And this Gareth, he's a good lad and doesn't give up. So after Christmas he stops by the farm and he says, 'What about London, Owen? Shall we go have ourselves a good time in the city?' It was winter then. And I thought to myself, I can't go in winter. In winter the farm's quiet. It's the only time I have to get out and do things that I want to do. I walk sometimes. Down by the river in the valley. Last winter I made those bird tables by the back door. I think, truth be said, I like winter the best of all seasons. And so I had to say no to Gareth. I didn't want to go. The last time Gareth asked me was in May. He comes and says, 'Owen, it isn't summer, so London can't be too hot, and it isn't autumn, so the harvesting's done, and it isn't winter. Will you come with me to London for a weekend?' And I thought to myself, how can I go in spring? Have you seen a spring here? So I said to Gareth, how can I go away from here now? And he said, 'Owen, it's only for a weekend.' He said, 'I don't think you want to go.' And he was right. I didn't want to go to London.''

I was smiling. His story reminded me of a song I'd heard. The singer had been unable to find a season in which to leave the woman he loved. And if I remembered correctly, as the story that had inspired the song progressed, it was the woman who betrayed and left him.

I looked over at Owen Jones. ''But still, haven't you ever just wanted to know what London was like?''

''No.'' He turned his head to look at me. ''I've seen it on the telly. You can see things ever so much better on the telly anyway. That's the way it always is. Like the rugby matches. Same thing. I'm warm and comfortable in my own sitting room, and I can see better what's going on than all those blokes who are there.''

I studied my fingernails. ''But it isn't the same.''

''Good enough for me.''

I extracted lichen from under my nails with a sliver of slate. ''But what about music and things? And plays. Wouldn't you like to go to London and see a really professional production in the West End? Or a live concert? Or go to a really nice place to eat?''

He shook his head.

"Wouldn't you want to go just to *be* there? Being really honest now. Just once? Just to say you'd actually been there for yourself?"

Again he shook his head. "Why would I go?" he asked and turned enough to see me again. "What would there be for me to do? Mortar and bricks. That's all it is. With all those streets and buildings. A rat's maze, that's all. Nothing to it but mortar and bricks, mortar and bricks, everywhere you look. Why would I go there when I have this?"

His contentment with life on the farm made Owen Jones's memories of my mother and father stand out all the more vividly. Living up in the cottage for the major portion of his youth, my parents had seemed wildly exotic figures to young Owen Jones, not only because they were foreigners, but also because they had come and lived among the locals and become like them and still in the end were able to leave.

Owen Jones had loved my mother desperately and unashamedly. All throughout his childhood Owen Jones had made the trek up to the cottage from the farmhouse just to be near Mama. He told her about school and chapel and life down on the farm. He played word games with her to strengthen her vocabulary. He sang for her in his high, schoolboy soprano, which she loved most of all. And Mama, for her part, kept him there with her smiles and her laughter and her exquisitely spun tales of Hungary and Dresden. Owen Jones, I discovered, knew as much about Lébény as I did myself.

Mama, for her part, I suspect, did nothing to discourage him. He was undoubtedly her favorite among the three boys. It was easy to hear that in his stories, although he never said as much. I reckoned it was more likely because he was nearly the same age as Klaus than anything else, and Mama was making do with a make-believe son, but I never said that to Owen Jones. Whatever the reason, knowing Mama, I had no difficulty imagining her enchantment upon discovering this bright-spirited boy, who sang with the voice of an angel.

"I sang in the chapel," he said to me one rainy Saturday afternoon. He was repairing the tractor, and I was sitting on hay bales against the wall and keeping him company, the way I used to do with my father when I was small and he was out in the garage working on the car. "The Lady loved to have me sing to her.

"This one time in particular I remember," he said from under the tractor. "It was summertime and most of the men were away on their holidays. The choir in the chapel was only twelve or fifteen strong because almost everyone had gone somewhere. It was a big choir normally, with maybe thirty men in it. The tenor, the man who usually soloed, was away too. So they chose me to sing the solo. I didn't sing with the big choir on most occasions. Just the children's choir. But they chose me to come in on Sunday morning and sing with the men."

He slid out from under the tractor specifically to look at me. "Was I proud?" he asked rhetorically and laughed. "The buttons on my shirt wouldn't stay on!" Back under the machinery he went, and the clank of metal against metal momentarily disrupted his tale. "I was only eight, like. Only a lad. And so proud to be chosen to sing in the big choir. To solo. So, you see, I wanted her to come hear me.

"When I came home from choir practice, I remember saying to Emyr that I was going to ask The Lady to come hear me sing on Sunday next. He says back, 'Owen, you're daft. The Lady'll not come. The Lady never comes to chapel.' Emyr, see, was older. He knew The Lady wasn't a believer. But I was only eight. I didn't know. I mean, I didn't understand. I knew she didn't go to chapel but I never thought about it. But Emyr was thirteen. He'd asked her, so he knew. And he says, 'You're daft, Owen, if you think she'll come just to hear you sing. You're daft as a Blaenau sheep.'

"So, I went right up to see The Lady. I said, 'You must come to hear me in the chapel Sunday next. I've been chosen to sing "Dafydd y Garreg Wen"—"David of the White Rock"—with the men in the big choir. I want you to come hear me.' Then I said, 'But Emyr says you won't come. And Mam says you won't come. And even Dai *bach* says you won't come. But I told them they're wrong. I told them you will come because you'll be wanting so bad to hear me solo.'

"The Lady looked at me. She says, 'I don't go to chapel, Owen *bach,* don't you know that?' I said, 'Not even for me?' She says, 'I don't go in the chapel.' And I said, 'Not even to hear me sing the solo in "David of the White Rock" with all the big men behind me with their deep voices? Even when I've been chosen specially to sing with them and no other boy is?' And she said, 'No, not even to hear you, Owen *bach*. Because I do not go in chapels.' "

Owen Jones came out from under the tractor. He sat in silence for a few moments on the cobbled stone floor of the barn and wiped the grease from his hands with a rag. "I was shattered. I was absolutely shattered," he said without looking up at me. "I had to hide my face from her. I was too big to be crying about such things, and I didn't want to be ashamed of having her see me. But I was simply shattered. So she knelt down beside me and said, 'But you can sing "David of the White Rock" for me here and it will be a song for just the two of us. That'll be even more special.' But I told her that there'd be no men's voices to come in behind me when I'd finished, and that made it not so good. I said, 'Please, please come down to the chapel on Sunday next and hear me sing, because I want to sing the song for you. Please,' I said. But she said no.

"I told her I hated her. I was only eight, you know, with only a lad's heart. I was crying. I said I would never come up to sing to her again. I said I hated her and was done being friends with her. And so I left.

"I hid in the barn the rest of the afternoon, so Mam wouldn't see me crying. Right up there I hid, in the hay." He pointed upward toward the loft. "And worse, I was afraid of seeing Emyr, of having Emyr laugh at me because I'd been so certain The Lady would come just for my sake."

Then a smile touched his lips and he looked over at me through the murky dimness. "But you know what happened in the end? I didn't see The Lady for the whole of the next week. I was still unhappy, but mostly, I had to practice with the choir. So I didn't see her. Then I was in the chapel on that Sunday morning, and it was time to sing. The master pointed to me and I stepped out and began. And there was The Lady. Way in the back. Your dad too. Both of them together in their Sunday clothes. Came to hear me sing, she did. And I sang my heart out for her.

"Afterward, I said to her, 'You were only teasing me!' And do you know what she replied? To just a little lad like I was then? She said, 'I had to come, Owen *bach*. You are my smile. How could I live in the cottage, if you never came there anymore to make me happy?' "

Owen Jones rose up and went over to the barn door. He pushed it open into the rainy half-light of the afternoon. "I was so proud," he said, pausing before going outside, "to think that someone like The Lady couldn't do without me. It made me prouder than singing with the men in the choir had.''

He stepped out into the rain and went to get a tractor part from the shed. Left alone in the gloom, I leaned back into the scratchy hay and thought of Mama and little Owen Jones. With no difficulty, I could picture the incident clearly. It was so like Mama, so like the scenes from my own childhood. Mama never saw things from another point of view. She saw them in her terms and that was that. Yet, because her selfishness was so guileless, you could always forgive her for it. Again and again and again. Things never changed. Whether it was Owen Jones or Elek or Daddy or me, it made no difference. Mama took us up, breathed life into us with her stories and her dreams and her great, unharnessed vitality, and then in the very same breath, sucked life out of us. And yet in the end she left us always feeling like little Owen *bach,* that we couldn't have been luckier.

Those were three easy months that summer. They were almost dreamlike for me, so radically different were they from the tumult of my family. It was hard for me to realize that both Wales and Kansas existed on the same planet.

I worked very hard physically. I cut wood and moved coal. I helped Owen Jones with the haying. I weeded the garden, helped clean and process mountains of vegetables for the freezer, made beetroot pickles by the gallon, dreamed of watermelon and tried to describe for Angharad how you made pickles from the rind.

During the warm, muggy days of July, I ranged the hillsides with Eirian and Siôn Twm, scaring the silly sheep and watching the bare, rocky slopes grow familiar. Some days we played pretend games, being spacemen or pioneers or pirates. Sometimes the pretending was all mine, and I would imagine that they were actually my little boys, that like Mama or the girl on the train, I had become a mother in my teens. Once, one afternoon in late July, I even thought I might tell Eirian as we were sitting, eating apples by the stream, that we were going to make believe his name was Klaus and Siôn Twm's was József. But when that thought had fully formed in my mind and I realized it, I found myself sick with horror to be thinking it. I looked at Eirian, bright-eyed and curious, running barefoot through the stream, and I thought of Toby Waterman. I really was sickened by how easy it had been to want to make him Klaus.

As the summer wore on I learned to muddle along in Welsh. It was an odd language with some very peculiar features, such as the fact that there were no words for "yes" or "no." Worse was the discovery that the first letter of many, many of the words had the disconcerting habit of changing, so that any single one of them could have as many as five different beginnings and still be the same word. The English called this aberrance "mutating" but the Welsh, in their own language, called it "wandering" and did it, they said, because it made the sentences sound more beautiful to them.

The days ran on, one into the other, without my ever noticing. In the beginning I remembered to write letters to my father and Megan. Then my correspondence deteriorated to postcards. Finally, the days got away from me altogether. The only person I continued to write to was Paul, even after mid-August when he left Kansas for Ohio State. As Wales grew more familiar, Kansas grew more distant. I lost the ability to evoke vivid mental pictures of home. Sometimes I would try to re-create the image of something very familiar, such as my room or the kitchen, but with surprising suddenness the sharpness faded and my visions were dark and hazy. In the same

way, the emotions that had surrounded the time just before my departure also faded. I hardly ever thought about
things at home then, and the wide, arid plains became
more and more like something in a dream until in the end,
it seemed possible to me too that Kansas might be a place
no more real than the Emerald City.

# Thirty-Three

THE FIRST AUTUMN GALE broke at the very end of August. I was already in the cottage when the wind rose from the northwest and the rain started. At first the storm gave me only a sense of cozy well-being, since I had my little pocket radio turned on for company and the fire burning hot. There were no trees nearby to blow over, no electricity to lose. I turned up the volume on the radio. Then I threw more wood on the fire and drew closer.

It was the wind that made this storm different from the summer squalls. Hurricane strength and winter cold, it roared across the hillside. The slates on the roof of the cottage rattled. The plastic on the windows blew loose from their tackings. Rain, driven down the huge chimney opening, puddled on the hearth around the grate.

With a piece of slate I tried to hammer the plastic back over the windows. Obviously, it wasn't going to hold, so I took a blanket and reinforced the plastic with that. Then I put stones and loose slabs of slate on the windowsills, weighting the bottom of the blanket. Water began to leak into the back room through the roof. I'd noticed that when I'd gone in to get pieces of slate to put against the windows and hadn't been particularly concerned because the roof in there always leaked during rainstorms. However, before I had finished with the windows, I could see the wind was beginning to drive rain through the makeshift repairs in the roof over the main room. Water started to run down the far wall in discernible rivulets. I got down from the windowsill and went to move my sleeping bag. Bang! A gust of wind had caught up one of the slate roofing tiles. It clattered over the rooftop and then crashed to the ground somewhere beyond the cottage. Rain guttered in through the hole it left. I moved my sleeping bag again.

This was not fun. The fire, dampened by constant rain down the chimney, was more of a sizzle than a blaze. The floor was wet, one of the walls became background to a minor waterfall from the roof. Everywhere, it dripped. I stopped for a moment, clutching my sleeping bag to my chest, holding it above the floor to keep it dry. With the fire nearly out, there was no light in the room except for my flashlight. I was cold, tired and soon to be soaking wet.

It occurred to me then that it might be best to go down to the farmhouse. Holding the flashlight up, I looked at my watch. Not quite 10:00 P.M. However, I didn't cherish the idea of the steep, mile-and-a-half hike down the mountainside in the dark and the driving rain. Sitting down within the confines of the old fireplace itself, sheltering under the ancient, overhanging beam, I wrapped the sleeping bag around my shoulders. It was the first time since I'd arrived that I wished I had a telephone. Or a warm bed. Or even a light.


"Hallo? Hallo? Lesley, are you there?"

Asleep with the soggy sleeping bag still around my shoulders, I struggled to consciousness at the sound of Owen Jones's voice. Thud! Thud! came the sound of his fist on the door. I felt around for the flashlight.

The storm was still in high gear. Owen Jones rattled the door, and then it blew open with a bang, and a blast of freezing wind came into the room with him.

"Come down to the farm," he said. "I have the Land Rover at the edge of the forest. Come on. Quickly."

I searched for my anorak.

"The water's up," he said. "It's over the footbridge already." He set his lantern down on a windowsill and began lofting my things up onto the sills or hanging them on the old nails in the ceiling beams. "Put your sleeping bag up," he said to me. "There'll be half a foot of water in here by daylight."

I thought he was joking.

"Put it up," he said. "The bloody stream'll have washed your floor for you by the time you get back."

Alarmed, I looped the bag over a rusty hook inside the fireplace.

"Come on, hurry, or we'll not get back across the water very easily."

I ran after him, shutting the door behind me and dashing down the garden path. The small stream at the bottom of the garden was normally not more than a foot across and only a matter of inches deep. Now it raged down the mountainside, already too wide to step across. Owen Jones waded into it and leaped to the other side. Once over, he held his lantern high for me to see my way. Then he leaned out and tried to reach for my hand.

"Just jump," he said.

"I can't."

"Here, take my hand," he said, wading back into the water. "And just jump."

"I can't do it that way."

I was afraid of the water. I couldn't see in the darkness how deep it was or even precisely how wide. It made a deafening noise, which was all the more disconcerting to me, since normally it made hardly any noise at all.

"*Jump!*" Owen Jones shouted without much patience in his voice.

"I'll run," I said. "I'll get a running start and jump," I yelled back into the furor of the storm.

Running and jumping was the way some idiot from Kansas would cope with getting across a mountain stream on a wet slope. Wildly sprinting across the slippery grass through blinding rain, I attempted to span the water and couldn't. I came down with a splash, slipped on the rocks beneath, fell and was pushed several yards down the mountainside by the power of the current. Embarrassed to a point of tears, I crawled out, sputtering and soaked.

"Are you all right?" Owen Jones asked, his eyes still wide with amazement at the act.

"Yeah, I'm okay," I said and stood up.

Mostly, I *was* okay. However, as I was walking down through the forest after him, I realized I'd cut my foot on the sharp underwater rocks when I'd fallen. In the chilling rain, it was too numb with cold to hurt, but my sneaker darkened and filled with blood.

We were greeted at the farmhouse door by Angharad, wrapped up in a worn blue chenille bathrobe. "Look at you!" she said as I struggled gratefully into the warmth of the kitchen. "I told Owen to go fetch you earlier. I said, it's a big storm, Owen, and it's going to flood the cottage. I said that. Every gale, that cottage floods. That's why no one lives there. I told him he'd lost his silly head, leaving you up there through the night." She was laughing amid what I assumed was mock anger. Then she saw my foot, still bleeding through my shoe. *"Iesu Mawr!"* she cried and said something to Owen Jones in rapid Welsh that I couldn't get the gist of.

"Ay, we'll need to bathe that," Owen Jones replied calmly. "Where's the plastic basin?" He was over by the cupboard, already spooning tea into the teapot. Bending down, he opened the fire door of the cookstove and poked into the embers with a pair of tongs. He stuffed two thick pieces of wood in, one right after the other.

His wife again spoke to him in Welsh, and there was a few minutes' exchange between them—something to do with how I cut my foot. Unless people spoke slowly and very distinctly, I couldn't really understand much of what was said in Welsh. The Welsh had a tendency to run their words together worse than the French ever dreamed of.

"You'll take a chill in those wet clothes," Angharad said to me. She left the kitchen, and I could hear her footsteps on the stairs. When she returned, her arms were full of towels. "We'll draw you a bath, once your foot's been done. But in the meantime, you can dry off with these." She looked over at Owen Jones. He was pulling down cups and saucers from the dresser.

"Owen, leave us so the girl can get dry. The tea'll wait."

Angharad peeled my wet shirt from me and wrapped me up in Owen Jones's wool bathrobe, as if I were a little girl. She toweled my hair with deft, no-nonsense movements and then draped my wet clothes over the railing in front of the cookstove. Steam rose.

I was flooded with a very satisfying feeling as I leaned back on the bench beside the table. The robe was heavy and smelled of shaving cream and wool. The kitchen, dimly lit against the darkness outside, was humid from my damp clothes and very warm. In a sudden, quirky mental bounce I thought, Mama had it all wrong. *I* had been the stolen child, taken from here in the wet and wild mountains where I belonged and flung out with some strange family on the plains of Kansas.

When Owen Jones returned he was carrying a green plastic dishpan full of water. He knelt beside me and undid the laces of my sneaker.

"It doesn't really hurt too bad," I said and realized it

did when he moved the shoe. My foot had gone stiff while I was sitting.

"Yes, but we need to wash it. Wouldn't do to have it go septic."

The pain was a deep throb, and it seemed to make the room pulsate slightly. When Owen Jones eased my foot out of the sneaker, blood sloshed across the floor. Here, as at the cottage, the floor was of slate, and my blood washed across it in brilliant contrast.

Carefully, he lowered my foot into the dishpan. There was disinfectant in the water, which I suppose I should have expected, but I didn't, and when it touched the open wound, I shrieked in surprise and jerked my foot away involuntarily. Equally surprised, Owen Jones rocked back on his heels. He grinned at me. Then as if I were simply an uncooperative ewe, he snatched my foot and shoved it back into the pan with one sure movement. Clenching my teeth, I closed my eyes and wondered if I would faint from the pain. I thought I might. In fact, I hoped I might. But it didn't happen. Finally, he lifted my foot out and wrapped it in one of the towels.

Owen Jones did not apologize for the pain he'd caused with the disinfectant but he was gentle to a point of tenderness with the bandage. He wrapped the foot tightly and propped it up on a cushion on the bench.

Then came steaming cups of tea and a jug of rich milk. Angharad brought the toaster over to the table and supplemented our tea with slices of toast and butter. Owen Jones spread his thick with orange marmalade.

At one point while Angharad was up, slicing more bread, Owen Jones leaned his head back and closed his eyes.

Angharad looked over. "Will you be wanting your breakfast now?"

"No," he replied and straightened up. He reached for

the last slice of toast. "I want to go up and see if Bryn Derw's flooded. I'll eat when I come back."

The silence around us grew thick and sleepy. Owen Jones chewed his piece of toast thoughtfully, gazing at it between bites, shoving bits of marmalade back on with his fingers. I could see how tired he was.

So could Angharad. She rose. "Do you want a cup of coffee, Owen?"

He shook his head. "What I'm thinking," he said, "is that this about finishes it for the cottage."

"What do you mean?" I asked.

"The autumn's here. This is an autumn gale. From here on, it'll be one gale after another." He ran a hand wearily over his face. By American standards, I thought, he would be considered an ugly man, with his worn features and his bad teeth. But here he fit in so naturally that, like the slate or the lichen, his rugged appearance seemed well made. When he looked over and saw me watching him, he shook his head. "The stream comes up. It does with every gale. The mountain just funnels it down, and there's water in the cottage all winter."

"How did my parents live there then?"

He shrugged. "I don't know. The roof was better then. Your dad was a good one for keeping the roof sorted out. But they were forever having trouble with the stream. I remember that. I remember helping them with the sandbags one winter. And the place always smelled of damp. They couldn't keep it out."

"Oh."

"It's too bad, really," Owen Jones said. "It's a lovely little piece of work. It's a pity it's had to go to ruin. But whoever built it never knew the mountains."

"Well, maybe it was different in those days," I said. "Maybe the forest was all the way over the hillside then and the stream didn't do that."

Owen Jones pursed his lips pensively.

"I mean, they wouldn't have called it Coed-y-Bleiddiau if it had been built on a barren hillside, like it is now. That wouldn't have made much sense. So I reckon the landscape must just have changed over the centuries," I said.

"Yes, perhaps you're right," he said.

Once again we fell into silence. I adjusted my foot on the pillow. Angharad unplugged the toaster and moved it back to the counter. She paused to riddle the grate in the cookstove.

"You know," I said, "I can see now where they got the name for the cottage."

Owen Jones lifted his head.

"I'd always imagined something entirely different. Mama would go on and on and on about the sunflowers, about how there were sunflowers all over when they came. And I guess that I always thought of the forest in the name as being made up of sunflowers. I pictured this whole forest of sunflowers."

With a grin, I shook my head. "It's funny, really, how you get things in your mind like that. But now that I've been here, I can see what they really meant by their forest of flowers. Seeing all those rhododendrons in bloom when I first arrived, I can really understand."

Bewilderment was all over Owen Jones's face. "What *are* you talking about?"

"The cottage. I was saying that after seeing the rhododendrons in bloom, I can understand the name. It really *is* a forest of flowers."

His expression became a frown.

"I know you don't like them," I said, "and maybe they do make a lot of trouble. But I can see why whoever built the cottage thought to name it that. I think I would too."

A sudden smile lit up Angharad's face and she leaned over and spoke in Welsh to her husband. Owen Jones gave way with a loud guffaw. Ho, ho, ho, he went, just like Santa Claus. "Is *that* what you thought it meant? Forest of Flowers?"

"Coed-y-Bleiddiau, yeah," I replied.

Ho, ho, ho, he hooted. Ho, ho. At least all the laughter was waking him up.

"What's so funny?" I asked.

"You thought *bleiddiau* meant flowers?"

I nodded.

"Oh no. No. Forest of Flowers would be *Coed-y-Blodau*. Your Welsh is good enough for that, isn't it? You knew that, didn't you?"

I stared.

He was still laughing. As if I'd told the joke of the century, "Oh no, no, no. It's a much older cottage. The rhodos have only been here since the beginning of the last century. No, the cottage was built ages and ages ago. The name means Forest of Wolves."

"That can't be," I said.

"Oh ay, Lesley. *Bleiddiau* means wolves. Didn't you realize that?"

I sat, stunned into horrified silence.

Angharad smiled gently. *"Blodau, bleiddiau.* They sound very much alike. If you didn't know the language, you could easily confuse them."

Dumfounded that Mama could have made such a terrible error, I remained speechless.

"It's an understandable enough mistake to make," Angharad said.

Slowly, I nodded. "Mama must not have understood. She was Hungarian, you know. I guess she must have mixed up the similar sounds."

"You mean The Lady?" Owen Jones asked.

I nodded.

"The Lady?" he asked again cheerfully. "Oh no, not The Lady. She knew what it meant. She could speak the old language. Quick to learn was our Lady. In no time at all she could talk it. Well as my old *nain*. Ay, The Lady was a right wonder.''

I gaped at him. ''You mean my mother knew Welsh?''

''Oh, ay, that's what I'm saying. The Lady, she knew.''

# Thirty-Four

THE SENSATION of impending tears came up the way nausea does before you vomit. It started in my hands with pins and needles; my palms went clammy. My stomach clenched. Suddenly chilly in the warm kitchen, I shivered. My throat grew too tight to swallow.

Owen Jones was still chuckling, and I hated him for it.

Without excusing myself, I dragged myself off the bench, stood up and struggled toward the kitchen door.

"Where are you going, Lesley?" Angharad asked. Owen Jones's merriment halted abruptly.

"Lesley?" he called after me. But by then I was out of the kitchen and I shut the door firmly behind me. The cast-iron latch clicked into place, shutting off the sound of their voices.

Where *was* I going? Where could I go, wearing no more than my underwear and Owen Jones's bathrobe?

"Lesley?" The door from the kitchen opened.

I limped onto the front porch. Spying a pair of Wellington boots, I pulled them on and clumped out into the farmyard. The wind had died, but it was still raining steadily. I hobbled as fast as I could across the yard. Behind me, someone had already reached the front door.

Stumbling into the darkness of the barn, I groped for the light switch. Unable to find it and full of desperate urgency to keep away from whomever was behind me, I felt my way along in the blackness until I came to one of the pens at the end. I opened the gate and fumbled my way into the hay.

The barn door swung open, and Owen Jones's silhouette appeared in the doorway. He turned on the light. There was only a single, naked bulb to illuminate the entire length of the barn, so I was still in murky shadows.

"Lesley?" He came slowly down the aisle of stalls and pens.

My only conscious thought was one of humiliation. Ridiculously dressed in a man's bathrobe and a pair of rubber boots, sitting in a sheep pen, I felt like a fool. Not being seen that way suddenly took on bizarre importance, and I scrambled backward over the hay.

Owen Jones appeared at the gate of the pen. "I'm sorry," he said. "I wasn't laughing at you."

"Just go away, all right?"

"I was tired," he said. "It just struck me funny. But I didn't mean to hurt your feelings."

"They're not hurt. I'm all right. Just go away."

Rain pattered against the roof. Nervously, Owen Jones shifted from one foot to the other, his bewilderment undisguised.

"I'm sorry," he said again. "I don't know what made me laugh like that."

"It wasn't the laughing."

Silence.

I picked bits of hay from one bale.

He watched me.

I twisted a long piece around my finger.

No sound but the beating rain.

"She *told* me it meant Forest of Flowers."

"Who?" he asked.

"Mama. She told me the name of the cottage was Forest of Flowers."

His forehead puckered. "Ay, but that's not such a big thing, is it? Maybe she forgot."

"She didn't forget. My mama didn't forget things."

"Well," he said gently, "maybe not. But it's not a very big thing. Not a matter worth an upset, is it? It's just a name."

"It's *not* just a name, believe me."

He said nothing in response.

"What it is, is the last straw for me," I said. "This is the very last thing I can tolerate."

"Why?"

"Because it's a lie." I looked down at the hay, picked at it. "Because it's suddenly made everything a lie."

"Well . . ." he said with gentleness still in his voice. A moment or two passed, and he failed to complete the thought. He moved his weight back to the other foot. Looking away, he studied the timber of the stall beside him, then he looked back at me. Another weight shift. "Well," he said again, and the nagging discomfort of not knowing what to do echoed in his voice. Finally, he unzipped and pulled out his waterproof jacket. "Here. You're going to take a chill sitting out here. Put this on."

I let the jacket lie where it had fallen. "Please, just leave me alone."

He did. My attention was on the hay, and when I looked up again, he was gone.

The barn was damp and cold and smelled of sheep. It was an unwelcoming place to be. Reaching down for Owen Jones's jacket, I put it on. The rubber lining felt clammy against my skin.

Where tears should have been, there was nothing. I had no idea about what to do with myself. I sat, numbed. Everything in the world seemed wrong. Everything suddenly seemed tainted to me. Nothing had value.

\* \* \*

The rain stopped. I stood in the doorway of the barn and watched the mist lift off the immediate hillside. Dawn had come sometime during the previous hour and the sky had gone from black to leaden gray, a color it might remain all day.

Wearily, I leaned against the door frame and tried to think of what to do next.

The light was on in the kitchen. Siôn Twm and Eirian were up. I could see their small shadows bobbing on the wall by the window. A longing to go in and be with them overtook me. The kitchen would be warm and scented with bacon and toast. Siôn Twm would still be bleary-eyed with sleep, his teddy bear in his arms. He wasn't an early riser. Eirian, though, would be chattering, shoes on the wrong feet, shirttail untucked, like every other morning.

When I looked across the yard, I noticed the Land Rover was gone. I hadn't heard Owen Jones leave, but the tracks in the mud were full of rainwater, so he must have gone before the storm stopped.

Going back into the barn, I took down one of Owen Jones's shepherd's crooks from the wall. I zipped the waterproof jacket, shut the barn door and made my way through the farmyard mud to the steep path leading toward the cottage.

The journey back was difficult. I was tired and my foot hurt. Even with the shepherd's crook to support me, progress was slow over the sodden, slippery grass of the incline.

In the forest I found my way blocked by a fallen tree. It was an old oak, one that had been half dead previously. It lay sprawled over the path so that I had to retreat into the underbrush to get around it. A lot of branches were down in the forest, all of them oak or beech or maple. The supple, evergreen rhododendrons stood, untroubled, in the aftermath of the gale.

The clouds remained low and heavy against the breast of the mountain. Soon it began to rain again, gently but persistently. When I reached the fork in the path at the edge of the forest, I paused and looked across the hillside to the cottage.

There was no way to reach it. The stream had grown into a small river, crashing noisily down the hill. All the flat land around the cottage was swampy.

Forest of Wolves.

It was ugly. It was godawful ugly, really. It always had been. Gray walls against gray roof against gray rock against gray sky. Gray and swampy green. At least she'd been honest about that. But the cottage was nothing more than a man-made pile of rubble, desperately trying to revert to its natural state. My three months' occupation had done nothing to stem the tide of decay. It was almost a relief, I thought as I leaned against the shepherd's crook, not to have to pretend any longer that it was lovely.

I continued to stand, supported by the crook, my mind completely without thought. The rain strengthened. Thick cloud curled in around the cottage, and the gray stones softened and blended into the mist.

I began to cry, and the cottage and the hillside and the wild little stream dissolved entirely behind tears. Turning, I walked slowly up the path over the ridge, pulling myself along with the shepherd's crook, picking my way around lichen-covered slate outcroppings that glistened in the rain. All the heather was in bloom, a muted purple contrast to the stone and grass.

Above me a rook rose up from a gorse bush, circled and called overhead.

The rain continued.

Upon reaching the upper ridge, I crossed into the high pasture. Weary and in pain from my foot, I finally stopped at the wall on the far side. The pasture ended abruptly there on the rim of an ancient, disused slate quarry. Below the wall, the gouge in the mountainside dropped away in sheer terraces for hundreds of feet. On a clear day the spot afforded a spectacular view of the small, quarried cwm garlanded with heather, as well as the adjoining valley that widened westward toward the sea. Opposite rose the large mountains that formed the heart of Snowdonia, and when the clouds were lifted, the mountains ran away, one after another, as far as the eye could see. However, on this morning, there were only gradations of gray. Below me, the valley was completely obscured by fog.

Leaning against the wall, I wept.

The clouds thinned and lifted slightly, shredding apart on the rocky pinnacles of the mountain opposite. The rain slackened and then stopped altogether. But the sky never lightened.

A flock of wood pigeons was started up from the forest below, and they flew into the air in a great group, the sound of their wings carrying across the hilltop. I raised my head to watch them. Like a single being, they all turned midair and then dropped out of sight below the ridge.

With my attention on the pigeons, I did not hear her. Not until she had come clear through the pasture and was only yards away. Startled by the sudden awareness of movement, I turned.

Angharad wore a thin, blue plastic raincoat, the kind you buy for 50 pence at the seaside when caught in an unexpected shower. She had her skirt tucked into a pair of Owen Jones's heavy waterproof trousers, and it occurred to me upon seeing her that she never wore pants.

She came up beside me. Without speaking, she leaned against the wall and looked down into the cwm. Gently, she lay her arms between the sharp, spiky slabs of upright slate along the top of the wall.

Silence prevailed for several minutes.

"I used to come up here," she said quietly. "When I was younger."

She leaned farther over the wall. "See down there?" she pointed. "See that farm? You can just make it out through the mist. By where those trees are."

The mist cloaked everything that low in the valley. I strained to see.

"That's where I was born."

A pause.

"And I used to walk up here sometimes. It's about three miles. Straight uphill."

Somewhere behind us a bird began to sing a beautifully fluid song. Angharad turned her head toward it. It stopped. I gazed into the sheerness of the quarry. Sheep, as surefooted as mountain goats, climbed up the stony terraces to nibble heather.

Angharad looked back toward the valley. "I was about sixteen or seventeen then," she said. "I climbed up here to see if I could see beyond the mountains. I came up quite often for a while."

She lifted her eyes to the mountains beyond.

"It's the closest I ever came to getting out of this valley," she said.

I studied the mountain opposite. It looked mammoth in the mist, and mysterious, a mystery I knew would be dispelled in bright sunlight.

"Did you know," Angharad said, "that the Welsh have more words for 'mountain' or 'hill' or some other barrier in the landscape than the Eskimos have for snow?"

"I don't really want to know anything about Welsh right now," I replied.

"I think it must be because there are more mountains and hills in Wales than any other thing. They couldn't manage with the few words the English have."

"Then they must have a million words for sheep," I said without humor.

Angharad smiled anyway.

The silence returned. I felt full of sodden tiredness and braced my head with one hand. Angharad remained motionless against the wall, her gaze fixed on the shrouded mountain across the valley.

Far below in the quarry a ewe cried. Another ewe called out too. She was near to us and had a late lamb with her. It butted anxiously at her, and she watched us warily, without trust.

"Doesn't your father miss you?" Angharad said.

I shrugged.

"You're such a good help. Doesn't he miss having you home? Especially now, when he's alone and has the little one to take care of."

"She's not so little. She was ten on August eighth."

"But he must be lonely," Angharad said.

The ewe was still bleating. Many other sheep had joined in and the small cwm below us filled with an almost deafening sound, like cheering at a ball game. Their voices varied greatly. One was gravelly like an old grandfather's. One was deep. One was almost a Bronx cheer. One was melodic as a song. One was the voice of an infant crying. Back and forth across the cwm they called, their voices funneled up the steep sides of the quarry for perhaps the better part of ten minutes. I'd always meant to ask Owen Jones why they did that, because every day, at some time or another, I would hear them bleating all together.

"You want to know something, Angharad," I said.

She turned her head slightly but did not look at me.

"Do you want me to tell you how my mama died?"

My heart began to rush in my ears.

"I don't know how to say it exactly, how to tell it so that it makes sense to anyone." I paused. "My mama was in the war and she had her little boy taken away from her then, in Germany. And for some reason, I don't know what, she got to thinking this child in the town where we live now, this child in Kansas, was that little boy of hers. She just got the idea into her head, and no matter what we did to try and convince her that he wasn't, she went right on believing this was him, her son. We did everything we could think of. We tried and tried and tried to make her change her mind. But it did no good. She thought they were Nazis, the boy's parents, and that they were keeping him away from her.''

I took a deep breath. The mountains and the mist faded, and I was back in Kansas, trapped once more in the terrifying vortex of those days in April.

''I guess she must have thought it was better for him to be dead than to live like that, away from her,'' I said. ''Anyway, she took this gun. It belonged to my boy-friend, and he'd left it at my house one afternoon while he and I went out. And my mama took it and she went to where these people lived and she killed them all, the boy and his mother and his father. Then the police came to arrest her and my mama still had the gun. They shot her and she died.''

I looked down at the stone wall. Beside me Angharad did not move.

''Everything about it's so horrible,'' I said. ''About what she did. About why she did it. About the fact that these perfectly blameless people should get killed for something that happened forty years ago in another country.''

Angharad had her head down. The end of the cord from her raincoat was between her hands and she twisted it, first around one finger and then around another. Around and around. From her expression, I was unable to tell what she was thinking.

''I keep trying to figure out why this all happened to

us,'' I said. "I keep trying to make sense out of it. My whole life has fallen apart, and I just wish I could at least understand why. But I can't.'' I touched the lichen on the stone. "I don't seem to understand anything anymore. I thought I did. I thought I knew everything. At first, I thought Mama was just an innocent victim, that it was all the fault of those wicked people during the war. Then I thought the fault was my father's because he could never deal with Mama's problems. Mama was a law unto herself with Daddy, and I thought it was all his fault. Then sometimes I thought I caused it. I thought of all the things I had done, you know, and the things I could have done or could have said to her. Or shouldn't have said to her. I thought if only I could have done better, all this wouldn't have happened. And then I'd start all over again and blame the Nazis. And so on and so on and so on, because there wasn't an end to it. But the truth is, I don't really know what I think. I don't know what the answer is.''

Angharad touched the smooth wood of the shepherd's crook with her fingertips. "Is that why you came here?'' she asked.

I shrugged.

"What did you want from us?''

I shook my head. Silence came between us, faintly textured by the noises of the sheep. The mist was growing thicker again. It did so in a slow and even fashion, starting nowhere in particular. The valley floor melted away into grayness.

"I wanted to be happy,'' I said softly. "Mama was happy here.''

Angharad said nothing.

"But now I find out that it's all an illusion. Forest of Flowers never existed.''

"Perhaps it's time for you to go home,'' Angharad said.

The mountain on the far side had receded into the

clouds so that only the shape of it, darker gray on gray, was visible. The mountains beyond it, like the valley below, were indistinguishable in the mist.

"I always thought my mother was the most wonderful person in the world," I said. "I thought she was the bravest and the best, you know, for all she survived. Now I wonder how I ever felt that way. All I've learned, it seems, is that she must have sold her soul a million times over."

Angharad nodded. "I suppose we all do that," she said.

# Thirty-Five

GOING HOME, I flew from winter back into summer. The captain told us, as the plane banked in brilliant sunshine, that it was ninety-four degrees in Wichita. Across the broad plain below us all the fields were golden brown, a patchwork of somewhat imprecise squares and rectangles, as if the task of drawing them up had been given to a six-year-old, just learning to make straight lines with a ruler. Long before the curvature of the earth hid the land from view, it had disappeared into heat haze.

I sat with my face pressed against the small window and watched for the appearance of Wichita amid the miles and miles of farmland. I was energized with the crawlly sort of nervousness that overtiredness brings. I hadn't been able to sleep on the transatlantic flight, and I'd come to Wichita from New York via Dallas, following one of those puzzlingly circuitous routes that airline companies seem to prefer. The whole journey, including the nighttime train ride from North Wales to London, had taken twenty-seven hours, and I was desperate just to stop moving.

The plane leveled off. The outskirts of Wichita came into my view for the first time. Then the long, spidery arms of the Mid-Continent Airport reached out for us. It was a huge airport for the amount of traffic. Brown brick concourses, supported on concrete pillars, sprawled out from the main terminal. No need to economize on space here. Space was not something Wichita was short of.

With a peremptory bump, the wheels of the plane touched the ground. Wing flaps went up. All conversation in the cabin was momentarily drowned out.

I had forgotten the sheer hugeness of Kansas. In Wales, nurtured by the mounds and rises, like a child cuddled to its mother's breast, the world was intimate and well defined. Here, you could feel only your own smallness. In a place one-tenth land and nine-tenths sky, there is no other way to feel but exposed and insignificant.

Slowly, the plane taxied toward the gate. Below us on the tarmac men with ear protectors and orange paddles waved us in. We were within minutes of deplaning.

Now what?

I tried to imagine. I tried to picture meeting my father on the other side of the barrier. What should I say? What should I do? Would I kiss and hug him? Was I glad to be home? Would I say that? Was I?

I felt nothing. Empty. Numbed by exhaustion, I couldn't mobilize any emotions. Just the numbness, tinged perhaps by a lesser feeling, a sort of sad, hazy longing, although for what I wasn't sure.

Megan was standing at the very front of the group of people beyond the gate. She was wearing red running shorts and sneakers without socks and a T-shirt saying "My parents went to Chicago and all I got was this lousy T-shirt." Her hair had been cut. Not really short, just to her shoulders, but it was pushed back away from her face with a plastic headband. I very nearly didn't recognize her.

But she saw me. "Lesley!" she shrieked and bolted over the rope barrier. I stumbled from the unexpected power of her hug, and passengers behind me crowded up, attempting to get by.

"I thought you'd never get here. I thought that plane would never, never, never get up to the gate," she said as I dragged her back around the barrier. "We watched the whole way. From when you were just a little bitty speck in the sky till you landed. And it took *forever.*"

Then Dad was there, and the question of how to greet him was irrelevant. We clung to one another, squishing Megan unceremoniously between us.

"Your hair's long," Megan said to me as we all walked down toward the baggage claim area. "It's got really long over the summer."

"Well, yours is short. When did you get it cut?"

"Last month. For my birthday. Daddy and me went up to Auntie Caroline's for a vacation. And Auntie Caroline took me into Chicago to get it done. See, it's got blunt cuts so that I don't have to worry about split ends."

"Split ends?" I thunked her on the side of her head. "You've never worried about split ends in your life."

"Well, see, now I don't got to. See? Look at it. That's a blunt cut. It's just like Alison's got."

"Who's Alison?"

"She's this girl. She lives on Fourth Street, and her and me are best friends now. She got to stay overnight after my birthday party. Guess what kind of party I had?"

I shrugged, "How should I know?"

"Guess."

"Megan, I haven't the faintest clue."

"It was a disco party. And I got to invite every single kid in my class. A real disco party with lights and music and everything. It was super."

I grinned at her. "Were boys there too?"

"Daddy let me invite my whole class. Twenty-three kids. Everybody in the fourth grade. Well, I mean everybody that was in the third grade last year but were going to be in the fourth grade, but weren't yet, because it was summer. You know what I mean."

"You mean boys. How many did you dance with?"

She shrugged. "We didn't dance much. Mainly we ate junk. Sometimes me and Alison danced." She hesitated a moment. We'd reached the escalator going down, and she paused to run her hand along the moving handrail before getting on. "But it was a super party. No other kid's gotten to have a disco at their house. I'm the first."

"What about that one boy? You danced with him," my father offered and put his hand between her shoulder blades to shove her onto the escalator. "What was his name? Lenny?"

"*Benny*, Daddy. Benjamin actually. They just moved here from Goodland. And he dances real good. So I let him dance with me one time."

"You *danced* with a boy? Oh Megs, guess who has a boyfriend?"

"I didn't say that, Lesley. He's *not* my boyfriend. I just said he was a boy and he could dance good. That's all I said."

"I dunno. Having disco parties, dancing with boys. Sounds dangerous to me." I glanced over. "Bet you smooched him when Daddy wasn't looking."

"*Lesley!*" She turned, horrified. "I did not!"

"Meggie's got a boyfriend."

"Lesley, shut up. Shut up or I'll kick you. People're going to hear."

We were in baggage claim, waiting for the carousel to start. Megan moved away from me to stand on the far side of my father. She took his hand. "Dad, tell her he's not my boyfriend and so she better shut up. I don't even know him hardly. He's just a kid in my class. Besides, he's only nine and I'm already ten. Tell her he's not my boyfriend."

As we waited and waited for my bags to appear, Dad began inquiring about Wales. How had I found everyone? What about the farm? he asked. Was the old barn in the back of the house still standing? It was the one with the little white cupola and weather vane in the shape of a fish. Yes, I said, and we decided it must be in no better or worse shape than when he'd last seen it. Had they cut down the stand of three oaks up by the spring? Or were they still there? he asked. Someone had told him once that those trees were over three hundred years old. When he was helping old Jones with the farmwork, he used to take his lunch break under those oaks and he often wondered if they were still standing now. And what about the village? Was Mrs. Davies still running the post office? Was the village built up any that I could tell?

I found it almost eerie to be standing in the dim, air-conditioned lower level of the airport discussing the Jones farm and Bwlch-llwyd-ddu so casually with my father. The baggage area was solid and substantial, almost a concrete fortress in its construction, and by comparison, Wales had already grown indistinct and ethereal. Prosaic as all my father's questions were, I found it impossible to shrug off the rather disconcerting feel that we were discussing something we had both dreamed.

The heat outside the airport building was paralytic. I'd left the Joneses' farm at 9:00 P.M. at night, and it had been forty-three degrees. So I arrived in Wichita wearing a turtleneck and a pullover. The pullover I'd shed long before, and I'd yanked the sleeves of the turtleneck up, but as I waited in the parking lot while Dad put my bags into the trunk, I seriously considered whether or not I could get away with taking off the turtleneck and making the long trip back to western Kansas in just my bra. Dad went around the car, unlocking doors so we could get in, and Megan went around behind him, rolling down all the windows.

I sat in the backseat with the intention of being able to stretch out and sleep during the journey home. But in a burst of unexpected sisterly love, Megan hopped in with me.

"Megs, why don't you ride up front? It's too hot back here for both of us. You got a sweaty little body."

"But I want to ride with you," she said cheerfully. She snuggled up against me.

"Megs, ride up front. I want to sleep. I'm exhausted."

"No. I want to ride with you. You can sleep if you want, but I want to ride back here."

"It makes Daddy look like a chauffeur with both of us sitting back here. If you're not going to sit up front, I'm going to."

"No, stay here, Lessie. Geez, it's been practically three whole months since I've seen you. I want you to sit with me." She slammed the doors and locked them.

Too tired to argue further, I collapsed back onto the seat.

Once we were out onto the highway, I slid down on the seat so that I'd have the benefit of the breeze through the window and so that no passing motorist would see me in my bra. Since the trip would take the better part of three hours across uninterrupted plains, I folded my sweater into a pillow, stuffed it into the corner and prepared to go to sleep.

"Dad," Megan said, leaning over the front seat, "can we stop at a Wendy's? I want a Frosty."

"I don't know where there is one, sweetie," my father replied. We were already well out of Wichita and into the countryside.

"How about Kingman?" Megan suggested. "Let's stop when we get to Kingman and buy everyone Frosties."

"I don't know if there is a Wendy's in Kingman, Meggie."

"Well, when we get there, let's find out, okay? Please?"

"We'll see," said my father. There were a few seconds of silence. "And Megs, sit back please. If you're going to be back there, I want you sitting all the way back. Don't hang over the front seat. And put your seat belt on."

Megan slid back.

I closed my eyes again. The motion of the car was friendly and familiar. Within moments I slipped into a doze.

"Daddy?" Megan said.

"Hmm?"

"Can I play the video games? If we stop at a Wendy's, I mean."

"Megs, to be honest with you, I don't think we really need to stop anywhere for a while. Maybe when we get farther down the road. We'll have to stop for dinner anyway. But I don't think we need to stop before then."

"But can I play the video games? I got my own money along. I got more than five dollars with me. It's from my birthday money. I got it along because I was thinking maybe we could've stopped longer in Wichita and I could've bought something I needed. Like maybe a new notebook for school. I need a new notebook. You know. One of those ring-binder ones, like Alison's got."

"We'll be able to find plenty of notebooks back home, Megs," my father replied.

"But anyway, I got my own money with me. So can I play the video games when we stop?"

"If you think you're going to spend five dollars on video games, young lady . . ."

"Not the whole five dollars, Dad. I didn't say that, did I? I just said, can I? Not the whole five dollars. Just a little bit of it."

"We'll see."

"Does that mean yes?"

"It means we'll see, Megan."

I was watching Megan as she talked to my father. The haircut did make her look very different. It was attractive, right at shoulder length like that, so that her thick hair swung cleanly away from her face. But it took away from her that untamed aura. It made her look ordinary, with her little pink plastic headband.

Megan, to me, had always more closely resembled Mama than I had. In spite of my fairer coloring, Megan had always seemed more like her. I thought of that as I watched her, and what occurred to me was how ordinary Mama probably would have looked, if she'd cut and curled her hair the way middle-aged women usually do. But of course, Mama never had.

"I'm hot," Megan said and flopped back against the seat. Sliding way down so that her back rested on the seat part and her bare legs were thrown over the seat in front, she waggled her feet in the air.

"I'm having a hard time understanding how you've got your seat belt buckled when your feet are up here with me," my dad said.

Megan giggled.

"I've about had it with you sitting back there, Megan. Now sit up right and put that belt on. I mean it."

"But I'm hot."

"I don't care if you're being grilled on a barbecue. Do as I say," he replied.

Reluctantly, Megan straightened up, found the two ends of the belt and buckled them. Looking over at me, she wrinkled her nose. Silence reigned for perhaps thirty seconds.

"I wish we had air conditioning," she said. She leaned forward. "How come we don't have air conditioning in our car, Daddy? Everybody else has it."

"Because it's an old car and the people who bought it first never had air conditioning installed."

"But why don't we put it in?"

"Because it costs too much money, that's why. Just roll down your window."

"I got my window rolled down. We got every window in the whole car rolled down. I'm still melting."

"You'll survive," my father said.

"Oh look! Look, Dad, there's the sign for Kingman! Can we stop for Frosties? Please, Daddy? Please, can we?" She had her seat belt off again and was leaning over to make sure he saw the highway sign.

"I said we'll stop later, Megan, when it's dinner time."

"But I'm *hot.*"

I nudged her with my foot. "Clam up, would you?"

"Come on, Daddy, please? Please?"

"Megan, shut up," I said again.

She was bouncing up and down on the seat. "Please? *Please,* Daddy?"

I kicked her.

*"Ouch!* Ow! Owie. What did you do that for?" Grabbing her leg, she fell back hugging it tenderly. "Owie. That hurt."

"Because all you're doing is talking. Talk, talk, talk. You haven't shut up since we left Wichita."

"Dad," Megan said in wounded voice, "Lesley just kicked me. Hard, too."

"Meggie, Lesley's tired. She's had a long trip. Now just let her be."

"But she kicked me. I'm going to have a bruise."

"Yes, okay. Les, don't kick her again." The car slowed, and he turned to look over his shoulder at her. "Look, sweetheart, why don't you come up here and sit with me?"

"I think I will," Megan replied sulkily and prepared to climb over the seat. But before she did, she turned and stuck her tongue out at me.

The journey, like the plains, seemed to go on forever.

The heat was unbearable to me. Saunalike in its strength, it sapped what little energy I had left. I lay sprawled over the backseat, my muscles anesthetized with exhaustion, and tried to sleep.

I couldn't. Even after Megan had finally shut up and fallen asleep herself, her head resting heavily against my father's arm, I was still awake. Somewhere west of Macksville, Dad tuned the radio to a country-western station from Tulsa and, under his breath, began to sing along with Crystal Gayle. I lay, suspended halfway between slumber and wakefulness, dreaming vivid but troubled dreams while at the same time being conscious of the car, the music and the heat. In fact, as the miles passed, I became more and more awake and lay with my eyes open, staring at the pattern in the upholstery. I discovered I was still feeling the same tainted numbness I'd felt on the plane when it was landing, only this time the other emotion that underpinned it was more perceptible. It was a desolate feeling, strong enough to color my half-awake dreams.

What came to my thoughts as I lay was the paradox of change. On one hand, I had expected no change. I had expected my father and my sister to be caught up in the same turmoil I'd left them in in June. I'd expected them to still be as embroiled in it as I was, yet, clearly they weren't. Whatever the depth of the wound Mama had inflicted on the family, for Megan and my father, it was obviously healing. On the other hand, I *had* expected change. I felt I had changed so much over the last months. I felt I was an entirely different person. And I'd expected them to be too. But they weren't. Nothing was different. Megan was still Megan. Dad was still Dad. Kansas was still Kansas. Time had gone by, that was all.

About half past five we stopped in Dodge City for hamburgers in a roadside café. Afterward, Megan and I walked up and down the famous main street and peered into the windows of the tourist shops. Since it was early Saturday evening, most of the museums and shops were already closed, but we looked anyway, just to be out of the car for a while.

The rest of the trip I rode in the front seat with Dad. Megan sat in back, trying to play ''Yankee Doodle Dandy'' with a piece of tissue and my father's comb. West of Garden City we turned north on Highway 25 and followed the same route Mama and I had used that day in April when I had taken her to see Dr. Carrera.

The flatness grew more familiar. First on the right side of the car and then on the left, sunflower fields came into view. Acre after acre after acre. There was no wind, not even the merest breeze to ruffle the golden petals. They stood, silent and motionless, their heads all facing the sinking sun in the west.

Megan leaned forward between the seats as we came into town. Her arms were hanging through the gap, and she drummed on the gear shift. Main Street, First Street, Second Street, Third Street, she read out as we passed them. Berg Street, Bailey Street, our street.

I was home.


All I wanted was to take a bath, wash my hair and go to bed. It was only about a quarter of eight, but I knew that would be the extent of what I could manage. While I went upstairs, Megan ran after Dad into the kitchen, harassing him about letting Alison come over. Come on, Daddy, come on, she was saying. I told her she could, I said so, I said I'd call her when we got back. Come on. *Please?* It isn't very late; it isn't a school day tomorrow. Please, Daddy, *please.*

Alison was there even before I got into the bathroom for my bath. She was a funny-looking little kid with striped overalls and fat, brown braids that stuck out like sausages at uneven angles to her head. Her face was full of dun-colored freckles, as if a sparrow had tracked over it. That's my sister, Megan was saying, pointing at me. Alison burst into giggles, and the two of them went tearing up to Megan's room.

I ran the tub completely full of water so hot I could hardly put my hand in and then threw in generous scoops of bath crystals to create a bath unlike any I'd had since I left. Pinning my hair up, I stepped in and carefully slipped down under the surface until the water was against my chin. Picking up the copy of *Cosmopolitan* I'd bought in the airport in New York, I opened it to resume reading a deliciously graphic fiction excerpt that I'd started on the plane.

The bathroom door rattled.

"Are you going to be in there all night?" a voice inquired.

"Megan, I've been in here exactly ten minutes, counting running the water."

"Well, how long you going to stay?"

"Until the water gets cold. Until I feel like getting out, that's how long."

A sigh followed beyond the door.

"You've been in there ages already, Les. Not just ten minutes. And I need to go to the bathroom."

"I'll be out in a bit."

"Can't you let me in there now?"

"Just hold it."

"But me and Alison are playing Monopoly and I want to get back. But I got to go. Come on, Lesley. Let me in there."

"Megan, honestly. Just wait."

Silence. I could hear her breathing outside the door.

Throwing the magazine down, I climbed out of the tub and dripped water over to let her in. "Damn you. Get in here and hurry up and get out," I said and stomped back to the tub. "And shut the stupid door."

Megan paused in front of the mirror. It was steamed over, so she took a towel and wiped it off. She picked up the hairbrush.

"I thought you were in some kind of rush to use the toilet."

"I am," she said absently and brushed her hair.

My bathwater was already lukewarm. My magazine had gotten wet around the edges. I was just preparing to yell at her for being such a pest when I too got caught up in watching her image in the mirror, already fading behind the steam again.

"Megs, how come you cut your hair?"

She shrugged and went on over to the toilet. "Daddy wanted it. He said he'd always thought I'd look nicer with shorter hair."

"He did?"

"Yeah. So when we were in Chicago, I went with Auntie Caroline and got it cut." She looked over. "Do you like it?"

I nodded. "It makes you look different though. I almost didn't recognize you when I got off the plane."

She flushed the toilet and was absorbed momentarily in tucking her shirt into her shorts.

"I didn't know Daddy ever wanted you to have short hair," I said. "He never mentioned it before. I always thought he liked it the way it was."

A shrug. She wiped off the mirror with her hand. "I dunno. I like it better too. This way it's not so hot. I used to get really sweaty in the summer. Besides, now I can wear headbands and clips and stuff. I couldn't before because every time I bent forward, my hair knocked them out."

"Mama wouldn't have liked it this way, though," I said.

Megan gazed at her image in silence. "No, I suppose

not,'' she said and lifted her hair off her shoulders. "But then Mama's not here anymore.''

Another quick flick with the hairbrush and then Megan replaced the pink headband. Starting for the door, she paused before opening it. She turned.

Silence.

"What's wrong?'' she asked. She crossed back to me in the tub. "How come you're crying, Lessie?''

"I'm not,'' I said and lifted the dripping washcloth to my face. "It just looks like it because I'm so tired, that's all.''

Her brow puckered.

"Honest, Megs. I'm just really, really exhausted. Nothing's wrong.''

Pensive a moment longer with her lower lip sucked between her teeth, Megan regarded me. Then she reached out and touched my hand. "Anyhow, I'm awfully glad you're home. I missed you a lot.''

I got into bed, absurdly grateful for sheets, after three months in a sleeping bag. The room was dark and overwarm but not hot. Beyond my room, the house was full of lively sounds.

I closed my eyes and waited for sleep that still seemed unwilling to come.

"Les?'' It was my father's voice outside the door. "Are you asleep yet?'' He was speaking very softly, in case I was. I almost didn't hear him.

"No, I'm not,'' I answered.

The knob turned and he pushed the door open. Light from the hallway spilled across the carpet.

"How're you doing?'' he asked and crossed the room to my bed.

"All right.''

"Do you want anything before you go to sleep? A snack? Maybe a glass of milk or something?''

"No, I'm okay. Thanks, though.''

There was a brief pause. He was standing over me, his shadow cast across my face. Because the light was behind him, I was unable to discern his expression.

"Meggie says you were crying earlier," he said.

"Not really."

He studied my face.

"I'm just tired. That's all it was. I told her that. But I'm okay now."

"You sure?"

"I'm sure."

Silence.

I sighed. "I'm so tired I can't even sleep. I feel like I'm crawling out of my skin."

He sat down on the bed beside me. Reaching over, he pushed back the hair alongside my face. "How was your trip?"

"Okay."

Unsaid things crowded into the darkness around us. Tears rose up into my eyes. If he could see them, he didn't say, but he was watching me very closely. The tears stayed but did not fall.

"How come she lied, Dad?"

"What do you mean?"

"Mama. How come she lied about Coed-y-Bleiddiau. I know now that it doesn't mean Forest of Flowers. You did too, didn't you? That's why you never called it anything but by its Welsh name. You knew all along, didn't you?"

He said nothing.

"So, how come she lied? If everybody knew *bleiddiau* meant wolves, why did she keep saying it was flowers?"

He gave a little lift of his shoulders. "She wanted it to mean flowers."

"But it didn't."

"I know it didn't," he said gently, "but she wanted it to."

"But it still didn't."

"Sometimes things are like that, Lessie. We long for them to be a certain way and they just aren't. And occasionally we want them different so badly that it's simply too hard to ever accept them the way they are."

"She lied about the sunflowers too, didn't she?"

He didn't respond immediately.

"In the garden of the cottage, there were no sunflowers, were there?"

"Once there were sunflowers. In one other place we lived," he said. "In Texas. There were wild sunflowers there."

*"There?* Those sunflowers?"

He shrugged. "I think she just confused them. Just mixed up one place with the other."

"How could she, Dad? That was Texas. Without a hill for a hundred miles. Without rain for months on end. How could she mix up Texas with Wales?"

Lips pursed in a thoughtful expression, he lifted his shoulders again. "I don't know. Maybe there were sunflowers in Wales too. There may have been. It was a long time ago, and my memory's not so hot either."

"There weren't, Dad. I'm sure there weren't. It was just another lie."

Silence.

"Were any of her stories true? Or did just the horrible stuff happen to her?"

"She never meant her stories to hurt."

"They were lies."

"No," he said. "I don't think they were meant to be lies either. She only wanted the world to be a little better than it was for her. They were just dreams she shared. They were never meant to hurt."

"But they hurt me, Dad. Can't you see how much they've hurt me?"

"Yes," he said simply.

The room grew quiet. I lay, listening to him breathe. Megan and Alison were audible down the hallway. Although the door to Megan's room was closed, their voices still carried clearly.

"I don't know what to do anymore," I said. "I don't know what to think. I don't know what to feel. Nothing's gotten answered for me. Nothing's gotten clearer. I went all the way over there and spent all that time and, if anything, it's made me understand less."

He reached his hand out and took mine.

"I kept thinking before all this happened that if only we—you and me and Meggie—could just love Mama enough, we'd be able to make up for everything. I kept thinking that she was innocent through all that, only a girl really, and so brave and strong to have endured so much. I thought if we could love her enough, we could forget the past and it wouldn't matter. But that didn't work. And now all I can see are her faults. I think to myself, how did she even deserve our love? I want to keep loving her. I do still love her, I guess, but all I can see is how much of this whole disaster was of her own making."

He tipped his head away and looked down at the floor. Thoughtful silence surrounded him. Megan and Alison had become quiet at whatever they were doing, so the silence grew rich and deep around us.

"Yes, maybe so," he said quietly. "I don't know. But I don't think it's really a question of love. Love and perfection don't have anything to do with one another. You don't love people as a reward for their being good or whole or perfect. Or as compensation, to make up for all the suffering there is in life. You just love them."

"But what's the point of it? All it does is hurt you in the end. If it doesn't make up for things, if it doesn't change people's faults and make them better, if they still go on suffering anyway, why bother?"

"Because when you come right down to it," he said, "it's the only real act of free will we have in our power."

The tears, still in my eyes, swelled, and I turned away from him to keep them from falling. "That isn't very much," I said to the wall.

He did not say anything.

"I guess I just wanted more than that."

"Yes, I think we all do," he said quietly. "But in the end, it's enough."

He continued to hold my hand, and with his fingers, he gently traced the topography of my knuckles. I turned my head to look at him. He was watching me, his features soft and vague in the darkness. He smiled, only faintly.

Wearily, I smiled back.

Just then Megan burst from her bedroom with a tremendous eruption of noise. She tore down the hallway to the bathroom. "Don't spill it, Alison!" she shrieked. "Let me get a towel. Wait, Alison, don't!"

"Oh dear," my father said in alarm and looked over his shoulder toward the doorway. "Now what?"

"Megan! Hurry!" Alison cried.

Dad rose up from the bed. "Just a sec," he said to me, "I'll be right back."

He never was.

I lay in my bed and listened. What my sister and Alison had been up to, I couldn't tell, but they were hysterical with laughter. My father was asking Megan just exactly what she thought she was doing, making such a mess, and there was a familiar note of exasperation in his voice. Megan was hooting like a monkey.

Tears still in my eyes, I lay and listened. Conversation was drowned out by the noise of wildly squeaking bedsprings, and I knew someone was bouncing on Megan's bed. Dad was telling them to stop, to get off the bed, to settle down for once. But his tone was only mockingly strict, and from the way things sounded, he was trying to catch the bouncers and they were taking turns at being caught.

Finally, when it became apparent my father was going to be in there for a while, I turned on my side to make myself more comfortable. Closing my eyes pushed out the tears that had rested there for so long and they slid over my face and down onto the sheet. I don't remember falling asleep but I must have, very quickly.

# BIRDY

## by WILLIAM WHARTON

### Hailed by reviewers coast to coast

The story of a guy named Birdy and his buddy Al—
their amazing adventures in a suburb of Philadelphia
before World War II, and the very different passions
that fire their spirits.

A story about dreaming and surviving, friendship
and family, love and war, madness and beauty,
and most of all—freedom.

"ENCHANTING"   *The New York Times*
"A MARVEL"   *The Village Voice*
"IT SOARS!"   *Time Magazine*
"TO READ IT IS TO FLY"   *People Magazine*

47282-1  $3.50/CAN $4.50

An **AVON** Paperback

# HASIDIC TALES OF THE HOLOCAUST
## Yaffa Eliach

"Many of these stories moved me and will remain with me." Rabbi Harold S. Kushner,
Author of *When Bad Things Happen to Good People*

This is a collection of true personal accounts, by turns moving, magical, chilling and heart-rending, as they tell of life in the Nazi Kingdom of Death. Based on interviews and oral histories, these 89 tales comprise the first new collection of Hasidic tales in over a century, and reveal the intensity of faith, fervent mysticism and joyous optimism which characterizes the Hasidic Jews of Eastern Europe. Winner of the 1983 Christopher Award.

"Moving celebrations of courage in adversity and faith in both god and mankind." *The Atlantic*

"The stories told here offer to us a perspective we rarely see. An important contribution toward giving voice to this very large group of Jewish victims." *Choice*

In this "beautiful book...Yaffa Eliach's tales are a victory over statistics. By a combination of historical and literary skills, Mrs. Eliach has recounted the destruction of the Hasidism of Poland as it was for those who were being destroyed." *The New Republic*

**64725-7/$4.95**

**An AVON/DISCUS Paperback**